The Burning Candle

A Medieval Novel

By Lisa J. Yarde

THE BURNING CANDLE
Copyright © Lisa J. Yarde 2012

ISBN-10 1939138000
ISBN-13 978-1939138002

www.lisajyarde.com

Cover Artwork
Francesco Hayez's *Il Bacio* (The Kiss), 1859
File source: Creative Commons, Attribution License
http://commons.wikimedia.org/wiki/File:Francesco_Haye
z_008e.jpg

Cover design and Alhambra Press logo by Lance Ganey
www.freelanceganey.com

Also by Lisa J. Yarde

On Falcon's Wings (2010)

Sultana (2011)

Sultana's Legacy (2011)

Long Way Home: A novella (2011)

The Burning Candle (2012)

The Legend Rises - HerStory anthology (2013)

Sultana: Two Sisters (2013)

Dedication & Acknowledgments

For Karen, my beautiful sister, another woman of great personal strength.

The completion of this novel would not have been possible without the assistance and knowledge of Jane Beckenham, Julie Cox, Anita Davison, Sandy Frykholm, Anne Gilbert (RIP), Shelia Lamb, Mirella Sichirollo Patzer and N. Gemini Sasson.

I am incredibly grateful for the helpful insight and patience of my beta readers: J.S. Dunn, Mirella Sichirollo Patzer, Veronica Reinhardt, and Kristen Taber Wood. The editorial advice, time and talent of Tara Chevrestt and Jessica Lux helped shape the final version of the novel. Lastly, Donna Schaal offered a detailed proof of the work, for which I am very grateful.

My thanks especially to incredible friends and best writer buds, Mirella Sichirollo Patzer and Anita Davison, who saved the earliest drafts of the manuscript and allowed me to continue working, after I thought Isabel's story was lost forever.

Foreword

The Burning Candle is a fictionalized account of the life of Isabel de Vermandois. There is little verifiable information about her life. To construct the best portrayal of Isabel, her possible experiences and the men who shaped events around her, I relied on a variety of sources.

Jeffrey L. Singman's *Daily Life in Medieval Europe* offered a general understanding of medieval society and traditions and the prevailing influence of the Roman Catholic Church. Jonathan Riley-Smith's *The Crusades – A History* revealed the plans and exploits of Isabel's father Hugh de Vermandois after he undertook his journeys to the Holy Land. *Medieval Costume and Fashion* by Herbert Norris aided in describing the appropriate attire for the characters. Trevor Rowley's *Norman England*, while very short, provided a concise overview of how the arrival of the Normans altered the country. *The World of Orderic Vitalis: Norman Monks and Norman Knights* by Marjorie Chignall gave general knowledge of the lives of monks within and outside monastery walls.

For an understanding of the court of King Henry I of England and the sovereign's interactions with his nobles, the account of his life in C. Warren Hollister's *Henry I*, part of the Yale English Monarchs series, was invaluable. Hollister's book provided incredible detail about the movement of Henry's court and information on one of Henry's illegitimate daughters, unmentioned in other sources. *The Royal Bastards of Medieval England* by Chris Given-Wilson and Alice Curteis imparted vital information on the number of Henry's illegitimate children and the roles several of them played in their father's life and the history of England.

Sally N. Vaughn's *Anselm of Bec and Robert of Meulan: The Innocence of the Dove and the Wisdom of the Serpent* provided an in-depth analysis of the life of Isabel's husband and his conflict with the Church, in particular his and King Henry's erstwhile nemesis, the archbishop of Canterbury, Anselm of Bec. *The Beaumont Twins: The Roots and Branches of Power in the Twelfth Century* by David Crouch informed about the lives of Robert and Isabel's children, as well as their interactions with William de Warenne and his eventual heirs. It also offered a wealth of information about household officers and retainers who would have served during Robert's lifetime, men whom Isabel would have known or encountered during her marriage.

Lisa J. Yarde

Act I: Sparks

(February – September 1096)

Chapter One – Blood Moon
Crépy-en-Valois, France: February 1096

A billowing shadow, the color of dried blood, crept across the face of the full moon and devoured it. Isabel eyed the astonishing spectacle from a frost-covered castle courtyard and clutched her blue mantle around her. Still, frigid evening air plucked at her body beneath folds of ermine and wool. Even the soles of her leather shoes offered little protection.

After Vespers, a brilliant moon had dispelled the gloom of dusk and bathed the snowbound landscape of Crépy-en-Valois in its golden glow. Then the light faded before the ominous darkness shrouded the sky.

The blood moon captivated rather than frightened Isabel. Her father's guards and men-at-arms stood in circles and ignored her presence. They whispered and gestured toward the strange display in the sky. Fear whitened their features and subdued their voices to bare whispers. Why should such a sight have terrified men hardened by years of service to her father?

Isabel dismissed their cravenness and glared at the blood moon. "I am not afraid. I do not fear anything of the mortal world." The lie would never ring true. She said it all the same with the fervent hope that someday fear would not rule her.

From behind her, a tremulous voice beckoned. "Come out of the night air! You should be sleeping. Your parents shall be furious if they discover you're out of bed, child."

Isabel squared her shoulders, despite the warning at her back. "I am no child. You told me there have been eleven summers since my birth."

"Must you always be so disagreeable?"

Isabel said nothing.

"Do you hear me, milady?"

"I have ears to hear you, Claremond."

"By the grace of our Lord Jesus Christ, you would try the patience of all His saints."

Isabel turned and stared at her nurse. Claremond shuffled her ponderous bulk across granular deposits of ice, which cracked with each of her footfalls. A green mantle trailed in her wake. She held a rushlight aloft in its iron holder. The dim flame illuminated the sagging jowls of her pallid face. Deep folds carved around her opaque eyes and the fleshy wattle under her chin betrayed her advanced years.

Isabel pointed at the rust-colored moon. "Tell me what it means."

The older woman made the sign of the cross and averted her gaze from the spectacle. "First, there were the fires in the sky last April and now this, another sign of God's displeasure and judgment."

Isabel bridled at the thought of righteous anger raining down brimstone and fire on the heads of the wicked people of France, as her father's chaplain often preached would happen. If God truly punished evil, how had men such as her father lived so long and found favor with Him each day? When would God chastise those persons who truly deserved it?

Her nurse draped an arm across her shoulders. Isabel pulled away and listened for an exasperated groan. When none followed, she glanced at Claremond, who offered her a smile that softened her wizened countenance. Isabel's gaze narrowed in anticipation.

As she expected, Claremond began, "Dear child, you would not want your parents to grow angry with me?"

Isabel turned her back on her nurse. "When I do not submit from the first, you always try to make me feel guilty. I do not care what my father does to you or me."

Claremond clucked her tongue. "You are a perverse liar, not the least among your childish sins. Another is your disregard for your parents' will. They would want you inside, for no good could ever come from any occurrence this night. I am fearful for you, my Isabel."

"You're afraid for me? Do you have reason to be?"

Claremond did not answer, even when Isabel groaned. Though she bristled inside, she tried a new approach. "Are my parents with the priest who arrived earlier today?"

"Brother Thorold is not a priest."

"He cannot be a monk living outside the walls of his order. He wears the habit of the Benedictines."

"Despite his habit and cowl, milady, he does not live in a monastery. Brother Thorold serves as a clerk—"

"My father has his own clerks. Why then is he meeting with the Benedictine?"

"Patience, milady, you must learn patience. You must never appear too eager for anything, including knowledge."

Isabel rolled her eyes, exasperated and glanced at the blood-red moon again. "How am I ever to learn anything? You, my father and my mother keep everything secret from me, even matters of little import. I am not an ignorant child."

Her nurse patted Isabel's lean shoulder. "Milady, Brother Thorold is the clerk and a devoted friend to Robert de Beaumont, the Comte de Meulan. He is one of the richest men on both sides of the Channel and a comte of the Vexin."

"For all his titles and land, the man is likely no more than a Viking savage."

"Comte Robert hails from Normandy. His ancestors have long surrendered their pagan faith and held lands in the duchy for several generations. He is a great warrior and a powerful magnate who has served the interests of the ducal court and English kings faithfully. I do not doubt he is an honorable man, despite his heritage."

"Can it compare with mine? I bear the blood of Capetian kings."

Claremond's touch fell away. "Milady, you are overly proud. I have oft said pride shall be your undoing. It makes you unpleasant."

"Your opinions tire me. Why has this Norman comte sent his clerk here?"

"I believe Brother Thorold shall finalize plans for your marriage, milady."

Isabel's heart leapt. All her concern about the portent in the sky vanished with her nurse's pronouncement. Finally, a chance for possible freedom loomed as alluring as the strange moon.

"My marriage? Oh, I cannot wait to be wed and escape this place forever!"

Isabel picked up the trailing edge of her mantle and dashed toward the fortress.

"Wait, milady! Milady, please. French ladies do not run!"

Isabel ignored Claremond, who gasped and panted, her bulk slowing her.

In the midst of two wooded valleys, the stone-built fortress of the comtes de Vermandois rose above the snowbound landscape. Eleven years before, Isabel's maternal uncle, Eudes, had completed a square tower of gray stone that served as the residence of Isabel's family and their retainers. Her gaze swept up the height of its walls. She clenched her fists and her jaw tightened. Myriad emotions roiled in her gut as she stared at the place. It had never been her true home, but more so a prison. Now the prospect of marriage offered her a chance at independence.

"Milady, wait for me! Where do you think you're going?" Claremond clamped her hand on Isabel's shoulder.

She struggled against the nurse's hold. "Let me go! I must see my parents. I want to learn when I may marry."

"You dare not ask! You should be resting at your parents' command. What would they say if you appeared in the hall at this hour?"

"Why haven't they told me anything before now? Am I to marry one of Comte Robert's sons? Is it a grandson of his instead? I suppose, since he fought the English years ago, he must have children and grandchildren of a suitable age to wed. Whom have my parents chosen from among them?"

"You misunderstand the matter, milady. Your parents made the arrangement with Comte Robert years ago—"

"If I misunderstand, it's because you're wasting my time with concerns about my parents. They can't do more to hurt me, not if I know for certain I shall leave this place forever."

Isabel dashed toward the entryway.

Claremond called out, "Milady! Do not interrupt your noble father and his guest!"

The guardsmen opened the carved, wooden door, which creaked on its hinges. Inside, iron wall brackets supported beeswax candles colored a dull brown. Isabel pressed a hand to her pulsing heart and inhaled a deep breath. A sweet, familiar fragrance like honey wafted through the air, as if welcoming entrants to the tower. How deceptive.

She plodded a few steps into the hall. Every breath from her lips escaped in a thin stream of white smoke. Cold dampened the innermost sanctum of the walls, despite numerous tapestries. The chill seized her heart, made the breath hitch inside her throat. She willed courage into her very soul and steeled herself for the encounter to come. Her parents would be furious with her for not being abed. Yet, she had to know their plans for her, even at the risk of their irritation.

Her parents sat in massive chairs on a raised, wooden dais, opposite the entrance. Isabel crossed the hall in rapid strides. Beyond the central hearth in the midst of the room, stood the black-robed, tonsured Brother Thorold, who spoke to her father and mother in low tones she could not overhear.

She darted past the thin, sallow-faced monk. His gasp echoed through the cavernous chamber. She ignored him and dipped into deep curtsy, greeting her parents.

Comte Hugh de Vermandois gripped the gilded arm of his chair and leaned forward. He appeared larger than usual, draped in an ankle-length blue tunic embroidered with gold at the hem and neckline. A gold-studded belt encircled his thick waist. Beside him, Comtesse Adelaide appeared bored as she fingered several of her rings. An array of topaz, sapphire, cornelian, beryl and sardonyx set in gold shimmered on her long, delicate hands.

Adelaide noticed Isabel first. Isabel flinched and shrank away under her mother's narrowed gaze as though already struck. Adelaide regarded her husband in silence before she returned her attention to the jewelry.

Isabel straightened and averted her stare. Stillness suffused the room, broken then by Claremond's footfalls. With a slight wheeze, the nurse also curtsied and stood beside Isabel, who avoided her stern gaze with an intent study of the rush-strewn floor.

"Why are you here, Isabel? Has willfulness tempted you from sleep and lured you here, against your parents' wishes?" Hugh's baritone rumbled through the hall.

"Forgive her, milord—" Claremond began.

An impatient wave of the comte's burly hand silenced her. "I addressed my daughter, crone. Not you!"

Isabel flushed and dared a glance at her father. His moon-shaped face had flushed red. Black brows knitted and framed his deep-set eyes, gray as a storm cloud. His stare often revealed the nature of his moods. Hard and cold like steel when he was merciless, murky and dark when he was angry, or like a tempest when cruel thoughts ruled him. The color was the only trait he shared with Isabel. Otherwise, she was nothing like him.

Her mother ceased her inspection of her bejeweled fingers. Her long nails tapped against the chair arm. "Answer your father, Isabel."

The childlike whisper of Adelaide's voice belied the strength of her steely gaze. Isabel cowered, wondering at the madness that had driven her to this precipice of danger. Her father's frown deepened. She froze in place and forced a response for him, while knowing it would only earn his further disapproval.

"The moon is a strange color tonight. I wanted to see

it."

"It warns of great evil. I wonder why it should have attracted the interest of a child of God."

Isabel turned toward the sonorous rumble of Brother Thorold's voice. Torchlight gleamed off his baldpate. His blue eyes, set beneath a fringe of golden hair, met her stare before he frowned. "Why was the child out of bed at this hour?"

Hugh's gaze hardened and filled with condemnation before he glowered at Claremond.

Isabel stepped between them, partially blocking her nurse from his view. "She did not know I was outdoors. Do not punish her for my sake."

Thorold mused, "The child is willful, hardly a desirable attribute in a female. When the will governs the soul, the path of sin is clear. I would suggest if her nurse is too old to supervise her, the woman should not travel with us to Paris."

"Paris? Why am I going there? Claremond must be with me. Please, you can't mean to have me leave her behind?" The inquiry slipped out before Isabel could refrain from it. She received stares of rebuke from both her parents.

Adelaide rose from her seat. Her russet-colored, woolen robe, draped in loose folds around her trim figure, swept across the floor. She descended from the dais and stood beside her daughter. She studied Isabel with slate-colored eyes. "The child knows nothing of these circumstances. We expected Isabel would have had more time to ready herself."

"She is eleven years old, is she not? A suitable age at which most Norman girls prepare for marriage," Brother Thorold pronounced.

Isabel asked, "Am I truly to be married? When? Where?"

Adelaide raised her auburn-colored eyebrows and peered down her aquiline nose at her daughter. Isabel closed her mouth and her head drooped again. Inside, she chafed. She also knew better than to persist.

Disobedience and questioning her parents had likely just earned her the usual chastisement. As if on cue, a dull ache suffused her shoulders. She ignored the sensation and concentrated on her surroundings.

Her mother sniffed and continued, "My daughter is no mere girl, Brother Thorold. She bears the blood of kings of France from Charlemagne onward. Her father is a prince of France. Her uncle is king of the French people. Your Comte Robert aims high in this match."

Hugh rose and nodded to Brother Thorold. "Forgive the Comtesse de Vermandois. She forgets your lord Robert bears the blood of an ancient and noble line. He is a descendant of the comtes of the Vexin, Amiens and Valois, as is my wife."

He glared at Adelaide briefly before he took his seat again.

"I forget nothing, Hugh!" His wife's shrill cry rang around the hall. "The blood ties between our daughter and the Comte de Meulan remain a matter of concern for me."

Thorold said, "When Bishop Ivo of Chartres prohibited the union because of such blood ties, Comte Robert directed his envoys to Rome. We may expect the Holy Father will issue a papal decree regarding the matter of consanguinity."

Hugh scratched at his thick beard. "His Holiness the Pope may also look with favor upon the request when he hears I have undertaken the Holy War against the Saracens. I shall fulfill my pledge and brave the travail of many months at sea, on horseback and across burning desert sands. I shall never stop until I have rid Jerusalem of the Saracens."

Adelaide snorted. "All by yourself, hmm? Your valor is boundless."

Her husband scowled at her. "Do not mock me, woman. Pray, instead, for my pledge to satisfy the Church."

News of her father's departure startled Isabel. Would he leave Crépy-en-Valois before or after her marriage?

She could not imagine the place without his domineering presence within it. Nor could she fathom why he would journey to the Holy Land for her benefit. He did not care for her. Why did the Holy Land and the Saracens concern the Church? In the previous autumn, Pope Urban II had proclaimed the mandate for true Christians to liberate the Holy Land from the Saracens. If Jerusalem was as far away from France, across burning sands as her father had described, matters there could not be of real concern to the Church or Hugh de Vermandois.

She eyed him from beneath lowered lids. Her father always yawned and fell asleep while leaning on a column during Mass. He never had any use for the Church before now. Why was her union with Comte Robert's family so important for her father to undertake the journey? Why should he care so much about the union of their royal blood with that of the Normans?

"Does the Comte de Meulan understand her value, what he gains by this union?" Her mother's voice banished her speculation.

Thorold nodded. "With the wealth of milord's French and English estates, the match is worthy and a blessing to your daughter. If you can subdue her inclinations toward vanity and pride, I do not doubt her betrothed shall be satisfied."

Adelaide sneered. "Comte Robert likes his females docile, does he?"

Thorold inclined his head. "It is the natural state, for some women."

Adelaide turned her back on him.

Isabel grasped her nurse's hand. "You shall be with me wherever I go. You must be."

"Claremond shall not go with you," Hugh interjected. "More suitable arrangements must be made for your companionship."

Isabel willed the useless tears away. "I want Claremond."

"What you want is irrelevant." Her father glared at his wife again. "I swear each and every day, she grows more like you."

"Good." Adelaide regarded Isabel once more. "Then she has my fortitude and none of your weaknesses." She ignored her husband's snort of disgust.

Isabel stared up at her, openmouthed. Once, she had marveled at her parents. Comte Hugh was large and bovine compared to her mother, who stood tall and slim as a reed. They seemed ill suited for each other. However, she had learned over time how callous indifference to the feelings of others bound them in a perfect match.

"My daughter, three years ago on the occasion of your eighth birthday, your father decreed your betrothal. You are to join the household of the Comte de Meulan, an advisor and friend to an English king. He has great estates."

"Must I live in England, milady?"

"I should hope not, child. It seems an incredibly dull place. There is lingering resentment among the displaced English people for their Norman oppressors."

Isabel glanced at Hugh. So far, both he and her mother had practically indulged her presence and questions without dire consequences. Did she dare press further?

"May I ask if you have ever met my betrothed, milord?"

Hugh grunted. "I did, a few years ago. He came to do homage to your uncle, King Philip of France. The man attended the assembly of nobles at Poissy."

Isabel nodded as a sense of relief flooded her. The evening had proceeded in a better manner than she could ever have hoped. If she could escape the hall without any punishment for having disobeyed her parents, she would consider herself fortunate. Indeed, she felt doubly blessed to know her father had seen her betrothed. The man had also rendered homage on behalf of the Comte de Meulan to the king for his family's French lands. Acceptance within the cultured French court implied certain favor. Would Philip of France have shown inclination toward an unworthy young man?

"Please, tell me more about my betrothed, milord. How shall I know my future husband? Tell me of his appearance and his manner."

Her father frowned at her demands. "He is tall with yellow hair. I do not remember much else of him. Why does his appearance or demeanor matter? His wealth shall keep you in comfort."

Isabel persisted. "Is he an elder son of Comte Robert?"

When Adelaide frowned and her husband guffawed, Isabel realized her horrid mistake at last.

Claremond shuffled beside her. "It shall be a great honor, milady, to be the wife of the Comte de Meulan. Your parents have made a fine provision for your future. I am certain your betrothed husband shall be mindful of your tender years and treat you with care, despite the difference in your ages."

Isabel looked at her parents, horrified. A tremor shuddered deep inside her. She held back the scream of denial. She had been so wrong to assume she would wed one of Comte Robert's relatives. Instead, her parents intended for her to marry an old man who would have no patience with her youthful years and ensure her continued suffering under brutal hands. Her legs quivered and threatened to give out from under her. She remained on her feet by some unknown strength. Her gaze drifted to Claremond, who hovered beside her, face ashen and drawn in mute pity. Then Isabel eyed her parents again.

Hugh's lips tugged upward at the corners. He met her confusion and horror with a malicious leer. Her mother observed her with a stark gaze, her countenance unchanged. Did neither of them truly care about the hell they had consigned her to, as the wife of a decrepit relic of the conquest in England?

Isabel whispered, "You can't! You cannot mean it."

Hugh turned another sneer on his wife. "What does she say? Is her mind addled?"

Adelaide gave her daughter a pitying nod. "You understand her shock perfectly, milord. You have delighted in her confusion for long enough. Clearly, Isabel shares my sentiments. Comte Robert has lived for over fifty years. The man is even older than you are, Hugh. Far too old for our daughter."

"Why should his age matter?"

"It may when everyone blames her for not bearing his children. Do you hear me, Hugh? The man may not be capable of siring an heir. Then people shall accuse our daughter of failing him. How do you believe her fate would reflect upon us?"

"She comes from good breeding stock. You have borne me several children. How could anyone think Isabel is barren? With God's mercy, she shall give him a son or two before his end."

"I won't marry some old man!" Isabel's voice echoed through the hall before deathly silence fell.

Her parents glowered at her. She could not believe her own daring.

Until now, she had avoided punishment. She would not retire from the hall tonight without chastisement. Claremond patted her shoulder. Isabel resisted the temptation to bury her face in her nurse's skirts. Futile gestures would not avail her now.

The harsh glint in Adelaide's gaze turned on Claremond. "The child has not bled yet?"

Isabel kept silent. She had bled enough under their cruel whippings for minor infractions in the past. Now she sensed a different meaning behind Comtesse Adelaide's question. Now, she leaned against her nurse and glanced at her in hope of understanding.

"Well? Has the girl bled or not, crone?" Hugh demanded.

Claremond pressed Isabel closer to her. "Her courses have not begun."

If they had been alone, Isabel would have demanded more information. What were courses? Why did her father and mother deem them so important and why was there blood involved?

Then Thorold took two steps toward Hugh. Isabel had almost forgotten the monk still stood at her back. A red flush had colored his cheeks. He had no reason for appearing so ill at ease, not when she faced the uncertain future alone with a husband older than her own father.

The Benedictine said, "Milord Robert expects he must make some allowances for his bride's youth. He has no reason to bed a child. However, milord shall never accept such a wayward nature in the mother of his future heirs. If you do not take the trouble to check her pride and temperament now, I do not doubt the Comte de Meulan shall attend to the task himself."

Isabel's tiny fists shook as she held them against her hips. All her life, she had bowed to the will of her parents, endured their cold cruelty and harsh punishment. At least here within her home, she knew the terrors awaiting her. What promise of gentleness or kindness could a stranger offer as her husband, when she had never gained the love of the mother who bore her or the father who sired her?

She drew apart from Claremond, eluding the nurse's furtive grasping. "If you wish me to marry this old man, you must force me. I do not want him, cannot take him willingly for a husband."

Her nurse sobbed beside her. As one, Adelaide and Hugh met her defiant gaze. Her father hefted his burly bulk from the chair. Her mother's hand swung wide and delivered a stinging, backhanded slap across Isabel's face.

Tears sprang to Isabel's eyes and her lips quivered. She clutched at her right cheek, where something warm and wet trickled. She observed the thin streak of blood on her palm from a watery gaze. One of Adelaide's rings had scraped her skin.

Her father pronounced, "You have no choice, child. You shall do as you're told."

Even as Isabel shook her head in denial, her mother's hands entwined in the auburn-colored plaits trailing to Isabel's waist. Adelaide grabbed them and set Isabel's scalp aflame.

"Do not quarrel with me! Do not challenge your father! Disobedient, ungrateful child!" With each word, Adelaide smacked both of Isabel's cheeks until the girl sobbed.

Claremond's cries vied with those of her charge. "Please, milady, I beg you! Mercy, milady, mercy for your child."

Adelaide's scowl twisted her features. "I should have you flayed to the bone for your neglect. You have permitted, even encouraged this willfulness in her. You have never chastised her, as I demanded. This is as much your fault and hers. Fetch the hazel rods!"

The nurse covered her mouth with a trembling hand. "Milady."

"There is no need to send the servant." Hugh joined his wife, holding a bundle of slender hazel switches, tied together with sinew and soaked in water.

As Isabel stared at the wood, the flesh on her back quivered with echoes of past hurts. She bit the inside of her jaw before a plea escaped her. She knew, as Claremond must have also determined, her parents would not offer clemency now. She had pushed them too far. She had never expected mercy in the past and saw no reason to hope for it now.

Her mother's fist tightened and tore hair from the roots. Isabel stifled her whimpers.

"Even now the spark of defiance is in your eyes. By the help of God, I shall drive this obstinacy from you. You will learn submission. On your knees, now."

Adelaide shoved Isabel forward. The powerful grip of Hugh's fingers on the hazel twigs tightened until his knuckles turned white. Isabel shuddered at the expectation of the blows delivered by his massive forearms. She extended her fingers, as her palms and knees hit the stone floor covered with dirty bull rushes. Resigned, she hung her head. Both of her plaits fell on either side of her face.

A shadow fell over her. She peeked at the hem of

Thorold's Benedictine robe. He intoned a murmured prayer, "Hearken. We beseech thee, O Lord, to bless thy servants Comte Hugh and Comtesse Adelaide de Vermandois."

Deep in her mind, Isabel cursed the monk. Her heart warned against such blasphemy. Thorold entreated Almighty God on behalf of those who sought to wrong her, who had abused her with frequent beatings for the smallest and greatest infractions and neglected the barest display of a parent's love and affection for her. Was there truly a God? If so, why had He ignored Isabel's prayers all of her life?

Claremond's harsh sobs nearly drowned out Thorold's voice. Isabel did not dare look up and comfort her nurse, who had witnessed the same scene countless times by now. She must learn to accept it, as Isabel had done. Afterward, she would be at Isabel's side, with a poultice of herbs for the fat, red welts on her back. Isabel relied on her nurse's care, no matter how poorly she treated Claremond.

Despite all her fear and the memories of prior beatings, nothing prepared her for the first heavy wallop from the hazel rods across her shoulders. Her back dipped before her mother's nails clawed at her scalp again. Isabel bit her lower lip and held herself rigid, despite the sudden pressure of her mother's knee at the center of her back.

"Give me the rods, Hugh," Adelaide ordered. "I shall teach this wayward girl of ours respect for her parents and her new husband. Lift her skirts."

Isabel quaked anew as a cool current drifted over her bared buttocks. Usually, her parents lashed her with the switches on her back. Before she could steel herself for this new form of punishment, the hazel rods sliced across her tender skin. Her screams and sobs vied with Claremond's own.

Isabel remained abed for two days before Brother Thorold came to the nursery with a summons from Hugh and Adelaide. Her nurse's loud gasp stirred Isabel, who slept on her stomach. She cradled her head on the thick pallet stuffed with goose feathers and eyed the monk in the doorway. He held her stare.

Claremond withdrew the hand she had clasped over her mouth. "They cannot truly think Isabel is being lazy and unrepentant. She is not ready to kneel and pray for hours in the chapel."

"It need not be hours if the willful child would comply with her parents' wishes."

"She can barely move! Are you a servant of God? Have pity upon her."

"This is the command of her parents. Shall I tell them the child's nurse has refused to comply?"

Claremond protested, "Isabel needs more time to recover her strength!"

The monk stared down his hooked nose at her. "She shall have it when she submits to her parents' commands. I await you both outside your door."

He pulled it shut on Claremond's astonished face. The nurse turned to the pallet. "Ready yourself, child."

Isabel washed her face and pulled on a clean robe over her chemise. Every movement drew a groan or wince. With shoes on her feet and a mantle covering her, she stepped out of the nursery and found Brother Thorold awaiting her.

He looked beyond her at Claremond. "You may wait outside the chapel for the girl. I am to speak with her alone."

They went to the private chapel reserved for the family. Isabel hugged her arms beneath the mantle, grateful for the wool that warded of the chill, even if the cloth fibers raked at her back through the linen robe and thin chemise of chainsil. Brother Thorold shut the door and blocked Claremond's frown from view. Isabel stood in the center of the chapel.

"You will kneel, child." Thorold commanded.

Her knees hit the bare, cold floor of roughhewn stone. Pain shot through her thighs, but she kept her back ramrod straight. Thorold circled her, while she remained stalwart under his inspection.

He finally stopped and demanded. "Prideful, even when you bend your knees. Why have you set your will against that of God and your parents?"

"God wants me to marry your master the Comte de Meulan?"

His frown and grunt of impatience answered her. He resumed circling her before he said, "It is the duty of children to submit to their parents."

"Is there no duty of parents to be kind and loving to their children?"

"Such sentiments are reserved for obedient children."

"Love and kindness for the obedient only? Did not Jesus himself take pity on wayward sinners and love them as much as his disciples? My father's chaplain told us Jesus loved Mary Magdalene most of all, even though she had sinned."

"The Magdalene sinned and repented. You have not done so before your father."

"Would he show me the same love Jesus blessed Mary Magdalene with, if I submitted and married the Comte de Meulan?"

"Your father is not Jesus. You cannot have the same expectations of him as of the Savior."

"Jesus is the example by which the chaplain teaches us of the duties of a father to his children and of a lord to his people. My father has forsaken the lessons."

"We are not here to discuss your father! We speak of your failures as a child." The clerk halted, his baleful stare fixed on her. "I see you may require further inducement to change your wicked ways."

Sharp tingles spread in waves across her lower back, flaring into a slow burn. She sucked in a harsh breath and regretted it instantly when he smiled. How could he relish the possibility of her pain? "My parents cannot hurt me any further than they already have."

His chuckle brought the scent of wild onions to her nostrils. "We shall see. Bow your head and pray for the forgiveness of God and the mercy of your parents. You are a disgrace to them. This stubbornness of yours will not avail you for long."

Her knees pressed to her chest, silent tears trailed along the bridge of Isabel's nose and pooled in the rushes beneath her cheek. The Benedictine's sallow-faced visage taunted her gaze. Pain blinded her to little else except his blue eyes, filled with familiar reproach. She blinked hard, her hatred focused upon him. During Mass, she often offered penance for her murderous thoughts about Thorold and every evening, she cursed him under her breath before she went to sleep. For three weeks, she had endured a cycle of beatings and lectures. When her mother and father were not wielding the hazel or birch rods, the clerk Thorold scolded her for her non-compliance.

Footfalls shuffled near her head before two fat, watery droplets smacked her forehead, followed by a heavy grunt. "Leave her there. Let her think upon the error of her stubborn ways for another night. Do you hear me, Claremond?"

Hugh's gruff voice preceded his stiff departure. He could barely lift the massive hand that gripped the hazel rods. Wisps of cloth and crimson stains clung to the wood. Still, Hugh attempted a dismissive wave again and ordered everyone out, even Isabel's mother. Beads of perspiration trickled down his temple. Adelaide snorted, as if she rebelled against her husband's command. She retired all the same. Her parting glance held a final sneer for Isabel. Thorold trod beside Hugh, who looked over his shoulder at Claremond. Her hands clasped in supplication, a soft sob escaped her before she followed her master. Even the few men-at-arms who had remained during the beating withdrew with stone-like gazes fixed on the ground, shuttered against Isabel's pain.

Claremond returned to her at some hour of the night, when the torches gave scant light. Isabel must have fallen asleep in the rushes. The nurse touched her arm and heaved a sob.

"Poor, foolish girl. How much more of this do you think you can bear? Don't you see? You have no other choice. You must submit." She set a bowl of congealed fish soup and a hunk of bread on the floor. "Come, child, you must rouse yourself and eat. You have had nothing for two days since your mother forbade me from bringing food to you, until you repented. I had to lie to the cook and ask for an extra portion from dinner for myself. No one must know I brought it for you."

"Take it away," Isabel whispered.

"Obstinate child! Do you think your mother will care if you starved to death? She would offer another of your sisters to the Comte de Meulan. You must eat and gain strength for the trials ahead. They will not cease until your parents achieve their aim—your compliance. You could have spared yourself this abuse if only you had not set your will against your parents' own."

Isabel stifled a pain-filled gasp and glared at the woman. "What would you have had me do? Accept this union and hope my future husband is more tolerant than my parents could ever be? What reason would I have to pray for such? Why should I cling to foolish hope?"

"It is not foolish! My Isabel, there is always hope. There are other means to achieve your goal. You may find the path lies in acceptance of this marriage."

"How can you ask me to submit to my parents and this stranger?"

"It is likely any man you wed would be a stranger. Who is to say he would treat you more poorly than your parents?"

"If he does, I gain nothing by marrying him. What if my mother is right and the old man chastises me for not giving him sons? At least I know what to expect from my parents when they are disappointed. I have survived their beatings before. Always the same punishment, no matter how grave or small my actions might have seemed."

"If the chastisements continue, you will not live much

longer, girl. Your father forbade me from taking you out of the hall. He never said I could not tend to you. He has broken the skin this time. You cannot leave the hall lest your parents learn of it. Await my return here."

"Hurry, Claremond!" Isabel shuddered, her spine bent. Her limbs were heavy. She could not have moved even if she tried. The torches slowly died down. Wisps of cold air nettled her back. She held the cries back until her throat throbbed.

Claremond returned, faster than she might have ever come to her side before. The woman set a brass candelabrum at her feet, a scant distance from Isabel's head. She sucked in her breath.

"Oh, what have they done to you?"

The pity in her nurse's voice stirred fresh tears. Isabel squeezed her eyes tight and held them back. Her cries had not granted her a moment's pity from her parents and if they heard them now from above stairs, her father might return with the hazel rods.

A cool cloth probed one of her cuts. Isabel could not contain the scream deep inside her throat. She jerked away from Claremond and fought for control over her uneven breathing. Waves of heat flared across battered muscles beneath her tender flesh. The pain rippled from her nape to the waist. Claremond soothed and hushed her, her touch lighter than goose feathers upon the tortured flesh. Isabel whimpered and pressed her lips together while she bore Claremond's attention. When even the faintest touch seemed unbearable, she would have sobbed anew, if not for the familiar feel of the cooling poultice and strips of linen that often soothed her ravaged back.

Isabel whispered, "My father may have broken flesh. He cannot break me so easily."

Claremond kissed her forehead. "Oh, he can, my dearest girl. He can and he will. He holds the power of life and death over you. Your father will not stop until you give your consent. Do you want to survive his brutality?"

When Isabel heaved a long, low sigh, Claremond bent close to her ear. "To live for another day, to escape this torture, you must surrender. Give your parents what they want. Marry this Robert de Beaumont so you may be free of their control forever."

"I shall have to submit to my husband's control."

"The lot of every woman. Whatever his faults, he cannot be as cruel as your parents."

Isabel raised her head. "Tell me what I must do."

"First, you must eat. It's cold, but it will nourish you." Claremond pushed the bowl toward her.

Morning arrived faster than Isabel would have hoped. Her father's chief steward entered the hall with two servants and ordered the fire lit at the hearth. The men attended their duties and ignored her. Dizziness almost overwhelmed her. Claremond snored against a stout pillar. The candelabrum at her feet held stubs of tallow. Faint wisps of white smoke spiraled from the blackened wicks. Claremond must have carried the food bowl back to the kitchen in the night.

Isabel groaned while she rested on her forearms and elbows. A dull throb weaved a dizzying path of pain down her back. Tears flooded her eyes and she lacked the strength to wipe them away. A fat one rolled down her cheek. Movement hurt as much as breathing.

She had to try. "Please God, if you are there, if you have pity on me, please help me!"

She pressed her palms flat on the ground and pushed herself almost into a sitting position before she froze. A creak in the wooden door gave scant warning. Then, her tormentors entered. Her father led them, resplendent in garments dyed with indigo and a black mantle trimmed with glossy sable fur on his shoulders. No sign of his exertions on the previous evening slowed his surefooted steps. His eyes gleamed once his gaze fell on her. Comtesse Adelaide wore a scarlet robe, the color much like the flecks of Isabel's blood dotting her garments and cheek the week before. Thin fingers glittered with her favorite rings, including the one that had scraped her daughter's cheek. Brother Thorold followed them, his tonsured head bowed. He lifted his gaze to Isabel's own and made the sign of the cross, as if he intended to ward off evil. If Isabel had the strength, she might have done the same, if only for protection against him.

Claremond snorted and opened her eyes. She blinked harshly at the intrusion of sunlight. Until she realized she and Isabel were not alone. She took a hesitant step toward her charge before pausing in midstride. Her cheeks reddened under Comte Hugh's unrepentant stare. Cowed, the old nurse stood with slumped shoulders against the marble pillar. Likewise, the steward and servants scurried like rats.

Hugh approached Isabel. He stood with his massive legs spread apart. She said nothing, could not have spoken for the dryness inside her mouth. Her hands curled into tight fists, the knuckles pressed hard against the dirtied floor. A whimper died inside her and she lowered her head.

His finger fastened on her chin. "Has this night's unpleasantness taught you to obey me, child?"

She closed her eyes in a futile attempt to shut out his presence. She felt rather than saw Claremond's gaze hard on her tortured back. Her sobs remained trapped in her throat.

"Look at me! Insolent girl, you will look upon my face when I speak to you."

When she glanced at him again, her father bared his teeth in a feral snarl. "Answer, damn you! Do you yield at last? Will you marry Robert de Beaumont?"

He had bedeviled her with the same question after each chastisement. Always, she had maintained her stubborn silence and vowed she would never accept the match. Even as her parents took turns beating her until she lacked strength for little more than curling on the floor into a shuddering heap. She knew powerlessness in those moments. Perhaps as Claremond had said, if she submitted, she might gain come measure of control over her fate with her future husband.

She whispered. "I yield."

His jaw slackened before he grimaced. "Louder, so everyone can hear you."

"I yield. I will marry Robert de Beaumont." The dull monotone sounded like another girl's voice from faraway.

Hugh released her and directed a satisfied smile at her mother. "I told you she would give in if I wielded the hazel rods."

Adelaide glared at her husband from beneath a puckered brow.

Thorold came forward, his narrowed gaze squinting at Isabel. "Can you be so certain, milord?"

Hugh sneered. "Would you have me beat her to death to ensure she'll submit to your lord? A dead wife would do him little good for her dower would remain in my control."

Isabel's breath quickened and her heart thumped. The clerk continued. "You should not rush to trust her word so soon, milord. Let the girl prove herself by devotion and prayer each day and night in your chapel. Then you may be certain she has repented of her wickedness."

When her father, mother and the monk left, Isabel sagged. Claremond nodded. "Do as you must, milady, if only to be free of this place."

Chapter Two – The King's Court
Paris, France: August 1096

Isabel endured the confines of a horse litter with Claremond and Petronilla, a young maidservant aged three years older than Isabel. The trio journeyed to the court of Philip of France in the ensuing summer. Beneath a canopy of leather, with tassels tied to the wooden sides of the litter, Isabel jounced and sweltered in the cramped conveyance.

A jarring turn on the road slammed her against the side of the timbers. She moaned as slivers of wood tore through her robe and raked at the reddened skin beneath. Her chastisement under the unrelenting cruelty of her parents had worn her resolve as thin as the remnants of cloth clinging to her back after each beating. Nearly five months after she had learned of her betrothal, she set off for Paris where her father would convey her to Robert de Beaumont, who attended the French court at the behest of his king.

She had survived the brutal whippings and Brother Thorold's censure. Now an uncertain future awaited her. Whatever lay ahead, she took some comfort in the attendance of familiar servants on the journey. With a few lies, she had earned her freedom from her parents' oppression and secured Claremond's company. She did not intend to let her nurse return home, despite her mother's wishes to the contrary. Her future husband might not make such allowances for her. She had to risk the possibility.

Her soul had paid a heavy price even after the beatings had stopped. She bore the burden of signs of false devotion, pleas for God's forgiveness that nearly choked her before she uttered them and murmured blessings upon her parents. If God existed, He would pardon her lies, spoken only for the benefit of release from her beleaguered existence at Crépy-en-Valois.

"We should be happy your father ordered the horse litter for our comfort," Claremond murmured, lifting her gaze from the embroidered lace on her lap. "I am grateful Comte Hugh considered my aged state before settling on it. Our retinue left Crépy-en-Valois four days ago. We must be at the outskirts of Paris by now. Be content the journey was not overlong."

Isabel pressed her lips tightly together. She would be damned to hellfire before she ever expressed gratitude for anything her father did again. A few moments passed in silence. Then she snatched off the blue linen covering her head. Auburn hair cascaded around her. The sight drew a long groan from Claremond.

Isabel muttered, "The cloth makes me hot."

Her nurse's steadfast stare offered only rebuke.

Isabel wrenched the fine linen back on her head. Petronilla's stifled giggle warned her she had not accomplished the task well.

Claremond cast a baleful glare at the girl beside Isabel. "The little lady has forgotten the importance of appearances. Attend your mistress." The maidservant sprang from her position. She fetched a boar's bristle brush and a small silver gilt mirror from a satchel. Isabel grasped the mirror.

Petronilla pulled the rough bristles through Isabel's tresses. "The color is the same as Comtesse Adelaide's own."

Claremond hushed her. "Be quiet, fool girl! You do not know what you are saying. Isabel has the Russian's hair. Anne of Kiev wed His Grace, King Henry of France, God rest his soul, when I was a girl. My mother often spoke of Queen Anne's beauteous crowning glory, fire and spun gold. Mark me—Isabel has her grandmother's hair."

"You wished I had her humility also." Isabel nodded toward Claremond.

"Milady has the impudence of childhood and shall learn to control it. Marriage to the Comte de Meulan shall teach you this."

"If it means I must be his servant, I'll never learn humility."

Claremond's features reddened in dismay. "Milady has little choice. Such is marriage for women—casting off a father's yoke for your husband's own. Do not forget what Brother Thorold has told you of your betrothed these past months. You shall submit to your husband because you have no other choice."

Isabel clamped her mouth closed and refused any reply. Claremond's gnarled hands continued their toil. The brush strokes Petronilla applied to Isabel's hair whistled through the otherwise silent space.

She thought of her future husband. What did he look like? Even if his age disgusted her, she must bear her husband's attentions and his children with pride, despite her mother's somewhat bewildering attempts at explanation of what awaited Isabel in the marriage bed. Adelaide had only taken further delight in frightening her. If Isabel could endure and bear her lord a son, he might be kind to her.

Isabel remained daunted by the tasks ahead of her. Not only would she have to endear herself to the stranger she must call husband, she would have to influence him to treat her with care, in and out of the marital bed. She understood the purpose of the courses she had yet to experience. She also knew from her mother how a man and woman created their children. She remained less certain of her future husband's expectations. Her mother had told her to lie still and if she did not fight the man, he would take his pleasure and leave her. He would come to her bed each night except for when her monthly bleeding occurred.

"If you are fortunate to escape him even then. Lord knows your father has never spared me his attentions," Adelaide had added. However, Isabel's new husband might once she quickened with his child, preferably a son. Her mother also promised birth would be difficult and painful. At his great age, Comte Robert might be satisfied with one son and Isabel would not have to endure him often.

Somehow, she doubted men and women shared a bed

and did the things her mother had described for the sole purpose of children. There had been a certain malicious delight in Adelaide's tone whenever she spoke of such matters with Isabel, her eyes glistening as though she relished her daughter's tears and horrified gasps. The advice, if Isabel could call it such, could not be true. Otherwise, the nightly sighs of passion and delight she had often overheard drifting from her parents' marital bed would seem odd. Why would any woman accept her husband's attentions knowing the pain and difficulty of childbirth awaited her? She might ask Claremond, who had been married to the Comte de Vermandois' seneschal. He had died fifteen years ago during a skirmish at the walls of the fortress. Claremond must remember some details of her marriage, Isabel mused as she shifted her sullen gaze to the nurse at her embroidery.

After some consideration, Isabel reasoned Claremond would not wish to speak of the marital bed. The nurse and the seneschal had not suited each other, for they had only produced one living son, who had perished beside his father.

Isabel lifted her chin. Her marriage would be different from any other she had known. Her husband would find contentment in her devotion and treat her with the respect all wives deserved. He would never be a brutish man like her father.

Petronilla's quizzical stare preceded a question. "What do you brood over so, milady?"

"Girl, do not question your mistress!" Claremond's sharp rebuke and smack across Petronilla's knee drew a sharp cry from the attendant.

Isabel said, "I was thinking of my husband-to-be."

Claremond smiled at her. "You should, milady. If you are mindful of his needs, not your own, he shall be pleased with you in the end."

"Brother Thorold does not think so. Each day, he condemns me with his sneers and mutters. He believes I am nothing more than an impudent child."

"He is not so far from the mark, milady."

At Claremond's voice, Petronilla halted her brushstrokes in midair. She could not stifle a giggle, even though Claremond threatened another slap. Isabel looked at both their faces and wondered, not for the first time, why her nurse always seemed bothered by anything Petronilla did or said.

The horse litter jerked to a halt. Loud commands issued from beyond the canopy.

"We must be here!" Isabel peeked through the leather folds. As she swiped unruly hair from around her face, her nostrils wrinkled at the smell of the black Percherons glistening with perspiration. The rank odor of the horses mingled with a musty whiff of river water.

Behind two stone-built walls, the bailey of Paris' fortress-fort thronged with people, including Comte Hugh's mounted retainers and men-at-arms on foot. They waited below a rectangular gate tower at the north. A square-shaped great hall towered above their heads. Mid-afternoon sunlight glinted off the lime wash. She wondered whether the layers of lime wash hid deep golden-colored stone, flecked with creamy white and brown tufa as at Crépy-en-Valois. Small, shuttered windows pierced the second floor. Wooden structures extended in a haphazard semicircle from the outskirts of the hall. Grotesque stone effigies lined the inner wall at intervals, water seeping from the carved mouths.

Between the buildings, masses of people lingered, women and children interspersed among the men. From the poorest infantryman to mounted knights, each man bore a red cross, sewn on his tunic or mantle at the right shoulder. Some of the warriors brandished their weapons in mock battles or ate their dinners and argued with each other beneath the shelter of poplar and willow trees. Many of the women encircled a disheveled man and gazed at him in rapt attention. His bare head glistened in the sun. Dirty feet peeked beneath his coarse robe. He held the people enthralled with his wild gesticulations and speech.

He was no different from the other holy men who had often appeared at Crépy-en-Valois, preaching of damnation and hellfire. Such men believed they spoke the Word of God. If He existed, why had He chosen disheveled, crazed men as heralds?

Isabel's father dismounted with a grunt and shook dust from his black mantle. He rounded the horses. His frosty glare met Isabel's wide stare. She ducked inside and snapped the leather canopy closed. She could not escape her father. He extended his jeweled hand between the curtains of the litter. He grabbed and crushed her fingers in a powerful grip. She winced and slid from her confinement. The trailing edge of her green mantle caught at the wood before she tugged it loose. She fell into step beside her father. He dragged her to the hall.

"Let us make homage to King Philip of France." Hugh's rough baritone rumbled over her bowed head. "Remember the courtesy owed to him. Do not speak unless he addresses you. Do you understand me, girl?"

She tamped down her natural inclination to withdraw from his vile touch. She would have to endure it a little longer before she could be free of him forever. "I understand, milord."

She looked behind her. Brother Thorold's resolute stare met hers. He had joined those who accompanied her father to Paris. He remained mounted on his mule. Even as she walked away, a tingling sensation warned her how his gaze followed her every movement. She wished he would leave.

Beside her, Hugh said, "Many of those who have taken up the cross gather here to receive the blessing of Bishop William of Paris. Some shall never see the Holy Land. It is a journey of many months over mountains and through treacherous waters. From here, I am bound for Italy, the Balkan passes and then the waters of the Bosporus. Then I am to travel by boat to Constantinople."

Shocked that her father offered any information

about his journey, much less spoke with her in a civil tone, Isabel hesitated before she asked, "Does the king of France also journey to the Holy Land?"

He halted and glared like a stone sentinel at her. His mercurial temper kept her uncertain as always. She edged away from him until his grip on her tightened. "His Grace cannot partake in the expedition. Pope Urban excommunicated him last year."

Concern for the king's immortal soul occupied Isabel's thoughts. The Holy Father's censure barred a person from receiving the sacrament of Communion and condemned the spirit. How had he earned Rome's wrath? Why had he refused repentance and shunned God's divine grace? Did such a thing even exist?

Her father urged her inside and toward a cavernous, smoke-filled room, from which shouts echoed. Guardsmen lined the walls outside.

A woman with flushed cheeks exited the chamber. A dark blue robe peeked from beneath the folds of her mantle, trimmed with ermine. Six attendants and a page followed.

Hugh halted and Isabel fell into a deep curtsy. He said, "Your Grace. I did not expect to see you so soon."

"Rather, you hoped you would see little of me, Hugh. There is no need to dissemble. Your brother has eagerly awaited your arrival, if only for the sake of the daughter you have brought with you. I see she bears her mother's loveliness. How unfortunate for you, but a blessing to her betrothed. Is your daughter cursed with Adelaide's vile temperament, or have her years at Crépy-en-Valois subdued her?"

Isabel's heart thudded, her gaze on the floor. She shivered when sharp nails grasped her chin. Carnelian, red jasper and sapphire set in gold filigree shimmered before her gaze. The woman tipped Isabel's face up for her inspection. Light green eyes met Isabel's own. Thin lips curved into a smile.

"At least the eyes are yours, Hugh. Welcome to Paris, Isabel." Queen Bertrade de Montfort's smooth voice washed over her. "Come with me, my dear. We have much to discuss before this proposed union between you and the Comte de Meulan takes place."

Isabel followed the royal retinue down the long corridor in silence, watched by guardsmen who leered at her. Queen Bertrade paid no attention. Isabel ascended stone steps just behind her, entering a long corridor without windows. The pageboy preceded them, holding a rush light aloft. A cool draft pervaded the hall. Isabel shivered beneath the woolen mantle and expelled a harsh breath in a puff of curling tendrils. Tapestries hung on the walls and in recessed niches, now illuminated by the passing light. Isabel looked behind her. The queen's attendants trod the long passageway in two pairs of three, their faces in shadow. Isabel wondered why they appeared so grim.

An arched, double door loomed, with crosses carved around the knockers. The leaf-shaped iron hinges groaned when the page opened the portal. Queen Bertrade ushered in her entourage, who fanned out along the timber floor. They unfurled the wooden shutters of the rectangular windows. Sunlight bathed the chamber in gold. Semicircular lunettes rose above each window, brightly painted in indigo, green and vermillion. The light revealed chests along the edges of the room, wooden pegs hung with cloaks, two low stools and the benches beneath each window.

Turning in a wide circle, Isabel admired the space until she realized King Philip's wife studied her. Her Grace, the queen, stood in the center of the room, her bejeweled fingers clasped together. Isabel fell into a deep curtsy. Blue linen cascaded around her shoulders.

"Come here."

Isabel rose. Wood scraped the timber floor as two of the attendants settled the stools beside the queen, who gestured to one seat for Isabel, while she took the other. Isabel settled beside her. The royal attendants returned with a pewter decanter and tankards.

"Take some wine."

"Comtesse Adelaide would not approve, Your Grace. She never let me or my brothers and sisters drink wine, even when watered."

A thin smile curved Bertrade de Montfort's lips upward. "Your mother is not here. Wine improves the humors. It is no small wonder your mother restricted its consumption. I do not believe she drank enough wine in her lifetime." Isabel stared in puzzlement at the queen, who continued, "Still, you are here with me, not her. You shall do as I command. Drink the wine."

The queen's tone indicated she would accept no refusal. Isabel accepted the tankard and brought it to her lips. The queen waved her attendants away with the canter. The wine's warm sweetness lingered on Isabel's tongue and coursed through her belly. "It's lovely, Your Grace."

Isabel took another sip before she settled the tankard between her fingers on her lap. "You said my betrothed is here."

Queen Bertrade grinned and revealed crooked teeth. She tasted her wine before answering. "He has coin, men-at-arms, horses and armaments to make war on the Saracens. He refrains from the journey himself. He has fought in countless battles. A warrior's courage must have abandoned him in his advanced years."

Isabel cleared her throat. "How old is the comte, exactly, Your Grace? He has lived more than fifty years. Is he so old he cannot fight? I asked Brother Thorold before we left Crépy-en-Valois. He considered my question impertinent and reproved me for it."

"Who is this Brother Thorold?"

Isabel detailed the arrival of the Benedictine monk, who had arrived in the month of the blood moon. "He believes I am unworthy to wed the Comte de Meulan. I am determined to prove him wrong," she finished.

"I do not doubt it. Has this mere clerk informed you of his disapproval? Has he been so bold?"

"His eyes told me, Your Grace."

When she fell silent, the queen made no comment.

Silence stretched until one among the royal attendants spoke of the impending dinner hour. Isabel sipped her wine. Her hand started shaking and a little crimson stain dotted her skirts. The queen snapped her fingers for one of her attendants, who blotted the cloth.

Queen Bertrade said, "You must not appear discomfited or nervous at your debut. The courtiers may want to observe you, the fair daughter of Comte Hugh de Vermandois."

"I am famed?"

"For your beauty, dear child, as was your mother in her time. You must appear before the king, your uncle. He has not seen you since you were two years old. What has your father told you of the king?"

"Father hardly speaks of His Grace, King Philip."

"It does not surprise me. There was always a little rivalry between Philip and his brother, or so my husband tells me. Philip said Hugh wished he might have been firstborn, destined to inherit his father's legacy. Philip reviled his birthright for a time and once showed little interest in the duties of a king. His power has availed him little in these years."

Isabel drank the last of her wine. "Do you mean in his dealings with Rome?"

Queen Bertrade proffered her tankard to one of her ladies, who poured the wine from its pewter canter. The woman also filled Isabel's cup.

"The wine has loosened your tongue too much, child. I suspect your lack of forethought is a sure sign of your mother's influence."

Isabel clenched the tankard between her fingers. "Please, forgive me. Father always says I must think before I speak, yet I never do. He blames my mother. I do try very hard to be careful of what I say. I cannot pretend to be unaware of the king's troubles with Rome, Your Grace"

The queen fingered the tasseled ends of her indigo and gold girdle. "Pretense is wise, especially at court. When you are older, you shall learn to temper the thoughts that swirl in your mind and spill from your lips too easily. You require greater mastery of your passions and will, lest they lead to your downfall. A woman requires a strong mind for the fulfillment of her desires. I feared for your upbringing with a mother like Comtesse Adelaide, a woman governed by cold reasoning alone. No passion in her at all, except for beating her underlings into submission." She paused and looked at Isabel, who sipped her wine. "You are not the same as her."

Queen Bertrade twisted her cup of drink in her hands. Her eyes were downcast and her lips drawn into a tight smile, bordering on a grimace. "I can foresee you shall be a woman of great beauty. Beware of men enthralled only by a woman's visage, Isabel, for they turn on her when familiarity and old age lessen her charms. A woman must have more than her allurements to secure her place beside a man, if she wishes to rule his heart and mind."

Isabel stared, bewildered. Was that what she should desire, to rule her betrothed's thoughts and feelings? The queen met her gaze. "Drink your wine and then you may have some more."

At the entrance of the smoke-filled hall, Isabel curtsied on wobbly legs before her father. He halted his steady pacing and bowed beside Queen Bertrade. Then he glowered at Isabel, his hands tightening into bulging fists at his sides.

"I began to fear you would not come, child."

The queen laid her jeweled hand on Isabel's shoulder. "You do not begrudge my time with your daughter. If so, your quarrel is with me, Hugh."

Isabel shuddered, certain the woman could feel the fear coursing through her. A tight knot coiled in her stomach, growing tauter each moment. She licked her dried lips, tasted the wine on her tongue again and wished she had some more to improve her humors in the manner the queen suggested.

The comte's face whitened. "I would never seek an argument with you, Your Grace."

She chuckled. "Your lies are still so discernible. Why do you trouble yourself with them, when you know I will never believe you? Escort your daughter into the hall."

With a nod, Queen Bertrade and her attendants preceded them. Comte Hugh grabbed Isabel's arm. A tiny flinch escaped her. She hid it while desperately clearing her throat. When her father snapped his gaze toward her, she returned his stare. "It is the smoke from the hearth, milord."

"You shall grow accustomed to it. Philip is impatient."

Through a white haze and a cacophony of voices surrounding them, Isabel and her father tread between long lines of trestle tables. Pillars on either side of the cavernous hall supported the timber roof. The narrow slit at the center of the ceiling hardly eased the conditions in the room. It proved unbearably hot. Perspiration trickled from beneath Isabel's head covering. She dared not remove it. She willed her feet forward in her father's wake, aware how every step brought her closer to a moment she anticipated and dreaded. Together, they mounted the dais.

"This is the beauteous daughter of the Comtesse de Vermandois?" A raspy chuckle issued from directly before her.

Isabel sank into a deep curtsy and remained there. Her father's voice boomed. "Your Grace, I present my daughter, Isabel."

All conversations ceased. Isabel quivered with the realization of how every gaze in the room lingered on her. Her heart hammered and pounded. She clenched her tiny fists and drew in a deep lungful of air.

"Well, does the child speak?"

Laughter unleashed in a rippling wave and Isabel cringed. Her father tugged her until she stood beside him.

"Is she so modest she cannot speak? Let me see your face, girl. You are my cherished niece, after all."

When her father's hold tightened, Isabel blinked back tears. Her stare traipsed across the rush-strewn stone floor, to the trailing edge of a white tablecloth, stained and tattered. Finally, she encountered the steady black-eyed stare from a corpulent face, which reminded her of her father's own. Familiar fleshy cheeks and a bulbous nose emphasized the resemblance, as did the dark short hair.

King Philip of France murmured, "She is well-favored with her mother's beauty."

Queen Bertrade, now seated beside him, laid a hand glittering with gems and enamels in gold on his shoulder. "Did you not desire Comtesse Adelaide yourself for a time?"

The king covered her fingers with his. His stare remained on Isabel. "Only until I knew you, my queen."

His wife chuckled and the noblewomen at her back joined in her merriment. Isabel looked away, feeling as though they mocked her and her mother.

The king said, "My knights shall compete in a tournament of arms at the beginning of next month, so we may test the strength and skill of those who would fight against the Saracens in the Holy Land. Hugh, you shall join us in the melee."

"The Holy Father has decreed the date of departure for all who would fight against the Saracens as mid-month. I must prepare for the journey, Your Grace. I have no time for your war games."

"You dare not refuse me. Since His Holiness has forbidden my participation, it is your duty to represent France's interest. You will prove yourself worthy in the melee, Hugh."

The king's tone held no request—only a command. Her father bowed. The pressure of his hand on her arm increased. She could hardly stifle the cry in the back of her throat as he muttered, "If Your Grace wishes it."

The king waved them off. Isabel sank down on the bench she would share with her father, grateful for its support. A server offered a wooden bowl of water for hand washing. When the meal began, Isabel's father grabbed fine cuts of the roasted capon and pork. He gave her a quarter of what he claimed for himself. Isabel chewed the bread in silence. A cupbearer offered her father wine, which he took. When the page did the same for her, Comte Hugh gave him such a baleful stare the young man nearly spilled the canter in his fright. As it was, she remained grateful and thankful she had not spewed the contents of her stomach. Her gaze followed the servant to an elegant table fountain, featuring enameled walls and encrusted with jewels.

Just below the dais, a man garbed in crimson and gold stared across the expanse at Isabel. She might not have noticed him, except for his stare as he brought the cup to his lips. His narrow features suited the hooked nose. Deep lines crinkled the corners of his light-colored eyes. Whitish-blond hair cut in a severe, bowl-shaped style topped his high forehead. His open regard startled her. No man, no one had ever thought her worth such interest. Who was he to stare at her so? She sucked in a breath and jerked her gaze away only to meet the watchful gaze of another impertinent admirer, seated a few benches apart from the first man.

This one's visage hinted at his youth, more comely than most of his fellow peers, favored with a high brow, large eyes and dark hair in curls almost to his shoulders. He flexed powerful fingers before grasping a tankard in his hand. The contents sloshed over the rim. He raised the cup to his thinned lips and drank in one long gulp, while ignoring a thin stream of dark liquid that spilled down his trim beard. He brushed the droplets away from his indigo-colored tunic, yet his regard never wavered from hers. After lowering his cup, he licked his lips.

She turned from the bothersome sight of him to her father. He shoved a large piece of venison pie into his mouth. He guzzled the last of his wine and dirtied the tablecloth with his grease-stained hands. A scruffy hound with a twitching tail whined beside him, eager for any of the gnawed bones piled high next to the trencher.

With a low snarl, Hugh kicked at the dog, which scampered off. Isabel wished herself far away from the company of men.

Chapter Three – The Melee
Paris, France: August 1096

A mood of exhilaration suffused the court on the morning of the melee, which also marked the start of the third week since Isabel's arrival in Paris. She could not hide her curiosity. "Your Grace, please tell me, what is the melee?"

In a circle of noblewomen, Queen Bertrade looked up from her embroidery to where Isabel sat on a bench beneath an opened window. "Something no gently-bred girl should be curious about or wish to see. It is a bloody display of men's folly and pride."

Isabel looked toward the large meadow in the distance. An army of men and horses amassed in the field. Their war cries and bellows, the snorts and trampling hooves of their mounts echoed across the landscape. She leaned slightly out of the window and wished she had a better view. As it was, the poplars to the left of the window partially blocked the site.

"Dear girl, come away. Heavens, what would I tell your father if something happened to you? Think of your poor mother! I am certain she would be so devastated if you fell and broke your neck. She has such a tender heart for her children."

A loud guffaw followed. Isabel turned sharply though not in time to catch the one who laughed. The queen had just mocked her for all her supposed concern about Isabel falling to her death. Whenever Queen Bertrade spoke of her mother, an underlying tone of sarcasm laced her voice. Isabel recognized it in her father's speech when he did the same, so she could not fail to observe similarities in the queen's behavior.

Still Isabel said, "Thank you for your concern, Your Grace." She settled against the cool stone beside her. She had slept poorly the previous night and not just because of the loud snores from the royal attendants and pages. The queen's revelation at dinner about her mother had disturbed her. Had Comte Hugh and King

Philip been rivals because of her mother? She perceived the queen felt some latent jealousy about her husband's interest in Comtesse Adelaide. Had her royal uncle truly preferred Isabel's mother? How did he feel about his brother marrying the woman he might have wanted instead?

Isabel hugged her knees to her chest and laid her chin on them. To think, if the king had sired children on her mother, she might have truly been a child of France.

A deafening crescendo of trumpets blared. Isabel jerked from her seat. "What are they doing?"

Queen Bertrade clutched her chest, muttered briefly under her breath and then returned to her embroidery. "Men's follies are of no concern to us."

Isabel ignored the queen and braced her arms on the windowsill. She imagined rather than saw the chaotic scene unfolding beyond the stone bailey. Hooves thundered across the field and a loud clash of metal resounded. Frustrated by her poor view, Isabel anticipated the worst.

Throughout the morning, the trumpets blasted again, jarring the occupants of the room each time. Until midday, when instead of the sounds from the field, a booming knock came at the door. The royal consort calmed her panicked attendants and gestured toward a pageboy, who answered the door. The poor boy quaked, the tendons in his slender neck standing out as he swallowed. He hastened back from the entryway as a squire bypassed him, his red and gold tunic splattered with mud. He bent on one knee and bowed his head.

"How dare you intrude upon the queen's privacy?" King Philip's wife drew herself to her full height and peered at the young man.

"I beg Your Grace's pardon. I bear a message for Isabel de Vermandois." A shrill tone escaped him.

Isabel stood on shaking legs, her senses heightened. "I am she."

Queen Bertrade glowered in her direction.

Still, Isabel waved the squire on. "Please, what news?

Has my father been harmed in the melee?"

Despite his cruelty to her, she still cared. Sometimes she wished she could hate him as much as he hated her.

"The Comte de Vermandois is well and among the victors, milady. Your betrothed, the Comte de Meulan, suffered a grievous injury to his head. The king's chaplain has been with him since mid-morning. He has prayed for milord's soul and remains watchful for signs he is worsening."

The queen gasped. "He receives the final rites?"

"He does not. The king's own physician attended to him. He believed my master would benefit from the opening of his skull, a relief from the bone pressing on his brain."

Isabel gasped in wonderment at the possibility of such a procedure. "Could a man survive?"

The squire said, "I would not know, milady. He suffers gravely. I hope he may survive. However, in the uncertainty of his future health, he insists you should come now, before the operation is performed, so you may be married at once."

Queen Bertrade moved beside Isabel. She dug her talon-like nails into Isabel's arm and asked, "Without the king's permission?"

Isabel winced, as much at the painful grip as the fury in the queen's tone. Her father had committed her to this course. None of them could undo it. She had given in to her parents' chastisement to gain her freedom. If she did not marry now, Robert de Beaumont might die and ruin her fragile hope. She could imagine a fate more distasteful than marriage to some old man whom she had never met. She might have to live in a nunnery or worse, return to her father's house indefinitely. Both possibilities terrified her. She had to marry Robert de Beaumont now and pray for the strength to tolerate him and the will to meet his expectations.

As she readied to affirm her agreement, her father stormed into the room. Isabel fell silent.

The queen said, "Have you heard the latest demand

from Isabel's betrothed? The fool man has injured himself in the melee and now seeks a hasty marriage. The Church has forbidden it."

Hugh chuckled hoarsely and swiped a hand over his face, smearing grime and droplets of blood. "You and my brother would know much about how to defy a pope, Your Grace. The consequences never stopped you."

Queen Bertrade reddened and she released her hold on Isabel. "Impudent cur! I should have you dismissed from court permanently."

"Try, Your Grace. Philip still needs me. At least, he needs my money and men to deal with his enemies in France and Rome."

The queen stamped her foot. "What do you intend to do about Robert de Beaumont's demands? Isabel cannot have such a hasty union made under duress, Hugh."

He snatched a tankard of wine from one among the queen's attendants. "I am her father and I alone decide her fate. Not even Philip may gainsay me, Your Grace. The betrothal agreement stands. Isabel may wed Robert at his choosing!"

His hardened gaze swept over Isabel. She lost the ability to speak or even think, rooted to the spot beneath his unrepentant glare even though she wanted nothing more than to flee from him. He downed the cupful of wine before demanding more.

"The man gains nothing by his fidelity," the queen insisted. "Even if he marries your daughter, Hugh, he is unlikely to consummate the marriage. Only the birth of a surviving son can secure her future."

"I do not care whether the man proves himself, as you say, or not. My honor is at stake. I gave my promise to Robert so he might marry Isabel. I am a man of my word. If he wants her, he may have her."

"You would dispense with the formalities and the consent of the king, the papal dispensation—"

The Comte de Vermandois hurled the tankard against the wall. Blood-red wine splashed on the floor, sopped up in the rushes. "Spare me your false piety, Your

Grace. When have you ever cared for popes? My brother suffered excommunication because he would not give you up as the Holy Father demanded. The formalities and Philip be damned to hellfire as well! Do not think I am unaware of his objections or yours to my plans for Isabel. You both would see her wed to your brother, Amaury, lest royal blood bolster Norman interests in France. Your wishes do not matter when the betrothal has spanned three years."

Isabel stared between the condemning glares her father and the queen shared. Daughters were of little consequence to fathers except in their marital prospects. To have her father confirm it tore at her heart. Did he truly believe she held no value beyond this union? If so, she would have to prove her worth to the Comte de Meulan.

Her hands fisted at her sides. "I am here to honor my father's pledge. I will wed the man he has chosen now, if my betrothed desires it."

An uneasy silence followed her words, spoken with a halting crack. Queen Bertrade's scowl deepened. When she finally regarded Isabel, her features had altered and reminded Isabel of the monstrous stone carvings along the walls outside. "You are a treasure, dear child. Be sure the Comte de Meulan never forgets what he gains by this union with one of royal descent."

Then she gestured to the squire who brought them such terrible news. "How was your lord injured?"

The squire shuffled on his feet. "He fell from his mount during the melee when a fellow combatant unhorsed him. His helmet rolled away. They were fighting in very close quarters, you see and as such, anything can happen in the heat of the contest." He hesitated before continuing. "A courser's very strong and fast, though he's easier to control than milord's destrier. The courser's hooves struck milord in the head."

Isabel gasped in horror. Her father's grimace fell on her. She recalled her impressions of the deafening charges across the field, the sights and sounds of men and horses crashing together. She covered her mouth and almost reeled from the shock.

The queen asked, "What can be done for your master?"

The squire did not answer immediately. Isabel looked at him. "Is there hope for him?"

"Hope remains, milady." He sniffled and scratched the bridge of his nose. A lock of wheat-colored hair fell over his large eyes, the curls cut in the bowl-shaped style of the Normans, severely shorn at the sides.

Though Isabel did not know him, her heart ached at his sorrow. "What is your name, squire?"

Queen Bertrade stared at her as if she had grown another head atop her shoulders.

"Please, tell me." Isabel stepped toward him. She noticed the smear of blood on his ruined tunic, half-hidden beneath the mud.

"I'm called FitzRobert, milady."

She said, "Then, FitzRobert, please tell my betrothed I shall meet with him so we may be married at once."

The squire bowed and retreated. Isabel glanced at Her Grace who was once again glaring at Isabel's father. He met her regard. Isabel suspected some bitter, unspoken argument continued between the pair.

For her part, she asked no questions, lest her father think her brazen and pummeled her head. She would soon gain her freedom. She only had to be patient and dutiful. It could not be such a hard task to accomplish.

Besides, she wanted to know something else. "Who unhorsed him, milord?"

"William de Warenne." Comte Hugh accepted more wine, which he gulped with the same fervor as the first two. Issuing a loud belch, he shoved the tankard at the closest of the royal attendants, who backed away as though her skirts were on fire.

"Who is he, milord?"

"Another of the Norman magnates who came to power in England, much like Robert." Isabel's father relaxed on the bench she had earlier occupied. He clasped his grimy hands over his rounded belly. "William de Warenne is richer by far than Robert, for he holds an English earldom." With a grin, he nodded to Isabel. "I should have wed you to him instead. You could have been the countess of Surrey in England instead of the Comtesse de Meulan."

"I would not marry him!" Despite the shocked stares of her father and the queen, she continued, "He was cruel to unseat my betrothed. He is the cause of the pain Comte Robert suffers. I wouldn't marry such a wretched man."

"There are no rules in the melee. You would have little choice in the matter of your marriage. You would still marry as I dictated," Hugh warned.

Isabel nodded. "Still, you chose the Comte de Meulan for me, above all the men of France. He must be worthy and good enough to be my husband."

A little laugh escaped Queen Bertrade. "Hugh did not choose your husband for his goodness or worthiness. You are not as intelligent as I had thought, my Isabel."

"I am sure my wisdom shall increase with time as the comte's wife." Isabel's sharp tone rang through the room. The queen eyed her with an unwavering stare, suddenly turned cold and embittered.

Isabel ignored her and continued. "Even if the Comte de Meulan survives, I shall hate this William de Warenne as long as I live."

The queen rubbed her brow as if an ache plagued her head. "This display of loyalty is strange, my girl, when you have never met your betrothed or the man who bore him to the ground. How do you know your betrothed has earned such devotion or his opponent such abhorrence? As your father said, no rules govern the melee. Your anger is unseemly when Comte Robert's horse might well be at fault for not bearing his rider. Would you hate the beast too, Isabel?"

Isabel sniffed. Whoever this William de Warenne might be, his careless actions had almost wrecked her one chance to escape her parents. She would never forgive him.

In a crimson mantle edged with ermine, Isabel followed her father from the fortress to the grounds of the melee. Two royal attendants trailed her with six men at-arms, three each on either side. The men carried torches to light their way as evening approached. Flames sputtered in the cool wind. A chill ran down Isabel's spine and she clutched her mantle closer to her body.

They approached tents bivouacked on slippery ground ringed with gorse shrubs. At the center of the encampment, the squire FitzRobert looked up from the battered shield he held on his lap. He shoved it aside, scrambled to his feet and bowed before he ducked into the nearest tent. A tentsmith repairing a tear in the top of the yellow and red fabric did not notice them.

Isabel looked around her, aware they drew the attention of others. Men stared openly at her with expressions she had never seen before. Their determined stares, idle winks and lopsided grins left her uncomfortable. It seemed as though she stood naked and exposed before them. She tore her gaze away and looked ahead. The tent seemed small even for one person. She glimpsed three figures through its opening. Two persons knelt on either side of another individual, prone on a pallet with large feet jutting through the opening. Then the tent flap fluttered and a tonsured Brother Thorold emerged. Torchlight illuminated the creases and folds of flesh sagging beneath his large eyes.

Her hands tightened into fists. The fingernails sunk into her palm, a trifling pain.

The black-robed monk studied them before he acknowledged her father. "I greet you in the name of God."

"I have brought my daughter at the behest of Robert, for the fulfillment of his pledge."

Brother Thorold's stare widened and a deep flush suffused his features. "Milord wishes to wed the girl? Now? Bishop Ivo of Chartres has said the marriage cannot go forward while the consanguinity issue remains. We must wait for the papal dispensation."

Hugh ignored the Benedictine. "How does your lord fare this evening?" His inquiry carried a tone of impatience.

The monk clasped his hands together. "The Comte de Meulan lives, though his wound pains him. I am surprised he had the presence of mind to consider fulfilling his marital vows now. He may have to surrender his soul to God this night."

Isabel whispered, "His squire said there was hope."

Her father whipped around and eyed her, his mouth a thin line of disapproval. Brother Thorold pursed his lips.

She looked at each man, emboldened by the need to secure her future. "Brother Thorold, when you arrived at Crépy-en-Valois, you told me all you knew of the Comte de Meulan, how he was first bloodied in the conquest of England thirty years ago. He has won many victories since then. I cannot believe a man of the comte's vigor, who has survived brutal battle against the English, would surrender his life so easily. There must be hope he'll live."

The clerk condemned her naiveté with his stony silence.

She refused to accept his judgment as the last word on the comte's future. "As his friend, his clerk, you should urge him to seek God's help and mercy, to pray for strength."

Thorold said, "Milady, one cannot question the will of God."

She refused to accept his blind devotion. "With faith, hope and prayer, anything is possible." Her father's priest had taught her such prattle, even if she did not believe it wholeheartedly.

"Thorold." A pained grunt escaped the darkened tent. "You may debate my betrothed on matters of faith later. Let me see her."

FitzRobert stepped out into the evening air. "I told milord milady was here with her father. He would speak with you, milady, if your father would allow it."

"I permit it." Comte Hugh gestured toward the tent and Isabel curtsied. She also ducked inside, despite being even shorter than the Comte de Meulan's squire. Her eyes adjusted to the dimness quickly and she gasped at the sight of the man. Whitish-blond wisps of hair stuck to a thick crust of blood on his head. His gaze fell on her, the same brilliant eye color as she recalled from the night before. He was the first of the two men who had admired her in King Philip's hall during dinner.

"Forgive me, milady." His gruff tone belied the amusement in his expression. "I had not planned our first meeting would occur under these circumstances."

"You do not need my forgiveness. It's not your fault you were hurt." Isabel knelt at his bedside. He expelled a labored breath. She was glad, in part, for the near darkness in the tent, for it hid all other injuries he suffered. A warm, burly hand enclosed hers. Though unexpected, she did not flinch in surprise. He remained a stranger, but his touch soothed her frayed nerves.

"Then you must forgive me my haste in seeking to wed you."

She rubbed her arms. "Milord, why do you wish to wed me?" At his low chuckle, she continued in a rush of words, "I understand the betrothal contract binds us. I would marry you at any time and place in which you would say. Still, should we not wait until your injury is attended?"

He laughed again, a display of slightly yellowed teeth and drew her hand to his chest. His heart thrummed beneath his tunic. "We cannot. Before the king's physician starts boring holes in my head, I would have my wits about me long enough to exchange marital vows with you. I am honor bound, though I would regret if we married today and you next became a widow."

"Please, milord, you must not speak of death. Believe and you may yet live."

"Do you think so?"

"It is my fervent wish and prayer."

"I am no fool, Isabel. I am a man of fifty years—old enough to be your father." His smile widened. "I am older than your father. Can you bear marriage to such a man? You must know I may die long before you do."

"Not this night, or for many nights to come, if you'll only allow someone to care for you now. I do not want you to die. I wish to be your wife."

She prayed he would believe her words, spoken for her benefit as much as for the father who must be eavesdropping on their conversation. The comte's sudden frown suggested otherwise.

"What you want is irrelevant. Your father has commanded it."

"Still, I wish it."

"Why? Were you unhappy in your father's home?"

How could he have already guessed at what she would not say? Her father stood outside the tent. He must have heard the bold question and she dared not give the full truth to her betrothed within earshot of her father.

Comte Robert released her hand and reached tentatively for her cheek beneath the linen covering her hair. She did not recoil from his caress, though she barely knew him. His caress conveyed sympathy and understanding of her plight, which she had yearned for in the husband her father chose. At least he had allowed them this moment of privacy. Hugh would have disapproved of their familiarity.

She clutched her betrothed's fingers against her skin. His candor appealed to her, so unlike the deception and stark cruelty she had always known. "Were you never married before?"

His smile vanished in an instant. She straightened, certain the question had displeased him. Only when his cool hand sought the warmth of her skin once more, did she risk leaning into his touch again.

"I should have married Godehilde de Toeni. Instead, she chose a lustful fool, Baldwin, son of Comte Eustace de Boulogne. I believe he shall undertake the cross same as your father. Godehilde may accompany him."

Despite her own uncertainties, Isabel found sympathy for the plight of her would-be husband. Had he loved this faithless Godehilde de Toeni? She must have chosen Comte Eustace's son. Why would she have done so? Her betrothed had proved gentle so far. It would be an honor to wed him.

He continued, "If I were to die unwed, it would not displease me if my brother Henri inherited my wealth and estates. He is more than a beloved brother. Henri has brought great honor to our family. Before I saw you, I could have gone to my grave knowing Henri remained to carry on our bloodline. From the moment you entered the great hall of your uncle Philip of France, I knew I must have you as my wife, Isabel. Your father's opinion of you makes it clear to me he finds little value in daughters. I see it as my honor and duty to offer you some sign you are worthy of love and adoration. I suspect you have yet to learn this fact."

Isabel blinked back tears. He understood her misery so easily. Was her suffering so apparent to others?

He stroked the softness of her flesh. "You are good and kind, Isabel. You do not recoil from an old man such as me. Instead, your generous nature comforts my heart. You think first of my wellbeing. I expect such devotion. I demand it." His hand cupped her cheek. "Lest you imagine me selfless, it would be a source of great pride for me to wed you. I would be the envy of every man in the kingdom of France and the duchy of Normandy, rightly so. We shall marry tonight, Isabel, without the benefit of the Holy Father's dispensation. I pray God shall grant us a full measure of happiness together. I will require one more thing from you."

She waited with trepidation for his demands. What could such a powerful man want with her?

"Children. You will give me children if I survive this day. A firstborn son to inherit my honors and titles, with brothers to aid him. I suspect daughters will come. Your mother has several of them, Thorold tells me. I need sons. I understand you are unready to receive me, as a wife should. I am willing to wait. Have you had your first show of woman's blood?"

When she did not immediately answer, he snapped, "I mean your courses! Have they begun?"

Mortification fanned waves of heat across her face. He had seemed so gentle before that the coarseness of the question shocked her. Despite an understanding of its importance for her childbearing future, she could not hide the blush on her cheeks.

When her gaze fell, his hand grasped her chin. "Never lie to me, Isabel."

"*Non*, I have not had my courses."

When his frown returned, she rushed on, desperate to avoid the possibility of his displeasure. "My nurse feels certain it will be soon. You must not worry. My mother has many children. When the time comes, I shall give you heirs."

"Give me the sons I want and you shall know only happiness as my wife."

The space between them hung heavy with the consequences if she should fail him.

Just after Vespers, in the private chapel of Queen Bertrade, Isabel stood before the bishop of Paris William de Montfort, who was the younger brother of the royal consort. Isabel wondered how the queen had influenced her brother's position with the Church, especially given his obvious youth and the ill will between the Holy Father and King Philip.

Her father gave a huff of impatience. His billowing breath reeked of wine. She turned from him and glanced at Comte Robert at her right. He shuddered as a pain-filled gasp escaped him. His brows knotted with evident discomfort. She would have reached for him, while knowing her father would have deemed it improper. Her betrothed managed a smile just for her.

Bishop William addressed him first. "Robert, Comte de Meulan, wilt thou have Isabel to be thy wedded wife, to live together after God's ordinance in the holy estate of matrimony? Wilt thou love her, comfort her, honor and keep her, in sickness and in health and forsaking all others, keep thee only unto her, so long as ye both shall live?"

"I shall." A groan escaped Comte Robert as he spoke and he wavered on his feet, before his squire bolstered him with a hand at his elbow. Isabel drew a deep breath, full of fear he might faint. A thin streak of blood trickled from beneath a strip of linen wound around his head. She jerked her gaze away from it and found Bishop William frowning, likely at her inattentiveness to the ceremony.

"Isabel, wilt thou have this man Robert, Comte de Meulan, to be thy wedded husband, to live together after God's ordinance in the holy estate of matrimony? Wilt thou obey and serve him, love, honor and keep him in sickness and in health and, forsaking all others, keep thee only unto him, so long as ye both shall live?"

"I shall."

As the benediction began, Isabel's heart soared with the knowledge she would finally escape her parents. With all her heart, she promised obedience and joy to her husband for all his days, if only he might survive this night.

Lisa J. Yarde

Chapter Four – The Comtesse
Paris, France: August 1096

Isabel groaned and rolled away from the insistent voice in her ear. "Please, milady, you must awaken."

Morning could not have come so soon. Isabel had just fallen asleep a moment ago, or so it seemed. After Matins, following a night of fine feasting and too much of the queen's wine, Isabel went to bed. Long after two of the queen's attendants removed her garments and ushered her under the coverlet, she stared up at the shadowy rafters. The evening's merriment drifted from the long hall in the echoing strains of the jongleur at his lute and the braying laughter of drunken noblemen. Too many people crowded the room, food littered the floors and the guests spilled more drink than they drank – all in celebration of her marriage.

"Isabel! You can't linger abed all day."

A rough shake now accompanied the incessant voice at Isabel's ear. Isabel tugged the coverlet up to her shoulders.

"Dearest child, do get out of bed this instant. Have I raised you to be so lazy, especially on the Lord's Day?"

Groggy, Isabel sat up and rubbed her eyes. The harsh glare of the midmorning's sun intruded when a shutter banged against the wall, thrown back on its hinges. When her vision cleared, Petronilla curtsied beside her. At the window, Claremond crossed her arms over her ample bosom and heaved a wearied sigh.

Isabel threw back the coverlet and crouched at her nurse's feet, grasping her ankles. "Oh, Claremond, I haven't seen you for weeks. Where have you been? Why haven't you come to me before?"

Claremond's pudgy fingers rubbed Isabel's shoulders, grasped them and helped her stand. "Your father said you would not need me hovering at your side in the queen's presence. He provided lodging along the banks of the Seine, where Petronilla and I waited for word of our return home. I'm here now, milady."

"You must never leave me again. I must see my father. He can't separate us again, not when I need you now." She turned to Petronilla. "Fetch my best blue robe, the silvery-blue brocade. I'll have a silver circlet for my hair."

Her nurse patted her arm. "Milady, your father isn't in Paris. He informed me of your marriage and left this morning."

"It is mid-month. He had said the Holy Father commanded his leave-taking should occur at this time. I suppose there was no reason for him to stay longer, especially now that I am married. He didn't say farewell." A lump swelled inside her throat. "He has truly never cared for me." It was a foolish hope that he might have loved her after all, one he had answered many times over with his threats and beatings.

Claremond's gaze watered and slid away. Petronilla idled before she turned to arranging the bedding. Tiny dust motes floated through the room.

Isabel hugged herself tight. She turned from Claremond and leaned against the wall at her back. The coolness of the stone chilled her.

Her nurse said, "You must not be sad, milady. God shall keep your father safe. In time, he shall regret that he has not always treated you as a father should have."

"I am not sad, Claremond, nor do I wait upon my father's regrets. He has gone to Jerusalem and I am to sail the Seine today. I know I shall never see him again." Her stomach tightened at the thought. She clutched the fold of her nurse's mantle. "You must come with me, you and Petronilla."

"Your father arranged my return to Crépy-en-Valois this week. Brother Thorold insisted upon it. You do not remember. At Crépy-en-Valois, he said I was too old to be of use to you." Claremond's brows furrowed deeply. "Petronilla can attend you. Believe me, I do not wish to leave you, milady. I should not abandon your younger sisters."

"Please stay. You've always said my sisters are even

more ill-tempered than I am.”

“They are. You ask to me stay and choose the lesser evil. What of your mother? She may be angry if I do not return as her husband instructed. I dare not go against her expectations.”

“Comtesse Adelaide can find another nursemaid for my sisters. Somehow, I will convince her there are no other women in the comte’s household I trust to serve me loyally.”

“That is a bold lie, milady. You have not met your husband’s household retainers.”

“At Crépy-en-Valois, you told me to do as I must to be free of my parents. I will do what I must to have you at my side. Even if my mother does demand your return, I won’t give you up.”

Claremond displayed a wide grin. “You have the strength of your mother, as intractable as she when your mind is fixed. Tell me then, where are we going?”

“We travel north to the comte’s castle at Vatteville.”

“Must we go so far from home? I’ll miss Crépy-en-Valois.” When Isabel frowned at her, she rushed on, “As you say, my place is with you.”

Isabel threw her arms about the rotund woman who hugged her in return.

When they drew apart, the nurse continued, “Milady, I heard of your lord’s injury in the melee. Can he undertake such a journey now?”

“The comte remains in Paris until he can join us at Vatteville. Brother Thorold and milord’s constable shall escort us to our new home.”

Claremond pursed her lips. Isabel suspected she knew what the elderly woman was thinking. She dreaded any time spent in the grim Brother Thorold’s company.

After meeting her husband yesterday, she wondered why such a tolerant man, as he seemed to be, withstood the dour Brother Thorold’s company. After the marital ceremony, when Comte Robert kissed her forehead before they parted, his clerk viewed their embrace with a cold glare. She drew apart from her husband when she would have done otherwise. Brother Thorold's frigid stare held hers, his lips curled with disgust even as he followed her new husband and the squire FitzRobert from the chapel. The monk's dissatisfaction with her had started at their first meeting at Crépy-en-Valois. The source of his dislike for her remained unclear.

At the behest of the king, Isabel's husband resided in the care of Benedictine monks at the Abbey Saint-Germain-des-Prés. The king's surgeon had trepanned Comte Robert's skull in the hours after the wedding. Isabel delayed her departure for a week until she could see her husband.

Before noon on the date of their departure, Comte Robert's constable provided horses so Isabel and her attendants might visit the abbey, situated just outside the walls of the city. Beside her, Claremond grunted and grumbled each time her palfrey jostled her. Petronilla held her nose at the stink of muck rising from the Seine. Isabel groaned at the complaints her nurse and attendant offered, while urging her own horse through waterlogged fields.

Upon their arrival, Claremond requested permission for a visit. The monk she spoke with seemed to think it an unusual appeal. He gazed at them with prolonged scrutiny, his face pinched with annoyance.

He asked, "Do you believe the monks of Saint-Germain are incapable of caring for Comte Robert? Women do not breach the sanctity of our walls."

Isabel sidestepped Claremond. "Your infirmarian must let me see my husband. I could persuade Comte Robert to grant a bequest to the abbey for your trouble."

His bleak countenance remained unchanged. With a loud huff, he opened the gate. Escorted to the infirmary, a long, rectangular building with a high roof, they waited outside the entryway. A garden of herbs and flowers bordered walls of rough-faced, gray stone. Two monks huddled together with the squire FitzRobert hovering between them. Though they spoke only with each other, the squire remained intent on their conversation.

Three other men waited nearby. The tallest among them, red-haired and green-eyed with a slash marring his left cheek, jerked his head toward Isabel. She averted her stare. "This must be the beauteous new Comtesse de Meulan, eh, William?" His words drifted beyond the cobblestone courtyard. He appeared intent on gaining her attention. "Yet another reason to envy Comte Robert."

In a grave tone, his black-haired companion replied, "It would be, Gerard, if my tastes tended toward children. Unlike Robert, I prefer fleshy, full women for my bedmates."

Isabel ground her teeth in frustration. How dare they speak of such things in front of her? Despite her youth, she knew the meaning of their jests, for it was a repetition of the bawdy talk in the king's hall on her wedding night.

"I've done well by my bastards, which is more than I can say for you."

"Your shrew of a sister swore to cut off my balls if another waif and its mother appeared at Gournay. Why did I ever marry Edith?"

"For the lands my father dowered upon her. Why else does a man marry any woman? Her worth lies only in what she might bring him."

His companion chuckled. "A woman's worth lies elsewhere, brother. If you bedded more than the usual whores, you might gain a finer appreciation for a female's charms."

"There's hardly a woman on this earth to tempt me, Gerard. Not even one with the promise of beauty such as the new Comtesse de Meulan possesses."

She jerked her gaze to the speaker. His fleshy lips curved in a smirk as he met her stare. His nostrils flared while he appeared to consider her. Then he yawned behind his burly hands and looked away as if bored. Something about his dark curly hair and large eyes sparked a memory. She had seen him before in the king's hall. A third man stood silent as a shadow behind him. He might have been his shadow with similar black hair and bulk.

"Milady." FitzRobert approached and bowed. "Milord hoped he might see you before you left for Vatteville."

"He's asked for me?" She struggled to hide the smile teasing her lips. "How he is? What's been done to aid him?"

FitzRobert's stare widened beneath his fringe of wheat-colored curls. "Milady, I wouldn't want to frighten you with the particulars. You might speak with the infirmarian instead."

She clenched her fists until the thin sharp nails dug into her palms. "I am the Comtesse de Meulan now, am I not? Milord's care is my concern. Please, FitzRobert, tell me what was done to help my husband."

The squire nodded, his eyes averted. "As milady knows, milord suffered an injury to his skull. When we came to the infirmary last night, they bored a hole into the top of his head. Milord was very brave. He did not cry out from the pain, though it must have been terrible. When it was over, he fainted. I remained with him throughout the night. The monks prayed for him. He thrashed and sweated. At dawn, he opened his eyes and asked for water. Then he asked for you, milady."

She covered her mouth with her hand. Claremond patted her shoulder. Her eyes watered at the thought of the comte's pain. He must have suffered so cruelly.

"By the heavens, William, she actually looks ready to cry." The red-haired man guffawed and bent over laughing. "Indeed it is a love match!"

Isabel strode toward the men. Claremond's yelp of fright and FitzRobert's cry echoed behind her. She halted before the men, whose companions idled along the wall. Each man eyed her with a lazy look except for the dark-haired stranger.

"How dare you eavesdrop?"

The red-haired man held up his hands in a placating manner, though he could not control the snorts, which nearly choked him. "Forgive us, little lady."

She ignored him and glared at his companion, who had not moved. He seemed as uninterested in her plight as he did his companion's mirth.

"Who are you?" she demanded.

He sketched a lazy bow. "Earl William de Warenne of Surrey." He folded his arms over his chest and leaned against the wall. Corded muscles flexed beneath his blue tunic.

Her heart hammered. "You have no right to be here. You are the cause of milord's hurt. Have you come now only to watch him suffer? Haven't you done enough?"

The earl raised a thick, black eyebrow. A spasm of irritation twitched across the angular planes of his face. "You have much to learn of me, milady."

"I do not want to know anything about you! You could have killed Comte Robert."

His expression hardened with each intake of breath. "Ignorant girl, he knew the dangers of the melee. All men do. I took no pleasure in his pain."

"Does he call you a friend?"

"We are hardly friends. We find each other tolerable. I respect him. After I learned of his injury, I thought it only fair to inquire after his health." He ground out every word between clenched teeth. He muttered under his breath, "By all the saints, I'm explaining myself to a child."

She said, "He's in the care of the brothers of Saint-Germain-des-Prés. He does not need you. You may leave us, milord."

His jaw dropped and he gawked in stunned silence. The braying snorts of his companion continued. He kicked the man and sent him sprawling backward on the cobblestones. His companion's hoarse, choking laughter followed.

His hands fisted, the earl edged closer. She stared up at him and forced courage into her heart. He advanced on her until barely a footfall separated them. "Are you dismissing me?"

"I am."

"What makes you think I'll go quietly? What can you do if I do not agree to leave?"

FitzRobert bowed beside them, his legs trembling as he straightened. "Please milord, forgive milady. Milady is overwrought by her concern for her husband."

The earl turned his cold gaze on the squire, while Isabel expelled a ragged breath. Once again, her foolish impulsiveness ruled her tongue and overrode her better judgment. She was not afraid of the earl. She would not allow him to hurt FitzRobert.

"Your lady hardly seems distressed, good squire. Still, it is good of you to remind me of the poor child's state." He swung back to her. "Otherwise, I would think she spoke without full awareness of the possible consequences. Children who speak coarsely against their elders should be chastised."

The veins in his thick neck stood out in livid ridges. She cringed before him. He bent toward her, his face a dark mask of fury. She forced herself not to retreat any further, though he stood closer than propriety allowed.

"Luckily for her, I do not waste my time frightening little children." He glanced at the squire. "I wish Robert joy of her. I hope for his sake, she grows out of her impertinence. Though I suspect he will have to take a firm hand to her before long. Come, Gerard, Rudolf."

He swept away. The billowing folds of his mantle swiped her face. Her cry of outrage followed him, his red-haired companion and the other man. Gruff rumbles of laughter echoed across the abbey long after the trio had disappeared from view.

"Milady, you were very brave." FitzRobert clutched his chest.

"Or very foolhardy," Claremond muttered.

When Isabel whipped around, her nurse's lips thinned in firm disapproval. Still, her icy censure could not compare to the hot fury glowing in Brother Thorold's eyes.

He stood framed in the doorway, his face flushed with

indignation. His scorching look confirmed her worst fears. He had seen it all.

Isabel plodded through the dimly lit infirmary on wooden legs with her head bowed and eyes averted. Hands clasped tight, her glittering wedding band flashed a brilliant gold in the windowless room. Tears stung her eyes. What would Comte Robert do when Brother Thorold told him of her encounter with the Earl of Surrey?

Afterward Brother Thorold's frosty glare had left her frozen in place, as he withdrew inside. When the bell for Sext pealed within moments, Thorold reemerged from the gray walls of the infirmary again. His beady black eyes stared out from a stone-faced expression. "The comte shall see you now."

She froze in the entryway. What would her husband think of her brazen behavior? Myriad images of possible punishments tormented her: a whipping, deprivation or confinement to a darkened room. She had experienced such cruelty from her parents. What hope could she hold of her new husband, a mere stranger? Would he treat her any better? How many times had her father demanded she hold her tongue? She seemed incapable of controlling the thoughts in her mind. When would she ever learn?

"Isabel?"

She yelped when the comte's voice rose above a whisper and he beckoned her closer. Nails digging into her palms, she picked her way toward him among the pallets stretched on the floor. The heady scents of comfrey, rosemary, centaury and lovage saturated the blankets of those confined to the infirmary.

She sank on her knees and awaited his judgment.

"Dare I hope this display of sadness is for me?"

When she looked his way, she found a bemused smile crinkling the edges of his mouth in deep furrows. When his large hand closed over hers, her awareness of the differences between them increased. At more than three times her age and with years of battle-hardened experience, his powerful hands could crush her with one blow. Yet, her uncertainty about him did not alter her sympathetic view. He reclined on his pallet with thick linen wound around his head. He must have possessed great strength and endurance while the surgeon worked on him. Perhaps God truly existed, for He had saved her husband.

"Vatteville is far from all you've ever known. I want you to be happy, Isabel. I want us to be happy. Can you try a little?"

She nodded, despite the lump stifling her throat. She could not trust herself to speak yet without bursting into tears. He must have thought she felt sadness only at the thought of going on to Vatteville alone. She knew nothing of what awaited her and little of the husband whom she must one day please with sons. The demands of her parents and her new husband's expectations burdened her, as did his thoughts of her after the introduction to William de Warenne.

He patted her hand and his fingers closed around hers. "Thorold escorts you to your new home so there will be someone of your acquaintance at your side. He spoke to me about you."

Isabel drew a harsh breath, fear coiling inside her.

His hold tightened. "You mustn't let his views upset you. Thorold is outspoken. I have always encouraged his thoughts. I respect the man, although I know he keeps a low opinion of all women. He does not believe you are worthy of my trust and respect. I see in you what he cannot, Isabel. You are worthy of kindness and love. I do not expect you to love me now. I hope for it."

She sat back on her heels. Why did he speak of love when all she worried about was how he intended to punish her? What had Brother Thorold told him?

A dry chuckle escaped him. "Have you decided I am unworthy of your love? Am I not even worth the effort? Your judgment of me is harsh and unfair, my dear. Will you not allow me the chance to prove myself?"

His words left her bewildered as to anything his clerk might have said about her. "I didn't mean you were unworthy. I only worried over what Brother Thorold might have said to you."

"You have no cause for worry. You are my wife, Isabel. Thorold shall never change my opinion of you."

"Did he speak of me today?"

"The only words we exchanged about you were this morn, regarding my request for your tutoring. I understand your father did not encourage your learning. He held much the same belief as Thorold, who says it is useless to teach a woman to read and write. I feel differently. There shall be times when we are apart. When I write to you, I want you to read my letters personally, to know my thoughts and feelings intimately. I also wish for you to share your own. Brother Thorold is to tutor you at Vatteville."

Though shocked by his interest in seeing her educated when not even her parents or her brothers knew how to read and write, she could not fathom his nonchalance about the encounter with the earl.

"Milord, forgive me. I do not understand. Didn't Brother Thorold speak to you about William de Warenne?"

"Of course he did. He heard raised voices earlier and went out to the courtyard. When he returned a moment ago, he told me the man insisted upon seeing me. I told him the earl might do so later. For now, the only person I wished to see was you."

She sat back on her heels, incredulous. Why had the clerk kept her furious meeting with the earl hidden from his lord?

"Dearest girl, you look worried. Don't you want to learn to read and write?"

His concern for her education surprised her more than his easy dismissal of the furious meeting with the earl. "You must admit it's unusual."

"Not for my mother. My father insisted upon it when they wed. When she alone held the defense of his castles, his correspondence with her proved invaluable. He shared with her what he would have told no one else. My wife must be educated in the same manner."

His gaze searched her face. She blushed and looked away, muttering, "If only Brother Thorold did not have to conduct my lessons."

A deep chuckle rumbled through his barrel chest before a wave of coughing overtook him. Isabel clutched his hand until the spasm passed.

He smiled again. "It seems neither of you is fond of the other. I understand your sentiments, but you must listen well to Thorold. He'll never neglect your education for my sake."

"You admire him."

Though it was not a question, he nodded. "Thorold has been very devoted to me since childhood. I trust him as I trust few other men. You shall be in his dutiful care in my absence. I would not commend you to him otherwise. Go with him to Vatteville. I'll follow as soon as the infirmarian deems it wise."

"May I beg your favor to have my attendants accompany me? My nursemaid and a servant journeyed to Paris with me. Claremond is old. She has served my family faithfully for generations. Petronilla is young, a little older than I am. She is loyal."

"You may bring anyone you wish to our new home. I'd like to see you happy there, my Isabel." He brought her fingers to his lips and kissed them. A shiver ran down her spine. "Now, go with God," he whispered. "We'll be together again soon."

"I shall live for the day, milord."

"Isabel, please call me Robert. You are my wife, by the heavens. Shall you think of me only as 'milord' all our lives together?"

"We've been married less than a day. I know so little of you. You are a proud and brave warrior."

"I am also significantly older than you. I am not your father, Isabel. I am your husband and you must never be afraid of me. I want to give you the joy you have granted me. You'll learn new things as my wife, many new things."

In the dim light filtering through the open doorway, his gaze warmed her. Her heart quivered. "I shall look forward to it, milord. Robert."

"Good. Now go."

He released her and she curtsied before him, hoping they would not remain apart for long. At the doorway, she lingered, still fearful to step out into the courtyard. Would Brother Thorold await her?

"Have courage, my Isabel." The mettle in Robert's tone emboldened her steps. If he believed she possessed courage she did not otherwise feel, he might inspire a measure of strength inside her.

She emerged in the courtyard. Claremond and Petronilla stood at a corner of the herb garden, the squire FitzRobert beside her attendant. Brother Thorold paced the grounds, his hands clasped behind his back. He halted and looked at her.

She nodded. "To Vatteville."

Vatteville, Normandy: August 1096

The full moon peeked between wispy clouds gathered over the motte and bailey at Vatteville. Isabel slowed her galloping palfrey as the weary riders entered the lime wash fortifications, under an escort of Robert's guard in the command of the constable William. One of Robert's pages, the constable's seven year-old son, Josceline, accompanied them. On the left bank of the Risle River, just south of Robert's castle at Brionne, the riders from Paris had met a detachment from the fortress. The two forces coalesced around Isabel and her attendants for the remainder of their journey to Vatteville.

Sieur Miles de Brotonne, the sandy-haired leader of the knights from Brionne, dismounted inside Vatteville's inner walls and began issuing instructions. Torches banished the encroaching darkness. Isabel's horse slowed when a pageboy grasped the reins. She alighted with the constable's assistance and thanked him. The balding, bearded man nodded and bowed before her. He took the steps of the castle two at a time with the vigor of a man half his age, as he went in search of the steward from Meulan. Claremond heaved a weary sigh and rubbed her rump, eliciting Petronilla's giggles.

"You must become accustomed to horseback, Claremond," Isabel grumbled.

"By the grace of God, may it be many years before I'm asked to endure such pains again. I am an old woman, milady, not like you and Petronilla. Have pity."

Isabel studied the timber-framed tower on the motte. Lime plaster had chipped in some areas, exposing the wattle and daub underneath.

Brother Thorold approached her, his features shadowed beneath recesses of his cowl. "You're the chatelaine of Vatteville Castle, milady. You may enter without fear."

Isabel recoiled from him. He frightened her with his gruff voice issuing from a black void. She wished he had remained at her husband's side, attending his duties as Robert's secretary. Why had her husband insisted Thorold would be the best tutor for her, even above his learned chaplains?

"I am not afraid." Isabel threw back her shoulders and held her head high. Her attendants and Robert's household officers followed her path. Sieur Miles bowed at the entryway and more torches blazed a lighted path to the castle's hall. The oaken doors creaked on their rusted hinges as the doorkeeper pushed them in.

Isabel stood in a cavernous room with columns on either side, topped by a timbered ceiling. Two windows set high on the eastern and western walls allowed natural light into the room. Tables and benches lined the northern wall. A draft pervaded the room. Gray ash littered the hearth. Isabel lifted the hem of her robe slightly when squeaks and scurrying disturbed the dank rushes strewn across a beaten earthen floor.

She turned to Sieur Miles. "This is a poor welcome to

my new home."

Behind her, Brother Thorold said, "For milord, Vatteville is one among many fortresses he may call his own. He's not been here in several months."

She cast a glance around the dilapidated room. "The neglect shows, Sieur Miles." She addressed him directly in hopes of avoiding the clerk's interference. "I do not understand how this can be, when my husband sent word of our coming more than one week ago."

The knight looked at his feet. "We received late word of your arrival. We were westward at Meulan, milady, when the herald brought news. We raced across the Vexin, arriving at Brionne Castle a day before sighting your escort along the road."

"Then there's no garrison permanently detached at Vatteville?"

"Milord's vassals provide service throughout the year."

Isabel wandered about the darkened great hall, assessing its pitiable condition. She fingered the wattle and daub walls, bare of the fine carpets and tapestries she had seen at Paris. The dampness permeated the room, in part because of several cracks near the base.

Claremond patted her shoulder. "We'll make this a comfortable home."

"This is not a permanent home, milady. The comte often travels among his estates. It's likely we won't remain at Vatteville for long."

Isabel turned to Brother Thorold as he spoke, his intent look piercing her heart like a sharp dagger. She did not shrink from his cold stare. He would not intimidate her.

The constable entered and bowed before her. "Milady, I beg your forgiveness. The steward is not in residence, as he often travels between the Comte de Meulan's castles. Had we sent word earlier of your arrival, I do not doubt he would have been here."

"Constable, you do not expect us to await the steward's return for a warm hearth and the arrival of a meal? Comte Robert's wife has not eaten since this morning." Brother Thorold clasped his hands behind his back.

"It is of little concern. I am not hungry." As Isabel spoke, Claremond's stomach gurgled loudly. Isabel rubbed her temples, wishing the earthen floor would crack and swallow Robert's clerk completely. Friend or not, Thorold's presence annoyed her.

Then she turned her attention to the lead knight from Brionne. "Tell me, Sieur Miles, of how long you have served Robert and this Brotonne from which you hail."

The knight looked at Brother Thorold before he answered, "I'm a foundling of the forest at Brotonne. I have served Comte Robert since childhood, milady."

Waves of golden curls softened his otherwise craggy features. Something about him seemed familiar, though they had only met within scant days. Then she realized the source of her feelings. "You remind me of milord's squire, FitzRobert."

"You're not the first to remark on the resemblance, milady."

His noncommittal tone sparked her interest, as did the sharp glare Brother Thorold cast the young man. Was there some connection between Sieur Miles and FitzRobert she had yet to understand?

The aged steward from Meulan, William de Fortmoville, shuffled into the castle and greeted Isabel three weeks later. His retinue included Anschetil, one of two butlers in Robert's employ. The steward supervised workers from the village in their labors. The dauber and his apprentice repaired the cracked walls. The blacksmith made new hinges for the hall's doors.

Isabel rode out with Petronilla and Sieur Miles once a week and learned about her husband's demesne and his people. While summer heat swelled, she wondered how the burgeoning wheat crop might fare during the harvest. She found Sieur Miles likable and respectful of her station, always deferential and polite. She could not say the same for Brother Thorold, who tutored her at Robert's behest.

Her lessons started on the day after their arrival at Vatteville. Just after the chapel bell pealed for Prime each morning, she met with Brother Thorold. Through the haze and fog of her daily grogginess, she listened as he instructed her in writing. He spoke slowly, enunciating as though she might be an imbecile. Still, she bore his patronizing ways with little complaint. Among his duties, he also taught her in the Norman language, somewhat different from the French she had spoken all her life. She struggled with the formation of some words, at least for his satisfaction. The monk's sighs and reproaches did not discourage her.

An hour after dawn, she struggled against sleep, seated beneath a shuttered window on the second floor of the castle. She hid her constant yawns behind her hands. The clerk's grimace of disapproval warned her. Thank heaven for Claremond. If she had had to confer with the bailiff on all the work without her elderly nurse and keep up with her lessons, she would never have managed it.

"Milady, idle thought shall not avail you in your lessons."

Isabel ignored Brother Thorold's chiding. Through the opened shutters, she glimpsed riders approaching the gatehouse. One head rose above the other, with hair like fine-spun gold. Her heart thrummed.

"It's Robert! He's come at last." She rose and shook her skirts, sending dust motes spiraling. "Why didn't he send word?"

She scrambled down the rough-hewn stairs to the ground floor and emerged on the steps. Robert had dismounted. He looked wonderful and reinvigorated, not a bandage in sight, striding toward her with the squire FitzRobert and Sieur Miles on either side of him. They chatted amiably, their golden heads close together. They seemed so comfortable in each other's company. Robert thumped Sieur Miles' shoulder. FitzRobert threw his head back and laughed at something her husband said.

A tingling sensation crept up Isabel's spine. Instinctively, she understood the close connection she sensed between the trio. She clamped a hand over her mouth and smothered a cry of dismay.

A shadow fell over her. Brother Thorold had arrived. A flush of genuine pleasure dimpled his cheeks. She had never seen him appear so contented. He met her gaze.

"Are you ill, milady? You are suddenly pale." Brother Thorold's sonorous tone belied his attempt at concern.

"I am not! You must know I bear only an ailment of the heart. Robert is their father, isn't he? That is why Sieur Miles and FitzRobert resemble each other, why my husband is so amiable with them. Tell me the truth. I demand it as his wife."

A smug smile thinned his lips. "Truth is often painful, milady."

"Don't belittle me."

Brother Thorold looked down his nose at her. "The Comte de Meulan has acknowledged his parentage of Sieur Miles and FitzRobert."

"What of their mothers? Who are they?"

"Neither is here to distress you. Why worry yourself, milady?"

"Are they his only bastards?"

"He has acknowledged others here in Normandy and in England."

Isabel whirled toward her husband, who halted at the base of the steps. He grinned and opened his arms wide, offering his embrace. She flinched, panting with fear and fury.

Time passed slowly, in which his brow knitted. "Isabel? Why do you recoil from me so?"

She stifled a sob and fled inside the castle.

Chapter Five – Secrets
Vatteville, Normandy: August to September 1096

"Why didn't you tell me?" Isabel trembled with rage, her breath ragged and raw. "You've betrayed me, Robert. How could you hide your bastards from me? Then leave it to Brother Thorold, of all people, to tell me about Sieur Miles, FitzRobert and the others? He witnessed my shock and rejoiced. I saw it in his face. I blame you. How could you do this to me?"

Servants stood silent with jaws gaping, the hall unattended after the morning meal.

Robert bellowed for the butler. "Get them gone, Anschetil and close the doors behind you."

The young man bowed and fled, shooing the servants as he went. Isabel ground her teeth together and turned aside, bumping her calves against a wooden bench. Robert's gaze narrowed, but she stood her ground. Cowering had never helped her in any situation before, so it seemed a useless sham to perpetrate now. The servants scrambled, sloshing water buckets, with wets rags leaving a trail of water behind them. The trestle tables remained splattered with food.

The hall's doors slammed shut. Robert clasped his hands behind his back and trod the rushes underfoot at a steady pace. "How exactly have I harmed you, Isabel? Have I forced the knowledge of my children upon you? Have I insulted you by keeping my *lemans* underfoot?"

The edge of impatience in his tone made her skittish. Her bladder felt full and heavy. Her father used to bellow and bluster, her mother's voice ascended to a frenzied falsetto. She sensed greater danger in Robert's brisk tone. Had she gone too far? She pushed aside the inherent fear. She wanted answers and deserved them from him.

"Are there other women here?"

"None. I would not sully my marital vows with other women, Isabel. The bastards who may claim me as a father are liaisons of the past."

"I should not forgive you. You didn't tell me about

your children."

"When should I have warned you, Isabel? In the hour where we met before we married or after the surgeon bored a hole into my skull. Or, while I recuperated on my sickbed and worried for your safety on the journey here?"

She winced when he spoke of the painful surgery he had endured in Paris. When he halted and stood silent, his gaze expectant, she bridled at his blatant attempt to rouse her sympathy. He did not deserve it after keeping such secrets.

"I have more than a child's understanding, Robert! I know you are not a man like Brother Thorold. I understand how men's lusts and appetites may rule them. My mother often complained about my father's other women. I've seen the children at Crépy-en-Valois who look like me or one of my sisters or brothers."

"Then why are you so angry with me if your own father's done no better?"

"You should have told me! Not your creature, Thorold! Your life is important to me. I do not want to find out about things in your life from your minions."

She turned away from him, tears blinding her. Her heart heaved with the true source of her agony. Still, she kept her stubborn silence. Robert would never know how much she had wanted to be the first to give him children. Vague images of nameless, faceless women tortured her, women who had stolen the honor from her. Robert had given her so much already: his trust, his respect and an escape from virtual imprisonment at Crépy-en-Valois. What could she give him now when he had sons?

He rubbed her shoulders. Though she gave a half-hearted struggle, he turned her around and tugged her into his arms.

"My Isabel, I'm sorry you have discovered the truth in this way."

She whimpered and buried her face in his tunic. His fingers stroked her hair. When he released her, she sank down on the bench and he knelt before her.

"I vow I never meant for you to suffer so. I had not expected this reaction from you. I suppose I didn't give the matter any thought at all, which was careless of me." He raked a hand through his hair and exhaled a ragged breath. "If Miles and FitzRobert pain you, I'll remove them at once."

"Please, do not. I can see how close you are to them. You must not send them away, not because of me. I like them both. Sieur Miles is kind. FitzRobert has your easy humor and temper."

His brow furrowed with deep lines, he eyed her with a long searching look. Her body stiffened in apprehension, her chest heavy. She clutched his hand. "Please, Robert."

He sighed. "You have wisdom and beauty beyond your years. It is easy to forget you are still a child. Miles and FitzRobert shall stay while I'm here for some months." He looked around the hall. "I have neglected this castle for too long and there is work I must do, as you rightly judged. My steward is here. I trust you've found him worthy of the title."

"He is. Please forgive my haste. I wanted this to be a comfortable home for you upon your arrival."

"Isabel, you shouldn't apologize for taking an interest in this or any other castle of mine. When I was last at Vatteville, I knew the stonemasons would be required sooner rather than later. I last stayed for three days, until a rebellion against the king demanded my attentions in England again."

"You're often at the English court?"

"Since my father's death, I have overseen my inheritance while my beloved brother, Henri, attends to our English estates. Duke Robert Curthose of Normandy pledged himself to the cross and lawlessness ensues in his absence."

"The duke has undertaken the cross as my father has?"

"He required some assistance from the English king in the task. The duke has mismanaged his coffers. He mortgaged the duchy to his brother in England for ten thousand marks so he might join the others."

She looked at him askance. A deep chuckle rumbled in his throat and he kissed her hand. "Forgive me. I speak of political matters when we should be celebrating our reunion. I've missed you, my Isabel."

She fingered a jagged scar at his temple, often concealed beneath a forelock of his pale golden hair. "I didn't see the resemblance before when I first met FitzRobert."

A sheepish grin curved his lips. "You won't let this matter rest?"

"I have other questions regarding these children you have claimed."

"Then make your inquiries. I'll tell you everything."

She swallowed against the knot in her throat. "What about their mothers? Sieur Miles told me he was born in Brotonne forest. Who was his mother?"

Robert's features twisted. Isabel touched his ashen cheek.

Had he loved her, this unknown woman who had mothered his bastard, or did the memory inspire bitterness? Such strong emotions crisscross his face as to stir Isabel's jealousy. Did she have reason to fear Robert's past and the specters of his past conquests?

He interrupted her musings. "She was a scullery servant. I was twenty-two, three years younger than Miles is now. She submitted because I was a lord's son. She could not bear the shame of my bastard. I had ruined her, you see." He glanced at her and she held her breath until he continued. "The baker's apprentice wanted to marry her. After I took her as my *leman*, she refused him. Henri and I were hunting on the day she bore the child and exposed him. My guilt demanded I raise the boy. He is my eldest."

She squeezed his hand. "You did more than most men would have done, more than my father did. Are Sieur Miles and FitzRobert your only sons?"

"There are also twin boys in England, raised as the sons of another man."

She sighed. If only guilt had contained his initial lust. By the heavens, four baseborn brothers for her own children to contend with someday. They must never know of their father's shame. If Sieur Miles or FitzRobert ever gave them cause for suspicion, she would deny it. "What of daughters?"

"All except one remains here in Normandy. The eldest is to take her vows at Saint Leger. I have had no word of the fates of the other two beyond my knowledge they are both alive at Meulan. I provide what I can. I'm a stranger, whom their mothers have whispered of in the night."

She nodded, though his admission knifed her heart deeper still. A lump threatened her ability to speak.

"One day, you'll give me strong, fine sons who shall grow to be honorable, worthy men and lovely daughters with the brilliant color of your hair." He touched her cheek where an errant dark strand of hair slipped from beneath the silvery-blue cloth covering on her head.

"I pray for sons, Robert." Her words of reassurance for him offered little personal comfort to herself. She had pledged herself as a dutiful wife and she would hold her vow. Robert might prove faithful in his marriage and she would learn the past no longer mattered to him.

It rained throughout the summer season, forcing Isabel indoors to her regret. Though Robert's company kept her entertained for weeks, she wanted to explore the countryside with him.

On the first day on which rain did not threaten, Isabel stood at the base of the tower steps beside Petronilla, while Robert, Sieur Miles and the steward huddled in a circle. FitzRobert held the reins of his lord's restless horse and patted the beast's neck. Isabel nodded to him and he flashed a smile.

Robert tramped across the muddy earth and bowed before her. "We're going out with my steward to inspect the fields."

Isabel looked past him to where the steward and Sieur

Miles waited. The young knight nodded to her. She asked, "Can't I go with you this time, Robert?"

"You've been awake since dawn at Thorold's lessons, my dear. You must be tired?"

She ground her teeth before mumbling, "I'm not easily tired."

"Crops wouldn't interest you. Now, let me kiss you farewell until later."

Though disappointed by his refusal, she pursed her lips and arched toward him. Holding her breath, she waited, anticipating. Today might be the day. Her heart leapt with hope, a surge of elation making her giddy. As usual, he chuckled and kissed her forehead, his lips barely skimming her skin. Her fingers clenched, nails digging into her palm. Disappointment soured her stomach. He bowed and mounted his horse with a farewell to FitzRobert. The company rode out. The squire joined Isabel on the steps. They watched until the men disappeared beyond the bailey.

"I would've liked to have gone with them," Isabel murmured.

"I'm sure milord believes you might find an inspection tour of little interest," FitzRobert commented.

"Why? I did them with Sieur Miles for three weeks before my husband's arrival."

Her voice sounded waspish, harsher than she intended. When FitzRobert looked at her askance, she refused to offer contrition. "Petronilla, another dreary afternoon in the hall awaits us."

She took the step, asking Petronilla as she went, "What shall we do today? Claremond keeps to her tapestry and she has warned us to stay away from her weaving. My mother's at fault for she never encouraged me to learn. We might sew more cushions for the hall. What do you think, Petronilla?"

When the other woman did not answer, Isabel turned at the entryway. Petronilla slammed into her, her rapt attention on the squire who admired her retreating form. The attendant offered Isabel a hasty apology, her eyes now averted while FitzRobert blushed. Though puzzled, Isabel continued onward to the hall.

How could Robert continue to treat her this way? He attended to her with great solicitude. If he really cared to know, he would see how her feelings had grown. It chafed her when he went out, he never asked her to accompany him. He often rode with Sieur Miles at the head of his company and at times, FitzRobert joined them. Except of late, when he hovered beside Petronilla and Isabel. Though she wondered at the strange scene between her attendant and FitzRobert, thoughts of her husband's evident ties to his children preoccupied her.

While her heartache lessened with the passing of the season, a tiny spark of fury and resentment flared when she chanced to see Robert with his sons. He never invited them to join him at mealtimes and he never sought out his bastards in her presence. She usually saw Robert outdoors with his sons from a castle window.

Engaged in worrisome thoughts, Isabel paid scant attention to her sewing, earning a scowl of displeasure Petronilla could not have hidden if she had tried. Exasperated, Isabel pulled the blue linen threads out and stood. "I can see you do not need my help."

Petronilla's gaze dipped to the neat embroidered stitches upon the leather cushion on her lap. "Milady should walk around the bailey."

"I have seen the bailey," Isabel muttered. She left the hall and almost collided with Brother Thorold at a sharp turn in the corridor.

His lips curled into a sneer at the same moment in which she gasped and jerked away from him. His jaw tightened while he swiped at his robe, as though the barest contact with her had soiled him. He grasped a rolled parchment in his other hand. She closed her hands into fists and fought a desperate desire to flee from his hateful presence.

"A letter has arrived from Crépy-en-Valois. Shall I read it to milady now?"

Chills swept over Isabel. Comtesse Adelaide had

promised to write. Isabel's fingers trembled as she held her hand out. "Give it to me. I shall read in private."

Thorold's smirk mocked her. He held up the missive with its broken seal of red wax. "Your mother wrote in Norman French. If milady had spent the last weeks in the improvement of your mind, rather than wasting the hours at embroidery and other fripperies, you might be able to read."

A tingling sensation swept up her cheeks, prompted by his baited words and the truth of them. She leaned against a column and crossed her arms over her flat chest. "What does my mother say?"

His mouth opened, but he said nothing. He glanced down the walkway to the opened hall doors. "You want to hear it now? Where all within may listen."

She shrugged. "These walls cannot hold secrets for very long. Speak."

Thorold stiffened, tension tightening the cords in his neck. "As you wish, milady." He unfurled the letter. "Greetings, my dear Isabel—"

Her loud snort interrupted him. Her hands dropped to her sides and she muttered the words to herself. Thorold's scowl deepened as he canted his head and then shook it.

"My dear Isabel," he repeated, folding a corner of the parchment to glare at her, before he resumed. "I expect you are in good health in the company of your new husband. Before your father's departure for Rome, he sent word of your hasty marriage to Robert, the Comte de Meulan. I am disappointed you have not also written. In the future, you will be mindful of my interest in this marriage and never leave me to wonder after your fate. You will write to me concerning the fate of your union. You shall do so in Norman French, so I may know how you have bettered yourself.

"Despite my favor concerning the match, the circumstances of your subsequent marriage displease me. Your father's poor judgment in permitting the wedding without the Holy Father's sealed approval leaves you to an uncertain fate. Whatever shall your husband do if the pope does not give his consent? Comte Robert cannot think he shall gain your *maritagium* without the benefit of papal dispensation. As I told Hugh, the comte aimed high in this match. If he expects to have your dower and your maidenhood without a proper conclusion to the formalities, I assure you he is mistaken, child. Before your marriage portion passes into his control, before the comte beds you, we shall have Rome's assent."

Though she felt the taint of a warming blush across her face, Isabel peered at Thorold when he spoke the last. A satisfactory frisson swept up her spine at how his pallid countenance reddened. She took some petty joy in his obvious discomfort and embarrassment. Her attention to the comforts of her husband's home had provided a reasonable excuse for avoiding her lessons, to her detriment. She would have to resume her studies, if only to end their necessity soon. She would not let Thorold compose letters to Crépy-en-Valois about her monthly courses!

The Benedictine cleared his throat before he continued. "The matter vexes me, Isabel. My waking hours are plagued with fear and my nights abed are tortured by thoughts of failure."

She snorted, wondering if there had been truly any day where concern for her children's fates plagued Comtesse Adelaide. Thorold paused. She endured his probing squint at her before he returned his attention to the letter.

"Then there is the matter of your collusion with Claremond. Do not think I am ignorant of how you have defied your father's orders and kept her at your side. You may bear the burdens of your old nurse's care. She is no longer welcome at Crépy-en-Valois. Before your father left, he charged me to finalize marital arrangements for your sister Beatrice. I cannot concern myself with such now. I have had to find another caretaker for your sisters who would control them, as Claremond could not. Did you ever consider the girls or if your selfishness might disrupt this household? You have demonstrated poor judgment in all matters leading to your marriage. If only you had not wasted several months in stubborn refusal, you could have arrived in Paris sooner, there to await His Holiness' permission. I blame your father, Comte Robert and you for allowing this union—"

"Me? She blames me?" Isabel scrambled to understand, her thoughts muddied. "She and my father almost beat me to death for my refusal. I did as they demanded and yet I am to blame!"

Thorold put the parchment aside shortly. "Your hysterics are unnecessary, child. Your mother's concerns are unwarranted. My master has had word from his envoys. They are sure the pope shall give his consent."

"When will they be certain?"

"Soon." His clipped tone brought her stare back to his sour expression. He rubbed the back of his neck and perused the letter before he resumed reading. "I blame your father, Comte Robert and you for allowing this union without Rome's blessing. You should have each considered the consequences. I insist you must withhold yourself from the marriage bed. I have sent word to your father in Rome to make a similar demand of Comte Robert. Write to me each month after you have finished your courses. I must be certain the comte has not taken advantage of you. I await your reply at Crépy-en-Valois."

Thorold looked up. "That is all. What is your answer?"

"Greet my mother in the name of God. Tell her I have done the duty she and my father placed before me. Tell her the Comte de Meulan has shown himself kind and patient. I am blessed to be his wife and hope the day will soon arrive when he may claim me as such with the pope's blessing."

She sidestepped him and walked along the windowless corridor.

"What of the rest?" he demanded.

She stumbled and righted herself in an instant. "What do you mean?"

"You've heard your mother's demand, what she wishes to know each month. What do I tell her now?"

Her skin felt impossibly hot. "My courses have not come. After you have finished the reply, send for me before dinner. I want to continue my lessons."

Thorold raised his eyebrows. She fled down the hallway.

Robert returned at midday during dinner. Isabel's annoyance peaked while she ate her bowl of frumenty alone at the dais. When her husband strolled in just before dinnertime ended, trampling mud through the hall, she forced herself to remain seated. He ate without comment, although she had asked the cook to prepare one of his favorite dishes, eels baked in red wine. After the meal, he played chess with Brother Thorold until the late evening, while Isabel and Petronilla stitched fabric for cushions. She often glared at them whenever Robert's laughter rumbled in the air.

Torches illuminated the hall. Robert dismissed Thorold and came to Isabel's side. "I know you find it difficult to remain here each day. Thorold tells me you will resume lessons with him. Would you like to learn something new now?"

She looked at him askance and he smiled. "You might enjoy chess. You have often watched my clerk and I play in the evening."

In truth, she had stared at them with envy, wishing Robert might choose to spend time with her. If learning chess might draw them closer, she saw no reason to refuse.

The servants left one trestle table in place where Robert and Isabel sat together, after she had bid Petronilla good night. She asked several questions, which he answered without the slightest hint of frustration at her inquiries. More importantly, he refused to let her win because she was new to the game, yet showed no obvious pleasure at her first loss. She challenged him to another game. When the sentry called the watch at midnight,

Isabel yawned behind her hands.

Robert stood and lifted her from the bench. Startled, she clung to him. "I can take the stairs myself."

"It delights me to carry you."

"You're treating me like a child. My father never did this, even when Claremond told him how I had fallen asleep in our dovecote the first time. She said he demanded she wake me up and make me walk back to the nursery."

He chuckled and mounted the stairs. "Why were you sleeping in the dovecote?"

"My brothers snored terribly, even as children." She laid her head on his shoulder with a sigh. "I could never sleep with them close by. When the sentry changed watch, I always went out to the dovecote to sleep."

"You were never afraid of the mice or rats?"

"I had my blanket."

In the previous month, Robert had ordered the second floor cordoned off into a smaller chamber directly above the hall. It served as sleeping quarters for him, Isabel and their most trusted servants. Candles in wall brackets lit the space. A thin curtain of chainsil separated his bedding from Isabel's own. Claremond slept on her pallet at the foot of Isabel's bed, as did Petronilla beside her. Isabel chuckled when rumbling gas escaped the old woman's rump. She buried her face in Robert's shoulder and escaped the foul smell.

"You're being unkind, my dear," Robert admonished.

Isabel smothered her laughter in his tunic. "Please, take me to your bed. I can't lie down with her just yet."

Robert gathered her closer, his gaze holding hers. She held her breath. A wave of anxiety made her stomach heave. Then he nodded and crept around the curtain. He stood beside a bed constructed of beech wood, similar to hers. Coverlets and wool blankets draped it, almost to the ground.

Her gaze returned to him. "May I ask something?"

When he nodded, she licked suddenly dry lips. His nostrils flared.

"You were a commander of King William's knights against the English. Tell me of the battle."

Redness suffused his cheeks. "I would hesitate to speak of it. A battle is bloody business, Isabel. It is not what you may be thinking, of knights and bravery. There are the screams of dying men and their blood everywhere."

"Were you afraid?"

"Men are always afraid in the heat of warfare."

She pecked at the neckline of his tunic and stared up at him. "Were *you* ever afraid?"

Laughter rumbled through his chest at her insistence. He clutched her closer to him. Laugh lines crinkled around his mouth. She had never felt so warm and safe, never been held before like this in anyone's arms, even her father's own. He looked down at her with a generous smile, his eyes like sparkling crescents. Up close, she noted the fringe of his golden eyelashes. The tips of their noses almost touched.

"I was most afraid at the battle's ending, Isabel. Harold the usurper had his household guards who still defended the ridge at Senlac. They swung long axes that could cleave a knight or his horse in two. Even when defeat loomed, they fought on. I stabbed one in the neck. His axe cut my mount's legs out from under the beast. There I lay, trapped between the muck-covered ground and the horse. The Englishman raised his axe again, ready to chop me to pieces. King William stabbed him and saved my life. Until that moment, I thought I would die. I had never been more afraid before or since the king saved my life."

"You loved your king?"

"He was a proud man, he believed in his purpose and my father Roger supported him. I admired William, but he was a rash man. His heir William Rufus is similar, although he tends toward his mother's jovial temperament. We enjoy the hunt and similar pursuits. We are well-matched."

She wanted to know more about the man she had

married, beyond his service to the English king. "How do you bear Brother Thorold then? He is unlike you."

He lifted his head and cleared his throat. "How so?" His smile had faded. His eyes bored into hers.

She drew a deep breath and willed away the knot in her belly. "He takes no joy in anything. Why must he be so hateful?"

He raised an eyebrow. "You judge him too harshly, my Isabel. I believe you only need time to know Thorold better."

She nestled within the comfort his arms offered and remained silent for a time, before she added, "I remember when he told me of your relationship to FitzRobert and Sieur Miles. I think he wanted to hurt me with the knowledge of your sons."

Robert sighed and carried her to the bed beyond the screen. He tucked her under the coverlet with a kiss on her brow. "These are foolish concerns. You should not hold such petty thoughts about my clerk. He is loyal to my interests, which include you."

"I know what I saw on his face. He enjoyed my tears. He wanted to see me suffer."

He pressed a firm finger to her mouth and leaned over her. His lips thinned, all traces of his earlier humor having finished. Her gaze flicked upward to his blue eyes, narrowed to thin, icy slits. A chill swept over her. His thumb and forefinger grasped her chin. She winced and held her breath.

"You are wrong, Isabel. You will not speak of this again. You will accept my bastards and be mindful of Thorold's value in my household. You need never concern yourself with his opinions or actions. He is under my protection, as are you. Stay here tonight. I shall sleep elsewhere."

He released her chin and straightened.

"Where will you go?" she whispered.

A tic pulsed along his jaw line. "Do not concern yourself. Sleep now."

When he left her, Isabel pressed her palm to her

heart. She would never have asked about Thorold if she had anticipated how much it would displease Robert. Her husband obviously felt some attachment to his clerk, even if she could not understand his reasons.

In the scant space of a few breaths, she had felt only fear in his presence. Robert's harsh stare and his rough hold on her chin had reminded her of how her father once treated her. In Paris, Robert had claimed he wanted her to be happy at Vatteville. Surely, he would not forsake the vow already. She had made vows as well, to obey and serve him. He was right, of course, for she and Thorold lived by her husband's graces. She would not raise the topic of Thorold's malicious cruelty again. She might have imagined it because she did not like him. Robert did not believe him capable of such vice.

She remained alone with her doubts in the poorly lit room for a long time. The candle in a brass sconce along the wall subsided to a stub, yet its golden flame still flickered.

Act II: The Flame

(October 1100 – June 1101)

Chapter Six – The Hunters
Brotonne Forest, Normandy: October 1100

Isabel wrapped her fur-lined mantle tightly around her. The ermine trim at the neckline tickled her cheek. An autumnal chill penetrated her leather gloves. Beneath the mantle, her icy fingers gripped the reins of her palfrey. Petronilla rode beside her with pale features barely visible under a hooded sheepskin cloak.

The riders ambled along a winding footpath. Sieur Miles led them, surrounded on all sides by Robert's knights and men-at-arms. Isabel and Petronilla followed, while Brother Thorold trailed astride a docile rouncey, just ahead of the servants on foot, who led their packhorses.

Sieur Miles turned in the saddle, his upturned nose reddened at the tip. "We'll soon arrive."

"Thank heavens, for I can hardly bear the cold much longer," Isabel grumbled. "Since we first came to Vatteville, it has grown worse."

"You have said the same every year for the past four years since we came, milady," Petronilla commented.

Isabel aimed a narrowed gaze in her direction. "It remains true. Would I speak otherwise?"

Petronilla said nothing, merely sniffed and stared at the shady canopy. A crisp breeze soughed through the beech trees and rustled their leaves.

Isabel said, "The weather and the journey have been wearisome. I am simply eager to reach home. Though we have traveled so often this year between Robert's castles, Vatteville seems more like home than any other place. Even Beaumont with its thick forests and valleys and the church of Saint Nicolas and the priory of Sainte Trinité can't compare."

When Petronilla did not reply, Isabel continued, "I believe Vatteville has a claim on your heart."

Her attendant dipped her head. The hood fell over her eyes, but not before a warming pink flush colored her cheeks.

"FitzRobert is handsome and you are fair, Petronilla. He shall make a fine husband. If only you would let me write to Robert on your behalf."

Isabel's servant peeked from beneath the hood. "Please, milady, stop. Would you bring down Brother Thorold's wrath on both our heads? You know he listens to everything we say. He's your husband's spy."

The Benedictine who served as Robert's clerk had been quiet since they had left the castle at Pont Audemer two weeks ago. He kept to himself along the northbound journey, even at the sole mealtime he allotted for himself. Isabel sometimes forgot he rode with them, except when a tingling sensation swept up her spine, as it did now. She jerked around in the saddle and found him staring at her back. His intense glare startled her. His lips thinned in a firm line of disapproval and she ignored him again.

Isabel said, "Robert would never put anyone to spying on me. He trusts me."

Petronilla sighed. "I'm not worried about your husband. My concern is the monk."

"You worry without cause. I do not believe Brother Thorold heard us."

"Don't be so certain. He hears everything, milady. Remember when we spoke of your father's failure?"

Isabel groaned, hardly needing the reminder. After her father took up the cross, he had helped capture Antioch by the second year of her marriage. Then instead of going on to the holy city of Jerusalem as his oath bound him, he returned home, concerned whether his spoils reached France. For his perceived cowardice, the pope threatened excommunication. Isabel had shared all with Petronilla while dining one afternoon.

The next morning, Brother Thorold concluded his lecture on French royal history with the comment, "A man's word is sacred. To break it is to break faith with God." Only later did she comprehend his meaning.

She focused on the present time. Petronilla's moist, pleading gaze met hers. "Please do not say anything more of FitzRobert."

"You are devoted to him and he adores you. You refuse my help. I could intercede with Robert and ask his permission to allow your marriage, at least when FitzRobert has attained his knighthood."

"Milady, FitzRobert hasn't asked me to marry him. He would not dare risk his lord's displeasure. He shall become a knight. I am only a lady's attendant. Please do not incur your husband's anger because of me."

"Why should Robert be angry? He can hardly be displeased by the devoted attentions of a kindly squire to a woman in my employ."

"If you'll forgive my hasty tongue, you've hardly known him long enough, milady, to guess at his true moods and feelings."

"Your tongue has grown hasty indeed and spiteful to remind me I haven't seen my husband in far too long. I have given you too many liberties. Be mindful of your station."

"Forgive me, milady." Petronilla ducked her head again.

Isabel reached for the servant's frozen fingers and tugged them into her grasp. "Don't be sullen. I cannot deny Robert's long absence in England does not hurt me. Only his letters have sustained me during these years. If only he'd return to Normandy, or at least to me, without concern for the commands of his king."

Although she had not seen Robert, their lengthy correspondence kept her aware of all his affairs. Within a month of arriving at Vatteville, he had returned to England at the behest of the English king, only to journey to France when the king invaded the Vexin in the following year. He had offered no promise of reunion with her upon the king's victorious ride from Paris. Still, Isabel kept watch every day for his appearance. When his next letter reached her, he had reached England again in safety. There were no more visits afterward. Isabel despaired for nearly a year, wondering when she might see him again.

In his letters, Robert charged her with a solemn duty, as chatelaine of all his estates in Normandy and France. Every year, she made her progress from Vatteville to the principal castles at Meulan, Pont Audemer, Brionne and Beaumont, residing for two months at each before returning to Vatteville in the autumn. Her studies with Brother Thorold continued. The duties of a chatelaine kept her occupied.

Claremond had not accompanied them this time. She had complained so for her aching back in the previous year, Isabel reluctantly allowed her to stay behind at Vatteville, where FitzRobert promised he would see to the elderly woman's needs. Isabel also regretted her inability to visit Elbeuf during her progress. The picturesque estate southeast of Vatteville was her marriage portion. Next year might offer an opportunity, when she could enjoy the fine cider the villagers brewed there.

She would have cast aside all the trappings of the Comtesse de Meulan, the furs, jewels and lands if only she might always be at her husband's side. Such comforts offered little joy absent Robert's presence. She would have to write another letter to her mother soon, to assure her the marriage remained unconsummated. Four years of Robert's absences had not engendered the compassion of Comtesse Adelaide.

"Milady, you've grown quiet." Petronilla drew her from her reverie. "I didn't mean to upset you when I spoke of your husband."

Isabel clenched her fingers. "You're worse than Claremond. Both of you still think of me as a child. I am sixteen now. I do not need your coddling, just to get out of this bitter cold." She jerked the reins of the horse and kicked the palfrey into a gallop.

Sieur Miles looked at her askance. "Milady, why do you hasten so? Are you unwell?"

She snickered at his kind concern and urged her mount to go faster. Sieur Miles' voice drifted on the wind. "Milady, please be careful!"

The dense woodland blurred into thickets on either side of the footpath. Behind her, Sieur Miles cursed and urged their company, who followed her lead. She laughed again, throwing her head back.

Two piercing notes penetrated the thicket. Isabel looked about wildly, startled by the sound. A boar burst out on to the footpath in a frenzied squeal. Isabel slowed her horse. The palfrey snorted and sidestepped.

Hounds crashed through the woodland from the direction of Vatteville, cornering the feral pig between themselves and the riders bound for home. Urged on by the master huntsman, the dogs yelped and barked. Desperate, their quarry lowered its tusks. Collared mastiffs held back at the curses and commands of the huntsman. Only the alaunts leapt at the boar, their squared jaws clamping down on the bloodied hide. A whining cry, swiftly cut off, signaled the savage death of a hound.

Sieur Miles reached Isabel and tugged the reins of her mount. She hardly noticed the knight's attention. The orgy of blood held her transfixed.

A large company of riders approached, their burly leader covered in a cobalt-colored mantle. "Get them back! By Christ's blood, this is my kill!" He dismounted with a spear in hand. He butted some of the dogs with a metal disc halfway down the shaft and bellowed to the huntsman. "Call them back!"

He dragged off his helmet and pushed black hair out of his eyes. Isabel yelped and stared at him, incredulous as memory evoked his name. He pushed his way through the dogs and raised the spear above his head.

"How dare you hunt on milord's lands?" Isabel's voice shook with rage.

William de Warenne, the Earl of Surrey, jerked his gaze toward her. A scowl darkened his countenance. "Lady, you have no business here."

"I am the Comtesse de Meulan. The forest of Brotonne is part of my husband's domain."

The earl lowered the spear. "You are Robert de Beaumont's wife?"

The hounds growled a warning before the boar sprang loose of their hold. The earl whirled just as the maddened animal charged him. Its tusk gored his shin. His roar of pain echoed through the trees, frightening birds into flight. He stabbed with the spear, the shaft embedding in the feral pig up to the edge of the metal disc. The hounds tore bloodied muzzles into their quarry and the earl scrambled out of their way. He collapsed on the footpath, clutching his oozing, torn leg. Isabel's hand flew to her throat.

"Look away, milady, please," Sieur Miles urged.

She could not. The growls and snarls of the dogs told her the boar's struggle had ended. Roused to anger at the earl's trespass, she stared at him in silence. He met her shock with upraised eyebrows. "Well? Do you offer me the hospitality of your hall, or shall I bleed to death this day?" He folded his arms across his chest, tapping his fingers impatiently on his brawny arms.

She could have laughed at his pouting lips and reddened cheeks. He looked like an obstinate child sitting on the cold ground.

"I have some experience in the tending of such wounds," Brother Thorold said.

She had almost forgotten him among their party.

He continued, "I shall attend the earl if he wishes it." When Isabel huffed, he nodded to her, "If milady permits."

His belated display of deference did not fool her at all. She inclined her head to him. "I'll permit it. Miles, help him mount his horse."

"I do not need help." The earl rose gingerly, biting his lower lip. He staggered to his horse, limping. A squire offered aid. He brushed the young man aside. With a grunt, he lifted the injured leg, aiming for the stirrup. Instead, he tumbled and fell backward.

A bark of laughter escaped Isabel's throat. Despite the dismayed stares of Brother Thorold and Sieur Miles, she could not help it. She maneuvered her mount beside the proud earl, who once again refused his squire's assistance. From atop her horse, she looked down at him, sitting on the grassy footpath. He clutched his injured leg before releasing the wound, as though daring her to turn from it. She ignored the obvious attempt to bait her and inspected him. His bloodied hose, tied below the knees with garters, revealed muscular legs, accustomed to horseback riding. His stubborn chin exuded arrogance.

"You are joyful at my misfortune. Have you no Christian kindness, milady?" With his black eyebrows drawn together over eyes the color of flint, he seemed monstrous.

"If I didn't, I would not suggest you wait here, while I ride on ahead and send a horse litter for your comfort. It is the least I can do, though you have offended my husband by daring to hunt on his lands. I would think the Earl of Surrey would know better than to abuse privilege."

He glanced around before eying her. "I do not see Comte Robert. Is he here to be offended?"

"I am here and as his wife, I bear his slights." Then she realized mirth crinkled the fine lines around his dark eyes. The wretch dared make sport of her.

She opened her mouth, ready to offer a sharp retort, before she thought better of it. Too many watchful eyes observed their banter. "The Benedictine monk in our company may attend you. Then you and yours may be on your way."

"Certainly kind of you, to offer such meager care before I'm cast out. Tell me, have we met before this day? You are well aware of my title. I do not recall you fully. I believe I've seen your face before, though I can't remember when or where."

She did not know whether he attempted another poor joke or not. Could he truly have forgotten their first encounter four years ago, after he aided her husband's injury in a brutal melee? Could he truly be so dim-witted or neglectful? She berated herself for recalling him with perfect clarity. If he deemed her so unimportant, why should she have thought anything of him?

He shaded his eyes against sunlight shimmering through the treetops and appraised her. His eyes raked over her form before they returned to her face. "We have met. I am certain of it now. Robert's bride was a child. I can hardly call you such now, can I?"

"Impudent fool, you do not deserve the hospitality of milord's hall!" She kicked her horse into a canter, hoping the dust kicked up by the beast might choke the arrogant earl. Christian charity bound her to offer him the hospitality of her husband's hall until he mended. She prayed he was a fast healer and would soon be on his way.

Over the pounding hooves of Sieur Miles' horse, which galloped beside her, the earl's answer echoed on the wind. "I shall have what is his all the same."

Vatteville, Normandy: October 1100

Isabel dismounted and stood in the shadow of the weathered façade of Vatteville's timber-framed tower. The damp earth mired her shoes in mud. On her first viewing, the tower dominated the western skyline, a forlorn relic atop the motte with crumbled lime plaster from the walls strewn haphazardly around the base. Now an air of mystery permeated the grounds, shielded by a thickening mass of fog around the mound. She tugged her mantle closer, shivering at the memory of the tower's drafty confines.

The smell of hot metal at the forge tinged Isabel's nostrils. The blacksmith shaped shoes for a horse, tiny sparks emitting with every blow of the hammer, while a groom kept the snorting and stamping beast calm.

Scullions hefted overflowing casks of water from the well, spilling more than they managed to carry. Twin girls with ruddy faces alternately helped and hindered their father drive geese to the fields. FitzRobert pushed his way through the bustle, descending a crescent-shaped, sloping bank. Behind him, a limestone building loomed which now served as Isabel's residence. Construction had begun in the spring after Robert's departure and ended just before Isabel's birthday that year.

"Welcome home, milady." FitzRobert bowed, golden hair falling over his eyes. When he raised his head, her chest tightened as it often did when he appeared. He might have been a younger version of Robert standing before her. The young man shuffled on his feet, avoiding her gaze. He looked beyond her. A frown marred his forehead with tiny lines. She followed his stare to where Sieur Miles aided Petronilla as she dismounted. Isabel's attendant smiled shyly at the knight before she realized FitzRobert watched her. Her smile widened briefly, before she averted her eyes and strode beside Sieur Miles, joining Isabel.

"It's good you've come, milady," FitzRobert murmured, his lips pressed tightly together. Sieur Miles greeted him. FitzRobert barely acknowledged his half-brother with a curt nod.

Isabel wondered at his jealous display. How could he not know how Petronilla felt about him?

She said, "Thank you, squire. I am glad to be home at last. I trust all is well?"

A new tension radiated from FitzRobert. He opened his mouth and closed it again, hesitant. She held her breath and waited. When she expected an explanation, none came. Instead, his lips pressed tightly together and a pained grimace shadowed his face.

"What's happened?" she asked.

When he did not reply immediately, Sieur Miles grabbed him by the arm and shook him roughly. "You'll answer milady."

While FitzRobert stirred from his torpor, blinking with eyes widened like an owl, Isabel glanced past him and looked around. Every sound echoed—the snorting of the horses, the incessant ringing of the blacksmith's hammer. Her heartbeat roared in her ears.

Shaking with a sudden chill, she reached for Petronilla, who grasped her hand and held her steady.

"Where's Claremond?" Isabel forced the words from her tightening throat. "She always welcomes me home. Why isn't she here?"

"She's abed, unwell, milady," FitzRobert answered.

"She was well when we exchanged messages at Brionne three months ago. Why didn't she send word to me at Beaumont?"

"Please, I do not know, milady." FitzRobert raked his hands through his hair. "You should go to her."

Isabel dragged Petronilla with her, hastening past servants who stopped and bowed in acknowledgment. The ground level of the new residence housed the kitchens, from which a whiff of fresh-baked bread drifted down the dim, windowless corridor. Although her belly rumbled in response, Isabel took the stairs at the right and nearly knocked aside a page struggling under the weight of table linens balanced on his arms. Through a large, open window, light flooded the passage outside the dining hall. At the southern end of the hallway, a door hanging fluttered.

Petronilla squeezed her hand. "Have courage, milady."

Their pace slowed and the pair walked through the hallway before entering the chamber. Chainsil screens hung on interconnected, wooden rods partitioned the vast room. A woman's labored breathing echoed from behind two curtains. Petronilla pushed aside the fabric. Isabel peered between the screens.

Claremond rested on a pallet with her eyes closed. Her bloated face and hands were barely recognizable. Her fingers twitched and she scratched at them, murmuring something unintelligible. Isabel knelt beside her, reached for her former nurse's hand and gasped when they touched, for the woman's gnarled fingers were colder than shards of ice. Though several thick, wool blankets shrouded her, Claremond shivered beneath them. Isabel bent close to her ear. "I'm here now."

Claremond's eyelids flickered and her rheumy eyes searched Isabel's expression before she smiled a lopsided grin. "Milady."

Isabel did not draw back from the foul breath even though it made her eyes water. She squeezed Claremond's hand despite the chill. "You'll be well now. I shall ensure it."

"No time for me now." Claremond wheezed.

Isabel blinked hard, forcing the tears back and kissed her former nurse's fingers. "I won't allow it." She glared at Petronilla, who sobbed quietly behind her hands. "Stop this! Claremond does not need our tears. They shall not strengthen her. We must be strong for her sake and trust in God to cure her."

Even as she spoke, Isabel questioned the soundness of her own words. Petronilla sniffled and wiped her wet nose with the back of her hand. Isabel patted her attendant's shoulder. "We can't give in to despair so easily, Petronilla. Bring FitzRobert to me. I want to know everything. Ask Sieur Miles to fetch Brother Thorold. My husband says the monk's mother taught him the healing arts. He may have some skill to aid my nurse."

"Shall I also ask Sieur Miles to send the litter for the Earl of Surrey? You promised the man, milady."

Isabel rubbed her forehead at the mention of the arrogant earl before she nodded. "I suppose I have no choice. Hurry, Petronilla."

The servant cast off her heavy cloak and rushed from the chamber.

Isabel spoke with FitzRobert while awaiting Brother Thorold. The backache Claremond complained of before Isabel's progress to Robert's estates had intensified over the last three months, forcing Claremond to keep to her pallet. Recently, she had endured brief fainting spells, constant tiredness and vomiting whenever she ate. The barber had bled her several times. FitzRobert refused the treatment when the bleeding left her weakened and listless afterward.

Under the blankets, Claremond's pallet stank of urine and Isabel ordered FitzRobert to find others who could help him lift the old nurse onto a new pallet. When he had done so, Isabel covered her nose from the stench and told Petronilla to burn the pallet and blankets. She would have to fetch new coverlets for Claremond, who shivered worse than before. Isabel's attendant shielded her nostrils also and peered closely at the dark stains on the foul-smelling pallet.

"What does this mean, milady? It looks like blood."

"I do not know. Brother Thorold may be able to tell us. Where is he? I summoned him."

FitzRobert looked up from where he helped Claremond settle. "He has arrived, milady."

"Then, Petronilla, tell Thorold to come here at once. Claremond needs him. Please, bring the new blankets for her."

FitzRobert ushered the other young men who had assisted him out of room. He halted just beyond the door hanging and bowed to Isabel. "Claremond wouldn't let me summon you. She did not want you to worry. She said she knew the importance of your duties."

"She is equally important to me, FitzRobert."

He hung his head, his face ashen. "Forgive me for my part, milady."

"There is no need for forgiveness. She shall be well again. Thank you for your kindness, FitzRobert and for keeping the barber away. I have no training in the healing arts. I am also uncertain whether bleeding would have helped. The monk shall know what to do. I'm sure of it."

"I only wish I could have done more for Claremond. She reminds me of the woman who raised me, my grandmother."

Isabel waved him off. He bowed again and left her. She paced the room and mumbled complaints under her breath about the clerk's delay. A coughing fit overwhelmed Claremond and Isabel knelt beside her. Often, Isabel's attention darted between her former nurse and the doorway. Patience eluded her. Just when she heaved a weary sigh, Petronilla returned, burdened with the coverlets draped over her arm. Isabel wrapped Claremond in the warm woolens.

"Where is Brother Thorold?" she demanded.

Petronilla stood, doe-eyed, her lips trembling. "He cares for the Earl of Surrey's injury, milady."

The last blanket fell from Isabel's grasp. "What did you say?"

Petronilla mumbled, "He said it's more important to see to the earl's injury."

Without another word and despite her attendant's pleas, Isabel walked the short distance to the hall. Earl William's hunting party lounged idle on benches at the fringes.

Beside the hearth, Brother Thorold bent his tonsured head over the wounded man, who sat on a long bench with his lips tightly compressed. A long slit in his hose from ankle to upper thigh bared his thick-muscled flesh. He looked up when she approached and a slow smile widened his lips. He lounged on his seat. When she stopped beside the Benedictine, the earl's insipid grin faltered.

"Brother Thorold, did you receive my summons to see to my nurse Claremond?"

"I did," the monk said over his shoulder, "As I told your attendant, the Earl of Surrey suffers and requires my attention first. I'll see to the woman in a moment."

She inspected the small laceration, now free of blood and grime. "For this trifling wound, you delay the urgent care my nurse needs?"

"Milady wouldn't be expected to understand. I assure you, my attention is necessary. Would you prefer the earl's leg became infected? I'm sure whatever ails your woman, it cannot be so grave." Thorold never acknowledged her while he washed the leg, though she stared hard at his back. His indifference infuriated her.

"Robert shall hear of your negligence. If Claremond dies for lack of care, I'll have you dismissed from our household."

Brother Thorold raised his head and regarded her. "You may try, milady."

His dark gaze bored into hers as did that of the earl, who eyed her impassively.

A moment's panic ensued, where she felt trapped between the apathetic stares of both men. She clenched her fists and retreated with her back held rigid. Once outside the room, tears stung her eyes. Petronilla gasped when she reentered the chamber and sank down beside Claremond. The young woman looked ready to speak until Isabel offered her a silent scowl.

Isabel did not know how much time passed until Brother Thorold strolled into the chamber. He ordered her and Petronilla to withdraw so he might attend to the sick woman in private.

Isabel stuck her chin out. "I won't leave her side."

The clerk's jaw tensed. He hovered over Claremond and questioned her ailments, while covering his nose against the fetid smell whenever she mumbled a reply. Then he asked, "Have you confessed your sins? You must confess and gain God's succor for the relief of your illness. For what is illness except a manifestation of evil?"

A frustrated groan escaped Isabel. "She shall perform all the religious devotions the Church prescribes when she is well. She has no strength for it now. Something, someone, must aid her. Can you do nothing except pray for her?"

Brother Thorold scowled. "Do you doubt healing by faith, milady?" His hard stare again challenged her. Behind him, Petronilla mouthed a silent plea between her hands.

Isabel ignored her attendant. "I would trust the hands of a skilled healer upon my Claremond more. She has had blood in her urine, Brother Thorold. You can see it on her old pallet just there." She pointed at the stain. "Have you ever treated someone with her ailment?"

"Where there are stones in the body, the blood may manifest itself in the urine. The brothers of Saint Pierre-de-Préaux suggest an infusion of juniper berries steeped in boiling water to aid such trouble."

Isabel turned to Petronilla. "Do you know where juniper grows?"

"At the southern edge of the trail through Brotonne Forest, milady."

"Have Sieur Miles escort you to pick the berries at once."

Petronilla curtsied and left them. Alone with Robert's clerk, Isabel patted Claremond's hand as her dear nurse drifted to sleep again.

"I bid you the Peace of God, milady," he intoned. "I can do nothing further here."

When he rose, Isabel eyed him. "Would you, if you could?"

His gaze jerked back to hers. "You must trust in God, milady."

"Brother Thorold, have you ever seen prayer and confession cure anyone?"

"If such is the will of God, it happens, milady."

"Did my husband heal by faith when he suffered his injury in the melee on the eve of our marriage?"

"God aided in his treatment, as milady is well aware."

"Do you truly believe the infusion of juniper can help my old nurse?"

"Only God may determine its usefulness. There is no guarantee."

Isabel rose from beside the sleeping Claremond, her fingers clasped tightly. "There is one guarantee. If by your neglect and delay, she has suffered further harm, I shall have you turned from this place. You shall never be welcomed in my presence again. Robert would never gainsay me."

Brother Thorold raised his eyebrows. He withdrew his

hands into his woolen habit. "You're certain?"

"I know you have little regard for me, for women in general. Robert trusts my opinions."

"Does he?"

She disliked the certainty in his tone as much as the impudent curve of his lips. "You believe he does not?"

"I would not know, milady, milord does not share confidences about his marriage with me. However, I have known milord since our boyhood. He holds me in high esteem. I will not be so easily removed from his household."

She stepped past him, her head held high. "We shall see."

Chapter Seven – The Hall
Vatteville, Normandy: November 1100

Isabel's heavy sobs filled the otherwise quiet room where her nurse's body lay. Face buried in her hands, she released all her pent-up fear and sorrow. Weary exhaustion seeped through her aching limbs. The familiar, light touch of Petronilla's fingers at her nape and her soothing murmurs offered a small measure of comfort.

"It is over now, milady."

Isabel peeked between her fingers, her cries subsiding to soft hiccups.

On her pallet, Claremond opened her eyes, awake for the first time in two weeks. Her red-rimmed gaze darted around the chamber, unfocused and filled with confusion. Isabel had spent nearly every hour of the past two weeks beside her former nurse, had even taken to sleeping on a pallet next to her. After Tierce this morning, when Isabel had visited the chapel for an hour, she returned and found Claremond stirring.

Isabel reached for the old woman's fingers, the skin stretched thin in smooth, dry folds. "I've been so fearful I might lose you. Have you truly come back to me?"

A croaking groan issued from Claremond's lips.

"Water, she needs water, milady." Petronilla darted from the room and returned with a small pitcher. She cupped Claremond's neck and raised her. After two sips of the water, Claremond coughed and sputtered. Isabel waved Petronilla off, while her old nurse struggled to speak. "Don't, please, rest your throat. We'll talk later."

Claremond's glassy eyes watered. "I was always with you, milady."

Isabel kissed the hands she held, though they were as dry as parchment. Her old nurse managed a weak smile.

An hour before Sext, Petronilla brought in a broth with thin slices of pork, minced sage leaves and parsley skimming the surface of the bowl. She fed Claremond a small spoonful. Isabel sat beside her, her rapt attention on her former nurse. Claremond rested much more comfortably, her chest rising and falling with each even intake.

Though Isabel hated to acknowledge it, Brother Thorold's juniper berry concoction had eased the woman's struggles. Despite Isabel's refusal to leave Claremond's side while Brother Thorold attended her, Isabel still never experienced more discomfort than in his presence. Always, she imagined his eyes watched, judged and condemned her. He had made his contempt for all women known from the earliest days of their first meeting. Isabel felt he reserved his full censure for her.

Why did he dislike her so much? He believed she did not suit Robert as a marriage partner. Why did Thorold view her as a threat to his relations with her husband? Was there yet something about their connection she did not know?

"Milady, the dinner hour approaches. You have ignored your guests since our return. You should go to the hall," Petronilla said, drawing her away from her morose thoughts.

Isabel rubbed her fingertips over sore, heavy lids. She did not need a mirror or Petronilla's sympathetic stare to warn her how haggard and unkempt she must appear. In her concern for Claremond, she had ignored her own needs, eating little more than the bread Petronilla brought up from the kitchen at dinnertime. Her blotchy, wrinkled robe hung limp in loose folds where two weeks ago, it had fit her snugly about the waist. She ignored Petronilla's attempts to arrange her hair, which still hung in a loose braid coiled at her back.

She glanced at her attendant. "I cannot dine with Earl William now. I wish he might hurry his recovery and leave Vatteville. Besides, how can I entertain him and his men? I must look awful."

When Petronilla nodded, Isabel grimaced.

Claremond sipped the last of the broth and let her head roll on the pallet, her eyes closing. "I taught you better, milady."

Isabel wallowed in misery, well aware of her own faults. She had proved a poor hostess and a terrible chatelaine of Vatteville to the Earl of Surrey and his men.

Then, she raised her chin a notch. Why should she care what he or his men thought? Each afternoon, the sound of their revelry drifts from the dining hall. They drank her husband's wine, hunted on his lands and devoured his food stores. Two weeks after his injury, how bad could the earl's leg possibly still be?

It was time for him and his men to be on their way. Isabel had had her fill of their excesses in her husband's hall.

She stood. "Petronilla, bring fresh water for a wash. I'll dine and return to Claremond later."

Isabel lingered just outside the oaken doors of the hall and licked her dried lips. She had never experienced such trepidation at the thought of entering the cavernous room and it bothered her she should experience it now. She smoothed the skirts of her robe, sewn in Robert's favorite colors and adjusted the pleated cambric draping her hair and framing her face.

Beside her, Petronilla whispered, "You look splendid, milady. The earl shall admire you."

Isabel whirled toward her attendant. "What makes you think I care for his opinion?"

Petronilla mumbled, "I only meant you do honor to your husband by your fine appearance before his guests."

"They're hardly guests. The sooner he and his men are gone, all the better for us."

"You should not seek to make an enemy of him. You've told me he's richer than your husband."

"What do I care for his wealth when the man is a brute?"

"He is not so mean, milady. He has increased our provisions for winter with his hunt."

"Now he eats the same stock he granted us, my

husband's game."

"When you did not appear in the hall, he has sent his men with inquiries after your health."

"Why do you defend him, Petronilla?"

"No person is wholly good or bad. All of us have the capacity for cruelty and kindness, milady. I think you would find goodness in the earl, if you let yourself see it."

"I have little reason to hold such expectations. The Earl of Surrey and his men have imposed upon us too long. Day and night, their carousing and drinking drains our wine casks dry. I wonder if we shall have salted meat or any food stores left to see us through this winter. My concern is for us and Robert's lands, not for the wretched earl."

Her head held high, Isabel advanced while Petronilla trailed behind her. At the entryway, Isabel received the greetings of Robert's newest steward, Morin du Pin, who served in the wake of William de Fortmoville's death. Morin, a wiry man with chestnut hair, had returned with her from Beaumont.

Isabel's gaze swept the room. The castle servants had draped the trestle tables with white linen, which now appeared dingy. One of the earl's entourage speared a loaf from a platter carried by a page, tore off a sizable chunk and crammed it in his mouth. Another bellowed for wine. At the table closest to the dais, Earl William lounged carelessly on a bench, the uninjured leg hoisted on the table. Mud encrusted the heel of his shoe. A man who resembled him, whom she vaguely recalled, guffawed at something the earl said before he looked up and noticed Isabel. He bent and nodded to his lord, who removed his limb from the table and leaned forward, leering at her.

She pressed her lips tightly together and then glared at Morin. He offered a sheepish grin before his beefy features reddened. He stared at the floor.

She said, "Morin, in the future, I trust you'll prove yourself better at the task of providing for our guests. I would not have them devour the entirety of my husband's stores."

The steward bowed. She approached the dais with Petronilla. Almost instantly, any conversations fell to a lull. Whereas most of the men sketched a bow or nodded, Earl William remained seated, his watchful gaze tracking her. His grin widened. She refused to let him bait her and returned his impertinent stare. Only when she neared, did he stand. He and his companion bent their heads. She took her seat and Petronilla curtsied. "I'll return to Claremond now."

Isabel quaked. "You would leave me alone?"

Her attendant chuckled and looked around the room. "You are not alone in the company of the earl and his men. Besides, I have not neglected my meals, as you have. Please let me see to Claremond instead."

"Go then. Come to me if she needs me."

Pages began the service with basins of water for the guests to wash their hands. Isabel thanked the small boy who attended her and signaled for the commencement of the meal.

Though she had often eaten meals absent the presence of her husband, today she pined for Robert's company. She had not received any news from him since her return to Vatteville and being so concerned with Claremond, she had not written either. Despondent, she hardly cared when the nobles closest to her gnawed at bones while they ate and belched loudly before demanding more wine.

She stirred her venison stew with little interest and waved away the page who offered a platter of roasted heron. When she did so, she looked up to find Earl William staring at her over the rim of his cup. He downed the contents and lowered his hand. His gaze never left her face. She returned the stare, mesmerized and confused. Usually, she found an easy betrayal of a person's views in their open expression. She could not discern anything from his steady regard.

Morin the steward interrupted their uneasy rapport. "Milady, a messenger has arrived from England with word from your husband."

Isabel gripped the edge of the table and rose. The Earl of Surrey also stood. She swept from the hall, her spine held straight. A tingling sensation warned her that the earl was watching her.

Later, Isabel knelt on the cool, straw-covered floor of the chapel after prayers ended, with Petronilla beside her. She made the sign of the cross and addressed her attendant, "Robert seemed so earnest in his desire for me to come to England and the court of its new king. How can I leave Claremond now?"

"Milord is your husband. You can't disobey him."

"I know, Petronilla. I only wish he had not commanded it now. I was glad to receive news of him, since we had not exchanged letters after my return from Beaumont. I do want to be with my husband. Four years is far too long to see us remain apart. What do you suppose the English king's court shall be like?"

"The same as any royal court, milady." Petronilla gazed in her direction beneath half-lidded, red-rimmed eyes.

With a snort, Isabel replied, "I hope not. I did not like the French courtiers in Paris. Still, something in Robert's message troubled me."

"What can you mean, milady?"

Isabel sat back on her heels. "In Robert's letters, he often mentioned his role at King William Rufus' side, as one of his counselors. He has hardly ever spoken of the then Prince Henry, who has now claimed the kingship. Robert worked hard to ensure Duke Robert of Normandy reconciled with his royal brother, William Rufus, for the sake of the succession. How, then, did Henry claim the throne?"

"The king could have changed his mind."

"I suppose." A deep sigh escaped Isabel's lips. "There's so much I'll have to understand. I will miss Claremond's guidance for a time. If she improves, she can join us in England. Until then, I charge you to remain with her."

"I shall, milady."

When Petronilla sagged and yawned behind her hands, Isabel dismissed her. "Seek your rest. I want to stay a little longer."

In a moment, the wooden door creaked and the chapel's dimness enfolded Isabel. Though eager for her reunion with Robert, she still worried about leaving Claremond behind.

She clasped her hands together and bowed her head. "Heavenly Father, grant us grace and mercy. Continue to watch over my beloved nurse and keep her from harm. She is dear to me. I could not bear it if I lost her. I pray it won't be long before I'm reunited with her in England."

"You're going to England?"

Isabel sprang forward at the unexpected, gruff voice behind her, scraping the heels of her hands across rough, cold stones. She looked around and found Earl William leaning against the doorpost. The breadth of his form prevented most of the evening's light from entering the chapel.

"It's rude to intrude or eavesdrop," Isabel muttered while she rubbed her palms. When she rose and brushed at flecks of straw clinging to her robe, he strode up the nave.

"Why are you going to England, Isabel?"

She gasped at the edge of impatience and the demand in his tone, as much as his familiar usage of her Christian name. Still, she answered, "It is my husband's desire."

His nostrils flared at her clipped tone. She rushed on. "I hope we may leave soon. My servant is still ill. My attendant cares for her. Are you often at the English court, milord?"

"When I've had business there in the past."

"What manner of man is the king of England? Robert has described his countenance. I wish to know if he a good king. Does he show my husband favor?"

"I suppose."

"Oh, I hoped you might know something of him. I

confess I am a little nervous about my presentation at court. Even with Robert at my side, it is daunting. I hope the king is a man of a temperate and kindly nature."

"What I know of him and his court is unfavorable. You would do well to keep away, Isabel."

She wondered that he took the trouble to warn her against anything. "Why?"

His lips pressed tight together, he muttered, "I merely caution you."

"You've hardly told me anything at all of the king or his courtiers. I believe you dislike Henry of England. You owe him your loyalty. Has he offended you in some way?"

"Why are you so interested in the court? Does your life as chatelaine of your husband's castles no longer hold interest? Are you not kept occupied by your duties as mistress of your husband's domains?"

"It is impertinent of you to ask such a thing, yet my Christian charity and the honor of my husband compel me to remain civil with you. The truth is I admire and miss my husband. It has been several years since I have seen Robert. He returned to England in the autumn after our marriage. I have never been to England. Indeed, I never even left Crépy-en-Valois until I married him at Paris." She clapped her hands over her mouth, mortified to find herself explaining anything to him. She lowered her hand and curtsied. "I bid you good evening."

As she rounded him, he grabbed her wrist. She attempted to jerk away. Still, he held her fast.

"Release me! You do not dare touch me. You have no right. You're a guest in my husband's home and a poor one."

"My enchanting hostess offers such censure. You have not inquired after my injury. Except for your Brother Thorold's attentions, I might have bled to death."

"He's not mine. You seemed hearty when we prepared to dine earlier, with your muddied feet propped up on the fine linen tablecloth. I hope you're on the mend and shall soon resume your boar hunting elsewhere."

His grip tightened when she spoke. She struggled against his hold. "I'll shout the rafters down if you do not release me at once."

He loomed closer so she could scarcely draw breath without inhaling the smell of wine and horses.

"Your husband's a fool."

"You drink at his table and now think to mistreat me and insult him?" She renewed her struggles. He let go in almost the same instant. She spun away from him, her chest tight and ready to explode.

He sketched a stiff bow. "Indeed, he is a fool, to leave you here alone for so long." A sardonic smile curved his lips. He strode past her, saying, "If you belonged to me, Isabel, I would never leave your side."

Flames crackled in the open hearth bordered by stone. Drawn to the inviting warmth, Isabel settled on a low stool, her back bolstered by a large, stone column. She swept her mantle off her shoulders and stared into the fire at the western edge of the hall. Across the chamber, Petronilla looked up from her embroidery lesson before Claremond demanded her attention returned to the task. Petronilla's weary sighs and stifled groans echoed in the near silence. In a huff, she tugged threads from the cloth, while Claremond urged patience and snuggled in her warm blanket.

A low whimper warned Isabel the three of them were no longer alone. Then a warm muzzle nosed her hand. An injured alaunt gentil flopped at her feet. The poor dog favored her uninjured foreleg, drawing up the other close to her underside. Earl William's boar hunt of three weeks past had ruined her.

Isabel stroked the coarse white hairs on the dog. The alaunt raised her sleek head before settling between Isabel and the hearth, her muzzle resting on her forepaws. Her eyelids drooped. Despite an occasional flick of the tail, she remained quiet.

The day after Isabel had resumed her appearances at dinner, she noticed the solitary dog. Unlike the other eager hounds, this one did not tussle over bones and scraps of meat, content to relax beside the hearth instead. Her ragged state and painful shuffling into the hall each day betrayed an enduring pain. The earl's master of the hounds had done his best and patched the gaping tear in the left leg. The man held little hope the bitch would ever hunt again. Isabel doubted his view, believing the dog needed only time and care. Each day, she fed her by hand and chased off any rival who edged too close. Isabel delighted in the dog's renewed appetite and hoped the alaunt might regain her strength soon.

"Milady, aren't you frightened of such a great beast?" Claremond's raspy voice stirred Isabel from her musings.

"Never, for she's as gentle as may be."

"Surely, not so in the hunt?"

"Alaunts are not bred for gentleness. Besides, she is not hunting now. I've no reason to fear her."

Then the bitch raised her head, her ears cocked, attention on the doorway. Earl William entered the hall.

Isabel stared into the flames once more. Her stomach fluttered and clenched as if dinner had soured inside her. She clasped her fingers together in her lap.

Unbidden, her thoughts strayed to the evening when they had stood alone. She recalled his heated, whispered words in the chapel. *"If you belonged to me, Isabel, I'd never leave your side."*

She banished the memory, which had haunted her for the past three nights. Her awareness of him doubled as he trampled fresh straw beneath his feet. His heavy footsteps halted a short distance from her. Her skin tingled.

When she glanced upward, the earl loomed, leaning against the column. As he bowed, a forelock of dark hair fell over his eyes. He straightened with a trace of a smile on his lips. Her mouth felt dry. Her tongue flicked over her lips. His smile faded, a hardened stare lingering on her face. He moved toward her, only to halt abruptly.

Her skin tingled beneath his impertinent gaze. When Claremond coughed, Isabel blinked and looked away.

"It's unhealthy to sit so close to the flames, inhaling all this smoke. Your vents are aloft, too high to spare you the worst." He gestured to the swirling gray wisps.

Isabel snapped her mantle closed around her shoulders and regained her composure. "It's cold."

He came around the column and stood directly across from her seat. The hound approached, crawling on her belly. She issued a loud, long-drawn-out whine. The earl chuckled and crouched beside her. Thick muscles bulged beneath his hose. He patted her head and stroked her coat.

"I'll miss her. She has been my strongest hunter for many years. She deserves her rest."

Isabel sniffed and crossed her arms beneath the mantle. "Then, you believe your master of the hounds? You presume she's outlived her usefulness?"

"The injury shall trouble her until her life's ending. It's a kindness for her to end her days in relative comfort, instead of dying at the end of a boar's tusk."

The earl returned his attention to the alaunt and tickled under her chin. She flicked her tail happily.

He said, "I'm grateful for your care. She has long been a favorite of mine, since she was a pup. You should have seen her then, fierce and daring amongst the litter."

His generous praise tugged at Isabel's heart unexpectedly. She wished she might have enjoyed such a close bond with an animal. The dog's proximity offered an odd sense of comfort she did not understand or question. Her father's hounds and hunting birds at Crépy-en-Valois were unimportant to the family. After her elder brothers had teased and taunted a dog until it snapped at them, her father forbade all of his children from approaching the hounds.

"She'll regain her strength soon, milord and resume the hunt."

The dog rolled on her side, inviting him to rub her exposed belly, her tongue lolling. The earl obliged her, glancing between the alaunt and Isabel. He said, "Even if she could, I cannot wait. I am leaving Vatteville in the morning."

Isabel gazed at him in silence and wondered why he would share his plans with her. Then she remembered how her tongue had betrayed her during their meeting in the chapel, when she rattled on about how much she missed her husband to a mere stranger. The earl must think her pathetic, starved for attention. Perhaps he pitied her.

Sympathy did not soften his intense gaze. In the dimmed hall, lit only by one window to the north and the vent for the hearth, the firelight betrayed his fervent attention. Beneath a furrowed brow, his candid expression studied her with widened eyes. She leaned forward on the stool. At his feet, the dog enjoyed his slow strokes across her stomach. His fingers smoothed the short white hairs.

Isabel tore her gaze away and folded her hands, suddenly aware she had said nothing in response to his leave-taking. Finally, after three weeks, he would leave her. The news brought no relief. Her thoughts churned as rapidly as her belly did. Nausea roiled inside her stomach anew. She had surely swallowed something disagreeable. The eels baked in red wine had tasted a bit more sour than usual. Still, the earl had eaten of it and applauded her cook's efforts.

She groaned. Why had she been unable to stop thinking of him since he entered the hall? For weeks, she wished nothing more than his departure. He should leave and take his men and dogs with him. When he departed, she could prepare for her journey. A long-desired reunion with Robert awaited her.

The alaunt's plaintive yowl drew her from reverie. When she looked up again, the earl had stood. His keen expression faded to a placid, stark look. He scratched at his chin and took a deep breath before exhaling slowly.

"I would beg milady's favor. That is, if you would wish it, she may remain here with you. She's my present to you in thanks for your hospitality, though it's a mere token."

Isabel stiffened. "How convenient for you to rid yourself of her in this way. Indeed, your guilt is greatly eased, isn't it, by making such a gift?"

The earl's jaw tightened and his fists curled at his side. "Do you refuse her?"

"I've grown fond of her, milord. I accept her with all gratitude."

"Then why couldn't you say so without trying to goad me? You try my patience repeatedly."

She studied him and wondered why he cared so much that she should accept his generosity. The man might never have known any woman who challenged his motives or offered him little more than simpering courtesies before.

With a sigh, he sketched a stiff bow. "Forgive me. I spoke without thinking and beg your favor. Your kindness has not only been to her, but to my men and me. I shall never forget you. I shall always be in your debt."

"You have no debts unpaid to me, milord. Good Christian charity compelled my kindness. I wish you and your men Godspeed."

His brow furrowed. "Then, I thank you for your good Christian charity. I shall trouble you no further." His clipped tone startled her, almost as much as his abrupt departure. A sudden wind snapped the trailing edge of his mantle.

The bitch dropped her head on her forepaws again and whined.

Isabel's eyes watered as dark wisps of smoke coiled around her. She swiped at her tears. She should be in high spirits at the hope of the earl's departure. The sentiment still escaped her, replaced by somberness and gloom.

From across the hall, Claremond observed, "Milady has lingered too long by the fire."

Just before dawn the next day, the bailey of Vatteville thrummed with activity. The horses in the earl's retinue stamped and snorted their eagerness. Pack animals groaned under the weight of provisions piled on their backs.

Isabel leaned against the doorpost of the castle, her hand resting lightly on the head of the alaunt beside her. Fingers of faint light crept over the land, mired in a silver mist obscuring the treetops. At the center of the courtyard, the Earl of Surrey and his dark-haired companion, whom Isabel guessed to be some relation, directed their pages.

Then, the man who stood beside him now approached Isabel. She straightened, her hands clasped before her. His smile widened beneath thick, dark hair. His long mantle, fastened on the right shoulder by a garnet brooch, trailed in the dust. When he became aware of this, he jerked a portion of the wool over his left arm and continued his advance. She moved just outside the door. He bowed.

"Milady, I am Rudolf, constable of Castle Acre. I wish to offer my humble thanks for your hospitality of these past weeks on his behalf. We shall trouble you no further."

She sniffed and looked beyond him. The earl's squire held the reins of a mount. Earl William approached the stallion and patted the muzzle before he spoke with his squire.

"Milady may not remember. We have met before, at Paris. Milady had newly married the Comte de Meulan and visited him at Abbey Saint-Germain-des-Prés, where he recovered from his injuries during the melee. I was then with milord and his brother by marriage, le Sire de Gournay."

Her gaze returned to the man before her. "I'm surprised you recall the occasion with such clarity. Your master did not remember it."

"William is a man often preoccupied with his thoughts. Having renewed the acquaintance, I doubt he shall soon forget you again. I know he is grateful for the kindness you have shown. For my part, at our first meeting, milady impressed me with her devotion to her husband. I thought at the time, how pleasant marriage might be if all wives were so dutiful."

"Indeed, if only all husbands deserved such devotion."

The constable chuckled. "Your wit is as remarkable as your kindness, milady. Your husband is fortunate in his choice."

She nodded in appreciation of his solicitude and peeked around his shoulder again, to where the earl had mounted his horse and begun directing his men. "Rudolf, come on." He growled over his shoulder.

The dog howled plaintively. Isabel stayed her. The earl's man bowed again and made his farewell. On horseback, he nodded in Isabel's direction and rode to the forefront of their retinue. Earl William rode the length of the column, giving orders to pick up the pace. The hounds followed the master, yipping and snapping whenever a horse strayed too close. The gentleness of the alaunt beside her gladdened Isabel's heart, as the last of the breed exited Vatteville.

At the sloped edge of the crescent-shaped bank, the earl waited for his servants with the pack animals and the last of his knights to clear the gatehouse. With the first rays of sunlight at his back, the mist created a golden halo around his head. Isabel stepped forward. Across the distance, his gaze lingered upon her. A smile smoothed his craggy visage. He raised a hand in farewell. She suppressed the eager urge to return the gesture and patted the whining hound instead.

The earl's smile never faded. As the rearguard joined him, he wheeled his horse forward and joined his men. He never looked back. Her eyes strained for the sight of him, until he became a faint dot on the landscape, suddenly vanishing into the haze.

Chapter Eight – Shadows of the Past
Vatteville, Normandy: December 1100

Short, shallow, pant-like breaths stirred Isabel from a light sleep. She gripped the blanket to her chest. A stony chill swept through the room, wintry dampness permeating the walls. Her blurry gaze flitted across the darkened room. Eerie shadows haunted every corner. She knuckled the corners of her eyes, disorientated and unsure of the source of the sound or if she had truly heard it. A week after the departure of William de Warenne and his men and the castle seemed too quiet. From the pallet at her feet, a few light snores and faint mumblings escaped Petronilla's lips. How dare her attendant sleep so soundly when Isabel had been unable to enjoy a peaceful slumber in several nights?

The raspy breathing returned, echoing beyond the borders of the chainsil screens Petronilla had drawn closed. Isabel threw back her coverlet in alarm and strained to hear the sound again. She did not, for an interminable time. When the sickening rattle rose again, she got to her feet unsteadily and parted the curtain. She ambled across the timber floor, covered with grit and rotting herbs. Something small and furry squeaked in protest at her footfalls.

Near the doorway, the lone torch in a wall bracket outlined the small mound of Claremond's weakened form. In the feeble light, she thrashed restlessly and tugged at the twisted blankets. Isabel knelt beside the pallet, her heart fluttering against her breast. Claremond reeked of sweat and stale urine.

"Rest now, nurse. Be at ease. I'm here with you now." Isabel ignored the pungent odors and gripped Claremond's gnarled hands, so cool to the touch. The waning torchlight heightened her nurse's graying pallor.

"Rosamund?" Claremond's voice issued in a soft, croaking whisper and she tried to pull away, though Isabel held her firm.

"Nurse, it's me, Isabel, your lamb. Do not fear. You're

not alone."

Why did Claremond call for Rosamund now, a woman who had died in childbirth almost twenty-three years ago? Isabel had never known Rosamund, but the gossips had revealed the troubled history between Claremond's husband and her twin sister long ago.

"Help me, please," Claremond pleaded. She jerked away from Isabel's grasp and pulled at the edge of her coverlet. Isabel aided her. Only then did the beleaguered woman relax on the pallet, her eyes closed, her hands clasped in prayer.

"I knew you'd come back just when I needed you, Rosamund."

Isabel buried her face in her hand. Tears pricked her eyes at her nurse's confusion. Just a week ago she had seemed on the mend, giving orders to Petronilla at her embroidery lesson and helping Isabel choose her robes for the journey to England.

The day had dawned and proceeded in the usual manner, except when Claremond fainted right after dinner. With Petronilla's help, Isabel helped her shuffle to her pallet, where she collapsed in exhaustion. She slept all afternoon and into the late evening, through the bells of the prayer hours. Isabel checked on her often and though she worried at finding her still asleep, it was possible Claremond had taxed herself too much in the first days of her recovery.

"Why did you leave me behind?"

Claremond's mewling pitiful voice tore at Isabel's heart. She patted her hand. There was only one way she might ease her nurse's troubles. "I never left you, Claremond, I was always with you."

The pretense left her hollow, until her nurse turned in the direction of her voice, her owl-like stare on Isabel's face. "You'll stay now with me, my sister?"

Though Claremond looked at Isabel, she still believed her sister sat beside her. Isabel could not disappoint her. "I shall, always. I promise."

Her gentle words calmed her nurse, who once again

quieted. Occasionally, she mumbled a few words, sometimes discernible. More often, her whispers were a litany of prayers. Soon the murmurs ceased. Certain she slept again, Isabel drew one blanket over the frail form. In silence, she watched her and listened for shallow, even breathing as the coverlet rose and fell.

Behind her, the door creaked. A soft whine preceded the footfalls padding across the floor. Then a furry tongue licked the side of her face. In the darkness, Isabel threw her arms around the dog. She buried her face in the short fur and wept.

In the morning, Isabel and Petronilla returned from Mass at the chapel. The dog trailed them, having whined and waited outside the door. Isabel told her companion of the previous night.

Petronilla gasped and halted. "Claremond called for Rosamund? She asked after my mother?"

Isabel nodded, though she had anticipated how her revelation might pain her maidservant. Petronilla barely recalled the mother who died giving birth to a second child when her daughter was barely two years old. Robbed of her, Petronilla grew up in Claremond's care.

"Why now?" Petronilla's eyes watered. "She hasn't spoken of her in years. Claremond hated my mother."

"She did not!" Isabel refused to allow anyone to malign her old nurse.

"Milady, everyone at Crépy-en-Valois knew the truth. You can't deny it."

"It's best left in the past, for your sake and Claremond's."

"Now is the time for atonement."

"Atonement?" Isabel folded her arms across her chest. "How? Your father is dead and Rosamund long gone. How can they atone for their actions?"

"The burdens of the past must have haunted Claremond for years."

"Your mother and father carried such burdens on their conscience, not my nurse! She did her duty as a wife and mother, only to endure treachery. Her husband and sister betrayed her!" Isabel paused, indignation firing her blood. She paced back and forth. "Men have no control over their carnal appetites and women are often at their mercy. What can be said of a woman who willfully commits adultery, who knowingly betrays those whom she claims to love?"

Her maidservant stared, incredulous. "Life is never so simple, milady, least of all for a woman."

"What can be plainer than the heartbreak my nurse suffered? Rosamund deceived her and bore a child for Claremond's husband."

"Milady, you cannot know what happened."

"Neither do you. You were a toddling child."

"I remember my parents and the love they bore each other!"

"A selfish love, for neither of them considered Claremond's feelings. Your father thought nothing of the pain he might cause her. The bonds of sisterhood were trivial in comparison to Rosamund's lust."

"It was not lust! They loved each other, milady. You have no right to judge my parents for their choices, for matters beyond their own control. Love demanded their union."

"Love for Claremond should have kept her sister and Claremond's husband faithful. Betrayal of one's marital vows, of a beloved sister, could never be right in the eyes of God."

Petronilla cupped her forehead in her hand and smoothed the lines crisscrossing her brow. "I hope you never face the choice my mother did. You cannot understand the past, milady. You never shall. Not only the rich and landed have little choice in their marriages. Sometimes, the poor wed against their will."

She buried her blotchy face behind her hands and with a sob, returned to the house. Isabel stared after her, shocked at her uncharacteristic outburst.

At the entryway, FitzRobert met Petronilla. Though he immediately dropped the mail shirt hefted in his hands and offered her comfort, she pushed him aside and disappeared inside.

Isabel sighed. The dog nosed her hand and she patted the animal, before the alaunt settled back on her hind legs and stared at her intently.

"Have I been wrong, my pet? Is there more to my nurse's past than she led me to believe?"

The dog whined and flopped down on her belly in the mud.

Only Claremond knew the truth that would grant her peace.

Isabel kept a vigil beside her nurse's pallet throughout the night. Claremond refused all offers of food, even water, during the day. Now Petronilla knelt and offered a bowl of broth to Claremond, who turned her face away and murmured under her breath. Isabel leaned closer to listen. She could not understand the mutterings. Claremond's raspy breathing followed and then she fell asleep.

Petronilla heaved a weary sigh and sat back on her heels. "She could drink some more of the juniper berry steeped in water."

"Didn't we brew the last of it?"

"I think so. I could fetch more, if Sieur Miles would escort me."

"At this hour? You risk too much."

Petronilla nodded and sniffled, her eyes downcast and her shoulders slumped. "I would risk it, for her." Silent tears tracked down her cheeks.

Isabel folded her hands in her lap, unsure how to comfort her. She regretted their earlier conversation, how it pained her attendant.

"Even if I cannot understand Claremond's anger toward my mother, I know it must have been terrible for her, to care for me. I am a symbol of my mother's betrayal. Claremond has hated me all these years because of it."

Though she wished to spare Petronilla further more

anguish, Isabel knew Claremond's feelings about her sister's sole child were complicated, at best. Claremond never expressed the attachment their close kinship might have implied.

"My mother hurt her. I wish they could have forgiven each other—"

"Before the end." Isabel sighed and rose. "I'll go to Brother Thorold. The bell for Compline has rung. Likely, he still offers his devotions in the chapel. He may have some more of the juniper berries we might brew. Otherwise, in the morning, you will search the Brotonne Forest under Sieur Miles' protection. I believe the Benedictine can help us, though it troubles me to ask him."

Petronilla swiped at her cheek. "You also risk too much, milady."

Isabel squeezed her shoulder gently. "Stay with Claremond. I'll return soon."

"It's so dark and cold, milady," Petronilla protested.

"I won't be alone." Isabel snapped her fingers and the alaunt who sprawled at the foot of the pallet rose to follow its mistress.

Isabel stepped out into the crisp night air, her mantle billowing around her. The dog loped at her side, panting, with its nose to the ground. She approached the chapel, her shoes squishing in the slippery mud. The moon rose and bathed the stark grounds in a silvery glow. The hound sniffed at the outskirts of the door. Isabel reached for the handle. Her dog whined and nosed her thigh.

"You must stay here. You know Brother Thorold shall chase you out of the chapel." Isabel bent and patted the soft white head. Each day when she attended Mass, the dog tried to trail her inside.

As she rose, the alaunt tugged the hem of her mantle, tearing it. Alarmed, Isabel jerked the cloth away. "Heavens, what's wrong with you? I said you couldn't come inside."

The door creaked and opened. Brother Thorold stood framed in the doorway. A golden glow crowned his head in a halo of light. Isabel looked past him. Innumerable candles glowed all throughout the chapel. Beneath his cowl, he stared in silence. Behind her, the dog issued low, menacing growls. Isabel silenced her pet with a stern look and a wave of her hand.

"Brother Thorold." She hesitated and swallowed against the dryness tickling the back of her throat. "I need your help."

He withdrew from the doorway. He ushered her inside with a wave. She hesitated and looked over her shoulder. The dog sat back on her hind legs, her growls subsiding to a low whine. Her mournful whimpers echoed long and low through the night.

Isabel rubbed her arms, wondering why her husband maintained his chapel in a separate building within the bailey. At Crépy-en-Valois, morning mass had occurred only two doors down from her father's hall. She never ventured outdoors for worship, not when her father's chapel remained reserved for the family's private use.

The location and construction of Robert's chapel were not the only differences. Candlelight bathed the chancel on the eastern wall in a golden glow. There were candles burning everywhere, set at the foot of the marble altar in iron candlesticks. At the north-south crossing, they stood impaled on vertical spikes. Beeswax sweetened the air. Isabel frowned at the aroma.

"This seems an extravagant waste, Brother Thorold. Why must you burn so many candles and some so near the altar cloth?"

She glanced at him when he did not answer.

He stood beside the stone-carved baptismal font, enclosed on both sides and topped by a wooden canopy, with motifs of animals and foliage. His lips pressed tightly together, he waited with his hands clasped behind his back. He had removed the cowl he had worn upon opening the door, revealing his tonsured head. He seemed in deep concentration on the stone slabs at her feet. Then his gaze met hers. His large eyes caught the candlelight, giving them an almost otherworldly appearance.

She shivered when he stared in silence, before saying, "The urgency in milady's voice suggests graver concerns than my activities in the chapel."

She bristled at the arrogance underlying his smooth even voice and crossed her arms, emboldened by his daring. "Whatever your activities, you can't justify wasting my husband's bounty. Robert has hidden nothing from me. I have reviewed the household accounts with Morin at year's end. My husband has never denied you anything."

"He is concerned with his immortal soul, milady," the monk intoned.

"What does this display have to do with Robert's immortal soul?" She gestured toward the sanctuary. "It is inexcusable. I am sure my husband would never allow it. In his absence, his interests are mine. You'll not waste beeswax like this again."

He barely inclined his head in some semblance of a nod, which irritated her even more. Claremond needed his help. With an exasperated huff, Isabel looked away.

A long curtain of coarse linen hung between two paneled walls behind the altar. When the cloth fluttered on an air current, she suspected it covered an entryway to another room, possibly the sacristy, where sacred vessels were stored. Then she noticed the recessed cupboard on the north wall, which held the chalice, a wine beaker and more beeswax candles. Again, she considered the linen curtain, wondering what lay behind it. Before she could ask, Brother Thorold said, "Now, does milady wish to tell me how I may help her?"

His conciliatory tone notwithstanding, Isabel doubted he really cared. Likely, he wanted her gone so he could return to his devotions.

"My old nurse, Claremond, is ailing again." She exhaled in a loud sigh. "I think she's dying. The juniper berries you had brewed for her seemed to help. I'd like some more for her."

"As you know, the cold has descended, milady." He

paused and she looked at him again, holding her breath. Dear God, could it be his supply was exhausted or the wintry weather made the procurement of more impossible?

What could she do for Claremond then? Her mind raced.

"I've dried the remainder, which is admittedly less potent." His soft-spoken words jarred her.

She released a sigh of relief. Though he stared impassively, his cold stare judged her as always. She sensed he viewed her display of compassion and worry as a weakness. She hated any show of weakness before him and could never consider her devotion for her nurse a failing.

"Praise be to God. I thank you. Please, brew them for her. Anything which can help would be a blessing from God."

Again, he barely intoned his head and gestured toward the altar. "Milady wishes to pray for her servant's soul?"

When he lifted his hand, a thin rivulet of blood ran from beneath the black sleeve of his habit. It trickled on the stone slabs. Isabel gasped. "Good heavens, Thorold! Have you injured yourself? Look. Your arm's bleeding."

He bent his arm and swiped at the blood with his other hand. "It hardly matters."

She stared at the blood spatter on the floor. Her spine tingled with uneasiness. She glanced past him toward the chapel door. The sudden need to escape his unsettling presence overwhelmed her. Instead, she lifted her chin. "I'd best wait outside."

When he raised an eyebrow, she rushed on in a shaky breath, "The dog, she'll be missing me."

Thorold clasped his hands together. Her gaze darted to his sleeve again, where the blood flow had stopped. What had he done to injure himself? Why did he seem so unperturbed when it disturbed her so? A place of worship was an unusual place to see blood droplets.

"I have never understood how people care for such

animals." His casual tone surprised her. "Your husband had a fondness for cats in his youth."

"Oh, I never knew."

The instant she spoke, Isabel regretted it. Brother Thorold's mouth curved into a nasty smirk. "Indeed? I assumed he had spoken of it, since he hides nothing from you."

He dared to mock her.

She ignored the provocation. "He has no reason to hide his past from me. Still, I would be pleased to hear anything about milord's past. Did he have a favorite cat?"

"All the castle's cats sought him, the strays." His countenance suddenly downcast, he paused before sighing, "I never understood his affection for them. It was beneath him."

"I disagree. No other living creature is beyond another's notice. We're all God's creations, Brother Thorold, as the Church teaches us."

"The comte's father did not agree with the Church's views. When Robert neared the age of seven, before his father fostered him, he refused to leave Beaumont-le-Roger without at least one among the animals he adored. Robert's father went into a rage at his son's stubbornness. He had the cats drowned."

She covered her mouth with both hands. "All of the cats? How cruel!"

"It taught milord a valuable lesson. Attachment is useless. Everyone, everything we love leaves us."

Her hands fell and she stared in disbelief. He had spoken in such a bland monotone she did not doubt he believed his own words. Her husband could not share Brother Thorold's beliefs. Such morose thoughts could not rule his life. She still did not know him as well as she wished. In her heart, she felt Robert had grown increasingly attached to her.

"His father was cruel. My heart aches for what he did to Robert."

"Then your heart is too tender and you will learn

disappointment soon enough."

"How can a heart be too tender? Did a seven-year-old boy truly need to learn such a lesson?"

"It helped form the man he is today, milady."

"He feels love and compassion, enough in him to have raised two sons born out of wedlock, where other men would have done less, or nothing. He didn't take to his father's message, wouldn't you agree?"

Thorold answered with silence. Then he looked away again. He seemed preoccupied at odd intervals throughout their conversation. Something clearly sparked in his memory when he spoke of Robert's childhood. She wondered at what it could be. It was foolish to pry into the monk's past. He would not thank her for such solicitude and, in truth, what she had seen of him in four years disturbed her enough.

Icy fingers of cold crept through her layers of clothing. "If you'll excuse me, I should attend to my pet. I await your return."

When she moved toward the door, he blocked her path. "The animal has probably wandered off now, found some warmth by an open fire, rather than brave the cold. You would do better to remain here and pray for your nursemaid. You must be more concerned for her wellbeing than a dog's own."

His disdainful tone stung her. His mood had changed from resentful of her intrusion to judgmental. Until a moment ago, she was also certain he wanted nothing more than for her to go. Now he did not seem to mind. Although the chapel offered little warmth, the night air would not do her any good.

She hoped her pet had found a warm shelter. "Very well, I'll stay."

He waved her toward the altar. She hesitated, then spun on her heels and sank down on her knees before the rood at the entry to the chancel. The image of the Blessed Virgin hovered above her. She made the sign of the cross.

An interminable amount of time passed before she

heard Brother Thorold's exit. It was more a feeling than a sound, in truth. While kneeling, she sensed his silent stare at her back. Though it unnerved her, she took deep, calming breaths and forced herself to concentrate on her whispered prayers. Then cloth rustled and a whoosh of air whipped past her before his footfalls faded. She opened her eyes, just as the curtain behind the altar fell back into place. Again, she wondered what the linen hanging hid from view and what Brother Thorold had done to his arm.

When Thorold returned, snapping the curtain closed behind him, he carried a beaker covered with a strip of cloth. Curling tendrils of warmth escaped the material. Isabel sat back on her heels and rose to accept the juniper concoction. She yelped when the warmth of the container scorched her hand. He went behind the altar again and returned with the beaker wrapped in cloth. Gingerly, she reached for it. The aroma was not as heady as she remembered. Thorold had said the remainder would be less potent.

"I thank you sincerely. I'll sit with my nurse and have her sip the brew."

The monk gave her a curt nod.

Though his calm unnerved her, she lingered. Thorold's mention of Robert's upbringing stirred her curiosity. He and Robert looked to be about the same age. They had known each other for so long, possibly been friends since their boyhood.

Did he perceive her as a threat to his companionship with Robert? Thorold might be jealous, having no wife of his own. If he kept women as some members of the clergy did, they remained a mystery to Isabel.

She stifled a laugh at the ridiculous thought. Thorold did not like women. She doubted even if he could have married, he would have found an acceptable wife.

"Was there something more, milady?"

His question jerked her gaze back to his face. She stammered, "I w-wondered s-something. My husband mentioned your mother was a healer."

"She was."

She gritted her teeth when he paused and failed to offer any elaboration on his answer. She should have listened to her own counsel. He was not interested in sharing anything of his past. She would not permit his easy dismissal.

"Where did your mother learn the talent for healing?"

"Her mother."

"You come from a line of healers then. How did you meet my husband?"

"We both grew up at Beaumont-le-Roger."

She nodded, sensing how her husband had formed a bond with the dour monk. "Where he was the lord's eldest son and you, a healer's child. Did you share an easy friendship?"

"Not always."

Isabel groaned. Why did he have to be so difficult? He had seemed talkative earlier when they discussed Robert's past. After the conversation turned personal, his reticence stifled it. He stared at the stone floor again. Understanding dawned. He always looked away from her at any mention of the past. His actions mimicked Robert's own from years ago. Clearly, their history troubled or even saddened both men. How could she have been so heartless to dwell on the topic?

Though she hated it, a twinge of sympathy sparked in her heart. She imagined how life might have been for him, a healer's son, not born to the upper nobility like her husband. Robert would have grown up in luxury and likely, Thorold's family might have been peasants, especially with a mother and grandmother as trained healers. Had her husband's compassion extended to a boy of similar age with a different background? Had their friendship began with some mutual regard in their childhood? What had Robert's father thought of their attachment? Had he tried to separate them, end their friendship? The monk spoke so bitterly before of attachments to others.

"Milady, if there is nothing further, then I must attend my devotions in private."

When he turned to go, Isabel clutched at the sleeve of his robe. "I'm not finished—" Her fingers grasped wet linen. She backed away a few paces and concentrated on her crimson-colored hands. Had Thorold managed to cut himself on both arms? The blood trail she had witnessed earlier dripped from his left arm, yet the right sleeve she had just grasped stained her fingertips with blood. What had he been doing before her arrival?

She looked up, determined to get an answer. His reddened face twisted into a monstrous mask. The flinty gleam in the monk's dark eyes frightened her more than anything she had ever seen in her life. She stumbled backward, nearly dropping the beaker. Rigid, he towered over her. She raised a hand and warded him off. He drew no closer.

"Don't. Ever. Touch me again."

Her flesh crawled and although shaking badly, she breathlessly whispered, "I'm sorry. I did not mean to do it. You startled me. Your arm!"

"It should not concern you, milady."

In the space of another breath, his brow smoothed and the grotesque, slashing line of his mouth softened. He clasped his hands together and bowed, before slipping his black cowl back into place. Isabel righted herself and went to the door. Though certain he no longer looked at her, she paused at the entryway. She would offer an apology for her offense again, even knowing his poor regard for her.

Brother Thorold knelt before the altar. The glowing candles illuminated a deep, spreading stain from his shoulders to just above his waist. The linen clung to the flesh beneath it. He pushed back the cowl once more, revealing his head bowed. He tugged aside the top half of his habit with a groan. The wrinkled cloth, belted by a cord, fell around his hips.

Isabel tumbled backward against the door. The contents of the beaker spilled through the cloth covering. The brew stained the stone slabs dark red, the same color as the blood on her fingertips. The bright hue of the scarred and shredded flesh covering Thorold's back.

Chapter Nine – The Favor of Heaven
Vatteville, Normandy: December 1100

Bitter wind swept across the courtyard and into the glowing recesses of the chapel. The candle flames flickered at the altar. Isabel doubted Brother Thorold even felt the chill. Horrified, she lay sprawled in the doorway. Her dog approached and licked her cheek. Isabel patted her absentmindedly, assuring the animal she was well. She felt exactly the opposite.

Thorold groaned and reached for something unseen beside the altar. His action splayed the wrinkled, reddened folds of striped skin on his back. Bloody rivulets trickled from fresh cuts into the mass of scars. How long had he been scourging his body in such a way? Did Robert know of his activities? Was this why he had constructed the chapel at a distance from her home, to allow Thorold his privacy at these blood-spattered rituals?

He chanted in a low murmur. She could scarcely hear what he might have said, except for, "I supplicate the Creator by the blessings of Saint Pardulph to mortify this weak and unworthy flesh—"

Great God, he intended to do it again. Isabel rose gingerly, patting her bottom where she had fallen hard. She feared him more than ever, especially given his outburst. The memory of his murderous tone when she had accidentally touched him frightened her. Still, an undeniable pang of pity again rose in her heart, as it had earlier when he had spoken of his childhood. What depravities had he endured then to make him seemingly immune to pain, to willingly embracing it?

With a shudder, Thorold closed a tight fist around long, thin strips of knotted thongs, bound at each end with rough-hewn white pieces of some indiscernible matter. Without hesitating, he brought the whip down on his back. Isabel closed her hands over her mouth, stifling a scream. If she cried out, she might never be able to stop. He whispered his penitence, the lash repeatedly scourging his brutalized flesh. Isabel fled, her original purpose long forgotten.

Later, Isabel's whimpering sobs echoed in the softly lit chamber. Petronilla rubbed her shoulders and crooned in a soft whisper, "It's over, milady. You're safe now."

"What sort of man is he? How can he bear it?"

"Don't worry for him, milady." Petronilla soothed her. "We cannot understand such a man as Brother Thorold."

Isabel jerked away from her. "I do not mean *him!* How can my husband permit these actions? Robert must know of the depravity his clerk inflicts upon himself. How can he keep such a man in his household?"

"Milady, you said they've been friends from their boyhood. Your husband respects Brother Thorold. He must be willing to tolerate it."

Isabel rose, as did the alaunt who kept close to her. "It has to stop. I won't allow it."

"What can you do, milady? Your husband is not here and he shall never let you cast Thorold from his household. You meddle in monastic mysteries which those outside the Benedictine order can never understand." Petronilla rubbed her arms. "In truth, I wouldn't want to understand any of it. Did he really whip himself into a bloodied mess, with you standing there?"

At her inquisitive stare, Isabel continued, "I said as much, did I not? I do not believe he noticed or even cared whether I witnessed him. I care not if his order requires scourging as a penance. I cannot understand why Robert would permit such a man to live among us, to reside at Vatteville with me, to be alone in my presence. Imagine if it had been our child, Robert's heir, who saw Thorold instead of me. How could I explain it to a child?"

Petronilla kept her silence, her head bowed. Isabel trod a frantic pace back and forth beside the chainsil draped around her bedding. "I'll speak to Robert. He'll understand my concerns."

"What if he does not?"

She halted and glared at Petronilla. "Robert cares for me. He won't allow Thorold to frighten me again."

"Milady, their friendship has held sway for many years. Your husband built his chapel as a sanctuary for—"

"A sanctuary of God, Petronilla! Not a place of wild mysticism, sullied by blood and brutal whippings. By Christ's bones, have you failed to grasp my meaning? Thorold was whipping himself before an altar. What man of God does such a thing? He may wear the habit of the Benedictines, but he lives outside heavenly grace."

In the days afterward, Isabel remained doggedly at Claremond's side. The old nurse neared death at last. Terrified she might expire at any time, Isabel sat with her daily and even slept fitful nights on a stiff pallet next to her. Fear often jerked her from sleep. Only when moonlight filtered through the shuttered window above Claremond's resting place, outlining her thinned lips through which shallow breaths whistled, did Isabel relax.

After the fourth night of Isabel's vigil, Petronilla protested her refusal to change her robe and chemise. The attendant collected the remnants of dinner, which Isabel had barely touched.

"Do you think Claremond will rejoice when you're there to greet her in heaven?" Petronilla grumbled while she threw a woolen blanket over Isabel's narrow shoulders. "She will not thank you for dying, you know. You won't be doing her any favors."

"Lower your voice. You might startle her," Isabel pleaded, her fingers caressing the parchment-like folds of skin crinkling Claremond's cheek. Why did her nurse have to leave her now?

"Hardly matters what I say or do since she can't hear me," Petronilla murmured. "Not when she sleeps the sleep of the dead these days."

She clapped a hand over her mouth and dropped the

additional blanket she had brought for Claremond on the floor. She bent and retrieved it. When she stood, tears pooled in her eyes.

"I'm so sorry, milady." She whispered through trembling lips. Isabel patted her hand.

"I cannot deny it either. She is dying, Petronilla. We must both accept the truth. We can do nothing for her."

"Except to see she receives the Sacrament."

Isabel nodded and blinked back her tears. "We must ensure she seeks God's grace and the forgiveness of her sins."

"Can Thorold minister to her?"

"He is a clerk, not a priest. We are here without the benefit of Robert's chaplains. I heard the church bells peal for Compline an hour ago. Dare I ask FitzRobert to brave snow and ice to fetch the priest? Would there be enough time? Thorold must attend Claremond now at her last. She must have the benefit of her last confession, even if the clerk would say holy mother Church does not allow him to administer the Sacrament."

"I can go to him."

"I would not have you alone with such a man!"

Petronilla shuddered at the fervor of her tone. Isabel sighed. "Thorold's disdain for all women is well known. FitzRobert can fetch him."

Her attendant covered Claremond with the extra blanket. Isabel clutched at her hand. "Please, hurry. I fear she may have little time left."

Petronilla bowed and scurried from the room. The white hound at the door lifted her head when Isabel's attendant swept past and then shuffled on her belly beside Isabel, who stroked her muzzle. "You're a dear companion. I'll miss my Claremond still."

The dog whined. A lone tear trickled down Isabel's cheek before she buried her face in her hands and sobbed softly.

"Don't cry, Rosamund."

Although Claremond's raspy voice sounded so far away, Isabel heard her clearly. The old nurse's confusion dismayed her. Many times when Claremond awoke, she seemed to forget where she was. Often, she imagined herself at Crépy-en-Valois and always asked after her sister. Once, when Isabel tried to make her aware of her current surroundings, Claremond turned her face to the wall and murmured, "Don't lie to me. I know she is not here because she has not forgiven me."

Now, Isabel took her nurse's hand in hers, marveling at the shriveled, weakened flesh. She glanced heavenward. After a silent plea for forgiveness, she bent close to her nurse's ear.

"Claremond? Can you hear me? I'm here, Claremond, it's your sister."

"Rosamund? Is it you? I knew you would come. We will soon be together with him. I loved him too, Rosamund. He was my husband."

The memory of her husband's adultery with Rosamund haunted the dying woman. With a gentle squeeze of her hand, Isabel hoped by such a small gesture to ease the pain.

"He should have been yours, Rosamund. You loved him and I stole him away."

Claremond looked up at the ceiling, though seemingly unseeing. Her voice croaked and gurgled as she drew a ragged breath. "I was outside the stable when he met you in the afternoon. You thought you remained hidden from everyone. I had followed."

Claremond's head rolled on the pallet, opaque eyes seeking Isabel. The dying woman managed a weak smile, a little spittle oozing between her lips.

"Still so fair, Rosamund, even after all these years. Remember how inseparable we were as children, how no one could ever tell us apart? The bishop swore identical twins were the sign our father was a cuckold. Mother and father, they knew he was a fool. Our parents hated when we would play games, me answering to your name and you answering to mine."

As she spoke of the happy past, her voice brimmed with vigor. Such delightful memories strengthened her against the tears.

"We were not children when you fell in love. I was jealous. He only wanted you. Even when he saw me alone, somehow he recognized me."

When Claremond fell silent, Isabel sighed, unsure she wanted this tale of remembrance to continue. She edged closer to a new truth about her nurse's past which she feared. The dog with its head in Isabel's lap became alert and growled low in her throat, her tail stiffening.

"I could not let you leave, Rosamund," Claremond whispered. "I stole Comte Herbert's wine and went to the stables the same night. I plied your lover with the wine and he drank, though he did not want to at first. He was drunk when I gave myself to him." Claremond sought Isabel's face again. "I quickened with his son. When our father found out and wanted to know who had fathered the babe, I lied and said he had forced me. He never stopped loving you and hated me each day."

Footsteps shuffled across the floor. Isabel swiped at her tears and looked up, into the stony, hard gaze of Brother Thorold. He lifted a Crucifix. "God damns liars and fornicators!"

The alaunt bared its teeth, lips drawn back in a snarl. Isabel hushed her pet and rose. "How long have you stood there and listened to her?"

"Long enough to know she is a vile sinner."

Isabel's hands became fists. "She sinned in her youth! My nurse has been a good Christian since my earliest days. Her devotion, her sorrow and regret are genuine. She seeks forgiveness for the sins of her past. She must have the last confession. We are all sinners, Thorold. Who gives you the right to pass judgment on a dying woman?"

"God."

He turned on his heel. Isabel charged after him. "How can you turn from anyone seeking penance? You are an evil man, beyond heaven's favor or grace."

"Your husband does not think so."

"His friendship with you blinds him. I wonder at how

you have imposed yourself upon him all these years and hidden your true nature."

Brother Thorold spun around so quickly, she almost slammed against him.

"Think what you like, milady. Even if I could, I would never perform the Extreme Unction on this or any other night for her. If she dies now, she does so in a state of disgrace, as her past warrants."

"Her confession is enough! God will forgive her!"

"Why? She's marked herself for a contemptible whore, as are all women."

When Claremond died within the week, Isabel ordered her burial near the chapel. She sent word to her younger sisters, who remained at Crépy-en-Valois, knowing they would also cherish the beloved memory of their former nurse. Then she prepared to leave Vatteville, despite Petronilla's protests.

"You can't go alone! The bitter days of winter lie ahead and what if you become lost?" Her attendant trailed her, as Isabel gathered her skirts on the steep stairs leading outside. Petronilla begged, "At least wait until Sieur Miles returns from Pont Audemer, or let FitzRobert accompany you. You're unprotected."

Tears stinging her eyes, Isabel swiped them away. She emerged in the full glare of morning, where sunlight glinted off the first snows of the season, which had fallen the preceding night.

Petronilla grabbed her arm just before she reached the mare, the reins held by an astonished squire. "Milady, you can't do this."

Isabel pushed past her attendant and mounted her horse. "I cannot stay here."

Petronilla stifled a sob and grasped her hand. "This is how you grieve for her, abandoning all those who love you, who would comfort you? She was my aunt, milady. How can your suffering be the measure of mine?"

Isabel grasped the reins and urged her mount forward. At the gatehouse, she demanded the guards let her pass, even without an escort.

The gatekeeper said, "Milady, let me find FitzRobert. The squire can attend you if you wish to ride out."

He left one guard on duty, who eyed her warily. Both of them looked past the gate as a rider approached. He identified himself as a herald from Pont Audemer. Sieur Miles was half a day's journey behind him.

Isabel knew Miles would never let her leave Vatteville. She had to take this one chance now. It would never come to her again. She glared at the sentry. "Open the gate. Would you have this man freeze to death atop his horse while he waits for the return of Sieur Miles?"

The man groaned and rubbed a hand over his reddened face. He opened the gate and she bolted. Her horse flew past the bewildered messenger. She escaped the confines of the place where only sorrow and regret held sway now, and vowed never to return.

Heavy hooves pounded the frozen earth covered in pristine snow. Isabel peered behind her. Her eyes widened in terror. A rider in black tracked her, a red cloak swirling and the hood pulled low, obscuring any facial features.

Her heart thudding in her chest, Isabel leaned forward, her icy fingers gripping the reins tighter as she whispered encouragement to her mount. Shafts of sunlight darted between the thick woodland. Ice mired the landscape. The brilliant rays reflected off pristine snow stymied her gaze. She prayed God might guide her.

"Milady! Stop! You'll harm yourself."

Isabel ignored the warning carried on the chill wind. She could not risk slowing the mare, not even for fear of icy patches. The mare snorted, her coat glistening despite the cold.

"Milady!"

Panicked, Isabel looked around again. Her pursuer gained ground, hurriedly closing the distance between them. A gust of air whipped the rider's hood back.

FitzRobert's fierce glower reminded her of his father. What would Robert say if he could see her now?

She slowed her mare and turned to meet the squire. "You cannot force my return to Vatteville."

His breathing ragged, FitzRobert joined her. With a nod, he grasped the reins of her mount. "I do not intend to force you."

"Did Petronilla send you after me?"

When he nodded, she looked away. "She worries too much."

"She is loyal to you. We all are. You are a good and gentle mistress."

"You only came after me because you feared my husband's wrath."

FitzRobert looked sheepish. "It's not the only reason. Milord would kill me if anything happened to you."

"He's your father. How could he ever—"

The squire's nostrils flared wide and he turned from her. Isabel groaned at her stupidity. How could she have embarrassed him so? "Forgive me, FitzRobert, I should not have spoken."

He could not meet her gaze. "How long have you known?"

"Since a month after I married Robert. I saw you, him and Sieur Miles walking across the courtyard. Your resemblance was unmistakable, as though younger versions of my husband strode beside him."

He glanced at her. "You've never spoken of it with me until now."

Her fingers covered his, encased in leather gloves. When he flinched, she drew back her hand. "I didn't want to shame you."

"I could never be ashamed to be milord's son." When her eyes widened, he cleared his throat. "Forgive me, but I am proud to have such an honor, too proud. Sieur Miles would say so if he were with us."

"You do not need to ask my forgiveness, FitzRobert."

"I must ask your pardon, for you are his wife. For four years, you have borne the burden of milord's past in silence. The knowledge must have pained you. I regret the sorrow my presence has caused you."

She pushed aside the memory of her discovery and her first argument with Robert. "It is in the past. You and Sieur Miles are a credit to him. I could no more hate you for your existence than I could despise Robert for having acknowledged and raised you. He did his duty as a father, which is more than most men would have done for their—"

"Bastards," he finished for her. No trace of bitterness tinged his voice.

"I meant to say, natural children. I was cruel to Petronilla when we parted this morning. When you return, tell her I am sorry."

When he sighed, Isabel smiled. "I won't go back to Vatteville, FitzRobert. You cannot persuade me to return with you."

"I know. I grieve with you, milady. Claremond was very dear to Petronilla. Your sorrow is hers. I believe she is more concerned for you than for her own loss. I can send any message you wish to her, once we arrive at our destination."

"Our destination?"

"If you shall not return home, then wherever you go, I'll go with you."

She looked along the trail winding through dense thickets and trees. Snowdrifts swirled and billowed with every puff of wind, obscuring the view.

"We ride east to my dower lands at Elbeuf."

FitzRobert removed his leather gloves and handed them to her. "You'll need these for the journey."

Elbeuf, Normandy: January to March 1101

Seated on the floor beside an open hearth, Isabel cupped a ceramic bowl brimming with golden cider. After two cursory sips, she stared into the crackling flames, the only source of light in the shuttered hall. Two village girls with heads bowed close together scattered laurel and rosemary, their voices barely rising above a whisper. From the corner of her eye, Isabel noticed they glanced at her. Something stirred and rustled among the oaken rafters above her head.

She sighed, missing Petronilla's company and the usual festive mood. The Advent season had passed without observing the fast days at Vatteville, while Isabel devoted her attention to her ailing nurse. When Claremond died two days before Christmas, the indulgence in traditional holiday celebrations would have been vulgar and inappropriate. Within the week after her arrival, Isabel sent a messenger to Morin the steward. He would have to supervise the usual holiday privileges she would have otherwise provided for her husband's tenants, including gifts to the village girls for Saint Nicholas' Day. With a gasp, she realized the Epiphany would arrive tomorrow. There would be no one to preside over the feast in her absence.

The hall door creaked, ushering in a blast of evening air, which preceded FitzRobert's near silent footsteps. Isabel sipped the cider again and eyed him over the rim of the cup. He walked with the grace and stealth of a cat. The village girls halted in their conversation and eyed him, tittering behind their hands.

"Milady, a party of riders under guard begs entry at the gate." FitzRobert bowed, golden curls falling over his eyes.

"We arrived less than two weeks ago. We're hardly prepared to offer shelter and entertainment to guests."

"I do not believe the lady and her party intend a long sojourn with us."

Isabel set down her drink. "A woman?"

FitzRobert nodded. "She has a dire need, milady. She is heavy with child. Last week's rains and the melting ice have flooded the roads to the north. Why a woman would undertake a journey in winter, in her condition—"

"Is not our concern, squire." Isabel finished. "Bring them in."

He bowed and Isabel issued instructions to the village

girls. She brushed rushes from her dour robe. The squire returned quickly, leading six women. Two at the forefront supported the gasping woman in their midst, who settled her bulk on a bench with a stiff groan.

Isabel curtsied. "I bid you welcome to Elbeuf."

"Who are you?" The woman clutched her rounded stomach, jutting beneath the embroidered mantle.

Isabel said, "The Comtesse de Meulan, wife to Robert de Beaumont." She waited in silent expectation for her guests to reveal their identities.

Beneath a pale blue *couvrechef*, the noblewoman's face grew flushed before she groaned. "Is there a wise woman in the village?" The words seemed wrenched from the depths of her.

"I'll see to it she comes at once." Isabel gave a stiff nod to FitzRobert, who scrambled from the hall. Isabel continued, "How may I aid you until she arrives? Would you take some wine to ease your pain?"

An elderly woman among the arrivals shoved an opaque jasper stone into the panting woman's hand before turning to Isabel. "Milady's time comes too soon. Are you aware of the rigors of childbirth?"

The question seemed impertinent. Still, Isabel shook her head, mute.

"Then it's unlikely you can do anything to help. We'll attend to her."

The elderly attendant turned again to her mistress, who groaned in pain. Isabel returned to the fire. The village midwife and her assistant arrived and the lying-in began later, during which Isabel retreated to the opposite side of the hall, near the doorway. Despite the draft, she kept far from the hearth while the wise woman worked. She had exposed the swollen belly of the noblewoman, whose cries and screams echoed to the rafters.

After some interminable time had passed, the midwife's assistant left first, a ragged bundle tucked silent and unmoving in the crook of her arm. Isabel lifted a hand to her mouth as the wise woman bowed.

"The child is dead, came too early. The noblewoman

is resting. It would be best not to move her tonight."

Isabel gazed, horrified, at the burden the other woman carried through the doorway. The healer followed her stare. "Be at ease, milady. It happens. The lady said she has a son and daughter at home. She'll bear this loss well."

Isabel nodded, though she did not see how any living child could compensate for a dead one. "Find FitzRobert at the gatehouse. He'll escort you back to the village."

She pressed a silver denier into the wise woman's hand and the midwife bit into it before bobbing her head. She followed her assistant.

Isabel knew women and their offspring could die in childbirth, having heard of the passing of Claremond's sister. A child's death must be more painful than the loss of its mother. She shivered and rubbed her arms. How could God have given a woman a babe, permitted its growth inside her and reclaimed the child before it had even lived outside the mother's body? Was the wise woman right in this instance? Would the lady bear the loss easily because she had other children? Isabel shuddered at the thought of how she might feel if she lost Robert's son before his birth. More than anything, she feared her husband's disappointment. She hoped such an awful circumstance would never be hers.

She remained awake when the hall door creaked again. She barely acknowledged FitzRobert's greeting while he draped a woolen blanket around her.

"We buried the babe at the crossroads, milady."

"Why?"

"The child was never christened or sprinkled with holy water. Its body does not belong in hallowed ground. Brother Thorold has said if anyone dies without—"

"Do not speak his name!" Isabel glared at FitzRobert. "I have no wish to hear anything of Brother Thorold or his teachings."

The squire looked away. "At your command. I'll start my watch, milady."

At her stiff nod, he bowed and left again.

The elderly attendant left the noblewoman at the hearth with her other companions, crossed the hall and curtsied. Isabel forced a smile. "How does your mistress fare?"

"She's sleeping now. She is strong like her mother and shall have many more children."

When she paused, Isabel nodded.

"I regret my abrupt tone this evening. I am Lady Judith. I have served milady since her youth. I worry for her as though she were my daughter."

Isabel's eyes watered and she sniffed, turning away. "I understand. I had a nursemaid once, who was also devoted to me." She wiped her cheeks and forced another grin, waving to the bench near the door. "Please, sit and take some wine or cider."

"I thank you for the wine."

Isabel poured from the ewer set on the dais into an empty cup and handed it to her guest. She sat beside her. "If I may ask, why was your mistress traveling at such a time in her state?"

Judith finished her wine and refilled the cup. "I advised her against it. My Edith is willful. A trait inherited from her mother, I believe."

Isabel managed a genuine smile, for her Claremond had often said the same of her.

"We went to Paris so she might reunite with her new husband. Her first husband, le Sire de Gournay, took up the cross and died for it."

Isabel did not dare mention her father had also attempted the same, for fear his disgrace had reached northern Normandy. She reproached herself for having forgotten to ask in her letter to her sisters whether Pope Paschal II had excommunicated their father on his shameful return.

Judith continued, "Milady cannot endure passage by boat. We traveled on horseback rather than on the Seine. I believe this made the child come sooner than she anticipated. We did not expect the birth for another three months. Her husband shall be disappointed. This would have been his child as milady already has children from her first husband."

Isabel kept her silence, still uncertain other children could soften the blow. Did the mother know her child did not rest in hallowed ground?

Judith continued. "We were grateful to find this estate inhabited."

"Normally, I would be at Vatteville."

"Where is your lord? Is he here with you?"

"My husband is in England, at King Henry's court for the Christmastide season, I'm sure."

Judith's limp lips puckered as if her third cup of wine tasted sour. "The English court is vile. It is no proper place for a young lady. Milady keeps far from it, unless her brother is with her. In England, she has a great manor at Caistor and estates throughout Norfolk, which her brother granted."

Isabel nodded, though she did not know where Norfolk or Caistor might be.

"Have you never been to England?" Judith asked.

"I have not, though my husband desires it."

Judith patted her hand in a familiar gesture, which belied her earlier hauteur. "You should go to him and pray he keeps you from court. If Earl William had not watched Lady Edith when she was younger, she would not be the good and virtuous woman she is today. William de Warenne is very attached to his sister and cares a great deal for her welfare."

"You mean the Earl of Surrey?" Isabel's heart pounded at the mention of the name. "Are you saying your lady is Edith de Warenne, his sister?"

Judith nodded. "Have you met him?"

"I have." Memories flooded Isabel's mind. "He sojourned at Vatteville this past season. A boar injured the earl. He soon recovered."

Judith relaxed and poured another cup. "Milady is devoted to her brother. Her heart almost cleaved in two at the announcement of her husband's death. She has the best of him in his children. Afterward, William arranged another marriage for her and eased her sorrow. He is a good brother to her."

Isabel doubted Earl William was a good man. She knew better than to voice such an opinion of him. "Where is the earl now?"

Judith hiccupped and giggled. "William went to England and left within weeks for Normandy again, before Epiphany. His determined efforts at wooing came to nothing and he departed from Castle Acre, embittered by his failure. The lady rejected all his proposals and chose another."

As her guest lifted her fourth cup, Isabel tapped her fingertips across her breastbone. Her mind raced, recalling everything she had exchanged with the earl short weeks ago. He had not mentioned his interest in marrying anyone. His future happiness held no meaning for her. The marital prospects of such a man were beneath her concern.

She could not help wondering, though, what sort of woman had refused the wealth and prestige Earl William offered?

Within a few days, Edith de Warenne insisted on resuming her journey, despite Isabel's assurance she might stay longer. Isabel bid the party farewell in the courtyard just after dawn. FitzRobert assisted Lady Edith in mounting her horse.

She settled with a groan, thanked him and looked down at Isabel. "I'll never forget your compassion."

"I pray God shall protect you on your journey, Lady Edith."

"Thank you. You're too fair and generous, as my brother William has described."

Isabel gasped. "The earl has spoken of me?"

"He sent a message to Paris two months ago. He told me he'd been injured in a boar hunt and found care in the kindness and solicitude of the beauteous Isabel de Vermandois."

Isabel tucked a strand of her loosely braided hair

behind her ear, certain a blush suffused her cheeks. "He was overly kind."

"My brother never resorts to flattery. We share a penchant for truth-telling."

Then Edith ordered her men-at-arms away from Elbeuf.

Isabel waved farewell until her hand fell listless. She clutched her robe and slowed her rapid breathing. Why had she reacted so to the mention of the Earl of Surrey? What had he told his sister of her?

Long weeks of winter gave way to an early spring thaw. Isabel returned from an early morning ride with FitzRobert and found Petronilla. Sieur Miles helped her dismount. Knights in his retinue milled about and eyed Isabel expectantly. She alighted from her mount without FitzRobert's help and ran to Petronilla, who embraced her.

Isabel said, "I've missed you so. Please forgive me for leaving you behind. I've been so foolish and stubborn."

"Indeed, you have." Petronilla framed her face in her hands and kissed her brow.

Isabel laughed. "Have you come only to chide me?"

"Your husband is very worried for you. He sent a messenger to Vatteville a few days ago. He demands you come to him in England, where he can be assured of your safety."

Isabel looked beyond her attendant to Sieur Miles, his mouth set in a grim line, reflecting his father's disapproval.

"I'm no child to be ordered about as my husband pleases." She extracted herself from Petronilla's embrace.

"You are his wife and you must obey."

She looked at the façade of Elbeuf manor, already missing the quiet and solitude she had found there. "Very well. Then we go to England."

Lisa J. Yarde

Chapter Ten – Reunion
Warwick, England: March 1101

Against the backdrop of a reddened sky, a square timber tower rose atop a steep, broad hill. The setting sun descended, casting an orange glow of embers on the nearby river. Isabel shielded her eyes against the glare. Behind a palisade, curious expressions focused on them, followed by a flurry of activity along the walls. At the base of the motte, another stockade encompassed the land and abutted the north bank of the river. Wooden buildings lined the stockade.

Isabel glanced at Petronilla, who quickly turned her baleful stare into an assessing one. "It's different from Normandy."

"Indeed, as the duchy differs from the whole kingdom of France. For now, England is home to us."

A graying pallor tinged Petronilla's features and her lips pressed tightly together.

Mounted on a palfrey, FitzRobert leaned forward in the saddle. "Do you suppose our messenger reached the castle, milady? Has milord been forewarned of your arrival in England?"

Petronilla glared at him.

Isabel lowered her hand and hid her smile. "He should have, considering our difficulties. He possibly expected us a week before now."

FitzRobert colored and his shoulders drooped. "I'm sorry, milady. I had told Sieur Miles not to entrust me with the duty of escorting you. He insisted I should have the responsibility."

Isabel said, "He would have led us to Warwick, squire, if he hadn't injured himself on the practice field at Vatteville. I pray God for his easy recovery. I do not blame him or you."

His sheepish grin widened. "I admit I'm a poor escort, milady. I am sorry we lost our way along all these rivers. Who knew there would be so many? I'd only ever been to England once before."

"I thought Robert might have sent a garrison to meet us. His letter at Christmastide instructed us to come here. He never mentioned why he chose Warwick. I am certain the hall is most impressive and comfortable. I shall be glad when we may retire. Are you ready to see our new home, Lovvet?"

Petronilla's brow wrinkled in vexation as Isabel reached down toward the white-haired alaunt beside her. The dog wagged her tail.

"Milady, I shall never understand why you named her," Petronilla muttered, shaking her head.

"I could hardly keep calling her 'dog' forever now, could I?" Isabel did not truly believe animals possessed emotions, but she could not deny Lovvet seemed pleased at their reunion. Isabel would never leave the dog behind again.

"Shall we continue on to the castle?" she suggested.

FitzRobert looked ready to say something. Then he lifted his hand and pointed. "Look, milady, they're sending someone out to us."

Isabel's heart soared at the vision of a man on horseback, a red mantle billowing at his back in the southwesterly wind. He led four others out of the gatehouse toward a wooden bridge across the river. Shielding her eyes with her hand again, Isabel gasped at her first glimpse of golden hair shorn in the bowl-shaped style of the Normans. Then the fluttering pennon on a lance drew her attention. The flag featured an image of a bear on its hind legs, bound by a collar and chain that held the animal to a long staff. "It is not my Robert."

Petronilla squinted. "How can you tell at such a distance, milady?"

"I recall every time my husband has ridden away from me. I would know him anywhere, for he is much taller in the saddle than the one who approaches us. What should we do, FitzRobert?"

Her gaze darted from the riders bearing down on them to the six men-at-arms who had escorted her. She pressed a palm to her chest. The men held their swords at the ready. Seven of them, including FitzRobert, could defend them against those who approached. Petronilla shied her palfrey closer to Isabel. Their escort encircled the women protectively.

After a moment, he sagged in the saddle. "It is your husband's brother, the Earl of Warwick."

The riders drew to a halt in the middle of the crossing. Their leader advanced alone to the south bank, his arms spread wide to show he intended no harm. FitzRobert inclined his head and greeted the Earl of Warwick, who nodded to him. He looked past him to where Isabel sat on her horse. She wondered whether the earl noted the resemblance between FitzRobert and himself. He opened his mouth, from which Isabel fully expected words would spring forth. Instead, he stared as though thunderstruck.

"Make the introductions, FitzRobert," Isabel whispered at his back.

The earl offered a beaming grin at the sound of her voice. "I bid you welcome to Warwick Castle. I am Henri, brother of Comte Robert. Are you his bride?"

She returned his generous smile with caution. "I am Isabel de Vermandois."

"Then I greet you as a brother, milady."

His candid expression reminded her very little of her husband's own. She urged her mare forward until their horses stood side-by-side. "I greet you as a sister, milord. My husband has oft mentioned you in his letters, with deep admiration and pride."

"He has spoken of you with much the same. I am honored and pleased to meet you at last."

His open charm belied an air of quiet reserve about him. He was shorter, sporting a smaller frame than her husband possessed, as she had surmised earlier. Their one similarity was the same golden hair. Glancing at FitzRobert, she recognized it must be a family trait. Warwick's eyes were wide, brown and warm. A general pleasant expression suffused his face. Deep lines scoured his brow. She knew much of him, for Robert often described his relations in detail. He had painted a thoroughly accurate description of his younger brother.

Henri said, "You must have witnessed my shock upon first sight of you. You are not at all the person whom Robert told me to expect."

"How so, milord?"

"My brother claimed he left a child bride at Vatteville. The changes in you shall bring him much pleasure."

Isabel strove against her furious blushes.

"I pray, milady," Henri rushed on, "do not think me brazen. My brother's descriptions did not lead me to expect such a beauteous woman as you."

"I do not think you are brazen. You are kind and generous, as Robert has described. You are too kind in your praise of me, milord."

"I am not. I speak only the truth. The sight of you pleases me greatly, for my brother's sake. If he still thinks of you as a child, then he has been too long at court and far from your side."

"It has been some time since I last saw my husband. When we parted, I *was* a child. I expect Robert remembers only the girl he left at Vatteville."

"Permit me to convey you to the castle, where there are others eagerly awaiting you, including my countess, Margaret." He pointed at the bridge. His horse cantered along the bank toward it.

Isabel urged her horse beside his. Hopefulness for a sweet and swift reunion with Robert sustained her. Horseshoes clopped in unison across the wooden planks. The rest of Isabel's retinue followed.

She asked, "Why is my husband not here to greet me? Is he unwell?" Isabel prayed it would not be so. A niggling doubt gnawed at her. The previous year would have marked her husband's fifty-fourth birthday. His service under successive Norman kings kept him active. The likelihood of grave injury or his death increased as he advanced in age. A dreadful future loomed if Robert died and left her alone, widowed without a son to carry on his name.

His brother interrupted her morose thoughts. "*Non, non,* milady. Forgive me if I have created a false hope. Robert counsels the king at Westminster regarding a matter of the former bishop of Durham. Robert is never far from the king's side for long. I find little reason to attend court, except when the king commands me. Robert often attests his charters and with each year, His Grace calls upon me less. It is as I wish, for I am a man best kept at the side of my beloved Margaret. She worries for me when I am with the king."

"Is court so dangerous?"

Henri smiled. "It is rife with scandalmongers, gossips and those seeking the king's favor. Men of such ilk would frighten a maid as gently raised as you must have been."

She did not take the trouble to correct him about her upbringing. "When we embarked at Le Tréport, we learned the king had newly married a princess of the Scots."

"She descends from the old English royal line. Queen Matilda is daughter of King Malcolm Canmore and his wife, Queen Margaret, a sister to Prince Edgar of the English."

"Is Robert so often at the king's side, even when His Grace is newly married?"

"The business of the kingdom cannot wait upon any man's happiness, including one lately in the throes of marital bliss. Robert asked me to entertain you at Warwick and, to bring you to him upon my return."

"Will it be a long journey from Warwick?" With yearning, she looked along the southwesterly course of the river.

"Not for mounted men accustomed to horseback." He slowed his horse when they reached the north bank. "I understand your eagerness to reunite with Robert and promise we remain at Warwick only for a few weeks."

Isabel blushed again. "You know a woman's heart, milord."

He nodded. "We are brother and sister. Call me by

my Christian name of Henri."

"Only if you shall do the same for me."

Inside the castle, which, as Earl Henri explained, rose at a bend of the river called Avon, Margaret de Perche, the Countess of Warwick, awaited them. Margaret's warmth and amiability matched her husband and Isabel judged them well suited. Their rapport and the countess' clear devotion to her newborn daughter made Isabel wistful about her future.

She did not sleep later, staring up at the ceiling beams of the drafty hall while Petronilla snored beside her. Even Lovvet breathed deeply at Isabel's feet, sleeping on her back with her paws in the air. Isabel envied their peaceful slumber. She sighed restlessly. Breath whistled through her parted lips in a white mist. The anticipated reunion with her husband occupied all her thoughts.

Henri and Margaret shared what seemed a pleasant, comfortable affinity, which suited their sedate personalities. Isabel wanted more than quiet companionship with Robert.

Beneath the woolen coverlet, wrapped in her chemise, she palmed her belly, as maiden-flat as the day she had married Robert. She longed to give him a son, a legitimate heir to carry on his name. Other women had stolen the privilege, which should have been hers alone. He had delayed the consummation of their marriage until she gave proof of her body's readiness to bear children. Her courses had started in the previous year. She would soon be sixteen, a year older than when her mother had her first child.

Her hand swept across the span of her hips, slim like her mother's own. Comtesse Adelaide had birthed nine children, including Isabel. If her mother had survived each birthing, there was no reason to fear it. She would have to surrender herself to Robert to give him heirs. It must be a pleasurable experience, or otherwise, women would not have babies.

She quested lower, touching the place where she would birth Robert's babies one day. Easing her legs apart, she cupped the fine linen against the warm flesh beneath. Here, their bodies would unite. She understood this much from having glimpsed her parents through the bed screen at night when they presumed she and her siblings slumbered. Her mother took obvious delight in those moments, despite all her outward signs of disgust with her husband during the day.

Petronilla rolled on her pallet, her limbs askew. Isabel jerked her hand away. Petronilla murmured in her sleep, an almost breathless whisper much like FitzRobert's name. Isabel smiled in understanding.

Westminster, England: March 1101

At noon, rain pelted the Earl of Warwick's party as they approached the thick walls encompassing the hall at Westminster. The sudden downpour had caught them by surprise just as they entered the city. Chilled to the bone, Isabel retreated into her hooded cloak. She sympathized with Petronilla, who muttered something very unladylike about what the English could do with their accursed rain. Riding just behind the women, FitzRobert urged them on. They entered the courtyard and groomsmen rushed to their aid. Isabel alighted and fled with the others inside, just as lightning arced and flashed across the murky sky. Lovvet shook her coat and rubbed against Isabel's thigh. She bent and stroked the hairs atop her head.

Henri said, "You'll find your husband awaits you here."

Isabel nodded. "I thank you for the escort, though I believe your countess was unhappy at your departure."

A smile softened his aged features. Still, he kept his features impassive. "My Margaret does not hide her affection for me. We'll see each other again at Easter, when the court travels to Winchester."

Isabel sighed. "Westminster, Winchester. How shall I learn of all these places? I must seem woefully ignorant of this land. Until I married, I knew no other place beyond

Crépy-en-Valois."

Lit torches cast their light into the gloomy recesses of the entryway. Double doors of solid oak planks swung back on the hinges. Through them, a massive, aisled room with large arches and windows beckoned. Isabel stared in wonder, for not even King Philip of France's hall at Paris was as impressive in size. Above the windows was a checkered pattern of light and dark stones. The painted walls hung with tapestries and between each hanging, a guardsman stood at attention. The focal point of the room was a raised dais at the southern end, around which a group of men clustered, speaking in turns to the dark-haired man who alone sat. A man garbed in a vermillion and gold *cotte* bent his whitish-blond head and spoke in low tones to the seated man.

"Robert!" Isabel's cry echoed through the hall. All the men looked to the doorway in alarm. Isabel did not care. She stifled a sob of relief with a hand over her mouth. The dark-haired man stood, his gaze assessing before he waved her husband away. Isabel forced herself to stand rigidly while Robert crossed the room in lengthy strides toward her. His stone-faced expression did not faze her. She saw only the husband she had missed for more than four years, unchanged. When he neared her, she could not wait to close the distance. She rushed to him, threw her arms around his neck and buried her face in his red and gold tunic.

"Robert, at last." When she looked up at him, his frown greeted her. She laughed cautiously. "Don't you recognize your own wife, milord? It's me, your Isabel."

"Indeed, it would seem so." He gripped her arms and studied her. "I didn't expect you to arrive here, sodden and bedraggled, interrupting the council. Remove your arms from around my neck. Your impetuousness is the act of a child, not the woman I had expected you might have become. As my wife, I expect a show of proper decorum in the king's presence. Do you understand me?"

Isabel's hands fell away to her sides. Her heart

sinking, she squeezed her eyes shut. She had intended a more joyous reunion than this one.

Robert's hold tightened. She winced and glared at him. "I understand you well, milord."

"Don't be angry with her, Robert. Your king commands it. Any man parted from his beauteous bride so long as you have been would wish for such a welcome." The dark-haired man advanced on them.

His voice boomed through the hall, tinged with a hint of delight, not anger. If he had not acknowledged himself as king, Isabel would have known it by the power he exuded in his tone and bearing and by his elegant dress. She sensed he was a man who, when he gave a command, expected total obedience. Such a man would be dangerous if anyone defied him.

When Robert released her, Isabel curtsied low before she stood, shaking, beside her husband. At the king's command, she rose again and looked into deep, bright eyes twinkling with amusement. King Henry was of medium height, shorter than Robert. The crown glimmered atop black, curly hair, which receded from his brow. He studied her and then nodded to Robert.

"You are congratulated. I dismiss you, Robert, though I expect you and your lady to dine with us." The king looked past them to Henri and gestured for him to join the council. The Earl of Warwick and Robert nodded to each other and then the younger brother followed their king to the southern edge of the hall.

Robert offered his arm. Isabel touched his sleeve hesitantly. At the doorway, FitzRobert bowed and Petronilla curtsied. When Lovvet nudged Isabel, who offered her a reassuring pat on the head, Robert raised an eyebrow. He led them down the passageway, the dog loping behind them.

A hooded figure stepped into their path. Lovvet growled low in the throat. Isabel gasped and clutched her husband's arm, sinking her nails into his forearm.

Robert glowered at the man. "Have a care before you frighten my wife to death, Thorold!"

The monk folded his hands across his chest and inclined his head slightly. "My apologies, milord, I did not intend to upset the lady."

It was too late. Isabel pulled away from her husband, glaring at him. "Robert, what is he doing here?"

She stifled a cry when Robert jerked her by the arm into the darkened alcove where Thorold stood. He bowed and joined the rest of Isabel's party, who conspicuously turned away. Lovvet whined when Petronilla tugged her by her collar and joined FitzRobert at the rear. The attendant looked on in dismay, before the squire patted her arm and spoke with her until she averted her gaze.

Robert shook Isabel, drawing her attention back to him. His eyes were hot sparks of fury, burning into her. She had never seen him so furious. A large vein in his neck pulsed rhythmically.

"Be mindful of your tone when you speak to me. I am unaccustomed to such displays of temper from a woman." He ground the words out in a tightly controlled voice.

"I am unaccustomed to your lack of caring for my feelings. How can you expect me to endure the pain which his," her finger stabbed in Thorold's direction, "presence has caused me? You have no idea how he's wounded me and you give no thought to my concerns."

"At least he obeys me." Robert edged closer. She would not shy away from him as he spoke. "He came to me at Christmastide when I commanded. You sulked and whiled away weeks at Elbeuf, with no thought except your own suffering or how I must have worried for you."

"Such neglect is unpardonable, milord, especially when I can see how much you're worried for my comfort now." Isabel rubbed her arm where he had grabbed her.

His body tensed. He flexed his fingers.

Isabel's heart hammered. She closed her eyes and awaited the blow. The Church gave him the right as her husband, much like her father's right of chastisement. She would suffer and survive Robert's maltreatment as she had done with Hugh.

She gasped when his hand touched her throat. Behind her, Petronilla's cry of alarm rippled through the passageway. Tears threatened. Isabel vowed he would not see them now.

"I forget at times you are a child, so easily wounded," Robert whispered. His caress swept down the column of her throat to her shoulders, where he rested his fingers. He pulled her to him, pressed her face against his chest. Isabel's heart and head warred inside her, one demanding she break loose from his hold, the other desiring nothing more than to find familiar comfort in his embrace. His hand stroked the limb he had gripped so roughly.

"Forgive me. I spoke without thinking. I never intended to hurt you by any of this, or by bringing Thorold here. He is my clerk. I depend upon him."

"You know what he's done?" Isabel searched his gaze. Beneath lowered lids, he returned her stare.

"I do. He's told me everything, Isabel."

"Did he tell you how he refused the Sacrament for my Claremond lying ill on her deathbed?"

Robert nodded. "He did and I berated him for it."

When she withdrew from the protective circle of his arms, he crossed his arms over his chest, his face blanched. "Thorold is not the arbiter of any man or woman's soul and I told him such. He was wrong to judge your nurse for any perceived sin of her past. He knows it now. He's done penance for it."

"Do you know how he does penance? Whipping himself in a bloodied frenzy?"

Robert flinched. "You were never meant to witness such practices."

"How can you condone such a practice?"

"It is common among many monastic orders, including the Benedictines." He raked his hands through his hair. "If he displeases you so, I'll dismiss him. He can return to the abbey of Saint Pierre-de-Préaux this afternoon. You shall never have to see him again."

Isabel looked to the monk, who stood with his hands clasped as if in prayer or contemplation, head bowed, so she could barely see his face beneath the cowl. Could it be so easy to dismiss the man she despised? Would Robert do it at her command?

"He offends me. I want him gone from your retinue."

Robert left her and stood before his clerk. "Your arrogance has wounded my wife. An injury to her is an injury to me. Gather your belongings and depart for the abbey this day."

A moment ago, Robert had chastened her, only to rise to her defense now. Thorold glanced at Robert from beneath his hood, a brief, incredulous look. He stiffened then and looked beyond Robert. His frigid stare met Isabel's own, his pale blue eyes glowing as though lit by fire within. She lifted her chin and stepped out of the shadowy alcove.

"As milord commands. If milady would allow it, I humbly ask her forgiveness for my offenses." He intoned his head slightly and then bowed before Robert. When he straightened, he made the sign of the cross. "I pray God be with you always."

He turned on his heel and left them.

Isabel released the pent-up breath she had held back. Though Thorold's retreating figure moved steadily away from them, she could not believe he was truly gone. Robert stood with shoulders drooping, his gaze downcast, eyes averted. When she touched his hands, his fingers were cold and pale in her grasp. He blinked hard. Her heart cleaved at his pained expression. Now she had wounded him, which she had never meant.

"Robert, I'm sorry. I spoke in haste. I know how much your bond with Thorold must mean to you."

"It means naught more than you." He crushed her to him and this time, Isabel did not struggle against him. "In time, Thorold shall learn the error of his ways. I cannot allow him to alter your happiness. I've missed you, my Isabel."

She sighed and nestled against him, desperate to

believe him.

The court dined less than an hour after Isabel's arrival. Robert escorted her, her fingers resting on his forearm, Lovvet trailing them, to the hall. Several times, her husband glanced over his shoulders, his features implacable. "The alaunt is attached to you."

Once Isabel slowed, the dog halted beside her and rested on her hind legs. Isabel bent and stroked the animal's muzzle. "She's endeared herself to me over time. I cannot be apart from her."

"I wonder that you find such joy in this great beast." Robert tucked her hand into the crook of her arm again. "William de Warenne was too generous with his gift."

Isabel stumbled and righted herself quickly. She resumed walking beside her husband. Robert stared straight ahead, as they approached massive doors thrown back on their hinges. Laughter and varied, pleasant scents drifted beyond the room.

She struggled with a response. "How did you know Earl William gave me Lovvet?"

"Thorold told me when he wrote before Christmastide."

Isabel stopped and turned to him. "I must know the truth of something."

"You may ask anything of me."

"Did you ask Thorold to spy upon me in your absence?"

"*Non*, I did not and he did not spy upon you. Thorold remained devoted to my interests. He never watched you at my behest or for his own purposes. He always kept me informed of general occurrences within my household. When the Earl of Surrey was injured in a boar hunt and stayed at Vatteville for nearly a month, Thorold thought his presence worth mention." Robert paused and cupped her cheek with his free hand. "Your charity toward William was admirable and I thank you for it, even though the earl is at odds with the king now."

"Have the earl and the king quarreled?" Isabel

despised the eager curiosity in her voice. She could not deny his mention of Earl William's troubles intrigued her.

"It's unimportant. Shall we continue in to dinner?"

She ground her teeth together at his easy dismissal. He behaved as though she should have no interest in courtly life, while it consumed his existence. When would he learn she valued his concerns as much as her own?

At the doorway, a page greeted and escorted them to the high table, near the dais at the forefront of the room, where the king and others sat on long benches. An open fire radiated its warmth from the center of the hall. Candles of wax stood impaled in iron candlesticks, attached to the walls with brackets. Robert seated Isabel and then joined her, with Lovvet sprawled on the floor at her mistress' side. The sewer supervised his underlings, each with warm water, wooden bowls and cloths. Isabel wet her fingers in the proffered water bowl in which flecks of sage and rosemary floated at the top. She expected a much more extravagant feast than she had ever partaken of in Normandy.

She glanced to the dais. King Henry met her gaze with his large eyes. The breath escaped her in a sharp sigh. Except for a brief flare of the nostrils, his expression remained unaltered. He nodded to Robert, who must have noticed his regard and inclined his head.

Isabel lowered her gaze and studied the king covertly. He spoke with a clergyman at his left, who wore a red mantle trimmed by fine dark fur. Robert identified him as Anselm of Bec, the archbishop of Canterbury, with an edge of annoyance in his tone Isabel would have questioned, except someone else drew her attention.

The woman at the king's right sat with a demure smile, though her stare was downcast. The richness of her attire, surmounted by a green mantle with a white border embroidered in gold, indicated her high status.

Robert whispered in Isabel's ear, "The queen of England is unlike any other. There is no woman who possesses her charm and dignity."

"Please tell me more about her."

"It's impolite to gossip at the dinner table."

She turned to him, surprised by the smile, which belied his chiding tone. "We are not gossiping, Robert. I must make presentation to the queen. Would you parade an ignorant wife who knows nothing? Please."

He stroked her fingers with his large hand. "You mustn't be frightened. If you listen to me, you shall find life at court interesting and Queen Matilda more so. She was born a princess of Scotland. Her father had named her Eadgyth at birth." He chuckled when Isabel crinkled her nose at his pronunciation. "She is a descendant of King Alfred the Great of England. She seemed destined for the veil, but swore she did not assume it. Her upbringing at the abbeys of Wilton and Romsey has ensured her grace and piety."

Robert spoke with such admiration. Isabel could not help the twinge of jealousy. "I'd never have expected you to speak with such reverence of her."

"Queen Matilda endears all. Others have sought her hand before she wed the king, most notably Count Alan of Richmond and the current Earl of Surrey."

Isabel looked away as her awareness shifted. When Edith de Warenne's nurse mentioned the earl's interest in a wife, Isabel could not have guessed the woman meant Matilda of England. Earl William had wanted to marry her and she had rejected him. Was her subsequent marriage the cause of his and King Henry's apparent estrangement?

Robert chuckled low at her shocked silence. "You seem surprised. Who would want the county of Surrey when one might have the whole of England?"

Isabel glared at him. "Robert, you're being unkind."

"I doubt the loss of her mattered to the earl. He is unsentimental."

When Lovvet stirred, Isabel felt inclined toward disagreement, for she had seen the earl's attachment to the hunting dog. She kept such an observation to herself as the king's chief steward signaled the beginning of the meal.

Isabel dined on roasted venison and ate sparingly of a dish of frumenty. While picking out the pungent, aromatic leaves of dittany from a salad, she noticed a noblewoman and a young girl dressed in russet. They sat at the lower trestle tables and shared a trencher. The girl laughed at something the woman said and when her cheeks dimpled, Isabel thought she was the most angelic vision she had ever seen. Clearly, she had inherited the beauty of the woman beside her, whose florid skin and fine features matched hers. Only the coloring of their eyes differed, the lady's own being a crisp blue and the girl's a dark brown. Isabel wondered whether they had the same lustrous hair, as wisps of almost black curls framed the child's face and billowed around her shoulders.

The girl's gaze wandered to the dais. Isabel followed her stare, in time to see the king wink in the child's direction. Her smile widened before the woman beside her whispered in her ear and drew the child's attention. When the girl looked to the dais again, the queen leaned forward, gripping a cup between her fine-boned fingers. A deepening scowl tugged her lips downward.

In an instant, something in the child's features seemed familiar to Isabel. "Robert, there's a child among us."

He did not look up from the meal. "I have noted her. She is the only child here."

Isabel hesitated, uncertain as to her husband's sentiments. Her curiosity piqued, she could not put aside further inquiry. "She reminds me of the king. Why?"

Robert sipped his wine. "She is his natural daughter."

"Who is the woman beside her?"

"She is the girl's mother. She is here so the king may arrange her marriage. At his command, she brought the child with her. I believe the king considers prospects for the girl's future husband. She nears a marriageable age."

Isabel sighed, understanding the emotions Queen

Matilda displayed all too well. She no longer resented Sieur Miles and FitzRobert, but remained unsure of how she would have felt if there had been a woman from Robert's past to contend with in Normandy. She pitied a queen faced with any rival.

Isabel knelt before Archbishop Anselm and received his blessing after the court dined. Robert's rigid stance beside her belied his amiable manner of greeting the prelate. Afterward, Isabel made her formal introduction to the queen. The monarch seemed curious about her at first. When a minstrel arrived, he became the center of attention for everyone. Bored, Isabel did not anticipate an afternoon with the court ladies at their embroidery and slipped from the room when she thought no one would notice her absence. As she stepped into the darkened passageway, the hem of a scarlet robe disappeared behind a pillar. When she approached, the dark-haired little girl from the dinner hour scurried down the corridor.

"Wait! Don't be frightened."

The girl turned, clutching a harp to her frame. As Isabel neared, the child gulped, her eyes widening.

"You must not run away. I would never inform Queen Matilda you were listening at her door to the minstrel. Please, tell me your name."

"Amieria, milady."

"My name is Isabel. You're a very lovely little girl."

"My *maman* tells me so."

"She should, for it is true. Do you play the harp?" Isabel indicated the instrument the girl clutched.

"Not as well as the queen's minstrel, milady."

"I would prefer to hear your verses instead of his at any time. Can you play for me now? Please?"

When the door opened and voices intruded into the passageway, the little girl disappeared. Isabel followed, not wanting anyone from Queen Matilda's retinue to see her either. She rounded a corner and slammed into King Henry's burly frame.

Chapter Eleven – The Queen's Displeasure
Westminster, England: March 1101

King Henry's grip on Isabel's shoulders tightened with unyielding pressure. She gasped and stared, flabbergasted by his amused expression. One hand released her briefly and instead, cupped her elbow. He said, "Have a care, lest you fall." Wine and mint leaves co-mingled in his breath.

He abruptly let go. She looked past him into a sea of faces, guardsmen and nobles, by their respective dress. Sniggers and smirks marked their features. Only one person did not mock her with his earnest gaze.

Earl Henri pushed past the king's men and bowed before Isabel. "Are you unwell?"

"We surprised her." The king waved a dismissive hand.

Robert's brother offered Isabel a last glance and she nodded her reassurance. He bowed and withdrew.

The king eyed Henri, Earl of Warwick sharply from beneath hooded eyelids before he regarded her again. "Why are you not with the queen and her ladies? You take no pleasure in the evening's entertainment?"

Behind her, tittering laughter and feminine voices warned the minstrel had finished with his audience. Isabel licked her dry lips.

The king's nostrils flared and he closed any perceptible distance between them. Something about his overly familiar approach and manner disturbed her. The amused appearances of the men behind him remained unaltered. "I'm weary, Your Grace and sought my husband."

"He is not in Westminster. I expect he'll return shortly."

Surprised, she wanted to ask where he had gone. Just then, the king turned aside. The little girl, Amieria, stepped out from behind him. She clutched her harp as if it were a prized possession.

Henry smiled. "Comtesse, I see you've met my angel."

Amieria glanced at the sovereign, who winked at her as he had done during dinner and patted her dark hair, so like his. Seen together, their resemblance was uncanny. None could doubt the girl's lineage when she stood beside her royal father.

Isabel's gaze jerked from her back to the king, who eyed her with a speculative glance. Licking her lips again, she said, "We spoke a moment ago. I had only the pleasure of learning her name and her delight in the harp."

"Indeed. It was my gift to Amieria for her birthday last year."

"Your Grace is generous and kind."

Behind her, the laughter and chatter abruptly stopped. She turned in time to catch sight of Queen Matilda, as she rose from her curtsy before the king. The pained expression the royal consort had worn during dinner returned now. Her cheeks colored scarlet.

If the king noticed, he made no comment. Instead, he bent and spoke to the child beside him in a foreign tongue, which was both strange and intriguing at once. The girl responded and the king patted her head again. This familiar gesture delighted her until she stared past Isabel, to where the queen stood.

She clutched the harp, fingers rippling the strings. Then she curtsied prettily, her dark eyes averted. Queen Matilda's lips thinned though she acknowledged the curtsy. She glanced at Isabel. Her countenance did not improve.

Isabel might have wondered at this, except the king addressed her again. "Grant me a kindness. Escort my Amieria to her mother. The child will show you."

Behind the king, Earl Henri cleared his throat. Isabel met his stare, as did the king. Henri's placid countenance betrayed nothing, despite whatever he might have meant to say.

Isabel said, "It would be an honor, Your Grace, to take your daughter into my care."

The king bent and kissed his daughter's forehead,

speaking to her again in the language reserved for their private communications. She curtsied before him and then walked toward Isabel. Amieria's gaze lingered on the queen, who reddened with each diminutive footfall the child made.

Isabel grasped the girl's shoulder and shepherded her along the passageway, placing herself between Amieria and Henry's consort. As she passed the court attendants, silent glares united in disapproval that mirrored their mistress' own.

A little ache stabbed at Isabel's heart, at the memory of her first having seen Robert with Sieur Miles and FitzRobert. She had sympathized with the queen because of her own experience. Isabel had never truly reviled the knight and squire sired by her husband for their low birth, as the queen did with the little girl. The child had no control over the circumstances of her birth. If anything, her father bore the blame. The courtiers could not see the truth because their loyalty to the queen precluded an understanding of the child's innocence.

"You shouldn't have done it." Amieria's low murmur jarred Isabel.

"Done what, dear child?"

Amieria looked to where the king and Queen Matilda spoke in low tones a short distance away from the others, who had all turned away. "She won't like you now, milady. She does not like having my mother or me at court. She may think less of you for being with me."

"Henry's consort should not be threatened by a child's presence. If she truly feels so, then she proves herself unworthy to wear the crown of a queen of England. Women must bear much in life. Your mother, I am sure, knows this better than most. She shows courage by her attendance at court."

Amieria halted. "You have not met my mother, milady. How do you know she has courage?"

Isabel paused and smiled at her. "Women have to possess strength if we are to live in a world of powerful men."

"The queen doesn't frighten you, milady?"

"I am the granddaughter of King Henry of France. The petty jealousy of a queen of England does not concern me. Now, may we share a proper introduction? I am Isabel de Vermandois, the Comtesse de Meulan. You may call me by my Christian name."

"Oh, *non*, I could not."

Isabel laughed. "Not even if I insisted upon it?"

"You outrank me, milady. My mother has taught me to show proper respect."

"She has raised you very well, Amieria. She should be proud."

When they exited the building, darkening clouds overhead portended another fierce storm. Amieria pointed to a lone, hooded figure standing beyond the gatehouse. "*Maman* waits for me."

Isabel nodded. "When you come again, bring your harp and play for me. This time, I insist upon it."

"If you wish, milady."

The little girl curtsied and scampered away, her shoes squishing in the muck. Isabel waited until mother and daughter reunited in a sweet embrace. Isabel rubbed her shoulders against the bitter cold, envying the apparent closeness between the pair. The woman stared past the gatehouse to where Isabel stood. Then she swept the child beneath her mantle and they disappeared into the evening gloom.

The next day, when Isabel and Robert attended morning Mass, he did not speak to her. His lips were a thin slash of censure. She wondered what she had done to earn his displeasure, since they had not seen each other the evening before. She did not know where he had gone or when he had returned. The sentry must have called the hour of midnight before Robert returned.

They stood a few rows behind the king and queen. Both had acknowledged her with faint nods, though the stiffness of the English queen's gesture belied any attempt at a pleasant greeting.

Instead, Isabel focused on her husband. "Do you

intend to ignore me all morn?"

Robert glanced at her once. A darkening look deepened the lines crisscrossing his forehead. "I begin to wonder whether I shall have to beat the impudence out of you after all."

"You may try. My father did." His threat did not frighten her. She had known worse as a child.

"How did he fare?"

"As you see."

A chortle escaped Robert. Congregants who stood nearby glared at him. He ducked his head. "Do not banter with me, milady. Let us talk at dinner."

Later, while they shared a dish of oysters, Robert said over the rim of his cup, "You are unwise to disdain the queen."

Isabel pouted, her gaze roaming the line of tables, until she spied Earl Henri. Her brother by marriage looked away from her quickly.

Robert grasped her hand. "You must know there can be no secrets at court. Henri did not speak of your meeting with the girl, the king and his wife. Others did. The queen cannot abide her husband's bastards."

"Amieria has done nothing wrong." Isabel kept her voice moderately low, though she seethed inside. "The king asked me to escort her to her mother. Would you have had me disobey him and earn the royal displeasure?"

"Dearest, you must be mindful of Matilda's opinions. She is Henry's queen."

She slid her hand from beneath his. "I'm not ignorant, Robert. I am also the descendant of kings and queens of France. I bear as much royal blood as she, if not more."

"Your birthright gives you too much pride."

Roused to anger, she turned away and snapped, "Without my birthright, I would have been a less favorable marital prospect. Admit it."

His cup clanked on the table, sloshing wine. He gripped her hand again and compelled her to look at him. "The Testament cautions us, 'If you allow yourself to become full of pride, you shall find yourself humiliated. Be modest.' Do not tell me your pride cannot bear it, for then I would think you incapable of mastering it. You can do anything when you set your mind to purpose."

Mollified, she nodded. "You do well to remind me to seek temperance. I fear pride governs me. My father always said it was chief among my faults and blamed my mother."

He touched her chin and raised her face to his. "Did he truly beat you?" When she nodded, he added, "I would never harm you. You must believe this. I am not like your father."

She gazed into his eyes and leaned closer. "I believe you, Robert."

Loud guffaws and ribald laughter interrupted the unison of their loving glances. Isabel blushed. Several nobles eyed them and encouraged Robert to kiss her lips. He surprised her by laughing, when she anticipated he would have been annoyed and embarrassed. He raised her hand to his lips and nipped her fingers, earning cries of dismay from his peers. He ignored them all and stared in admiration, having eyes only for her. She took comfort in his possessive hold, believing herself safe and loved.

After dinner, Isabel found Amieria again, or rather Lovvet found the girl. The dog scampered behind Isabel and Petronilla while they walked in the gardens, and then bounded out of sight behind frost-covered bushes. A squeal drove a spike of fear into Isabel's heart. She calmed upon seeing Amieria playing with the alaunt, who chased the girl around in circles. White puffs of breath floated through the air as the animal panted.

"The bold hunter snares her quarry again," Petronilla commented.

Isabel glared at her.

Amieria ran toward them, her dark hair billowing, Lovvet at her heels. The chill in the air had turned the child's cheeks pink. "Is she yours, milady?"

Isabel offered her hand to Lovvet and stroked the animal. The dog nosed her fingertips, tail wagging. "She's my Lovvet."

Amieria imitated her gesture and the dog rewarded her with an affectionate lick. "She is like a 'little wolf'. That is what her name means?"

When Isabel nodded, Amieria stroked Lovvet again. Isabel glimpsed the longing in her wide eyes. She introduced the girl to Petronilla. They continued a tour of the garden until they sheltered under a copse where Amieria sat with her harp. She played and sang for them with confidence, not with the shyness Isabel expected.

"Where's your mother today, Amieria?"

"She is with the king, milady. He has chosen the man she shall marry."

At Petronilla's curious glance, Isabel explained the circumstances, which had brought the little girl and her mother to court. She withheld information about the girl's parentage. She did not know why she felt such an affinity for Amieria. It seemed equally foolish to hide the truth from Petronilla, herself the product of an illicit union. Isabel refused to mar the afternoon by mentioning Amieria's baseborn heritage.

"How does your mother feel about the king's choice?"

"*Maman* must do what he says, milady."

Isabel could not fault the simplicity of Amieria's reasoning when Henry's control mirrored his power over the realm. "Where is your mother's dower estate?"

"We live in Kent, milady." Amieria plucked the harp strings and stared off into the distance at Lovvet patrolling the grounds. "My grandfather and uncle died in the revolt of Bishop Odo de Bayeux against King William Rufus. Now my *maman* must marry a man of the king's choosing."

"When do you return home?"

"After His Grace has arranged the wedding. I shall be glad to go, milady. I miss Kent."

"Shall you come to court again?"

"The king wishes it. *Maman* does not. She wants me with her."

Remembering the queen's disdain, Isabel could not blame Amieria's mother. Clearly puzzled, Petronilla frowned at their byplay. Isabel hushed her with a glance and waved her off. Petronilla wandered after Lovvet.

Isabel asked, "Amieria, shall you come and play for us every day until you leave court?"

"If the king permits, milady."

"Yesterday, I did not understand the words you exchanged with His Grace."

"We spoke in the old tongue of the English, milady. My grandfather was an English lord, loyal to Harold the Usurper. My grandfather fought at Senlac and lost most of his estates in Kent before he married my grandmother. She bore him twins, my uncle Harold and my *maman*."

"Then you are descended from the English."

"Did you know His Grace was born in England, milady? The first among the Norman kings."

"My husband told me." Isabel fell silent, wondering about Amieria's mother and the king. Clearly, they had shared no casual union. If Henry wanted Amieria at court, if he took care to arrange a respectable marriage for his paramour, he must have felt more than lust for the woman.

Regret flooded Isabel's heart as her thoughts on Queen Matilda wavered again. She had judged Matilda too harshly, for what woman could bear the proof of her husband's indiscretions every day, without feeling some bitterness? Still, the king bore the blame, not the little child. She sighed, disliking the perilous direction in which her thoughts turned. Henry's lusts had resulted in several bastards, similar to her husband's circumstances. At least in her case, there were no real or imagined women in Robert's past to worry her. She had no betrayal to accuse him of now.

She returned her attention to the child. "You are very fond of His Grace, Amieria."

"He is the king. I obey him in all things, milady."

Isabel wished she possessed the unwavering dutifulness of this child of the king. Robert had been right to chastise her at dinner. She could never have the goodness Amieria displayed if she did not learn to control her pride. It made her act without thinking too often. For now, she would risk the queen's further displeasure by spending time with the little girl. She resolved to exercise more caution at court. Pride would not be her downfall.

Saint Albans, England: June 1101

Seated on a low stool, Isabel arched her aching back and rubbed her sore neck. Since midmorning, she had worked tirelessly at embellishing her husband's *cotte* in the small room of an inn at Saint Albans. Sunlight filtered through a large gap in the wooden shutters, illuminating a blue and yellow checked pattern on the tunic's voluminous sleeves, shot through with gold-colored thread.

Isabel glanced at Petronilla, whose work already displayed a pattern of fine, glittering stitches on the left arm, before glaring at her uneven, loosely placed threads. Isabel removed the leather thimble and ripped the stitches from the fabric, muttering under her breath.

Her maidservant looked up from her work. "Milady, what's wrong? Please, be careful when you're removing the threads."

"I hate this! I shall never learn to embroider! What must Robert think of me? What sort of wife doesn't know how to do this?"

Petronilla reached for the material. "Milady, it's a very simple technique. The closer the threads are together, the more brilliant the colors of your husband's *cotte* shall be. If you would only learn to be patient and attentive to your task, you would not have such difficulty."

Isabel shoved fabric into her maidservant's hands and stood, kicking back the wooden stool on which she had sat for hours. "Attentive? Patient? How can I be when Normandy may come to strike against England at any moment?"

After dawn, a herald had arrived at Saint Albans, nearly five thousand furlongs north of Winchester. Ushered into the king's presence, he confirmed Duke Robert Curthose, Henry's elder brother, prepared for an invasion of England. Alarmed, the king convened his counselors, which included Isabel's husband. Days later, the alarming news spread amongst the courtiers.

"How can I think of anything else except the possibility Robert may go to war? What shall I do if he does not survive? With no heir to his name? I am a disgrace to the title of wife! I'm a failure, if I cannot even entice my husband to bed me so I may give him a child."

His tender care frustrated her. In his absence from Normandy, Isabel had blossomed like the lush wildflowers at Vatteville. After her arrival in England, Robert had purchased new textiles and dressmakers fashioned beautiful robes to replace ones she had clearly outgrown, which accommodated her hips and breasts. The new clothes included the scarlet garment she wore now, ornamented with an embroidered golden border at the wrists and hems. Otherwise, Robert seemed uninterested in her physical changes. He brooded on the realm's troubles instead.

Petronilla rose from her window seat and embraced Isabel, who clung to her.

"You can't know the torture I've suffered these three months since our arrival in England, all because of my virginity! You have not been there to see how the women of the court look at me with pity or scorn in their eyes, because my husband has not claimed me. Everyone knows it. There are no secrets here."

"Milady, calm yourself."

Isabel threw off her maidservant's hold. "For months, he has lain beside me long after I have slept and awoken before I have. We are hardly together. He disappears for hours each day, I know not where. When he does come to dinner, which is rare, he is little more than civil and polite."

"Be at ease, he is being kind and gentle with you, milady."

"I do not want his kindness only! I want his sons. How can I have them when he shuns me so?"

"He's preoccupied with matters of state. You have seen how His Grace relies upon him."

"Indeed, as has everyone else. Likely, they think Robert's so exhausted from Henry's demands, he's incapable of siring a babe on me."

"No one holds such beliefs, milady."

"They do, Petronilla, I tell you they do. The queen's ladies whisper when she is absent, for Matilda frowns upon gossipmongers. Sybilla Corbet of Alcester called Robert 'the great monk' when we stood together at Mass on Whitsunday. She believes I am not womanly enough for him. I cannot continue. I must give him a child, Petronilla."

"Lady Sybilla is beneath your concern. She's naught more than the king's whore," Petronilla said and at Isabel's horrified gasp, she continued, "If you'll forgive me for speaking so. The queen does not like her husband keeping his *leman* so close. The lady of Alcester returns to Warwick soon. I'm sure of it."

"I do not care for Sybilla. I fear the fault lies with me. Do I displease him in some manner? Am I to have naught more than his chaste kisses on my brow? What is wrong with me?"

As Isabel wrung her hands, Petronilla grasped and kissed them. "Milady, you are perfection. Any man with two eyes in his head can see your beauty. What more could your husband desire of you?"

"I wish I knew, but it is for certain, he does not desire me."

Petronilla squeezed her fingers. "Do you fear there is another who holds Robert's attention?"

Isabel laughed. The hollow sound echoed to the rafters. "Lord knows he has enough bastards to leave me unsure of his devotion. I know I should not judge him for the past. If Robert has taken a lover, he has kept me blissfully unaware of her existence since I arrived in England."

Chapter Twelve – The Marriage Debt
Saint Albans, England: June 1101

Embittered, Isabel set aside her embroidery in the early afternoon. She avoided dinner and spent the late hours until evening wandering the extensive garden in the shadow of Saint Albans' Abbey. Earlier, she had dismissed Petronilla, who probably had sought out FitzRobert. Isabel did not begrudge her attendant's happiness. Instead, Isabel wished she might find a measure of it with her husband Robert. Now leaning against a tree, she palmed her empty belly. Tears trickled down her cheeks.

"Why do you sniffle and sob, my Isabel?"

She turned at the velvet baritone sound of Robert's voice. "You've returned to me! Has the king had word from the coast of Normandy? Has the duke already set sail?"

He ambled toward her, twirling the stem of a blush pink bloom between his long fingers. He touched the petals to her damp cheek.

"You shall leave me again to war against the Norman duke, after we have been apart for so long. I can't bear it!" She avoided his gaze.

He pressed the flower against her palm. When she took it, he tipped her chin up and framed her face between his hands. "Do these tears mean you care for me, dearest Isabel?"

"How can you ask, Robert?"

"My parents did not truly care for each other. My mother did her duty, bore three children and defended my father's lands during his long absences at the ducal court. She respected him. He remained too devoted to the Conqueror's causes in Normandy and here to love her as a man should love his wife. I want you to love me as I have learned to love you."

She stared at him in silence.

He cupped and kissed her cheek so softly, the gentleness of his touch awakening an ache deep inside her. No one had ever shown her such tenderness or made her feel so loved. Her eyes watered again.

"I love you, my Isabel, your laughter and smiles, your tears and worries, your tender heart. Even your impudence and pride. I love watching you sleep for a little before I must leave you in the morn, the frown of concern marring your brow when I enter the hall late at dinner and the way you cling to me at night in your sleep, as if you wished I were always at your side."

"I do wish it, Robert."

The first appearance of the moon wove through the evening clouds. A cool breeze whispered through the garden. He tugged her against his body, fitted her form to him and wrapped his mantle around her.

"Then, my dearest, do you believe you can learn to love me?"

She shivered and leaned into him with a sigh, her arms around his shoulders. "Is it important to you? My parents did not love each other. They had many children together. I care for you very much. I want to give you the heirs you must have. I do not always know what you want of me. Robert, I fear sometimes I am not the wife you desire, the wife you should have."

He loomed closer, filling the shadows. "You are the only wife I shall ever want. Give me sons. Give me your heart also. I shall treasure it."

Isabel had loved her nurse Claremond, who had proved dearer to her than the mother whom had borne and abused her. She loved Petronilla, her dearest servant and companion. She also loved Lovvet, whom she could never bear to part from again. Could loving one's husband be so different?

When Robert bent his head, she cried out softly and leaned against him. A sudden uncertainty pulsated through her quaking limbs. Hesitantly, she locked her slim fingers behind his neck. His hands swept along her spine, curving around her hips and buttocks beneath the robe. Her heartbeat raced in a mix of fear and anticipation. She did not pull away from his wandering hands.

He stilled her. "Don't be frightened of me." He brushed feather light kisses on her brow and cheeks. When she leaned back slightly, exposing her neck, he kissed her there. Teeth nipped her skin.

"Robert—"

"Be at ease, now." He turned her around and pressed her against the solid trunk. The rough bark dug into her skin through her garments. Burly hands caressed her form, dragging the hem of her robe upward.

His hand dipped beneath the neckline of her robe, while the other held her hips still beneath his eager touch. Nimble fingers traced circles across her chest and downward, cupping her breasts. A heaviness settled in her belly as his hands encircled the nipples, until his touch became almost painful. Wordless, he drew her from the garden. They entered the small room they occupied at the inn, where Petronilla and FitzRobert slept at night on separate pallets. They had sought each other out, both seated on scattered, dried straw. A scant distance separated them, FitzRobert against the wall and Petronilla on her pallet. Their fingers almost touched on the ground between them.

Robert nodded to them. "Leave us."

Isabel lowered her gaze, her cheeks warming.

FitzRobert stood, reached for Petronilla and hauled her to her feet. She swayed against him before righting herself.

"Milady, milord, we await your summons below stairs."

Petronilla avoided Robert's stare and glanced at Isabel before she took hesitant steps toward the door. She lingered there with a final look at Isabel before Robert closed the door on her wrinkled expression.

"I did not expect them to be here alone together. That is not proper," Isabel murmured.

A slow smile curved Robert's lips. "I believe they are beyond such concerns."

She would have inquired after his meaning, if Robert

had not removed his hose. She sank down on the bed before him. The ropes supporting the thin mattress creaked beneath her.

"Did you have to dismiss them so abruptly?"

He tossed his hose aside and tugged his tunic over his head. The cloth muffled his response, but she heard it all the same. "Would you have preferred if they remained here and witnessed our lovemaking?"

She fisted her hands in the coverlet. A few months before, such words would have stirred curiosity and anticipation. Now, the certainty of his intent sent a wave of uneasy quivers rippling through her stomach.

He stood over her. A quick glance took in the pelt of yellow hair across his chest, tapering and thickening where the hair disappeared below his knee-length braies. She focused on his face and tried avoiding the obvious sign of his desire. His lips parted and a soft sigh escaped him. He grasped her fingers and tugged them. He held her hand against the bulge in his braies.

At her gasp, he laughed. "Does my desire surprise you? Age has not altered my passions or appreciation of my beautiful wife. Stand and let me see you as God has fashioned you. Remove your garments."

On unsteady legs, she rose from the bed with his help and turned her back to him. Tiny tremors quaked across her belly. "You'll have to undo the laces. I cannot reach the back of my robe."

The thin strings whistled through the holes. She jerked and swayed beneath his urgent hands. She shrugged the robe off her shoulders and peeled the tight sleeves down her arms before the garment slid to the floor. She removed the *couvrechef* and revealed her hair in two, fat plaits braided with ribbon. The coolness of the room made her chemise cling to her form.

"Turn to me, Isabel."

She did as he commanded. The thin chainsil revealed her body beneath the garment. Her arms crisscrossed her breasts. "Robert, please—"

He demanded, "You will show no shame before me.

Drop your hands."

When she complied, he said, "Now, remove your undergarment. Slowly. I would savor your beauty."

"Please be gentle with me, Robert. I know it will hurt at first."

His jaw tightened. "Why would I hurt you? Have I given you any reason to think I would wish harm or pain upon you? The Church teaches that if a woman is to conceive, she must gain her pleasure. I will ensure it tonight."

When she said nothing, he stepped back a pace. "You believe me, don't you?"

"I want to, Robert."

"Then do not make me repeat myself. Do as I have asked."

She tugged the chemise upward and revealed her legs to the knee.

"Stop! No higher." He crouched before her and stroked his forefinger from her toes up to her ankle. His callused hand slid upward and grasped her calf, kneading it. A startled shiver ran through her. His fingers covered her toes. She felt ridiculous and shameful before him, her arms aloft and holding her chemise up at his command. Her weddings vows taunted her. Had she not promised to obey him?

She became aware of each intake of breath and the tightness across her chest. He hefted her bare foot by the heel. She grasped his shoulder quickly and steadied herself with one hand, the other still clutching the hem. His thumb smoothed across the arch. When her breath quickened, he raised his gaze.

"You may continue. Raise it to the top of your thighs now."

"Why do you ask me to do this?" Her mind raced, searching for an answer. Did he seek to humiliate her or did he believe a demonstration of his power over her, even in their bed, would be necessary? Could he have found amusement in her distress?

"It is enough for you to comply. You will not refuse

me anything, my Isabel."

He wished to demonstrate the proof of his power over her then. She wished she might tell him such displays were unwarranted when she belonged to him by the laws of God and man. Instead, she hitched up her undergarment, revealing one leg. Satisfied, he repeated the actions of his hand from earlier, with a brief stop at the back of her knees. She sucked in a ragged breath as his fingertip pressed inward, before he drew circles along on her inner thigh.

He murmured against her flesh, "Like Saracen silk, the color of a pale, pink rose."

Robert leaned forward and kissed her knee. He inhaled. A flutter slowly spread across her stomach and her leg almost buckled. When she swayed, her fingers scrabbled for purchase and dug into his shoulder.

She whispered, "You do this as much for your pleasure as mine, I think."

He made no reply. Instead, he pushed the chemise aside and transferred his attentions to the other leg.

"Up to your waist now." His voice had grown huskier.

She almost did not hear him, her focus on his fervent touch. His palm swept across her hip and pushed the fine chainsil away. His fingers ran along her thigh. His touch was eager, a quest to discover her. She sighed and wished he might caress her like this always.

Robert sighed, "My own impatience bedevils me. Take it off, now."

She removed her chemise and let it fall from her fingertips. Both of his hands caressed the backs of her thighs.

He planted kisses along the inside of each leg, saying as he did so. "I shall give you joy, if you would only give me a son."

His lips found the dark thatch of hair at the apex of her thighs. The tip of his tongue flicked the cleft at her center.

"Robert!" His name torn in a whisper from her lips echoed in the room. Her nails sank into his scalp and raked across the rounded bump beneath the hair, where the surgeon had cut into his skull.

He palmed her hips, pulled her impossibly closer. "Shall I stop?"

She fought to slow her irregular breathing. "You cannot kiss me there! Surely, the Church does not consider such a thing appropriate for a woman's pleasure."

"I will not confess to it if you do not, my sweet." He dipped his head again and drew a long shudder from her. "As it is, the Church proscribes many things. The man atop and the woman beneath him is the only blameless path for the procreation of children. If I take you from behind while you are upon your knees, or permitted you on top, it would require a penance of ten days. Churchmen would say I should only share a bed with you when I want a son of your body." He chuckled. "They are all liars and fornicators themselves. I vow no priest has ever seen a woman of your perfection. If he had, he would forgive my lustful thoughts. I would gladly offer penance and live on bread and water for the rest of my life, if only for the sweet taste of you every day and night."

He ducked his head again, his lips at her thigh again. Her fingers tightened in his hair. "Please, Robert! Will you not kiss me as a man would kiss his wife upon the lips? Do not shame me so."

He raised his head. "I forbid you to feel ashamed because of my lust for you, no matter what the Church says. My desire for you is as natural as your pleasure. It is also necessary. You understand I shall do anything to assure myself you will conceive a son."

Her grip slipped and she tugged at his shoulders, emboldened. "If you kissed my lips, it would please me. I would like to learn how to kiss my husband properly."

When he stood, his hands framed her face. He loomed closer and his lips brushed her brow once, twice. She trembled at his unexpected gesture. Then he kissed her nose, her cheek, in a feathery touch. One of his hands slipped beneath her braids and massaged her nape. The other cupped the back of her head. She encircled his shoulder with her arm and squirmed against his chest, her skin gliding against rough hairs. When his lips grazed hers, she opened her mouth slightly. It seemed all the invitation his tongue needed to seek hers. She clung to him while his fingertips crept down her back and kneaded her hip. Then his knuckles grazed her front.

He lifted his head and broke the kiss. A whining moan filled her throat. He shook his head. "Heed me. Open your legs. Let me show you one of many delights I shall bring you this evening."

She did as he ordered, expecting there would be some pain or discomfort. None followed, more of a sudden tightening in her lower abdomen. She tilted her hips slightly toward him, seeking more of the unexpected sensation unfurling inside her. The slow, maddening strokes of his fingers teased and circled her cleft. He drew a whimper from her, swallowed up by his mouth. She felt slick everywhere he touched and rocked her hips against his hand now. He watched her beneath hooded lips. His ragged breathing almost matched hers. She was past caring for the shamefulness of her actions and wondered whether he gained satisfaction from touching her so intimately, until she could not think reasonably. Shards of pleasure stabbed her belly. Her hand covered his, urging him onward. His thumb circled a spot as hard and swollen as her nipples.

"Let your desires take you," he whispered against her neck. His teeth nipped at her throat. Her back arched and she clung to him until her whole body shook. She buried her face in his neck. Her heart exploded before lethargy swept through her limbs and left her weakened and dizzied. He kissed her brow, his ragged breath warm against her neck and rubbed her back. She struggled to draw breath.

She stirred at last when he whispered, "Isabel, my sweet Isabel."

He scooped her up with his forearms under her thighs

and placed her on the bed, as he had once done at Vatteville. This time he removed his braies and joined her. He pressed her on her back into the thin mattress and palmed her hip, which bucked against his. Her arm wound about his neck and she pulled him close, seeking his mouth.

"Christ's bones, you are eager. Have I fashioned a wanton wife, fit for my loving at last?" he murmured against her lips, before his tongue teased at hers. He draped her thigh over his while she touched his back and urged him closer.

"This is how I dreamt it would be between us," she whispered between kisses.

When he slid a fingertip inside her this time, his thumb finding the same sensitive spot as earlier, she rolled her hips and stared at him through a haze of her own desire.

His gaze narrowed and he stilled his movement. She arrived at the realization a moment later.

"Robert, what is it?"

"Your maidenhead must be lodged deeply. It may hurt more than I anticipated. Let us be done with it. I shall soothe the hurt afterward."

Before she might gain an understanding of how he intended to do so, she felt him probing between her legs. She realized it was more than the thickness of his finger. He eased inside her, slow and measured. She held her breath now, waiting for the pain her mother had promised. When only discomfort followed, she stared at the deep furrows lining his brow. Was there pain for men? It appeared so, otherwise why would such a grimace mar his features.

At first, the slow, shallow movements did not pain her too much. Soon he began to thrust deeper. An unpleasant burning sensation stymied her wonderment. She willed herself to relax and enjoy. His hips slammed against hers and tears sprang to her eyes. The muscles in her stomach tightened and she could not stifle the whimper in the back of her throat.

"Robert, it's hurting."

A faint sheen of sweat clung to his forehead. He closed his eyes and groaned at each thrust.

She pushed at his chest. "Robert, please stop, it hurts."

His eyes opened and he glowered at her, before slowing. His jaw tightened, as did his hold on the curve of her hip.

She blinked back tears. "I am sorry."

"Why do you hinder me? I have done naught except seek to please you this night," he muttered.

"You have, you are pleasing me, Robert. If you could just go slower."

He sighed and covered her mouth with his own again. She surrendered to the kiss and clutched at him. His knuckles brushed her breasts and stomach. His touch lacked the spontaneity of their earlier interlude. Now, it seemed almost perfunctory. She reached between their bodies and tugged his hand back to her breast. Her nipple tightened beneath his warm touch. He raised his head from their kiss and looked at his palm cupping her flesh.

She drew a calming breath before meeting his inscrutable stare. "Could you use your mouth and tongue there, as when a babe suckles at his nurse?"

"Would you instruct me on how to please you now, wife?" His low tone held a warning she could not ignore.

"Never! It's just, well, when you were kissing my leg earlier, your lips felt so good against my skin. I wondered if it might feel the same elsewhere."

A chuckle rumbled through him. "Innocence and wanton desire coupled so perfectly. I would kiss you all over, if you would only let me. It would please us both."

"How would you know? Oh!"

His tongue flicked her nipple. Another, less startled "Oh!" followed. Isabel arched against him and he groaned deeply. He kneaded one breast while he laved the nipple. Her fingers clenched in his hair. Every tug set a jolt rippling through her lower abdomen. Soon, he had her moaning again and her hips could not keep still. One hand grazed her belly and slipped between her legs. She squirmed beside him, seeking more. She did not know what to do with herself. In one instance, she kissed his forehead and clutched his head against her chest. At another, her nails scoured his back or tugged at his hip.

"I think I'm ready again. Now, Robert!"

He surged inside her once again, her leg still slung over his hip. "You are wanton for true, my Isabel. I may grow to like it."

She pressed her lips tightly against the anticipated pain. It receded to a dull ache. His fingers returned to those strokes that made her twitch, until even the discomfort faded. The leg draped around his hip imprisoned him. His touch rekindled those same fires as he had stirred within her earlier. She wanted nothing more than those intense waves of bliss, which had overwhelmed her. They seemed so close, yet still elusive.

Their bodies glided against each other, slick with perspiration. She dug her heel into his backside and urged him on. He lifted his head and she tugged his face to hers. His hip jerked against hers once, twice. The whole length of his body shook and a loud groan filled his throat. He collapsed atop of her, uneven breaths torn from him.

When she realized he would not continue, she felt strangely bereft and alone.

"My Isabel, mine. You have pleased me. Pray I have put my son inside you tonight."

His heated whisper left her chilled. Her eyes watered and she buried her face in the bedclothes. How could she have forgotten? She had thought this evening was about pleasing her. Robert only sought his son.

He raised his head. "You want the same, don't you, to bear my heir?"

After she nodded, his possessive hold tightened. He rolled on his side and dragged her with him. She rested her head on his chest, damp tendrils of her hair clinging to her temple. His heartbeat thrummed steadily beneath her ear. The sticky wetness between her thighs lingered, coupled with a deep throb. She could excuse his casual disregard this once and hope for more from him next time. He had not been cruel after all, only determined. Her mother would have laughed at her foolish tears and possibly said Robert was no different from other men. Isabel desperately wanted him to be, the sort of husband who showed her kindness and gentle care, one with whom she could respond in kind.

A tear trickled beneath her lashes. She smoothed the wetness away lest it evoke his concern. "Robert, promise me it will only be better and better for us."

His rumbling snore answered her.

Isabel lay still on the bed's thin mattress on her stomach, her lips pressed tightly together. Robert stood over her and she listened for his movements as he donned his garments again. Just before the bells of Saint Albans cathedral rung for Compline, the king had summoned him.

He huffed before his hand pressed against the small of her back. She winced and looked at him.

Robert asked, "How do you fare?"

Her hands curled into fists as she wet her lips. "I am well."

His gaze focused on her mouth. She steeled herself for the rough feel of his lips claiming hers. When he did not kiss her again, she pressed her body into the rough bedding.

"Do not hunch your shoulders like that. It makes you look slovenly."

She blinked, stunned by his cold reprimand.

He pressed his lips against the back of her knee. "I caressed you only, yet you bear marks upon your body. Did I hurt you so?"

"I have always bruised easily, Robert."

"Evidenced by these silver scars upon your back. The work of your father, I presume?"

"Both of my parents chastened me."

"It is no wonder you were so determined to wed. You did not deserve such pain, Isabel, not from your parents. You understand I shall never treat you so poorly."

His shining gaze held hers with a question and a plea. She wanted to believe him, but also understood there were other ways to be cruel.

Isabel whispered, "I will hold you to your vow, Robert."

His fingers trailed the edges of her scars and along her spine, a spark of admiration and the desire she now recognized in his eyes. She bit back a wince of disappointment. She wanted him just because he was her husband, not for what she might gain from him. A dull ache in her chest reminded her of how he lacked similar sentiments.

He continued. "I should have sent for you over a year ago, when you told me your courses had finally started. My desire for you almost bested me. It must never happen again. It is possible you have bewitched me, wife. Even now I would dally here with you, though the king summons me."

She refused to apologize for inspiring his lust, while knowing his need for a son rivaled all his feelings toward her.

"I did please you for a time?" he asked.

She took a deep breath and remained quiet beneath his questing hands, which now slid down her back. He palmed the curve of her buttocks.

"You did, Robert." She ignored the pit of unease in her stomach.

He bent his head. Light kisses ascended her back, so soft and soothing. His unanticipated gentleness tugged at her heart and brought a fresh flood of tears to her eyes. How could he be so generous and yet, so insensitive in turns?

His fingers teased between her legs, where they probed her sensitive flesh. She bit her lip, stifling a cry behind her lips.

"Still sore, hmmm? You will grow accustomed to the

length of me. God fashioned women to birth babies after all."

She shivered in response. His cold assessment chilled her to the core. All his talk of granting her joy this night had meant nothing.

He leaned over her. "You must be cold, my dear. Rise and put on your chemise. I must see the king. I shall find your maid and send her to you."

When he withdrew after a final kiss on her shoulder blade, Isabel rose from the bed and crumpled her torn garments into a ball. She had almost covered herself with the mantle he had left behind, before Petronilla entered the room with a muffled cry of horror at Isabel's naked body.

"Milady, there are marks on your hips, your neck, your waist. He has ravished you."

"Hush, please. Come in and close the door behind you. My husband did not ravish me. His lust was unbridled. He did not harm me. The bruises shall fade. My hurts always do."

When Petronilla closed the mantle at her throat, Isabel winced at the memory of Robert's teeth scoring her skin. She could not meet her attendant's concerned frown. "I was unprepared for my husband's passion. His desires overrode him. He has waited so long."

A doubt nagged at her. There had been some joy in the experience before Robert reminded her of his single-minded purpose.

Petronilla's horrified stare made Isabel's cheeks tingle and she knew a profusion of blushes dotted her cheeks. Robert had finally claimed her virginity, a natural consequence of marriage. She resented her own embarrassment at his actions. He had showed no such concern for how the wooden posts of the bed butted against the adjoining wall or might have echoed to the floor below theirs, or at how bruised and battered she had felt.

She wondered if all husbands were so fierce with their wives in the getting of sons. She had looked down at herself with some shame. A flurry of reddened and purple love marks covered her torso and legs. Her mouth throbbed almost as intensely as at the center of her thighs.

"Petronilla, do not stare at me. You'll make me think it looks worse than I feel."

Her attendant blushed. "Well, Sybilla Corbet would be shocked to find your husband possesses more stamina for lovemaking than she might have imagined. More than other men she has known. I do hear she's known her fair share of men besides the king."

Isabel clouted her. "You're an impudent wretch, Petronilla. Help me wash and bring me a new chemise for the night."

"Do you expect your husband will want you again when he returns?"

Isabel flinched and she hugged her body beneath the mantle against a sudden chill sweeping down her spine. "I shall be ready for him."

"Then I'll remain below with FitzRobert."

Isabel did not like that arrangement. No other choice remained.

In the last two weeks of June, Isabel said farewell to her husband, who informed her of the king's plans. Henry expected his elder brother would land at Pevensey, the same as their father when he undertook the conquest of England. Instead, Duke Robert's ships sailed to Portsmouth and by the next month, his army had encamped some distance from Winchester. Isabel had feared her husband becoming embroiled in a civil war. Instead, Henry's counselors met with their counterparts from Normandy at Alton, one hundred and twenty furlongs from Winchester. Each side negotiated the terms of a treaty and withdrew to Winchester for the signing of it.

Acknowledging Henry's right to rule England, the near-bankrupt duke accepted the sum of three thousand marks of silver in exchange for the king's promise. If

Henry died without an heir, his brother Robert would rule England in his stead. Isabel wondered whether the duke's Sicilian-born wife was also pregnant. Queen Matilda had announced similar news at Saint Albans.

Act III: Burning

(August 1101 – June 1109)

Chapter Thirteen – The King's Peace
Winchester, England: August 1101

Robert informed Isabel of the full contents of the treaty with Normandy, in between fervent kisses on her lips, neck and hands, when she met him at Winchester seven weeks afterward. In a darkened alcove outside the hall, Isabel returned his passion with a furtive embrace. When his hand cupped and teased her breast beneath the robe, stirring the nipple almost painfully, she covered his hand with hers and stilled him.

"Please, they're too sensitive."

Robert's hand closed tighter. "I remember."

"Milord! Please. Be careful with me."

He laughed low, nipping her throat, pressing his hips against hers. "My Isabel, my delicate flower. How I've missed you."

She groaned and pushed him back. She could not risk him hurting her again so soon, especially not now. "Would you harm your child?"

His laughter died away. He stared at her.

After a while, she pressed his shoulder. "I thought you'd be pleased. Petronilla was first to believe it, for she realized my courses did not occur in the month after you left. Each day, I grow more certain of the possibility."

When he remained silent, she cupped his face in her hands, desperate for some acknowledgment of his joy. "Will you say nothing?"

"Why did you not send me word sooner? You know how I long for a son. Why did you keep this from me?"

She withdrew her touch. Of all the responses she could have anticipated, this was not among them. She pulled her mantle closer as disappointment settled like a heavy shroud upon her.

"I had to be certain before I told you."

"I had you at Saint Albans each day before my departure. You did understand a babe might be a consequence of our frequent lovemaking?"

"My courses have been erratic in the past. Would you have had me send word before I felt assured? What if I had been wrong?"

He crossed his arms over his chest and stood rigid, a tic pulsing in his cheek. "You will be careful with my son. You will not take risks. You will not ride a horse. You will take walks only with an escort. Nothing must endanger my heir. Do you understand me?"

Isabel had envisioned this scene so many times in her head, the joy shining in Robert's face and his tender concern for her and their child. Now it seemed he regarded her as little more than a broodmare.

She whispered. "I would never do anything to harm the child. I shall give you a son, a true son you may call your own."

Windsor, England: September 1101

Isabel swayed between awe and concern over the changes in her body. The expanding girth of her stomach confirmed her pregnancy, as did sudden, uncontrollable flatulence, which embarrassed her and made Petronilla giggle. The court went on to Westminster for a few days, then to Windsor, where Henry convened a council of his loyal nobles and prelates including the duke of Normandy and his supporters. The king's peace prevailed and his brother appeared at ease among Henry's courtiers.

In the second week of September, Isabel's husband left for an inspection of Leicester Castle with Ivo de Grentmesnil. The fortress came under Robert's control through an agreement with Ivo. A staunch supporter of the cause of Normandy, Ivo remained sheriff of Leicester. The king had forgiven almost all his brother's supporters.

He did not grant Ivo the same favor for the sheriff had pillaged his neighbors' lands after the duke's landing. In exchange for pleading Ivo's case at Windsor, Robert took the mortgage of all Ivo's lands in England. Robert paid the sheriff a large sum of money, which Ivo intended for his second pilgrimage to the Holy Land early in the following year.

Two days before month's end, the court prepared the feast of Michaelmas. Several of the magnates in Normandy's retinue readied for departure from England with their liege lord, chief among them, Earl William. The accusations of others, whom Robert had not identified to Isabel, placed the Earl of Surrey's men at the heart of a series of countryside raids in July. Although he protested, Henry seized the earl's English lands, including his seat at Castle Acre in Norfolk. Isabel could have pitied him, if she cared for his pains.

On Saint Michaelmas Day, Petronilla received word from FitzRobert, who had accompanied his father to Leicester. Robert would not return until the last month of the year. The progress of Henry's court would find Isabel at Winchester again. The constant movement from castle to castle wearied her, though she had once done the same in her annual visits to Robert's domains throughout Normandy. He had not been with her during those four long years of relentless journeys from Vatteville, Brionne, Meulan, Beaumont and Pont Audemer. Still, loyal members of his household had surrounded her. England was a very different place.

Disappointed by her husband's long silence and anticipated absence, Isabel escaped from the dank corridors of Windsor Castle. Beside her, faithful Lovvet bounded. Not even the dog could ease the long months without Robert's protection. Isabel made her way through a mob of revelers strolling toward the king's hall, from which strains of the lute and harp floated. She felt adrift in a sea of spiteful strangers, many of whom she knew envied her husband's influence upon the king and secretly yearned for Robert's downfall. The men regarded her as they often did, with naked lust in their eyes. Their women usually shunned her as a result and did not attempt to speak with her now. How could Robert have abandoned her to this nest of vipers?

Sybilla Corbet barred the path, as she strolled on her husband's arm. Isabel would not be sorry to see her go after the feast, along with others in Duke Robert's company.

The yellow-haired Lady of Alcester looked down her nose at Isabel's small stature and with a snort, commented, "Finally, your husband's seed sprouts inside you. Your belly barely juts beneath your robe yet you are already as ungainly as an ugly toad."

Those who stood nearby paused and laughed at Sybilla's wit or whispered and pointed. The woman's husband tugged her away with a mumbled apology on his wife's behalf cast over his shoulder. Isabel had always known her pregnancy could not remain concealed from the gossipmongers. Still, she pressed a hand to her thickened waist as if shielding the precious child inside her from the flurry of speculations. The English nobles watched her. She noted the dark-eyed Edith de Warenne among them. Edith's brother, Earl William, stood with her.

He eyed Isabel up and down. His stark gaze lingered on her hand. Lovvet whined and circled at her feet, clearly eager to attain her former master's greeting. She awaited her mistress' permission. Isabel's hand on the alaunt's head stayed the dog.

The earl demanded, "Has Robert done his duty at last? You carry your husband's child?"

Edith curtsied. "Comtesse Isabel, please forgive William's bold inquiry. He forgets the courtesy due to a lady, especially the wife of the Comte de Meulan," she finished, with a sharp glare at her brother.

Isabel tapped her belly with her fingertips. "I would permit none but my husband to father a babe upon me." She glanced at William before her gaze returned to Edith's own. "Your brother's question would suggest otherwise. How could I excuse such recklessness?"

She left them and escaped into the inner bailey. The afternoon sun filtered through a gray sky and tracked Isabel's progress across the bustling courtyard, where the companions of Duke Robert prepared for the journey south to the port at Pevensey. Isabel kept her gaze averted lest anyone view the tears of frustration in her eyes. She fought for composure though her lips trembled.

Clopping hooves jarred her from misery. A hand on her shoulder jerked her back from a mounted man, who cursed under his breath. He glowered at her from beneath a hooded mantle. "Fool woman! Would you have the beast trample you?"

"Constable, have a care how you address the Comtesse de Meulan. I would not have her believe the worst of my most trusted man." Earl William approached, removing his gauntlets before he patted the rump of the palfrey.

The knight dismounted. On one knee, he doffed his mail hood, revealing dark hair akin to his lord's own. "Forgive this lowly wretch, for I did not recognize you from the first. I spoke without forethought and am heartily sorry for my affront."

Isabel gaped as she recognized Earl William's man Rudolf by the similarities between them. The man was likely a bastard relation. All great men seemed to have them.

When she glanced at the earl, his lips twitched. "Get up, man, you've not offended the queen." When the knight stood, Earl William thumped his shoulder. "Much better, though I believe Isabel is still in shock." He bowed before her. "How can I earn your forgiveness for my crass inquiries earlier?"

She ignored him. Lovvet nosed the hands of her former master who patted the traitorous dog's head and scratched her coat. The alaunt responded with excited barks and yips, her pink tongue lolling.

Earl William nodded to Isabel. "I see that I cannot at this time. I hope you will think better of me in the future.

The dog thrives, much longer than I could have anticipated. You have taken good care of her. I remain grateful for your compassion."

"You seem surprised by my devotion to Lovvet."

"Who?"

"The dog. I named her Lovvet."

Earl William's incredulous, silent stare drew her ire and a rumbling guffaw from Rudolf, who fell silent at his lord's glare. The earl dismissed him. A sheepish grin curving his lips, the constable bowed. "I'll see to the horses."

"Go on then," Earl William said, before he turned to Isabel again. "She has earned your loyalty. You will find none more faithful than her. I should not have parted with her so easily."

"How easily you regret giving her to me, especially when I have devoted such effort to her."

"I did not say I regretted the offer. As ever, you take great delight in vexing me with your ignorant assumptions."

"I could say the same for yours. Your foolish remark before the other courtiers almost scandalized me. The insolence you possess knows no bounds."

"I ask your forgiveness for my choice of words. I spoke without forethought. I had not expected your pregnancy."

"Children are the natural consequence of most marriages. Why should my state have shocked you?"

"The gossips had it that Robert was incapable of siring a child at his age. I have seen his bastards with him. He takes great pride in his sons."

She rubbed her abdomen. "He shall be a devoted father to this, his trueborn son, as well."

"If you believe so. You shall be a good mother, no doubt, evidenced by your attention to the dog. I am pleased the alaunt has thrived in your care."

"Still, a hint of surprise lingers in your tone. Did you think I would mistreat a dog because she once belonged to you? Should I have thereby mocked your generosity? I assure you, I would not have done such a thing."

Though she addressed him, she gave a dirty look to the alaunt ignoring her with her muzzle buried in Earl William's hand, while she licked his palm. Was Lovvet no better than any other female, eager for a man's attentions?

"I know better than to doubt you, Isabel, for I have seen you can do anything, once you've set your mind to it. You came to England even after I warned against it."

"I do not act according to your will."

"Indeed not. If you were my wife, I would judge you willful and disobedient."

She glared at him, his words evoking memories of how her parents had chastised her and accused her of the same faults when she had first refused Robert. She palmed her belly, feeling the same odd flutters she had experienced earlier in the morning.

Earl William pouted before his stark stare returned to hers. "You must be pleased at the departure of the duke's men, including me."

"How observant you are," she said, shaking her head. "With you goes the threat of warfare."

"You do not attend the feast of Saint Michaelmas, although you rejoice at our leave-taking after we have dined. Does your husband's absence trouble you so much that you cannot eat?"

"I am not hungry! Besides, I didn't think anyone else would notice if I do not attend."

"A blind man would notice you, Isabel."

"Your impertinence will never change. I bid you farewell."

He grasped her elbow before she could escape him.

She whispered, "Do not presume to touch me!"

His hand fell listless at his side. "You always turn away from me, Isabel. Am I truly so offensive? Have you no sympathy for me in my landless state? I am banished from England."

"Had you controlled your men, the king would not have deprived you of your estates. Great God, you owed equal fealty to the king and Duke Robert. You succored with Normandy's master and trampled your own people in England. Henry is as much your liege lord—"

"Never him! I took a knee before the usurper when he stole the crown because I would not lose my English patrimony. He has never been my liege!"

She stepped away, stunned at the vehemence of his whispered tone. "By the grace of God, Henry is our king. You held lands granted from him and then sided with others against the king's lawful reign!"

"His lawful reign? What foolery is this?" Laughter rumbled, shook him until he bent over, holding his stomach.

She glared at him, finding no humor in anything she had said to him.

He straightened, wiping at mirthful tears. "You have much you must learn, Isabel. Shall I tell you how Henry gained his throne?"

"I learned of the events in the New Forest from my husband, how King William Rufus met his end in a regrettable accident. There's nothing you might say, which could enlighten me further."

"Your husband speaks with you about political matters?"

"Do you think I'm naught more than an ignorant woman who must rely solely on my husband for understanding? England is our home now. Its politics concern my husband. My husband interests me." She drew a sharp intake of breath and frowned at him until her forehead hurt. "Your disdain for the king is clear, as are your sentiments about his court. You speak treason against Henry and I shall not listen to your lies about him for another moment."

When she turned away, he cupped her elbow between their bodies. "Henry is not a king by divine right. He claimed the crown by conquest."

"As did his father, the conqueror of the English people! You Normans are akin to the conquering savages your forbearers were, men who harried the kingdom of my ancestors in France and sacked Paris. You have always claimed what belongs to another."

"Is this how you think of us? I am sure your husband shall be pleased to hear your views of his people. He may prove you right."

She sobered instantly, hardly fathoming her own outburst. Where had it come from?

He chuckled. "I promise you, Henry did not look to repeat the exploits of 'conquering savages' when he stole the crown. He sought only to deprive Robert Curthose of England. Henry was hunting in the New Forest and when he heard of the king's death, he first hastened to Winchester, seeking the keys to the royal treasure. Henry and your husband threatened the castellan of Winchester, William de Breteuil and forced his submission. Henry's own brother, William Rufus, never wanted him to rule. William Rufus intended the crown for Duke Robert, to unify the Norman and English domains and force the nobles to recognize one master. Henry damned us to civil war when he seized the throne."

"Would you have preferred a land without its sovereign? My husband told me your duke had undertaken the cross, before King William Rufus died. No one knew with certainty when or if Robert Curthose might return."

"I tell you Henry stole the crown. It would not be the first or last time he claimed something that did not belong to him."

She recognized the indirect reference. After so many months, he could not feel so slighted by the queen's preference in her marriage partner.

Isabel had to know the truth. "Did you love Queen Matilda? Is that why you hate Henry?"

He snorted. "You remain too naïve for my liking. I sought a woman of wealth only, royal blood or not. I never loved her."

Shocked, Isabel clutched at her breastbone. "You are beyond all hope of redemption, milord. You believe

Henry may have wronged you. I pray God the king's seizure of your lands shall spare me your odious presence forever!"

She left him and returned inside the castle, hardly caring how Lovvet whined, until she loped and followed her mistress.

Westminster, England: December 1101

At Yuletide, Isabel waited on the snow-covered steps adjacent the courtyard at Westminster, while her husband rode through the castle gateway. Robert wore a grave expression, sagging in the saddle before he dismounted. She had not seen him for three months since his departure for Leicester. FitzRobert stood at his left and beside him, a second figure in a deep cowl. She cupped her burgeoning belly beneath her mantle. Her husband crossed the courtyard and kissed her brow.

"Milady. A messenger from France reached me. Your father died in a city called Tarsus, on his second pilgrimage to the Holy Land. He fought bravely against the cruel Turks. He was wounded and passed away two months ago."

She barely heard him, staring across the expanse at the deep-set gaze of Brother Thorold. The monk inclined his head in meager acknowledgment.

Robert followed her gaze. "I brought Thorold, so he might send any message you wished to send to Crépy-en-Valois. I do not expect you to compose your thoughts at this difficult time."

She looked up at her husband, incredulous. He reached for her. She pushed against his chest. "The news has not addled my mind, Robert. Nor do I fail to see what you have done. You tell me my father is dead and your first thought was to write to your clerk, my tormenter at Saint Pierre-de-Préaux and invite him to return to England. How long have you known of my father's death, Robert?"

He raked his large hands through glistening,

whitened hair. "Thorold met me at Leicester."

"When? When did you summon him to England?"

He sighed. "Isabel, he's always been here, shuffling between my English estates. I've been to see him several times, sometimes for a few hours in London, at others for a few days elsewhere."

"He's been in this country all the while, since the time you supposedly dismissed him to the abbey?"

When Robert nodded, she turned her back on him. He touched her arm. She shook off his hand and refused his comfort. "You promised. You swore. You said he meant naught more to you than I did. Instead, you have kept him here. He is the one whom you have visited in the long hours and days when you disappeared. I suppose it is a tender mercy you did not seek the bed of some *leman*. Still, I wonder what else you have withheld from me, Robert."

"I regret your suffering at the loss of your father, Isabel. If I have withheld certain truths from you, I did it because I knew you could not bear them."

As he spoke, she looked away, refusing a show of weakness before him. She would shed no tears, lest he thought her tears were for the loss of her father.

"Mass shall be said for your father."

She shivered despite all her wishes to the contrary. "My father did not love me, Robert. I can hardly mourn his loss."

"Still, there shall be prayers of remembrance of all the souls who lost their lives in the Holy Land. I have known the loss of a father. Mine could be a brutal tyrant to all those who served and loved him, even my mother. He taught his children about loyalty and duty, love also. I cherish memories of him. Sometimes, the men in our lives are not what we would wish for, but we never stop loving them."

She sniffled, fighting against her tears. "Milord, please leave me be."

"I cannot. Your distress sickens me and I wish I could comfort you, Isabel."

He cupped her cheek with a bare hand. She leaned into the warmth and tenderness of his touch with a sigh, until Lovvet yowled and pushed between them. She pulled away, not prepared to forgive him for withholding the truth about Brother Thorold.

"Go inside, we'll talk later, of Leicester Castle."

On wooden legs, she turned away. At the doorway, she looked for her husband. She caught a glimpse of his retreating figure headed toward the stables. Brother Thorold strolled beside him.

She could not fathom whether Robert's betrayal or her father's death pained her more. Though Hugh de Vermandois barely countenanced her existence and brutalized her, he had treated her with the same casual indifference and cruelty other fathers showed their girls. What were daughters except burdens to their parents unless they secured an advantageous marriage? She did not fault Robert for delivering the news with a paltry show of compassion. However, her husband's concealment of Brother Thorold and the clerk's return at such a harrowing time showed Robert held scarce concern for her feelings.

She wondered if the father who had browbeaten and ill-treated her was so different from an inconsiderate husband, whose behavior had shattered her heart into tiny fragments.

"Leicester Castle. What can he have meant by it, Petronilla?"

The next morning after Mass, Isabel trod the frost-covered gardens. One gloved hand rubbed her aching back and the other cupping her swollen belly. Petronilla played with Lovvet, urging on the dog, which chased her in circles.

"Will you two stop it? You're making my head ache." Isabel leaned against a tree, sighing. "I need help to understand Robert's meaning."

"How can I know, milady?"

"He thought it important enough to mention upon

his arrival."

"You should speak with your husband. It's useless to wonder at his meaning when he can simply tell you."

Isabel groaned. "I do not want to talk with my husband just yet."

Petronilla huffed, her breath billowing in threadlike streaks of white smoke. "You must at some time. Do not risk his wrath, milady. He tolerates your annoyance with Brother Thorold. What if he should strike out at you while you still carry the child?"

"Robert wouldn't dare. He wouldn't chance any harm coming to his precious heir."

"Nor would you, milady. You know the importance of a son."

"Do you believe I misunderstand my duty is to bear milord a son and be a loyal wife?"

"Is there no more joy than duty, milady? Haven't you learned to love your husband a little and the babe growing inside you?"

"I'd love it a little more if it did not kick me so hard!" Isabel groaned wearily and cupped her belly with both hands. "Robert has asked the queen's physician, Faritius, the abbot of Abingdon to care for me when he does not attend the royal consort."

"He is the queen's dearest companion. Can she bear to part with the monk?"

"I do not doubt Robert's generous endowment at Abingdon will inspire the abbot's consent."

"Very true. I wish you every joy, milady and hope you might find it in your heart to love your babe and your husband."

"In the way you love FitzRobert?"

Petronilla blushed. "When he is knighted, he may ask milord's permission to wed me."

Isabel sniffed. "He presumes I have no say in the matter."

"He meant no disrespect, milady. The decision is the comte's own. I hope FitzRobert may marry me someday. I believe God has intended FitzRobert for me. I shall be truly satisfied when I know the blessing of a life with him and our children. Are you afraid of childbearing, milady?"

"Why should I be? Women do so every day. God made us for such purposes."

FitzRobert trod a path toward them, his short mantle fluttering in the cool wind. When the squire bowed, Petronilla blushed.

He said, "Milady, your husband has asked for you."

"Why?"

His eyebrows arched at her short, sharp tone. "Countess Margaret of Warwick has arrived at Westminster with her children. Your husband insists you greet them, with him and the earl. I shall escort you."

Robert's command brooked no refusal, given FitzRobert's steadfast expression and stance. Isabel had grown genuinely fond of Margaret and her little daughter, Adelina, named for Robert and Earl Henri's mother.

Still, Isabel hesitated before Petronilla touched her arm. "Milady? FitzRobert awaits you."

"I have not lost my wits!" She walked with Petronilla, FitzRobert and Lovvet trailing her.

Her husband stood beside his brother, sharing a laugh. When Robert saw her, he immediately sobered. "I thank you for coming, Isabel."

"You offered little choice, husband."

He grasped her icy fingers and kissed them before nodding toward his brother. "As I've said, my Isabel is slow to forgive."

Earl Henri bowed, yet made no reply. Isabel's stare remained on her husband. "Must I be subjected to gossip even from you?"

Robert sighed. "Henri is part of our family. If I speak to him of your earlier displeasure with me, it is not gossip. If you cannot forgive me for Brother Thorold's appearance, I forbid you to greet my sister Margaret with such a dour air."

She removed her hand from his and stood beside him.

"I would never embarrass you, milord."

When Lovvet bounded beside her, she patted the dog's fur absentmindedly, her gaze on the riders.

Margaret and her daughter shared an enthusiastic greeting with Earl Henri, before Robert welcomed her.

Margaret's green eyes glittered with the fresh, crisp beauty of holly leaves. She embraced Isabel warmly and patted her jutting belly. "God's blessings, I'm so happy for you, dear Isabel. I pray you shall experience all the joys I have known with my Adelina and none of other women's sorrows."

The women walked arm-in-arm, following their husbands toward the hall for dinner, while Petronilla and FitzRobert remained behind with the countess' daughter, her retainers and Lovvet. Restrained by FitzRobert's firm grip on her collar, the dog whined loudly.

Margaret asked, "Have you enjoyed court, Isabel?"

"It is different," she cautiously replied. She had relished the first weeks of her arrival, spent with King Henry's daughter, Amieria. The months afterward grew too fraught with worry. She wondered often about the little girl, whether she enjoyed life with her mother's new husband and if she would ever see her again. Perhaps she could learn about Amieria's welfare from her father.

"You do not fool me, Isabel. Court has its pleasantries, to be sure. It shall be a blessing when you are at Leicester in winter and I must visit you. You'll need your friends at this time."

Isabel halted, a heavy unease settling in her stomach, which had nothing to do with the smell of baked eels drifting from the hall. "What do you know of my husband's plans for Leicester Castle?"

"Has he not told you, Isabel?"

"He has not. I am asking you."

"You must know."

"What must I know?" Stamping her feet in displeasure would not gain her the response she wanted, but the urge burgeoned.

"Your lying-in shall be at Leicester. Your husband

wants your first child born there."

Had Robert taken leave of his senses? Ivo de Grentmesnil remained the lord of Leicester. He only mortgaged the lands and castle to Robert.

"Robert cannot claim dominion over another's honor. He wouldn't do such a vile thing!" Isabel's shrill voice echoed in the vestibule. Several passersby ogled them or looked at her askance. She ignored them and sought her husband nearing the hall. "Robert!"

He turned, his eyebrows arched over a murky gaze. She closed the distance between them, Margaret at her heels. "God's mercy, Isabel, be careful before you lose your footing in such haste."

Before she reached him, Robert whispered to his brother, who reached for his countess. He drew her away, although she protested, "Why is Isabel so angry? Didn't she know?"

"Come away, my dear. Let Robert speak with her in private." Earl Henri nodded to his brother and entered the cavernous room.

Robert waited for Isabel. Before she could speak, he drew her into an alcove. "Is it the babe?"

She clenched her fists against a murderous rage. "You know it's not!"

He sighed. "Do not raise your voice at me. Be mindful of our circumstances."

She cared nothing for the eager attentions of the gossip. Let them whisper behind their hands, laugh and point.

"Have you stolen Ivo de Grentmesnil's lands? Please, tell me I'm wrong."

"You are. I have stolen nothing. I've secured our children's legacy."

She stumbled, fingers splayed against her breastbone. "For shame, Robert, how can you do this? You gift our children a heritage borne of wickedness. I'd never burden a child—"

He grabbed her arms in his powerful grip, shocking her into silence. "My child! Never forget, Isabel, you carry my heir! What future would you have for our children? Their destiny lies here, not in Normandy. Land is power. Why do you think Henri and I have risked so much, if not for our own honor and gain? We have earned much by our loyalty to three Norman kings. How long shall that high favor last? I do not know when I may die. Now is the time to seize in life for my heirs. I think only of the legacy my children shall inherit."

"You would grant them a legacy of lies! An inheritance garnered from your selfishness. You are only thinking of yourself. You are chief among the king's counselors. You have power and lands. What more can you desire? Don't you have enough?"

When he released her without an answer, she glared at him in ensuing silence.

What manner of man had she married? How could he teach the virtues of goodness to his heir, a child who shall enter a world of iniquity, crafted through his father's greed?

Chapter Fourteen – Broken Promises
Leicester, England: March 1102

In a haze of hot, white smoke, Isabel sweated and panted. Her insides knotted and felt ripped asunder. She panted with a halting breath, gripping Petronilla's hand tightly in her grasp.

Her maidservant patted her brow with a dampened cloth. "Have courage, milady. It shall be over soon."

Isabel shied away from her touch. "You cannot know! When have you ever borne a child?"

From the recesses of the great hall at Leicester Castle, shuttered and dimly lit except for the fire at the hearth, the midwife cackled. With a withered hand, she nudged her assistant, who approached Isabel's pallet with an earthenware cup. Isabel clutched at her maidservant's hand. Petronilla soothed her with a gentle touch. The midwife's assistant offered Isabel the steaming liquid.

Isabel moaned and pushed the brew away. "Petronilla, tell her I refuse to drink more of the vile concoction."

A crooked smile splayed across the servant's lips. "It is necessary, Wulfwyn? Milady says it a vile-tasting brew."

Wulfwyn bent close and whispered. "It aids the birthing, or so my mother says. She can be forceful. If the wise woman insists milady drinks this, then she must."

Wulfwyn offered the cup again. Isabel sniffed the viscous brown liquid, green herbs swirling on the surface. The second mouthful tasted even more repulsive than the first she had consumed shortly after her labor began. She glared past Wulfwyn with stubborn determination. In her blurred view, the hearth fire cast a harsh, ugly orange glow on every visible surface. She imagined the Pit of Hell in such a garish color. The midwife's bulging stare met hers across the distance.

Dear Lord, would the fiery inferno be her fate? Would the Lord consign her child and her to Hell for his father's folly?

She pushed aside her fear and focused on the

midwife. "You may not understand my words, Hild. Still, take my meaning well. If this foul potion of yours harms milord's son, if you hurt his heir, my husband shall have the very flesh flayed from your bones. I shall summon all the strength to wield the whip myself, if need be."

Wulfwyn glanced at her mother, before her astonished gaze returned to Isabel. "Mother has understood all your words up to this point."

Petronilla snorted. "If she knows every word, why have you translated all milady has said into your barbaric English tongue?"

Hild grunted and gave them her back. Nestled beside the warmth of the hearth, the old midwife finished crushing a bowl of fine herbs. She added them to a boiling pot. The crackle and hiss of the flames beneath it devouring the burning wood vied with the bubbling gasps from the iron pot.

Isabel muttered, her heavy lids fluttering. "Wretched woman, no help at all with her cursed plants and foul remedies."

Wulfwyn shrugged. "Don't judge her too harshly, milady. Mother is proud. She has reason for it. She has descended from a long line of midwives, all women of Leicester. Her pride forbids her to speak the words of the conquerors, though she understands them. She lost her man, the father I never knew, in the battle against the Normans. She cannot forget the horror of those first days, after your husband's people came. She has borne the lusts of a Norman man and birthed his daughters, my younger sisters Constance and Agatha. Her heart can also forgive. It can be filled with compassion for all who have need of her, even among the Normans."

Isabel huffed. When would these people stop thinking of her as just another Norman? "Tell her who I am, Petronilla."

"Milady is not Norman," Petronilla murmured. "She is descended from French kings, a line unbroken from the time of Charles the Great."

Wulfwyn smiled. The gesture conveyed only wistful

sadness. "My mother does not care so long as you are not English." She offered the brew again. "Please drink, milady."

Isabel's lips trembled. "It shall not hurt milord's son?"

"Never, milady, I promise you."

Isabel sipped and gagged at the bitter, earthy taste. Petronilla patted her hand. "What is it, Wulfwyn?"

The midwife replied, "Motherwort and valerian, among other herbs."

Isabel downed the last drop and sagged against the pallet.

Wulfwyn took the cup away and returned quickly. She folded back the silken coverlet and for a brief moment, linen scraped Isabel's legs and thighs before the stifling warmth beneath her covers ebbed. Wulfwyn exposed Isabel's jutting belly, muttering something like, "Foolish waste," then said, "I must examine you, milady."

Isabel ignored Wulfwyn's cold hands probing between her legs. She edged closer to delirium in her pain. "Why is the birth taking so long? I have been in agony since midday. What hour is it?"

Petronilla glanced at the shuttered windows, the apertures covered with woven silk and gold tapestries. "I cannot tell."

"It seems long, too long. What if something has happened to Robert's child?"

"Only Hild can know. She would tell you if some difficulty with the child arose."

"Would she? Instead, she should fear my husband's wrath. I pray God for the safety of his son. Still, Robert is to blame for the agony I endure."

Petronilla patted her hand and kissed it. "All women in their travail say such things, milady."

"I am in earnest and you must believe in what I say." Isabel licked her lips as a tingling sensation throbbed along her tongue. "We should not have come here. I do not want Robert's child born in such a place, stolen from its rightful owners. Robert should have listened to me!"

The doors of the great hall creaked. Countess

Margaret entered, her hands clasped as if in prayer. Seven attendants trailed behind her, the last shutting the room away in near darkness again as she closed the doors.

"My dear Isabel, still struggling, I see. It is nearly dusk. Your husband and mine, we are all worried for you. I promised Robert I would attend you."

Bending beside the iron pot, she looked into its contents and her nose crinkled. Isabel stifled a feverish giggle, before a spasm overtook her. When her grip tightened, Petronilla squealed. Isabel murmured an apology, her head lolling. Weariness flooded her body. Her limp hand slid from Petronilla's grasp. Her hair, freed from its usual confinement, hung around her shoulders. Damp tendrils clung to her cheek and temple.

"Countess, assure my husband he may soon hold his son in his arms, though I may not live to see it."

"Nonsense. You are not the first wife bearing her husband's son, nor shall you be the last."

Hild looked askance at the countess hovering beside the pot. Margaret muttered under her breath and slid away. At an impatient tap of her foot, Petronilla moved and Margaret took the maidservant's place. The Countess of Warwick's servants encircled Isabel's pallet.

Cloistered among the women, sweat coated Isabel. The stifling heat increased. She licked her dried lips. "I want this child freed of my body, so his father may greet him."

Wulfwyn peeked over her engorged belly. "Milady cannot know if she bears a boy or a girl."

Eight pairs of eyes turned on the midwife's helper in dismay. Isabel moaned, beating her fists against the pallet with effort.

"Robert must have a son, Wulfwyn. I must give him his heir."

Margaret patted her arm. "You shall, with God's help." She glared at Wulfwyn as though chastising her suggestion anything else could result.

Isabel's eyes watered again. She had never allowed

herself a moment's consideration of a daughter. How would Robert feel if she failed him? How could she bear the disappointment of all her hopes?

Rose oil wafted across the hall. Hild approached with a beaker, her expression limpid. Isabel stifled an urge to throttle her. How dare she appear so calm and composed, when the very future hinged on the birthing to come? The midwife could afford her serene state when she was not the one to push the child into the world.

Hild spoke with Wulfwyn, who nodded toward Isabel.

"Mother wishes to know something. She says milady always refers to the child as her husband's own. She never claims the babe. Doesn't milady want the child?"

"The impertinence!" Margaret's cheeks flushed red. "How dare you ask questions of the Comtesse de Meulan?"

Isabel ignored her sister in-law's fervor. She sought Hild's intent gaze. "I conceived the child and did my duty. I bear this agony for my husband's sake, to give him the heir he desires. I have taken your foul potions to ensure the life and health of milord's child. Isn't that enough for you, wise woman?"

Hild did not answer. Her rheumy gaze suddenly sharp, the midwife nodded and handed the beaker to Wulfwyn, before she returned to the fire and her herbal brew.

"Your time has come, milady." Wulfwyn said. "I shall massage you with rose oil. Afterward, you must sit on the birthing stool. Your maidservant can support you."

"I shall have the honor," Margaret said.

Wulfwyn said, "It matters little to me." Despite Margaret's scowl, she continued, "Come, milady and give your husband his child."

Tears of bitterness trickled down Isabel's cheek. Her sobs of misery gave way to silent cries and anguished moans. On a new pallet, she shied away from Petronilla's comforting hand on her back. Her months of confinement, hours of torture, counted for nothing in the end.

"Milady, you can try again. You can have more children," Petronilla whispered.

"Would another child compensate for this failure? How stupid you are, Petronilla. I cannot even bear milord the son he wanted. What makes you believe he'll want to sire another child on me, after this?"

The loud, lusty cry of an infant echoed to the rafters. Isabel covered her eyes, blotting out the wretched sound.

"Isabel, hold your daughter."

Through aching eyes, she looked at Margaret, who appeared beside her with tiny, squalling bundle in the crook of her arm, bound in swaddling bands. "She has a glorious crown of your hair. Listen to her voice! Won't you look at her?"

"Take it away! I do not want to see her."

Margaret sighed. "I was disappointed when I bore a daughter first. A mother's love for her child is natural. Give yourself a few days and you shall soon see I am right. I shall take the baby to Robert now."

Isabel moaned, wishing her sister in-law would not do so. Her worst nightmare had come to fruition. Would Robert forgive her? Her heart's desire was for Robert to have the legitimate heir he craved. Now, she had presented him with a mere girl.

He would be as disappointed as her own father was when the midwives brought him daughter after daughter. Robert would likely demand his husbandly rights once she had completed the churching ritual. She might fail again. He would blame her.

Behind her, the hall door slammed against the adjoining wall. Her heart leapt inside her chest. She steeled herself for Robert's anger and sat up on the pallet. Her eyelids heavy, she shielded them with a hand against the glare of the torchlight in the passageway. Petronilla hastily arranged a *couvrechef* on her head. When Robert entered the cavernous room, she gasped.

He held the child in his arms. Margaret and her husband, Henri, strode beside him, while his men at-arms followed, each cheering him on with thunderous applause. Grins split their faces. Their joyful faces vied with Robert's pinched expression. With each footfall, he closed in on Isabel. His impenetrable stare pierced her as acutely as the hunter's arrow in his prey's belly.

When Petronilla moved aside, he knelt beside Isabel and showed her the child. "Milady, I gave you pleasure. In return, you grant me a daughter."

Margaret seemed not to hear his clipped tone. She approached with a circlet of finely fashioned gold. At its center, a fiery carnelian sparkled. Inlaid around the circumference of the bands of gold were other precious stones, including emeralds, pearls, sardonyx, beryl and amethysts. With Petronilla's aid, she settled the shimmering circlet on Isabel's head.

"How lovely, just like your little girl." The countess moved beside her husband. She asked, "What will you name her, Robert?"

Isabel looked up at her husband. A cold blue fire simmered in his eyes. "I have decided to call her Emma."

Henri kissed his wife's hand. "Emma de Beaumont shall be fair like her mother. Come, dearest, we should leave Robert and Isabel alone to become acquainted with their new daughter."

At Robert's nod, the Count of Warwick dismissed everyone from the room. Isabel grasped Petronilla's hand, a silent plea on her lips for her attendant not to leave her alone with Robert. Petronilla kissed Isabel's fingertips before she shuffled from the hall, a frown of concern cast over her shoulder as she went.

When only Isabel and Robert remained with the child, the weight of her failure settled in her stomach like a stone. His frigid expression pinned her to the pallet. She looked from him to the babe.

"Do you wish me to hold her, Robert?" Her arms shook as she reached for the child.

"She will go to the nurse I have hired."

"Who is this nurse?"

"She is not your concern. You will not coddle the

babe. I thought we had an understanding made in the bed at Saint Albans. Why have you failed me? I expected an heir from you, Isabel."

Her gaze watered, blurred by unshed tears. She could hardly bear to look at Robert's face, contorted in a dark mask. She had failed him and he might never forgive her. "Please believe me, I shall try again and I promise we shall have a son next time! Do not despair, Robert. It was the same for my mother. She had a son after she bore my two sisters and me."

"Are you saying I must abide by your damnable failures and also wait patiently, while you whelp two more daughters *before* you grant me an heir? Your mother did so to your father. I am not a youthful man, Isabel! My days on this earth grow shorter with each year. I wed you with the hope of heirs, but spared you a hasty bedding ritual in consideration of your tender years. Now, you have repaid my kindness and patience with this meager girl. Christ's bones! How much longer shall I have to wait for you to fulfill your promise?"

The newborn whimpered and turned red-faced at the rage in Robert's voice. She let out an ear-piercing caterwaul. Isabel's shoulders shook as she also began crying, her noisome sobs vying with those of her baby.

Robert rose and said no more.

Isabel clutched her hands as if in prayer. "Please say you'll forgive me, Robert. We shall try again. Emma shall have a brother."

He continued to the door. The child wailed, tucked against the crook of his arm. Over his shoulder, Robert muttered, "You will see to it as soon as you are capable. You *will* give me my heir."

Isabel discovered Emma had her baptismal ceremony in days. Countess Margaret relayed her joy afterward and promised she would be a dutiful godparent along with her husband Henri. Isabel sulked in silence, for Robert had not forewarned of his plan to name his brother and his sister by marriage as godsibs. He even kept the knowledge of Emma's nursemaid a secret, though Isabel had asked twice.

She remained sequestered before the churching for almost six weeks after giving birth. She lived in a shuttered room above stairs, which Robert had appointed as their bedchamber. A screen of white chainsil concealed the bed from view of other occupants. Clothing chests and one stool with the chamber pot set beneath it lined the western wall of the windowless room, lit only by candles in the evening. Isabel did not know where Robert slept, nor did she ask Margaret or Petronilla during their daily visits with her.

On one such occasion, Margaret sat on the bed and took Isabel's hand in hers. Faint light from a candelabrum the countess had perched on the stool revealed thin, blue veins beneath her sallow skin. "You must not worry for Emma during this time. Her nurse takes good care of her."

Isabel rubbed at her sore, swollen eyes. Sleep had evaded her almost every night. When she chanced to find it, she often woke fitfully, trapped in a horrid nightmare where Robert, her mother, her father or Brother Thorold berated her for producing a girl. "Emma must be a very quiet babe. I never hear her crying."

Margaret's brow crinkled. "She is not in the castle, Isabel. Surely, you must have known the nurse has taken the child to the village, where she may attend to her at every hour. I have accompanied Robert when he visited the nurse and child and promise you both remain in good health. Your husband is attentive, holds the babe with ease and does all a father should for a child. He has provided the cradle, fine linens for swaddling, caps for Emma's head and slavering cloths. The nurse's eldest daughter is at hand to rock the cradle. Has Robert told you none of this?"

"I have only seen him twice in the last six weeks." Isabel slumped, hoping the countess could not guess at her misery. Isabel had hoped for a confidante in Margaret. Now she recognized the long-standing affection between Robert and Henri would not allow Margaret to think poorly of her brother by marriage. Robert had fooled them all with his displays of affection for the child, while he had berated the mother for bearing her. He wished others to believe him a good father and honorable man. Since her arrival in England, Isabel had witnessed enough facets of her husband's personality to know no single trait governed his moods or actions.

Margaret's fingers patted her hand. "During his gander month, Henri kept from my side after our daughter's birth. The Church ordains it. Do not be resentful. Robert follows the correct course. Besides, a woman needs time after her travail and yours is almost at an end. The old midwife has examined you and said your churching could occur this week. Robert shall soon return to your bed."

A shudder coursed through Isabel and she burrowed her head in the warmth of the bedding. Her hand shook in the countess' grasp.

"It is not such an unpleasant expectation, is it?" Margaret inquired. "I know the birth was difficult. Consider only the happy prospect. Worry and pain cease to be important once a child is born. Next time, I am certain you'll know only joy as mother to a son."

Isabel closed her eyes. She could think of little else except sons and feared Robert's recriminations if she should fail him again.

Three days later, Isabel entered the hall, clutching her rosary beads. The skirts of her new robe of blue samite, a gift from Margaret, swirled around her feet. A new *couvrechef* hid her braided hair from view and floated around her hips like a gossamer cloud. The countess and her attendants, Petronilla and the wise women Hild and Wulfwyn followed her.

Robert stood beside the hearth and spoke with his steward, his back to her. Isabel halted a short distance away and cleared her throat. She hoped he would notice her. Though he did not, his steward paused in his reply to Robert and bowed. "Milady."

Robert turned, his mouth pinched. When he did not speak, she made a pretext of showing him the samite. "A costly gift to be sure. Do you approve?"

A tic pulsed along his jaw line while he remained cold and silent. His rudeness mystified and saddened her. She denied him any outward sign of her heartbreak. He stepped toward her, his lips parted slightly. She froze at the same time he did. His gaze left her face, traveled downward over the bodice and skirt of the glossy silk. He heaved a ragged sigh, before the muscle beneath his jaw clenched again.

Caught in the hold of his intense glare, she blinked and forced the words from her mouth. "We are leaving for the churching, husband. Have you finished discussing the feast to follow with your steward?"

"I have not. You just interrupted me." Robert's clipped tone staggered her.

Then he said, "I am leaving in the morning for court. Henry needs me."

She readied to rail at him, a reminder of how their newborn daughter needed him, too, before she recognized how foolish everyone would have deemed those words. No babe needed its father's care, especially when a competent wet nurse provided comfort.

Instead, she asked, "When will you come back to Leicester?" He had already returned his attention to the steward. They spoke in low tones before Robert dismissed the man.

Robert looked at her again. Her soft inquiry about his anticipated return went unanswered. "What are you waiting for, Isabel?"

A long shudder coursed through her. She would have pleaded for his forgiveness again and begged him to stay, not to leave while discord simmered between them. That would have been almost as foolish as asking him to remain for the child's sake. Instead, she left him alone, her train of followers with her. Still, she sensed Robert's gaze upon her as she exited.

Isabel plodded the final steps of the route from the castle to the church of Saint Martin. She whispered the Paternoster, "Our Father, who art in heaven, hallowed be thy name," from rote, without dwelling upon the words.

Soon, the procession assembled in the presence of the parish priest in his liturgical vestments, with a clerk beside him. Isabel wrapped the rosary beads around her wrist. With the aid of Petronilla and Margaret, she knelt just inside the vestibule on the cold floor beneath a shelter of stone. She glanced at the baptistery, where the font held holy water. The priest's clerk carried a silver ewer, presumably with some of the water and an unlit tallow candle. He offered it to Isabel. She bowed her head and waited, her thoughts muddled by Robert's cold dismissal.

Fat droplets cascaded, surprising her. After he sprinkled the holy water, the priest intoned, "'Blessed art thou among women and blessed is the fruit of thy womb.' As the Virgin Mary brought forth her son, Christ our Lord and sought ritual purification at Candlemas, so must all women who endure the travail of childbirth."

Isabel had not felt blessed when she made her farewell to Robert. She recalled how his unkind, silent regard had raked over her from head to toe and reduced her to a quivering form. Long months and years without him had taught her endurance. It pained her to part from him now with disappointment and resentment in both their hearts. She doubted Robert felt the same. He had usually left her side without a backward glance, or a lingering look filled with hope of his swift return. After six years of marriage, she still did not fully understand her husband's moods and doubted she ever would.

Lost in her thoughts, she almost recoiled at the unexpected gesture the priest made, touching her wrist with the end of his white stole. "Enter now into the house of God and adore the Son of the Blessed Virgin Mary, who granted thee fruitfulness of offspring."

She blinked and looked up at him, dazed. His brow crinkled. He stood aside while Petronilla helped Isabel to her feet. The priest and his clerk led her to the altar. The women followed and surrounded her. Isabel knelt once again, while the priest turned his back on them and recited the Gloria Patri and Kyrie Eléison in Latin.

She paid the ritual prayers scant attention. She could not let Robert leave with such rancor in his heart. If her words could not appease him, she must find some other means to restore his good nature. As it was, she recognized his desire lingered in the way his lips had parted and in his steady gaze. He had stepped toward her before seeming to think better of it.

In better days, his hunger for her and attentiveness in bed had continued during her pregnancy, until she thought it unsafe. Robert had scoffed whenever she reminded him the Church also forbade the practice. Hild had not told her how soon he could share the bed again. Margaret presumed no restrictions after the churching.

Isabel would have to ask Hild, only to be certain. She could find herself with child soon again, a boy who would vindicate her in Robert's eyes.

Still, she seethed at the unfairness of needing his forgiveness at all. He dared heap castigations upon her head, unmindful of pains suffered for his sake. Most men would likely be happy to know they did not bear the burden of an infertile wife. A healthy child and mother should have been a joy to any man. Not for Robert. He had not even asked how she felt after the birthing, only raged over his damnable disappointment.

She muttered under her breath, "Miserable, wretched man!"

Upon looking up, she found the priest glaring at her. She looked around. Margaret's face beamed with pleasure and the rest of the women seemed bored. Only Petronilla, who stood closest to Isabel, ducked her gaze. The corners of her mouth twitched.

Isabel returned her attention to the priest. He closed his eyes and blotted out the sight of her. "Let us pray.

Almighty and eternal God, who by means of the Blessed Virgin Mary's childbearing has given every Christian mother joy, even in her travail, look kindly upon thy servant, Isabel de Vermandois, who has come with gladness into thy holy dwelling to give thanks for her life and the life of her child. And grant that after this life, through the intercession of that same blessed Mary, she and her child shall be deemed worthy of everlasting life through Christ our Lord. Amen."

As one, the women whispered, "Amen."

Afterward, the priest stood before Isabel and sprinkled holy water on her again, before he uttered, "The peace and blessing of God Almighty, the Father and the Son and the Holy Spirit, descend upon thee and remain forever. Amen."

The clerk brought another lighted candle from the altar and touched the burning wick to the one Isabel grasped. The orange flame sputtered. The women curtsied before the priest. Then he and his clerk departed, leaving Isabel and her companions alone. The women returned outdoors.

Isabel begged off from the repeated kisses on her cheek from Margaret and her attendants. "Please I must see the midwife."

Even now, Hild and her daughter Wulfwyn curtsied at the fringes to no one in particular and started down the muddied lane. Isabel rushed after them. "Stop, please."

Wulfwyn closed a hand on her mother's arm and halted her. The young woman asked Isabel, "Are you well?"

"I am." Isabel licked her lips. "I wished to know something from your mother." At Hild's stiff nod, she continued, "How soon may my husband return to our bed?"

Hild's rumbling chuckle shook the aged woman's bent posture, before she said something in English. Isabel frowned at her. A tense exchange followed between mother and daughter before Wulfwyn threw up her hands.

"I demand to know what Hild said," Isabel commanded, though uncertain she would like it.

Wulfwyn's brow furrowed and she avoided Isabel's persistent gaze. "It is not worth repeating."

Isabel insisted. "Still, you will tell me."

Wulfwyn murmured, "My mother said the Norman girl enjoys bedding her lord more than the consequences of the bedding. She wishes to know why you want your husband back in your bed so soon when you turned from the child afterward and have not visited her."

A sudden tightness constricted Isabel's chest. Despite the tears that threatened, she focused on Hild's face.

"I do not know where the child is! Robert took her from me and gave her to some wet nurse whom I have never seen! You dare judge me, old woman, when you know nothing of my circumstances!"

Hild scrubbed a hand over her face and then muttered a response, which Isabel awaited from Wulfwyn.

"My mother says milady should know the child is with Agatha. She is the younger of my two sisters and has five children with FitzMaynard, another of your husband's clerks. Hild also says it is not right for a father to keep a child from its mother and she would not beget another child for such a man." Wulfwyn paused and added, "As if she could have more children."

Hild pinched her daughter's shoulder at the last bit.

Isabel stifled her laughter. "I appreciate your concern, Hild. I know the duty before me. You asked me if I wanted the child. I do, but I still want a son for Robert's sake."

Hild grunted and shrugged. "I will not stop you, lady. Go to your husband. I hope when you give him the son he wants, you'll know a mother's happiness finally."

She ambled down the lane and left Wulfwyn briefly stunned into silence, until the young woman said, "She has not uttered a word in Norman French since Agatha and Constance's father died fighting in the Fens. My mother loved him though his people invaded our land."

Hild snapped over her shoulder. "Child, I do not give you leave to speak of my past to the Norman girl. Now come."

Isabel's shock outweighed her embarrassment. Wulfwyn mumbled an apology on her mother's behalf and followed the crotchety woman, both veering right at the crossroads for the village. Isabel chuckled and returned with her companions to the castle.

Dinner occurred just after noonday. Beneath the table, the warmth of Robert's thigh penetrated Isabel's silken skirts. He never acknowledged her otherwise. His conversation encompassed only Henri and Thorold, who sat at his right. Margaret shared a trencher with Isabel.

The countess said, "It saddens me to leave you today, when you'll be bereft of Robert's company tomorrow. I miss my children at Warwick. Henri is eager to return. You must visit us."

"I would be honored and pleased. You have been kind to me, Margaret. I'll never forget." Isabel turned and kissed the older woman's cheek.

Margaret sighed. "You seem in need of kindness. You are so timid and cautious at times, I worry for you. Then there are other times when fire and fury glows in your eyes after some hurt or disappointment. All women, especially wives and mothers, understand disappointment. We arrive at marriage and motherhood with expectations of our husbands and children. Reality falls far short of our long-held hopes. It is a prudent woman who makes the best of her circumstances."

Isabel looked down at the fingers resting on her lap. "My father often said women must be meek and accepting of all circumstances. During their marriage, my mother was not and he despised her for it."

The countess nodded. "A woman's agreeable nature is a boon to her husband, to be sure. She also has her own desires. I believe you are a woman of great pride and personal strength."

"My father would say pride is a fault."

"It is only misplaced pride, my dear."

Isabel wished she might let go of harsh lessons from the past that weighed upon her. "My mother taught that the will to endure childbirth is each woman's lot, part of her life's journey. It is not the only mark of a woman's strength. I wonder how I shall fare against other tests in new forms."

Margaret squeezed her hand and held her gaze. "You'll meet them with the inherent courage that dwells inside all women. It lies in our grace and endurance, in the personal difficulties we must each overcome. You have this strength. Let it guide your path."

Isabel remembered a conversation with Amieria long ago where she had ensured a little girl that all women held courage. It seemed Isabel's own had disintegrated beneath the burdens of Robert's expectations. Could she summon such strength again when faced with her husband's cold fury?

When the meal concluded, the countess asked Isabel to stay with her while she readied for the departure to Warwick Castle.

Robert's hand closed on Isabel's wrist. "I would speak with you now."

She had almost forgotten he sat next to her, the conversation between him and his brother having faded long ago. He leaned forward and smiled at Margaret. "I won't keep her from your side for long, sister."

The hall's occupants rose from the table. Many, including Margaret and Henri dispersed. The servants remained behind and cleared the tables of dinner scraps. Lovvet wandered in and nosed among the rushes for any remnants carelessly discarded. With the return of winter, amidst the dank drafts pervading the castle, she favored her leg with the old injury. Since their move to Leicester, the alaunt spent most of her time in a corner of the castle kitchen, unable to climb the stairs. The scullery maids and kitchen boys took as much liking to her as Isabel had and saw to Lovvet's feeding and care. Isabel feared she might not live much longer, as old age and aches took their toll on the loyal hound.

She held out a hand to the dog. Robert cupped her elbow. "Why is that dog here? Send her away," he said. "You know I do not like her here at dinnertime."

"We have finished the meal, Robert. Why should her presence trouble you? She is no burden upon our household. Everyone likes her, except you."

"You are too fond of William de Warenne's gift."

"Would you have had me reject her just because of him? Why must you mention him at all?"

He did not answer. His mouth tightened to a stubborn line that would not allow for refusal. Isabel beckoned a pageboy. "Take my Lovvet back to the kitchen, please."

When the boy tugged her collar, the dog whined. Still, she dutifully followed his lead.

Robert drew Isabel to the hearth and released her. She rubbed the samite where his hand had alighted.

"At times, I think you care more for your pet than me," he muttered, staring at the movement of her fingers against the silk.

She lowered her hand. "You are mistaken. I worry for Lovvet. She is getting older. The affection I have for her could never rival my feelings for you." She paused and drew a deep breath, willing the courage Margaret said she possessed in herself. Bitterness helped her find a measure of mettle. "However, when you snarl and shout or ignore me as you have done these past weeks, you cannot expect me to be happy for it."

He chuckled. "Obviously, you did not take to your father's advice regarding meekness."

She shuddered, realizing he had likely listened to her entire conversation with the countess, while appearing otherwise engaged. What had he thought of their exchange over disappointments in marriage? Her heart in fear's cold grip, she turned to the hearth and stretched her hands toward the warm flame, tilting her chin a little. "You are unhappy with me, Robert, for a cause not of my own making. God gave us a daughter. You have rejected me for my supposed failure, and then wonder at whether I care for you. I should hold such concerns instead of you. Have I not proven my devotion? Your wishes are mine."

Chairs and benches grated across the floor, as the servants set them against the wall or atop the tables. Robert raked a hand over his pale hair. "Out, all of you! I've had enough of this racket."

The household fled at his imperious tone, while Isabel pondered his mercurial moods, flippant in one instance and irritated in the next. Her husband's anger did not bode well for harmony between them this day. The obvious futility of any argument she could have offered left her fraught. How could she convince him when he refused to listen?

Her head bowed, she yelped as Robert touched her shoulder. He eyed her with an unrepentant stare. She wanted nothing more than to escape him as well and rushed to speak. "Margaret is waiting for me, Robert. Give me your leave to go."

"My good sister can wait upon my news, Isabel. While I am at court, I have arranged for the wet nurse to live here with our child."

She gasped and her fingers flew to her parted lips. His gaze lingered on her mouth. "Why must you appear so shocked? I am not cruel enough to deprive you of the girl forever, despite what you apparently think of me. You may hold our daughter for brief periods. Otherwise, let the wet nurse attend her. Under no circumstances are you to suckle her. She is accustomed to the wet nurse's milk."

"I would not alter the arrangement you have made."

"Good. You believe me a heartless wretch. I act to benefit our daughter and for our future. Women who nurse do not conceive. You must be ready to bear my son."

He grasped her arm again. Long fingers curled around the silk and tugged her toward him. "I have granted you a boon. What will you give me in return?"

She blinked rapidly and then stared at him openmouthed. Her hands flattened against his chest, where his heart hammered beneath the tunic. "I don't know what I could give you that you do not already have from me."

"You are mine, are you not?"

"You know I am. I have kept my marital vows. All I ask is for your kindness and gentle care."

"You do not inspire gentleness in me just now!" He grabbed the neck of the silken garment and tugged it downward. His action robbed her of speech, shocked in silence by the suddenness of his actions. In one motion, he had ripped her robe and the chainsil undergarment beneath.

"Robert, you've ruined Margaret's gift! You should not have done that."

He ignored her. He tugged the torn top of the garment downward until her breasts spilled from the cloth. "You will deny me, nothing, Isabel. I may have you when and where I please. Remember your vows. You will obey me."

He steered her toward a table and bent her over, his hands pushing aside her skirts. "This is not the time or place. You cannot mean to take me now, in such a way. The Church forbids it. You must take care. I have healed—"

Cool air stung her exposed back. One hand gripped her hip while the other tightened around her neck and held her down against the wood. "We have tried for a son in the ways the Church demands and I am still waiting, my sweet. In this way, you shall conceive my heir."

She had expected passion when they made love again, not this frenzied rush to claim her. A harsh, almost guttural cry escaped her when he lifted her hips and thrust against her roughly. She hung almost suspended by the startling pain, lank in his arms. Then she struggled against the pain he inflicted. His fingertips raked her hip. Stunned by his cold brutality, she stifled an agonized scream. While his body battered hers, she prayed to survive him and the mockery he had made of their marriage.

Chapter Fifteen – The Heirs of Leicester
Leicester, England: February 1104

Two winters after the birth of Emma, the windows of Leicester Castle's great hall stood shuttered again, as Isabel prepared for the arrival of her second child. The agony and ambivalence returned, coupled with a bitter resentment of Robert. He had left her for the remainder of the year after Emma's birthing and returned disappointed at Epiphany, when she did not greet him with news of another pregnancy. Over seven months of his erratic departures and returns from court, she bore his unceasing attentions and foul moods, while her body refused to cooperate. He demanded explanations from Hild and Wulfwyn, their assurances that in his absence, neither of them had provided Isabel with the means to prevent conception. Just after May Day, when Emma began speaking clear words, Isabel realized her courses had not arrived. She waited several tense weeks until she received confirmation of her second pregnancy, before writing to Robert.

Despite more than a year of motherhood, Isabel despaired at her muddled feelings. When Emma wanted comfort during the day, she howled and screeched until Petronilla held her. Emma rooted at another breast, belonging to Agatha, rather than Isabel's own. Not that Isabel could have nursed her. When Wulfwyn's sister Agatha set Emma down in the great hall among the rushes, the baby ambled toward her father and played with the tassels on his shoes. Robert tolerated it until he summoned Agatha to take his daughter away. Even Lovvet preferred the babe although her mistress stood nearby. The alaunt never bared her teeth when the girl pulled her tail or probed her ears with wiggling, fat fingers.

After a respite from her labor pains, seated alone on her pallet, Isabel stroked her engorged belly. This child might love her instead and she could grow to love him. Her sentiments regarding the child's father were more ambiguous. For the last three months before Wulfwyn anticipated her lying-in, Robert had often consigned her to their darkened bedchamber while her pregnancy progressed. She often ate her meals in the room, with Petronilla for company and seethed at her husband's rigid dictates. Only when lightning struck the roof of that section of the castle and set fire to the thatched roof and timber beams did Robert permit her below stairs again. While repairs continued, she became a resident of the hall.

Her travail started at midday, as it had at Emma's birth. The intense labor she had anticipated did not occur. Minimal pains and a growing discomfort across her back accompanied the heavy, swelling sensation around her hips. One month earlier, Robert had left Leicester Castle for a tour of the lands he had claimed. FitzRobert had gone after him. Petronilla summoned Wulfwyn, as old Hild had died last spring. Isabel awaited the appearance of both women. The castle's maidservants attended to her every comfort.

A shadow crossed the opened doorway. Isabel's hand halted on her belly mid-circle. She drew in a harsh breath at the haggard appearance of Brother Thorold. He stood thin and lank against the frame. In the winter months, he underwent a rigorous fast and she had mercifully seen little of him. His form, reduced to a shell of its former self, appeared skeletal and frightening beneath the black habit.

He gave a barely perceptible nod in her direction. She wondered why he bothered to appear at the hall door now during her difficulties, when he avoided all activity within since she had started spending days there.

"What do you want, Thorold? I am in no fit state for your company."

"As ever. The day ends and there is a strange star in the heavens. I realized milady must be without her usual attendant. It is an auspicious sight for the birth of milord's son."

"You thought to comfort me in Petronilla's absence

with news of this heavenly portent? You do not know how to soothe anyone, least of all me."

His hollowed cheeks whitened. "I would not trouble you, milady."

"Each day you remain with us vexes me. I wish you were gone from this place."

"Your husband cannot bear our separation."

She gasped at this. "Robert is blind to your faults. I am not."

He edged closer inside the hall. Instinctively, she moved backward a few paces and then stopped. She smoothed the creases in her robe, then looked up and found his cadaverous face focused on her. She had not fooled him.

"You have obviously come here to speak of more than omens from the skies."

"What do you think of your husband's plans for the lady Emma?"

Her spine tingled. If Thorold knew something about Emma's future she did not, she would never forgive Robert. Still, she could not deny her curiosity.

"Speak plainly, Thorold, if you can, of my husband's plans for our daughter."

"I should not have mentioned it, if he has not already."

Her nails cut into her palms. "What do you know?"

"Milord has instructed me to pursue further negotiations of her betrothal."

Isabel winced and flexed her fingers. "Whom shall she marry?"

"Amaury de Montfort, brother of Queen Bertrade of France."

Isabel recalled the mocking queen and her father's belief that Bertrade had wanted Isabel to wed Amaury. Instead, the queen's brother would have Emma for his wife, a man at least two decades her senior. The age difference would be slightly less than the one between Robert and Isabel. She worried for her daughter. The child would be uncertain about her future when offered in marriage to a significantly older man, as her own mother had been. If God existed, in His mercy, he might allow Emma some happiness in the fate her father had chosen.

"When did Robert decide this match?"

"A year ago. He has not pursued it, given other claims upon his attention."

"He thought it best to consult with you instead of me?"

"The comte values my opinion. It is God's will and her father's for Emma to be Amaury's wife."

Isabel turned away from him, fearing he could see the displeasure his news brought. At barely two years of age, Emma would be nothing more than her father's pawn, as Isabel had been for Hugh de Vermandois.

Within an hour of Wulfwyn's arrival, Isabel's labor intensified. The shattering pain robbed her of her breath and speech. She groaned on the birthing stool, Petronilla behind her offering encouragement.

When the midwife eased a red, slimy wetness from her body, Isabel sagged against Petronilla.

"Open your eyes, milady," Wulfwyn urged. "Behold your son."

Isabel sat up slowly, her eyes first taking in the birth cord still binding the child's body to hers. Then, she saw the unmistakable proof of the babe's sex. He shivered under Wulfwyn's gentle ministrations as she wiped him down. The midwife's younger sister, Constance assisted her. She severed the birth cord and took him away. Isabel's greedy gaze followed him.

"Milady, you have a boy." Petronilla wept hot tears on Isabel's neck.

"Indeed, at last, an heir for Robert," Isabel whispered. Relief flooded her.

As Wulfwyn tended her, a dizzy pain rippled through her side and the intense pressure she had felt returned.

She screeched, "It's happening again!"

"What, milady?" Wulfwyn probed between her legs

and then looked up with wide eyes. "It's another child, milady. Twins."

"Twins!" Isabel's eyes streamed with tears of horror. She clutched at Petronilla's hand. "Please, do not let Robert think I've been with another man. You are always at my side. You will tell him the truth. Promise me."

Petronilla nodded fervently. "I swear, milady. I'll swear on holy relics."

Wulfwyn's brow crinkled. "What nonsense is this?"

Petronilla whispered, "It's said if a woman bears twins, she's been with more than one man."

Wulfwyn threw back her head and laughed. "Such ridiculous prattle."

Despite the midwife's assurances, images of her husband's unwarranted rage and sentiments of disgrace tortured her throughout the delivery. Even when Robert's second son slipped into the world, her concerns did not abate.

Wulfwyn burnt the birth cord upon the hearth, before she and Constance cleansed both babies and brought them to their mother, who gazed in awe.

Petronilla touched the golden tufts of hair on each child's head. "I wonder what milord's present may be, for you have surpassed all his expectations in this birthing."

Isabel sighed despite her worry and lingering pain. "I have fulfilled my duty, doubly."

"Is duty all you can think of, milady, even at a joyous time like this?"

"It is all I have ever known, Petronilla."

Leicester, England: June 1108

Isabel arched her back and craned her already sore neck, peering into the nearly impenetrable canopy of elder trees. "I swear by the blood of our Savior, His heavenly Father and all His saints, if you children do not come down from the trees this instant, I shall have FitzMaynard whip the very flesh from your bones!"

Pealing giggles met this latest of threats, which had

issued first when the bells rang for Tierce. Now, exasperated and with her gaze blistered by the noonday sun, Isabel glared at Petronilla and Agatha, who sheltered under a copse just below the mound of Leicester Castle. Agatha held Isabel's second daughter, born earlier in the year, on her hip.

Petronilla suggested, "They certainly won't clamber down with the promise of chastisement, milady. You might try a different approach."

"Thank you for your helpful observation. Waleran, Robert and Hugh are my sons. I know how best to deal with them."

Agatha rocked the red-faced baby, who refused all comfort and wailed for her feeding. "Milady, my old husband's whip shall not do. The last time you ordered Lord Waleran chastened, he would not stand still long enough for FitzMaynard to ply the lash. My husband couldn't even raise his arms when I helped him remove his *sherte*."

"Old FitzMaynard can't catch us," twin voices lisped from among the crooked-branched trees. A conspiratorial giggle followed the taunt.

Hands akimbo, Isabel glared into the dense green foliage again. "Waleran and Robert, I warn you just once. Do not dare tease FitzMaynard because of his age. Don't join your brothers in such mischief, Hugh, or I shall thrash you all myself."

"You shall not."

Isabel recognized the defiance in four-year old Waleran's tone, a rallying cry soon taken up by young Robert and Hugh, who chorused, "You shall not. You shall not."

"They know you too well, milady, for you would never harm them," Petronilla said.

Isabel snarled at her. "Thank you again for confirming I'm as weak as water before my children." She returned her attention to her rebellious sons. "I promise you, my boys, you shall not join the court at Winchester if you do not come down. I shall leave you here."

"Milady! You cannot," Petronilla protested. Isabel silenced her with a brusque look.

"We hate court!" the twins shouted.

"Father's there." Although muffled in the dense, dark canopy, little Hugh's voice reached Isabel. At just over two years old, he worshipped his father more than he did his elder brothers, born two years before him.

Isabel smiled and strolled toward Petronilla and Agatha. "Farewell then, you naughty children. I shall be sure to tell your father how you have misbehaved in his absence."

The canopy rustled. "You wouldn't tell Father, would you, *Maman?*"

Isabel did not answer little Robert's plaintive appeal. She reached Agatha, who had loosened the strings at the nape of her robe and pushed the chemise off her shoulder. The baby's lips closed on her nurse's nipple and she made sounds of contentment.

Then Agatha gasped and looked beyond Isabel, who did not show any outward interest in what had drawn the wet nurse's attention.

Isabel's firstborn, Emma, a russet-haired beauty with her father's light-colored eyes, peeked around Petronilla's skirts. "At last you listened to *Maman*. You are naughty boys. I'm telling Father."

"You would, you little bitch."

Isabel turned sharply, her hand swung wide as it connected with the ruddy cheeks of her son Waleran. Startled, the boy clutched the side of his face before he burst into tears.

Appalled at the suddenness of her reaction, Isabel stared as if the same fingers did not belong to her. Then she caught her maidservant's nod and closed her fist. Waleran's caterwauling pierced her ears, piteous and heartbreaking. As she reached for him, Agatha cleared her throat. Petronilla's placid expression soured into a frown.

Although Isabel resented their silent encouragement, she finally resolved against coddling her darling son.

"Waleran, make amends to your sister at once." She forced a measure of steel into her soft voice.

"You can't make me!" The red-faced tyrant bawled behind his hands. His twin patted his shoulder before he stared at their mother. No spark of fiery rebellion glittered in his eyes, unlike his brother, only silent commiseration with Waleran.

Isabel glanced at Petronilla, who gave another barely perceptible nod. Isabel's heart sank. She also knew if she did not discipline her sons, they would grow unruly in manhood and cause her nothing but anguish.

She grabbed Waleran's *cotte* and hauled him against her. "Do not test my patience, you willful little brute. Otherwise, you shall have the thrashing you deserve, I promise." She met Robert's gaze then. "You shall have the same if you join your brother in his foolery. As it is, I forbid you both from play for your disobedience. Shall I banish you above stairs until we leave?"

Robert's eyes watered as his gaze fell away from hers. "Please do not. We will be good boys until we reach court. I promise."

She blinked harshly and forced back tears of her own. She had not missed her second son's half-hearted promise of good behavior only until they reached Winchester. She would not press for further concessions.

Petronilla placed a reassuring hand on her shoulder. Her twin sons mumbled apologies to their sister. Emma ruined the conciliatory moment when she stuck her tongue out. Robert and Waleran dashed at her and gave chase when she ran away, squealing. Hugh ran up the hillock toward the hall as fast as his pudgy legs might carry him.

Isabel sighed. "I never thought my children would be such headstrong devils."

"Only Waleran is a demon, until he incites Robert to join him. The rest are harmless," Petronilla murmured, before she smirked at Isabel's scowl.

"Mind how you speak of my children."

"The twins are spoiled, milady, a fact you cannot

deny. They test your will. If you do not check their behavior now, especially Lord Waleran's own, I fear you shall regret it."

"They are my sons, Petronilla."

"Emma and her sister are your daughters, yet you do not coddle them as you do Waleran and Robert. Even Hugh is as likely to escape your sharp tongue. If you continue to indulge the boys' behavior, you shall regret it, milady."

Winchester, England: June 1108

Two weeks later, Isabel shepherded her children as they traversed a narrow bridge over a channel of the River Itchen. Their company rode through the bustling streets of Winchester. A row of guardsmen protected Isabel's family. The children chattered and pointed at the sights around them, including the castle on its mound. They remained oblivious to any possible danger or the snide looks the English people cast their way. However, Isabel noticed the sneers and whispers. She considered whether it would not be best to appear in less finery, especially when many of Winchester's denizens appeared bedraggled. Isabel grumbled low under her breath about her husband's absence and looked around, assuring herself her family followed.

Petronilla and FitzRobert brought up the rear. Their mounts jostled each other. As FitzRobert murmured something to her, Petronilla blushed a bright pink. The maidservant nodded and cast him a demure glance before she lowered her gaze.

Their plight drew a sigh from Isabel. For several years, her maidservant maintained a steady attachment to the knight FitzRobert. Isabel did not doubt he returned the sentiment, always visible in his care and attentiveness to Petronilla. They were rarely far apart, even when Petronilla tended to her duties. Robert ignored their sentiments.

When Isabel had last seen him at Yuletide, he spoke

openly of his intent to have FitzRobert betrothed to an heiress by the summer. Later, Isabel had crept from her husband's bed to the shadows and draped her blanket around Petronilla's quivering shoulders. The memory of her maidservant's piteous sobs remained fresh in Isabel's mind. She would speak with her husband upon arrival at Winchester Castle. She had to do something or suffer Petronilla's heartbreak.

Too many in the world already bore the burden shattered hopes and fettered dreams. FitzRobert and Petronilla deserved their share of happiness.

"*Maman*, when may we see Father?" Emma's plaintive inquiry broke Isabel's reverie.

She glanced at her girl. "I hope it may be today. Your father has responsibilities to the crown."

"His duties have kept him far from us."

Isabel snapped, "Fathers have little use for daughters. You must accept."

Emma sulked and buried her chin in the warmth of her ermine-trimmed cloak.

Isabel turned her face into the biting wind. Her stomach roiled with regret at her callous response to her eldest child, a daughter much like her mother, blessed with an understanding beyond her years.

Often, Isabel found it a constant struggle to say or do the right thing for her children. Petronilla rightly accused her of a preference for her sons over the girls. She had witnessed her own parents do the same with their children, doting on her eldest brother. Painful childhood memories warned her not to take the same approach with her children.

She peered at her eldest daughter again and added. "Your father's service to King Henry is a great honor for us all. There are few in the realm who have shown such loyalty since the old days of the Conqueror."

Emma's chin rose a little higher and her cheeks colored. "Did my father truly know the Conqueror?"

"He did and he served him well. Your father has been loyal to each of the Conqueror's sons. He gives devoted service and his rewards provide us with the comforts we enjoy at home in Leicester."

The lie almost choked Isabel. She had never viewed Leicester Castle as her home and she never would. Robert's seizure of the castle from Ivo de Grentmesnil still tainted the birthplace of her children.

In the afternoon, Isabel went into Winchester Castle's great hall with Robert. The king had married his queen and she had birthed their son here. Now Isabel wondered whether the royal couple experienced happier times at Winchester than the reunion with Robert had allotted to her. After a murmured exchange of pleasantries with her, followed by a half-hearted, formal greeting of their children, Robert's demand for companionship at dinner startled her. His iron grip on her elbow at her left propelled her forward, even as she spared a worried glance at Petronilla, FitzRobert and her children before she left them.

Isabel permitted Robert's maneuvering. Still, his mood vexed her. Her instinct warned against questioning him. She ignored such concerns. She studied the lines carved into his sallow-skinned features and his purpled lips pressed together in a thin line.

"Something troubles you, milord? I have never seen you this overwrought after a return from Normandy. The journey has left you overtired."

He raked his brown-spotted left hand over hanks of grayed hair. The last vestiges of his former golden-haired glory had faded in the months of his abandonment.

"Robert, I pray, release me. You're hurting my arm."

When his hand fell away, she said, "You have been with Henry for months. I had hoped you would return home. Instead, you summoned us here. Why?"

"I should have asked for you alone, not the children. The king and I must return to Normandy within weeks. Your cousin, Louis of France, has ruled his country for less than a full month, yet he has demanded Henry's homage and the return of castles in the Vexin. Louis distracts Henry from the latest quarrel with Anselm of Bec. I wish Anselm would attend to his archbishopric and leave the monarchy in peace. You should not have brought the children at such a time."

"In your last letter, you asked me to bring them. I have done as you commanded."

"What do I care for such foolish whims when troubles afflict the realm?" His sharp tone pierced the wood-beamed rafters outside the king's great hall. Passersby glanced at them.

Isabel folded her arms across her chest. "The presence of your children after long months of absence should not be such a burden to you, Robert."

He grasped her shoulders, a gentler touch than she had anticipated. "Forgive me. I am overwrought and rightly concerned about matters between England and France, where I hold estates. I promise I shall have more time for the children and you, when I return. I have neglected you for too long."

His earnest gaze burned into her. He would likely claim his husbandly due tonight. The prospect did not warm her as it once had.

"Must you return to Normandy so soon?"

"I must."

"Does Henry intend to settle matters with Anselm before his departure?"

"It is unlikely he can. Look at how many years they argued over the investiture of lay prelates and homage due to the king."

Isabel gasped. "Does the king look toward the archbishop's exile again?"

"Anselm imposes his will in another matter when he should know better. When Henry wants something, it is best to give it to him."

"The archbishop is in his advanced years. One day, he shall leave all earthly concerns behind, including Canterbury and concern His Grace no more."

Robert's grimace altered his features. "Blasphemy, woman! Do you think Henry hastens Anselm's death?

The archbishop is the king's regent. Do not speak of matters where you lack the full understanding. Such concerns reside with the monarchy and the Church. Anselm and the king shall settle all troubles in due time."

She returned his scowl. He treated her as if she were an ignorant child. She tamped down her ill will and murmured, "I am no fool, Robert. Henry's troubles with the archbishop have bedeviled both men since I arrived in England. How can Anselm of Bec duly serve the will of God and the desires of the king without burdening his soul? You have never liked the archbishop. It is clear whenever you speak of him. You've never told me of your personal quarrels with him."

A tic pulsed along Robert's jaw line. "I have not."

After a short silence, her shoulders slumped in defeat. "You have no intention of doing so now. You should not keep secrets from me. I am your wife, milord."

"Have I forgotten?"

"I would not pry, Robert—"

"Then do not do so now, Isabel. You concern yourself with matters of the past beyond your understanding or care." His frigid stare froze her in place.

Resigned, she said, "Tell me, instead, the cause of Henry and the archbishop's quarrel of late."

"Negotiations of Henry's daughter's betrothal have left the men at odds."

"The Princess Maud's betrothal has been settled? Barely a girl of six and already destined for marriage. Why should Anselm object?"

"Maud's future is not the concern, rather another of Henry's children." Robert grabbed and tucked Isabel into a corner. His body shielded her from view against the cold, gray wall of flint. "Listen well, for a task lies before you. The king requires your service now. The children shall only serve as a distraction for you. You must leave them to the care of our servants. They do not need a mother coddling them, especially our sons."

Her nose wrinkled at the odor of stale wine and

onions on his fetid breath. "Of course, I shall serve His Grace as he desires. What could he possibly want from me where his daughter's marriage is concerned?"

"He seeks a woman of virtue as companion for his daughter. The archbishop of Canterbury raised some objection to the union. There is an impediment of the blood between Henry, as a descendant of the dukes of Normandy and his daughter's betrothed. A papal dispensation might resolve the issue."

"I do not doubt its necessity. The king has sired several children among noble families of England and Normandy. I do not doubt there are fears of consanguinity. Which one of his natural daughters shall be wed?"

When Robert stare narrowed at her causal tone, she regretted it, in part. She would not play the simpleton and pretend ignorance of the king's reputation with the wives and daughters of his courtiers, or the consequences of such liaisons. She also no longer viewed Henry's wife with sympathy. Life at the side of two of her husband's own bastards had taught Isabel the evidence of a husband's philandering did not always imperil marital relations. A woman could tolerate and accept the children of such unions, if her heart made the allowance.

Robert stated, "She is a black-haired girl from Kent. I believe you knew her some years ago."

Isabel's heart thrummed. She couched her deep-seated pleasure behind a fleeting smile, knowing of only one of Henry's daughters who might fit such a brief description.

"This girl, I think Amieria is her name, asked for you in earnest when she arrived at court." Robert eyed her intently. "The king has allowed her a little time at court with her betrothed. Henry often indulges the whims of his children, evidenced by Princess Maud's impetuous nature."

Isabel chuckled, "Maud is six years old, Robert. She has the arrogance of a child destined for a great marriage. I remember the same pride in myself as a child.

The years shall subdue her."

Robert eyed her. "As they have done for you?"

When she blushed, he continued, "The king cannot have his natural daughter and her intended husband found together, alone. Henry believes a woman of good repute, respected and admired by many and with children of her own, would suit his daughter's temperament. He has chosen you as the constant companion of his natural daughter, whenever she is with her betrothed."

"If the Lady Amieria would have me, I consider it a great honor and a renewal of our friendship. Nothing would please me more. Tell me, milord, who is the man she may marry?"

Robert's response died beneath a crescendo of horns announcing dinner.

"Come, Henry and his company have kept us waiting long enough. We must take our places and watch this farce of an evening unfold." He grasped Isabel's arm and ushered her into the stifling hall. The question of why he called the impending evening a charade died on her lips.

No sooner had they assumed their places at the trestle table than King Henry led a large retinue into the room. The king had grown fat. Gray streaked the dark length of his hair. In addition to the throne, he now claimed lordship of Normandy, having defeated his brother Robert at the battle of Tinchebrai. Isabel recognized few of the men with Henry, except for the tallest, most broad-shouldered among them. The Earl of Surrey followed the king, clearly at the sovereign's side now after he had abandoned Duke Robert's cause. He obviously cared more for his holdings than pledges to his former lord. How could Henry trust such a person?

Beneath a furrowed brow, Earl William's large eyes scanned the room and met her stare. She should have looked away sooner. He drew abreast of the king's table. For a moment longer than propriety would have allowed, the earl stared at Isabel, unwavering. She could hardly breathe, caught in the spell of his regard for her. A whispered gasp escaped her. His hard gaze pivoted to her husband, who stiffened beside Isabel.

Had Robert witnessed the indiscretion?

As if in answer to her silent query, her husband leaned forward and at the same time, he reached for her fingers on the table. He gripped them, almost painfully. Earl William's nostrils flared as though some malodorous scent had penetrated the hall. With a stiff nod to Robert, the earl found his seat close to the king.

Isabel dragged her gaze away from him and murmured to her husband, "Why does the queen not attend with her husband?"

Robert did not answer, merely jerked his chin toward the last of the king's company. A trio of young ladies appeared, the only women who had followed the king. Conversations ceased and silence descended as almost every occupant of the hall watched the last arrivals. Isabel stared too, wordless. With a hand pressed to her chest, she sighed.

If Isabel had ever believed angels might manifest themselves among God's people, then one must have chosen the form of Henry's natural daughter Amieria. Beneath a billowing, white veil, her ivory-skinned complexion glistened with joy. Her demure, dark gaze held the stark beauty of a doe's own. Her rounded cheeks colored a deep rose pink. Her garments suited her lean and graceful form. It seemed as though she glided, rather than walked across the rushes. Though Isabel had not seen the girl for several years, she would have recognized her anywhere by her generous smile and the harp she always carried. After Amieria took her seat across the hall, she favored Isabel with her warm smile. A spark of recognition and joy suffused her gaze.

After everyone washed his or her hands, the meal commenced at a wave from the king to his chief butler. The cupbearers and servers attended the king's table first, and then fanned out like an army of buzzing bees. Isabel ignored them when they proffered meat and drink for her and her husband. She would have dashed from her seat and rushed to Amieria's side at once, except Robert's hold crushed her wrist. She winced and glared at him. He raised her fingertips to his lips. "You must be hungry, my dear."

She settled herself beside him on the bench. Her husband's grip remained tight, as though he reassured himself of her presence. When had he become so possessive?

He quaffed a cup of wine and demanded more. She picked at a slice of pheasant, bit into the tender flesh and pushed the skin aside, slick with oil.

Beside her, Robert said, "William has grown overly bold. His daring only rivals his disdain for his fellow courtiers. I wonder why he troubled himself to stare at you for so long."

She swallowed before a piece of the fowl choked her. How could she have ever hoped he might not comment on the earl's actions? It was a fool's wish. "I care nothing for the earl's moods, nor do you. Why speak of him at all?"

Robert's hold on her hand tightened. She pressed her lips together against a brief moan of pain. "You're hurting me, milord."

"I do not mean to do so. When I look at you, I see my fair bride and the mother of my heirs. Does he see the same?" His grip never lessened. "Be sure you always have a care for my moods, Isabel and keep far from William. I did not like his gaze upon you. It was covetous."

"Hardly. The earl has no more regard for me than I do for him. You have no need to caution me. I promise you with absolute certainty I shall never suffer his company with a glad heart."

Robert released her abruptly and reached for his pewter goblet. As he sipped another cup of wine, he gazed over the rim at the earl, who had taken his place near the king.

Beneath the table linen, Isabel soothed her bruised wrist with her fingertips. If only she might still the furious beating of her heart. She grew frightened of her constant awareness of Earl William's presence whenever he appeared. The man had imposed himself upon her in the past only because he knew how much she disliked him. Otherwise, why did he often stare so impertinently at her, except it gave him some perverse pleasure?

Surely, sheer disgust inspired the emotions swirling inside her. Even now, as she stared at the frayed edges of the tablecloth, she could not ignore him fully.

How could she spend an entire meal in the same room with him? She despised the man's callous cruelty and taciturn nature. He was nothing more than a brute, the vile descendant of a savage race who had harried her ancestors in France for decades. If only she had never married Robert, she would have never met William de Warenne. Her husband was a man with his own culpabilities, but she could not justify any comparison of his behavior to that of the Earl of Surrey. They were different and her husband remained the better man.

With her husband's permission, Isabel escaped the festivities once a dancing bear arrived. Robert waved her away, his gaze on the king's table. Her husband seemed desirous to speak with Henry and she obliged him gladly. As she left her seat, her stare found Amieria across the room. The younger woman's brilliant gaze answered the silent question Isabel sought to communicate. Amieria spoke in turn to the ladies who had accompanied her. Isabel tried to hide a smile as she exited the room. With a sigh, she paced just outside the entryway. She did not dare peek inside, lest Earl William notice her. If the guards stationed beyond the hall observed her behavior, she did not care what they thought.

"Comtesse Isabel?"

Isabel halted and turned at the plaintive voice behind her. Amieria stood before her at last, more beauteous than ever upon closer inspection. Isabel thought herself a poor companion to this younger, more exquisite vision of womanhood. She pushed such morose beliefs aside and flung her arms wide. As she anticipated, Amieria knelt at her feet and grasped her hands only, planting a light kiss on each.

"Oh, do stand! You must embrace me as a friend, dearest girl." She tugged Amieria up from the cold stone floor and hugged her. "In truth, you are no more a girl than I was when we first met. Instead, a lovely, radiant young woman has returned to the king's court. I have missed you so."

As they separated, Amieria giggled. "In truth, I feared you might not recognize me or you would think me presumptuous to have dared renew our friendship."

Isabel clasped her in a tight hold and laughed. "I am more pleased than I can say. My husband told me of your request. It gladdened my heart to know you have chosen me as your loyal companion."

She grasped Amieria's hand and urged her down the dimly lit passage, away from the raucous noise of the feast. "What of your lady mother? Does she enjoy the match the king ordained? Has she come to court with you?"

Amieria sobered and her gaze fell away. Isabel half-regretted her foray into the topic, which clearly distressed her young friend. "Oh, my dearest friend, you must forgive me if I asked too much too soon."

"You did not. I miss my mother. She knows only the comforts of her husband's manor and the four sons she has borne him. She is content in her life and has no wish to leave Kent for the king's court, even for my sake. In truth, my mother is concerned for the match the king has proposed. She does not wish it at all."

"You deserve happiness in a suitable marriage."

Amieria colored at the compliment. "I hope for it. Nothing in life is certain, including the course and length of my betrothal."

Isabel sensed the guardsmen's eager interest in Amieria and their conversation. She drew the younger woman around the corner and into the recesses of a shadowy alcove. When they saw it already occupied by a young knight entwined with his male paramour, Isabel hushed Amieria with a finger to her lips. Hand in hand, they crept away and made for the opposite end of the vestibule, which offered total privacy. Both dissolved in peals of shocked laughter, holding their bellies.

Amieria patted her cheeks, already colored pink. "Now you must see why my mother is so concerned. She considers the king's court a little more than a nest of fornicators and catamites, vipers and scandalmongers. She rightly thought I would need protection in this place."

"You believed a married woman would best guard your virtue? Does your betrothed already pose a danger to your maidenhood?" Isabel teased.

When her friend's blush deepened, Isabel regretted her loose tongue. "You must forgive me. The wine gives voice to imprudent thoughts."

"You have never spoken foolery in my hearing, only the truth. Therefore, I cannot lie to you, though you may think me shameless. Indeed, until I first saw my betrothed, I had never even noticed other men, though I shall admit several made their attentions to me very plain."

"I do not doubt it, for your beauty would make any man forget his courtesies. Tell me of this fortunate match you have made."

"*Maman* believed the king aims too high for me. She warned me nothing good would come of this union he has sought."

Isabel nodded. "My husband mentioned an impediment."

"Some concerns regarding the king's bloodline, not my origins. The king has never hidden my low birth. Besides, everyone at court can see how he has honored several of his natural children. Robert of Gloucester is a favored son. Archbishop Anselm raised the question of consanguinity. My mother has made her own inquiries on my behalf with the abbey at Montivilliers. Her half-sister Cecilia is the infirmaress there. My grandmother had retired there until her death three years ago."

"Your loss pains me, Amieria. You might have a grand future ahead of you if only Anselm would permit it. I do not fault your mother for her attention to your future but beauty such as yours should not remain cloistered and hidden away."

"The king agrees with you."

"You speak of his desires, yet tell me nothing of your own outlook. Do you want this man because union with him would favor you and your family's fortunes, or do you desire the man because he has shown himself worthy of you?"

When Amieria laughed, Isabel guessed at the young woman's budding feelings. Still, she kept her own counsel.

"Oh, Comtesse Isabel, I can hardly understand how he makes me feel. I do want the marriage and the man. The very sight of him robs me of my breath, even the ability to speak. He is handsome and powerful. The king had considered a match for me with him years ago, except the man sided with Duke Robert in the invasion of England. All talk of marriage ceased and I rejoined my mother in Kent. After the battle of Tinchebrai, the king returned to England during the Lenten season. He wrote to me, proposing the betrothal of years ago. Near this summer's end, he urged me to Winchester. I have been with him since then. My betrothed arrived at court weeks ago with a large retinue. His sister Edith is even more courteous than her brother, who has been generous and gallant at every encounter. Even if he had not been, I cannot deny our union would improve my family's fortunes simply by our association with an earl."

Isabel nodded absentmindedly. Amieria would be a countess. The king's aspirations for his illegitimate daughter rose higher than anyone might have expected. Such base thoughts left Isabel disgusted with herself. Instead of considering Amieria's advancement, her focus should have been on her friend's delight at the happy expectations for marriage. A union with an earl must have exceeded all of Amieria's hopes. Even more startling, the young woman appeared disposed toward the man.

Amieria asked, "Comtesse, are you troubled by my practical feelings about the matter?"

Isabel said, "Forgive my silence, my dear, I only contemplate the happiness your future may bring. I could not bear to see you married to anyone who did not deserve you. You are a dear friend. You may be the only one I shall ever have at court."

Amieria squeezed her fingers. "As you shall be mine."

Her beatific smile warmed Isabel's heart. Whomever she married must consider himself lucky to wed with such a treasure. When she charmed him and became the delight of his heart, there would be no concerns about her low birth or wealth. The king would grant her friend dower estates, sparing her the humiliation of entering marriage with little to offer than a closer connection between her husband and the sovereign of England.

No one had ever inspired such a feeling in Isabel, as her friend described, not even Robert for all his declarations at the beginning of their marriage. Stark reality had ruined whatever hope he might have once inspired. Now, she felt as if he tolerated her at best and saw her as little more than a brood mare for the bearing of his children. Although she did not wish it, Isabel felt some resentment of Amieria's happiness. What manner of man held the power to rob a woman of her speech and render her so discomfited in his presence?

A memory intruded, her sitting beside Earl William next to the fire in Vatteville's hall, while Lovvet bedded down between them. She banished the troublesome memory from her mind before taking Amieria's hand in hers again. Why should the earl concern her now, when the very thought of him remained as odious as the earl himself?

A niggling doubt entered her mind. Earl William was not married. He had once broken with the king, who later restored his holdings in England. The king could not have considered a union with the Earl of Surrey for his daughter. Amieria, the image of angelic perfection, could not suffer such a union. The very thought of Earl William's brutish hold upon such a genteel creature, his babe rooting at her breast, made Isabel bridle.

She glanced at Amieria. "You have not told me your betrothed's name. I know of all the earls, most of them wed or ones I would deem unsuitable choices for you by their boorish manners. Has the king created a new title? Who is this man who inspires your devotion and stirs your soul?"

Amieria said. "He is Earl William de Warenne of Surrey. His seat is at Castle Acre in Norfolk. Oh, I have said something this time to trouble you. Your face has paled."

Isabel released Amieria. "Earl William? The king cannot intend a union between you and such a base creature!"

Chapter Sixteen – The Betrothal
Winchester, England: June 1108

Isabel realized she had gone too far, as Amieria's gaze fell away. Amieria murmured, "I did not know you held such hate for him."

Isabel turned away and rubbed at a tight spot in her chest, while she fought for every breath. The possibility of Amieria's tender, sweet ways crushed under the dominion, the crass attentions of Earl William, disgusted her. Had King Henry taken leave of his senses? How could he consign his daughter to a union with such a barbarous man?

She returned her attention to Amieria, whose eyes glistened with unshed tears. "Forgive me. I spoke too harshly of your future happiness."

"You must know how much I value your good opinion of me. You must be aware of how much your kindness and friendship mean to me. When I first came to court, when everyone knew I was naught more than another of the king's bastards, you shielded me from the queen's slights. You were the only person who cared for me, despite the fault of my low birth. Have your feelings altered so quickly, now I am to marry the Earl of Surrey?"

Seeing her friend's misery and her pale and trembling lips, Isabel reached for her and pulled her into a tight embrace. Amieria's hot tears doused her neckline. Isabel held her and rubbed her shoulders until the young woman ceased crying.

"I only wished you might be happy for me," Amieria murmured. "I do not know how the earl has given offense. There must be some explanation, some means to ease your displeasure. Won't you even try, for my sake?"

Isabel could not ignore the plea shining in her friend's watery gaze. How could she allow Amieria to marry such a brute and not fear for the young woman's future?

"My dear, I first met the lord of Castle Acre after he had borne my husband to the ground during a melee, a bloody contest of arms. Robert required a dangerous surgery to repair his skull and bears the scars to this day. In our next encounter, the earl hunted on my husband's lands without permission. At every opportunity, he has shown bad manners and questionable judgment."

"He can also be kind. He told me of his gift of the alaunt, your Lovvet. Is she not with you at Winchester?"

Isabel could not escape the earl even in the reminders of her grief. "She is no longer living. I should be grateful for her life and easy passing. It does not mean I miss her any less."

"I am sorry for your loss."

"Thank you, Amieria. I cannot fathom why the earl would have spoken of Lovvet with you. I am surprised he mentioned our meeting and the gift at all."

"He claimed Lovvet was his best hunter. He gave her as a gift to you rather than take her life. When I begged the king to summon you to court as my companion, my betrothed approved. He thought well of you. He mentioned your brief encounters, including the hunting incident, which brought Lovvet to you. He even expressed some fear you might think him an unsuitable match for me. I laughed then, for he suits me in every way."

He does not! Isabel wanted to screech the words. She held her tongue. How could Amieria think such a prideful, brutal man would do for her, when she remained too gentle and good for such a fate as marriage to the earl? Amieria's youthful fancies conjured the image of a gallant, worthy suitor. Isabel recalled only the callous, boorish nature of the man.

Amieria grasped her hands again. "Please say you shall try to accept William for my sake. I have never desired anything more in my life than to be at his side. I would have my dearest friend support me."

Isabel sighed. How could she refuse such a tender entreaty?

A few days after her arrival at Winchester, Isabel stood with her fingers clasped, while Earl William's lengthy stride brought him closer to her.

Non, she admonished herself. He had come for Amieria, who waited beside Isabel, wringing her delicate hands. The earl had returned with the king's retinue of nobles from an early hunt. The sunlight cast a golden sheen upon his craggy features. He pushed his way through squires, who hefted the carcasses of roe and red deer between them. Young pages also carried fowl and rabbits to the kitchens for butchering and salting.

Amieria whispered, "He must have claimed many trophies today. Look at the blood upon him." Admiration filled her voice, rather than disgust.

Isabel mused, "I do not doubt he can slaughter a trapped animal with ease."

When a little sigh escaped Amieria, Isabel rebuked herself for her callous statement. Tolerating the earl had proved more difficult than she anticipated two weeks ago, after Amieria revealed the news of their betrothal. Still, Isabel bit her lip and dipped into a curtsy as expected. Amieria followed the gesture. She looked very fair in a russet robe, which matched the dried stains on the earl's *cotte* and short mantle.

Earl William greeted them. "A good day improves as I find both of you looking so well!"

Amieria blushed and Isabel said nothing while the earl bowed. Thick dark locks fell over his eyes. Since the days of King Henry's predecessor, the noblemen of England had abandoned the bluntly shorn style of their conquering forbearers. Most wore their hair at shoulder-length as Englishmen did, except a few like the Earl of Surrey, who preferred the old fashion.

While he stood towering, by comparison to the petite frames of Amieria and Isabel, his gaze swung between them before he nodded to the latter. "Forgive me. I am not fit for anyone's eyes in such a bloodied state."

Certain he meant the apology for Amieria, Isabel wondered why his gaze had flitted to hers as he spoke. Nonsense! Why would he have worried about his appearance or odor in front of her?

"Your return is a happy one, milord," Amieria murmured. "I am especially glad to know you are not hurt."

He glanced at her and nodded. "Not for lack of trying on a buck's part. He gored a dog in an attempt at my life. His Grace's chief huntsman took the deer down. I am in the man's debt."

Isabel looked past the earl's bloodied figure to the king, seated on his horse and engrossed in conversation with Isabel's husband.

"Robert fared well in the hunt, though far less bloodied than I am," Earl William commented.

When his gaze caught Isabel's own, she huffed and looked away. She stared resolutely ahead, intent on ignoring him.

Why did he have to glare at her so? She wished he would not look upon her at all. He must know how much she disliked him. In fact, she grew increasingly sure he did it just to offend her. She had to govern her moods, free from his influence upon her thoughts and feelings.

She crossed her arms, fingertips tapping. "My husband is no savage."

Amieria gasped as her betrothed retorted, "You do not imply I am?"

His statement set her blood boiling. Only an ignorant oaf would not understand her deliberate insult. Amieria touched Isabel's shoulder. Earl William's mouth hardened in a thin line with each passing moment of silence. A tic pulsed at his temple. When Isabel realized how Amieria's fingers shook, she loosened her arms and grasped the young woman's hand in hers. For her friend's sake, she would bear the trial of the odious earl. She would also ensure he understood she was not some spineless simpleton.

She said, "When we first made our acquaintance years ago, you marked me for a girl who spoke without forethought. I have changed since then."

"I can see the physical improvements in you." His

gaze raked over her from head to toe. Before she could voice a comment about his insolent stare, he continued, "I am less certain how your moods have altered for the better. Your poor opinion of me over the years remains evident. Remind me of how I offended you from our first encounter."

"There is no need to speak of the past, please," Amieria whispered. Her eyes glittered with fearful tears, a silent plea meant for Isabel, as their mutual stares met and held. "I am sure the Comtesse de Meulan does not even remember."

The earl's rueful chuckle shattered the dour mood. "Amieria, the past yet governs us all. I cannot recall a time when Isabel has not made her displeasure with me well known. Now, I have found she is your dearest friend and you delight in her company, while she abhors mine. Your friendship with her shall endure throughout our marriage. I would not have my bride discomfited by her companion's poor views of me. I must know whatever I did to earn her ill regard." He nodded to Isabel. "Speak your complaints then."

"Complaints?"

"You must have several. I must seem a man of many faults in your view."

"All men and women have faults. It is those who do not strive to amend them who offend me."

He laughed again. "Am I irredeemable? Is there no hope for me? Should I be afraid of a litany of my poor behavior in the past, now spoken before my betrothed?"

Isabel glanced at her friend again. "Amieria has a sound mind, well-suited for forming its own opinions. I do not seek to influence her."

Earl William's mocking smile faded. "Come, then. Why are you so reluctant to speak of the past? If you have no fear of altering Lady Amieria's disposition, you cannot be worried I might bear you ill will. Men have called me worse than you might, Isabel."

"When first we met, you had borne my husband to the ground in the melee. You mocked my show of wifely duty to the husband whom I had newly married, when it is the province of a wife to show concern for her lord."

His black brows flared. "I earned your enmity for this petty offense?"

She shrunk from him and Amieria's light touch fell away. "I would not expect you to understand what you deem of little importance. Marriage to Robert meant more to me than you could ever have perceived! You do not know the cruelties I endured at Crépy-en-Valois. If Robert had died in the melee, you would have ruined my hopes.

"When you mocked me, my prior circumstances unknown to you, I marked you for a callous, indifferent man. You were clearly incapable of compassion. If your lance had taken Robert's life, I would have remained in the cruel clutches of a father who believed in chastising his children until they were bloodied and bruised. I bear the marks of hazel rods upon my back still. Union with Robert saved me."

Thin lines creased Earl William's forehead. His mouth slackened. "You love him."

Though he had not posed a question, she nodded. "I owe him my love and more."

His gaze slid away, though the tic still pulsed at his temple. "Then, forgive me now, Isabel. Accidents happen in the melee. I did not seek to cause you grief. I am not the heartless wretch you would deem me. If I seemed callous or indifferent in the past, it was never my intention to harm your interests. I would never hurt you."

His halting speech and kind words startled her. She blinked back sudden, foolish tears. "Forgiveness is not so easily won, milord."

"Then I shall do all I can to earn it." He dipped his head, dark locks falling over his eyes.

His solemn apology did not mollify her. Instead, her heart raced. Could she believe him? Why should it matter?

She realized she desperately needed to believe him,

for more than Amieria's sake. She sensed the turmoil within him and shied away from the thought she might have caused him some pain by speaking of her past.

He asked for the truth and she had provided it. Now, Amieria knew more of the nature of the man and might guard her heart against him. Would it have been better, less cruel to withhold the truth? Isabel might have ruined all her friend's hopes now. Dear God, what had she done?

Her mortification grew as she realized a lull descended over the king and Robert's conversation. Her husband's blue eyes focused on Earl William. Unmindful of his audience, the Earl of Surrey had straightened and watched her again as a man starved for something more than her good approval.

She weighed all the possibilities for his obvious interest in her and dismissed the most tantalizing one. She could not allow herself to consider that William wanted her for himself. He belonged to Amieria.

She curtsied. "I'll see to my husband now."

Her friend returned the gesture. "I hope you may believe the earl's earnest nature in time."

Isabel kept her silence before she left the steps, joining Robert and the king. She curtsied before both men. "Your Grace. Husband. I trust you both enjoyed the hunt."

While the king nodded, she concentrated on Robert's expression. She reached for the reins of his palfrey. The bay stallion shied away and nickered. The mount's fickle mood mirrored Robert's own. Her husband's frigid stare alighted on her and pinned her to the spot. She swayed as though her legs might give out from under her. Somehow, she stayed upright.

Anger etched itself in the craggy lines of Robert's hardened features. "You seemed engrossed in conversation with William de Warenne, my dear."

"You have not forgotten I am Amieria's companion and the earl is her betrothed?"

"I have forgotten nothing." He minced every word.

She reached for his fingers, seeking to soothe his obvious displeasure.

"See you do not either, milady." Robert jerked the reins and cantered his horse toward the stables. She stared at his retreating figure. Robert was jealous. She had never anticipated he might be. He could not think she invited William's eyes upon her!

"What do you make of the man?" The king's unexpected question drew Isabel's attention from her husband.

"Forgive me, Your Grace, but I do not understand."

With an impatient nod toward the steps, King Henry posed his inquiry again. "Do you believe William shall do for my Amieria?"

She avoided the dark gaze of the monarch. "I do not think I should judge the Earl of Surrey. Only Your Grace's opinion of the man matters now. You have deemed him worthy of Amieria. She does as you have bid, not only because you are king of England. It is a sign of her devotion."

After the space of a few breaths, Isabel dared a glance at him. His visage revealed nothing, not even his opinion of her comments. Then he nodded. "She is dutiful and respectful, more than some of my other bastards."

Isabel winced at his casual reference to Amieria's birth. "Your faith in her is not misplaced. She has the wisdom to recognize the great boon this marriage offers to her and her family. The earl would never risk your displeasure, Your Grace."

Henry snapped, "You forget how he first supported Curthose against me!"

"For which you would have forgiven him had his men not attacked English people. He supported you thereafter at Tinchebrai."

"You have obviously never heard his name for me, when I was a prince of England. He called me 'stag foot' for my aptitude in the hunt. William said my knowledge of the tines in a stag's antlers marked me better for a huntsman's son than an heir of the Conqueror."

Isabel lowered her gaze, fearing she might laugh as well. *Pied-de-cref*—she should have guessed the earl's daring extended to ridiculing a future king of England, although William could not have guessed Henry would one day rule the realm.

The lapse annoyed her. She could not allow thoughts of him in such familiar terms as to use his Christian name. The man was no friend of hers. Besides, he had roused her husband's jealousy.

She said, "Your Grace cannot hold the follies of youth against the earl. I am certain Amieria shall lack for nothing as his countess."

As she spoke, Isabel studied the couple with their heads bent close together. Adoration shone in Amieria's gaze. A smile teased at the corners of the earl's mouth before a chuckle emitted from his chest. His intended touched his forearm, unconcerned for the blood staining his garment. He covered her thin fingers with his larger hand.

Isabel heaved a long sigh. The earl would esteem Amieria as his companion and make her happy. As her friend, Isabel would learn to accept the match and enjoy Amieria's good fortune.

While the court prepared for the midday feast, Isabel fretted as Petronilla laced her into her robe. "The strings are crooked! You simply must redo them. Would you have me appear in the guise of the king's fool?"

"I would not, milady," Isabel's attendant whispered. She fumbled with the lacings at the side of the robe. Her fingers shook.

"What is the matter with you, Petronilla? First, you neglect to tell me Robert would dine alone with the king, though in truth, I should not blame you when my husband is at fault. Then you spill some foul-smelling concoction you were drinking on your robe, which you have ruined. Now, your hands are unsteady. What ails you?"

"Forgive me, milady. I am not myself today,"

Petronilla replied with a soft sniffle.

"Certainly not! You give no true answer. Why are you troubled?" Isabel turned and stilled Petronilla's hands. "Mercy, your fingers are as cold as morning frost. Are you in poor health?" She immediately loosened her hold, lest whatever Petronilla's malady or ill humor overcome her.

The maidservant hung her head. "I am not, milady."

Isabel took in Petronilla's puffy, wan cheeks. "Then why won't you look at me? Something ails you." Then she slapped a hand to her forehead. "Do not tell me you weep for FitzRobert's absence? He has escorted my children to Leicester at their father's behest. Your parting from him cannot be of such long duration as to sour your mood."

"He is lost to me forever." Petronilla pulled away and sobbed behind her hands.

Now certain of the source of trouble, Isabel reached for Petronilla's fingers. The woman shied away from her furtive touch.

Isabel pitied and envied her attendant's ability to choose the man she loved. "I understand your plight. My husband has arranged matters for his former squire. FitzRobert marries a woman of his father's choosing. He still loves you."

Petronilla cried harder, if such were possible and sank down to the floor. Her piteous wails echoed against the walls. Isabel turned away and brushed at her own tears. She had rehearsed the conversation with her husband about Petronilla and FitzRobert numerous times before arriving in Winchester. Lingering concern for Amieria's union with Earl William had distracted her from the goal.

How could Robert be so cruel or blind to the sentiments his own son bore Petronilla? How could he subject both of them to such misery? They deserved each other. How could Robert expect them to bear living apart forever? Fate's cruel jest had brought them together, only to deny them happiness. Was this to be the pathetic end of all Petronilla's hopes?

"I cannot let this be. Your sorrow moves me. I shall speak with my husband after he has dined with the king. Robert must see the love FitzRobert bears you."

Petronilla lifted her tear-stained face, her gaze wide and searching. Then her lips thinned. "What does the Comte de Meulan care for my happiness or for his bastard? I am a penniless, landless wretch. He sought an heiress for his son. He has found her. What do I have to offer FitzRobert? My hands can sew and clean, but they are empty. I have no gold, jewels or promises of riches to come. I have no lands."

Isabel crouched before her maidservant, disregarding the stains that would mar her own robe. "You cannot give up hope. It has not forsaken you. Nor has FitzRobert."

"He does as his lord bids him. When FitzRobert spoke of his future, I begged him to consider abandoning this life. We could have run away together. He is a worthy knight. Any lord would have taken him in."

"You would have abandoned your life here, knowing you would have faced my husband's wrath? Robert would never let FitzRobert leave his service, especially after my husband had arranged matters to his liking. Where do you think you could have escaped without Robert finding you? None in England or Normandy would dare risk his ire by sheltering you."

"Your husband cannot make claim to the entire world. There are lords of Outremer who require men-at-arms. How often did we offer travelers sojourn at Vatteville who spoke of their intention to take the cross or pledge their swords to the masters of castles in the Holy Land? FitzRobert could have made his way by Messina, offering his sword to any lord who would have him."

Isabel clutched Petronilla's hands. "Would you have shared in his miserable existence as a mercenary, the lowest sort of man, one who does the command of any lord who offers him enough coin? Would you have suffered his life as a despoiler of the Church and women? What would you have been to FitzRobert? His *leman?* Mother to his bastards? He could not have offered you marriage in his lowly circumstances."

Petronilla wrenched her fingers from Isabel's grasp. "What do I care for marriage? I already carry his child in me! Now FitzRobert has abandoned both of us. He shall not have cause for concern afterward. There will be no bastard for a bastard."

She clutched her robe between her thighs. A loud groan escaped her. "My babe shall be spared the shame, even if I may not be so blessed."

"How? What have you done?"

A lopsided grin vied with Petronilla's sullen tears. "Wulfwyn would have helped me, if she had been here. I did what I had to do, for my child's sake."

Isabel looked to the discarded, empty cup perched on the windowsill. A chill ran through her. She pulled Petronilla's hand away. A growing dark stain seeped through the maidservant's garments and blood coated her fingertips.

On wooden legs, Isabel entered the deserted minstrels' gallery at Winchester Castle. A draft seeped through chinks in the masonry and rustled the wall hangings. Dampness pervaded the dank air, even seeping through Isabel's hooded mantle and the soiled robe beneath it. Two torches revealed her husband and Brother Thorold standing in close conference. When Robert saw her, he abandoned the monk.

"She must leave your service, Isabel. A woman of such loose morals cannot remain within our household as your servant."

Isabel sagged against the balustrade. "You need not fear for Petronilla's morals, Robert. God has already passed his judgment. The poison she took to rob the child of its life has claimed hers. She bled for hours. The midwife could do nothing for her."

Thorold made the sign of the cross and came to

Robert. He pressed an age-spotted hand against his shoulder. "Thanks be to God. The taint of her shame cannot touch you. It need not go further than this wretched night. God's justice is done."

Isabel gasped at his callousness before she covered her face with her fingers.

"Do not weep for her!" Robert demanded. "She was a whore who strove against God's will, who sought to rise above her rank and burden FitzRobert with her bastard."

Isabel lowered her hands. "As you were burdened when he was born? Such concerns could not have troubled you in the getting of him. When you fathered Sieur Miles, FitzRobert, or any of your bastards, did you give any concern to the shame their mothers might face? You thought only of a man's pleasure. Not one care for the women who bore the consequences of your lust."

Robert yanked Isabel hard against him. When he raised his hand, she flinched.

"Do your worst, husband. My own parents chastised me more than you ever could. I thought you might be a better man than my father had been. He never acknowledged his bastards. I see you are also cold and unfeeling for the plight of your natural children. FitzRobert loved Petronilla as much as he loves you. You have torn his heart asunder. I do not blame him for what has happened. The fault is yours, milord. You shall never have my forgiveness in this, Robert, never."

He shoved her away from him and she fell. As she hit the wooden railing, a jarring pain flared across her hip. She clutched her side while Robert knelt, his features masked in a tight grimace.

"You forsake the vows of duty and obedience. I should remind you of them now. I have vowed you shall never suffer at my hands, even if you deserve it. As I have dominion over you, Isabel, remember all within my household reside there by my pleasure. I could have had the fool woman cast out years ago, when I knew of her perfidy with FitzRobert. How long do you suppose she has been letting him spill his seed inside her? Weeks or months? For years since she first accompanied you to England! She could not root out the babe as she has done in the past."

Isabel recoiled from him in horror. "Petronilla has never been with child before! I would have known! She was never far from my side. I would have recognized the symptoms."

Memories bedeviled her, of days when Petronilla took no food. At times, she had complained of an unsettled stomach and withdrawn to her pallet with excuses regarding her monthly show of blood. Rare days during which Isabel never questioned her maidservant's condition.

Had everything been a lie? She had a surfeit of people in her life who kept secrets from her. She had once thought she knew Petronilla best of all. The maidservant had deceived her.

Robert added, "I spared her and that English wise woman the king's justice for your sake. Henry's laws would have seen them both excommunicated for life."

Brother Thorold moved beside her husband. "God reveals all our sins. There is nothing we may hide from Him."

Robert grasped her chin. "She kept her licentious behavior from you. Thorold kept me apprised of all her activities, including her occasional visits to the midwife at Leicester. FitzRobert's dalliance with her did not offend me. I would not have cared if it had continued after his marriage. The whore should have known better than to encumber herself with yet another baseborn child, when she lacked the usual means to rid herself of it. God's wrath fell upon her. She is damned to hellfire, with the souls of those babes whom she robbed of life."

Isabel pulled away from him, even as he commanded, "To bed. The hour is late. We shall put this folly behind us. You have other servants in our household whom you may rely upon."

When he stood and offered his hand, she stared at him, aghast. "How can you be so cruel? You cannot be the same man I married.”

Robert scoffed. “My good humor remains reserved for those who deserve it. Your maidservant warranted no such kindness. You no longer bear the burden of her deceit. Find another to replace her. You'll soon forget her.”

“Never!”

“So be it. Remain in this dank hall and mourn her loss if you must. I seek the comfort of my bed and the coming dawn, which shall remove all trace of this night's stupidity. Come, Thorold.”

The monk stared in silence at Isabel before he followed Robert's lead.

She crawled away and secreted herself behind a column. She did not know how long she remained on the floor of the gallery with the cold seeping through her clothing. The retainers and servants of the castle returned to the hall below and sought their rest. The torches faded and snores echoed to the rafters of the gallery. Isabel drew up her knees and rested her elbows upon them. She never stirred, even when a mouse darted across her feet.

Later, footsteps resounded and a low whisper drifted over her. “Great God, have you been here all night?”

Strong arms cradled her body and encased her in comforting warmth. She burrowed her face in a woolen mantle, hardly caring for the impropriety. Exhaustion and grief weighed her limbs.

A strong hand caressed along her spine through her garments, before its owner said, “Tell me what ails you.”

She met the Earl of Surrey's dark stare. He sat on a stone bench carved from the wall beside a tiny window. She occupied his lap.

“Why must you always find me at my worst?” she whispered. “You have no right to hold me. Release me.”

“Not until you tell me why you are here alone at this time of night.”

“I could ask you the same.”

“I spent the evening with my sister. Edith suffers

cruelly from the loss of another babe."

Isabel lowered her gaze. "Please, I cannot bear hearing of another woman's tragedy. It is too much."

His hand cupped her cheek. "Do you care so little for others, for my sister's pains? You do not even ask after her welfare."

"I comforted your sister once, after similar circumstances had befallen her. If I make no inquiry now, it is because I know another who—" Her voice trailed off and she struggled against his hold. "Let me go. Someone might discover us together. Would you have the gossipmongers awaken only to whisper lies? Do you care nothing for your betrothed?"

He chuckled, a hollow and mirthless sound. His thumb stroked her flesh. "I do care for the lady. I am no fool. Any man would judge Amieria worthy of the honor of marriage, no matter her origins. I shall wed and strive with all my power to make her happy, even as I languish, my heart always in the keeping of another."

She pushed against his chest, a useless gesture. "You speak of a woman who is not your betrothed? You disgust me. Get away or I shall scream."

He leaned closer. A mocking smile curved his lips. "I doubt it. You fear rousing the suspicions of others sleeping below. Why should I release you when I have long desired nothing more than to hold you in my arms?"

A horrified gasp escaped her. He dragged her hand to where his heart thrummed beneath the mantle and *cotte*. "My torment has only grown over the years. To have you near, the dearest friend of one whom I must marry, is a grievous wound. You have pierced my heart and soul."

"You're mad!"

His smile widened. "If it is madness to think of you every day and dream of you every night, then I am forever in the throes of insanity. There is no hope for me. I shall never have your heart as you have held mine."

Her struggles renewed against him. He withdrew his touch with a sigh. She almost slid off his lap and scrambled away from him. His wistful look followed and pinned her to the spot.

Rage coursed through her body. "You are a lecher, the worst sort of man I have ever known! Duty binds me to my husband. For honor's sake, I would never betray the only person I may call a friend in England. Never touch me again!"

When he rose, she stumbled backward. He bowed before her and left the gallery.

She drew the hood of her mantle over her head. As she turned, a soft snigger echoed. She leaned over the railing. A sentry eyed her from his post below. His knowing leer hastened her departure.

Chapter Seventeen – The Meeting upon the Stairs
Winchester, England: July 1108

Isabel waited in the bailey of Winchester Castle while Robert mounted his horse before she joined him. She clutched his hand, despite the rough links of his mail glove cutting into her palm. "I pray you shall go with God, milord and return to us soon."

He looked down at her, his lips a thin, resolute line. His gaze had turned cloudy in recent weeks, yet she saw the mistrust and anger reflected in his eyes. "Brother Thorold shall remain here. I would have him speak with Faritius of Abingdon regarding the education of our eldest sons."

She refused to acknowledge the Benedictine, who stood atop the highest step from the castle, though the tingling along her spine warned her of his steady glare. "You would choose Faritius? His duties as the queen's physician claim all his attention."

"The queen is not in ill health requiring the hourly attendance of the abbot."

She licked at her dry lips. "As you say, milord. It would be a great honor. I shall send word of his answer while you are in Normandy."

Robert concentrated on her mouth again before he spoke. "Thorold may tell me himself in his letters. Besides, you have one task now. You must keep Henry's daughter entertained, especially in the absence of her suitor."

She lifted her gaze. "His absence? Is William de Warenne joining the king's retinue?" She hated how her mouth quivered as she spoke his wretched name. The earl had proven himself a lustful, deceitful cur. He wanted to take her away from her husband and ruin the vows she still held sacred. His sudden departure should have pleased her, yet tremors shook her hands so much, she clasped them tightly and stilled the furtive movement.

Robert's mailed hand closed on hers. She winced as

the chain links indented her flesh. He asked, "Did you not know of his leave-taking today?"

"Why should I have known? Amieria does not report on the earl's actions, nor do I care to know them."

Robert studied her in silence. A heavy weight settled on her chest and tightened.

"I thought for certain he must have shared something of his plans with you when you have chanced to meet with him alone."

"I have not sought him out."

"You have not?"

"Never! Robert, I do not like your meaning."

"I like it even less that the earl should have offered comfort in your distress over the whore Petronilla. Do you deny it? Think carefully, Isabel, before you speak a falsehood. If you lie to me now, I shall never forgive you."

He knew. Somehow, Robert knew of the night in the minstrels' gallery where the earl had accosted her. He must think the worst of her now because of it.

"I have no reason to lie. The Earl of Surrey did seek to comfort me, after you had forsaken me." Her voice warbled and she despised herself for it. "After you abandoned me to misery that night, the earl found me. We did not speak of his plans. I swear, Robert."

Her husband released his grip. She stared at the reddened marks dotting her palm, fearing her cheeks betrayed the same color under his intense scrutiny.

"Be mindful of your duties in my absence, Isabel and be wary of all else." He jerked the reins of his horse and joined the king, who spoke with his chaplain, Bishop Roger of Salisbury.

Their cold and solemn parting dismayed her. She would have dared run to him with promises of her enduring loyalty and faithfulness. The spectacle of Earl William stopped her short.

He strode beside his constable. Both men led their mounts, so engrossed in conversation Isabel could observe them unnoticed. Behind them trailed Amieria

273

and William's sister, Edith. The closeness of the women, locked arm-in-arm and laughing together, drew a huff from Isabel before she reproached herself. She should not be so resentful of their friendship. Amieria would marry Edith's brother. An affable young woman should enjoy good relations with the sister of her future husband. Why should the camaraderie between the women bother Isabel at all? She begrudged Amieria nothing, least of all the friendship of any other woman, even one related to William de Warenne.

Amieria spied Isabel and moved toward her, still in the grip of Edith's arm. The pair curtsied before Isabel, who returned the gesture. "Lady Edith, I pray you travel in safety to your lands in Normandy."

Edith smiled. "I trust the royal retinue shall protect us. Afterward, I may rely on my brother and his guards. William would shield me with his life against all dangers."

Isabel glanced at the earl who still spoke with his constable. "I envy you a devoted brother."

Edith replied, "I fear you have had ample reason to judge him harshly in the past. I assure you William is not a cruel man. If he was, he would not have won the heart of our dear Amieria."

Amieria blushed and said to William's sister, "I shall miss the chance to know you better now. When I am married, we shall have many opportunities. As much as your departure pains me, I shall be pleased when your brother returns to England."

Edith kissed the younger woman's cheek and hugged her again. "Do not worry." She looked over Amieria's shoulder at Isabel and murmured, "I shall not keep him from his heart's sole desire for long."

Her dark gaze locked with Isabel's frozen stare. Something in the depths of Edith's eyes conveyed adamant purpose before she released Amieria and walked toward her brother, leaving Isabel confused.

Amieria took Isabel's arm as she had done Edith's own. "I shall miss them equally. Your husband must also return soon."

"May it be," Isabel whispered.

Edith tapped her brother's shoulder. He turned from Rudolf, a smile for his sister transforming his grim-faced visage into a more youthful expression. He cupped his hands and boosted Edith on to her mount. She looked down at him with a grin and smoothed a forelock of his dark hair from his brow. He clutched her hand and pressed it to his lips.

Isabel had never expected such a tender display from the earl. She struggled mightily against the tears, her nerves frayed. When she blinked, the spell shattered, as Earl William and his men mounted their horses in response to the king's command.

Why should it matter what he did with his sister or any other woman? Isabel wished for nothing more than for him to leave, for a respite from the man and his betrayal. Amieria had given her heart to him, not knowing of his worthlessness. He did not deserve the girl's love. Could Isabel ever reveal the truth of his deceit? Could she risk hurting her friend?

She knew she could not do it. Amieria deserved the knowledge the earl did not love her, but it would kill her soul if she ever learned whom William wanted instead.

She could only guess at whether Amieria would believe or deem it a lie. Would she think less of Isabel, fearing she had deliberately sought to steal the only man Amieria had ever desired? Isabel did not want his love! It shamed her and humiliated them both.

No possibility of a liaison between her and Earl William could form in her mind. She belonged to Robert, body and heart, as Amieria would become bound to her betrothed in matrimony. His passionate declaration had left Isabel stunned and confused. She knew where her loyalty should lie. Robert had saved her from a miserable childhood, given her children and a life with him. For the sake of those gifts alone, she could never forsake him, no matter how he disappointed her and shattered her illusions of hope.

Try as she might, she could not dismiss the earl's adulterous vow from her mind. He had even shown a tender side when he offered comfort after her husband shunned her misery. She recalled how he had scooped her up in the minstrels' gallery, after she sat mired in sorrow over Petronilla's choices. Even when he goaded her to anger, she felt exhilarated by the challenge of arguing against his ignorant assumptions and shocking behavior. He emboldened her, whereas Robert sought only to bend her to his will. Another man offered what she could never have with Robert—a strong sense of herself and an even greater feeling of liberty. Only when she was with him did she feel at ease to speak her mind without fear of the consequences.

How could it be that a man who was not her husband offered her freedoms long denied? William should mean nothing to her. She had always hated him, had she not? *Non*, that was not the truth.

The sudden realization made her sway. He had always stirred powerful emotions within her. She could no longer attribute them solely to disgust.

Amieria clutched her side. "Are you unwell? Do not cry. Your husband will not leave you for long. You'll see him soon."

As the younger woman touched her cheek and held her gaze, Isabel saw her wretched, pale features reflected in Amieria's eyes. If only Amieria knew the source of her misery. Isabel promised to hold the secret from her forever, lest she burden such a tender heart with troubles, as Isabel's own had suffered since William's passionate declaration.

She swiped at her eyes and stared straight ahead. A column of noblemen and prelates, knights, men-at-arms and attendants on horseback followed the king from the bailey of Winchester Castle. Isabel lost sight of Robert as soon as his horse disappeared through the gatehouse.

Close to the edge of the column, William wheeled his palfrey around and looked to the steps. His gaze lingered as he raised a hand in salute. Amieria sniffled and waved to him.

Beside her, Isabel stared at the ground and did not look up again until her friend tugged her arm. "Shall we walk in the gardens and be of comfort to each other?"

Isabel nodded, knowing she would not find relief from her own jumbled emotions. The earl had meant the salute for Amieria. He intended his stare for Isabel alone. She had been the recipient of his lingering looks too many times to remain ignorant of their meaning now.

Winchester, England: December 1108 to January 1109

The first dreary days of winter found Isabel often alone at Winchester Castle. She should have withdrawn to Robert's manor in the town. Her eldest sons Waleran and Robert had arrived from Leicester at the start of December, in the company of Isabel's new personal attendants, Beatrice and Mabel. The boys began their tutelage under the abbot Faritius and their mother saw precious little of them except for a few hours at night and early in the morning when she awoke. At the manor, she would not have seen them at all.

The company of Beatrice and Mabel offered no comfort. Both women lacked the warmth of Petronilla and had never inspired the same confidence. They each claimed Meulan as a birthplace, where they had toiled as servants in the castle for over thirty years. One look into their familiar visages and ice-blue eyes warned Isabel the women could have claimed her husband as a father. She never questioned the women and they never volunteered the truth about their mutual heritages. Isabel knew the facts instinctively.

After the feast of Epiphany, at the behest of her mother, Amieria had returned to Kent. Likely, she had sought refuge from the queen's silent yet disdainful stares and despaired of her betrothed's return after some unexplained business kept him absent. After a seventh week without her friend, Isabel wondered whether

Amieria had forgotten her.

God afforded her one small mercy. She saw little of Brother Thorold, as he often kept watch over her sons and preferred the company of Faritius of Abingdon. Isabel did not doubt Robert had left Thorold as his spy.

Forlorn, she waved her attendants away and planned to wander the castle grounds. The court dined at the usual hour of midday. Isabel donned a fur-lined mantle and escaped via the stairs above an enclosed garden at Winchester. She trod a slow, gloomy descent and halted in mid-step at the second landing. Earl William, she chided herself, came up the same steps in lengthy strides. His stare widened as hers must have done.

An indigo-colored mantle draped across his shoulders and trailed to his feet. Dark hair fell over his black brows and a thick moustache almost obscured his lips. She would have recognized him anywhere by the wild staccato flutters within her heart.

She drew in a deep breath and stifled her inner response. "You have returned. Amieria remains in Kent. Did you visit with her?"

"You do not partake at dinner. Why?" He ignored her question, a frown of concern crinkling his brow.

His brazen interest in her and disregard for his future bride shocked Isabel still. After long months since his departure, he did not offer a word in greeting, only impertinent questions. Despite his betrayal of Amieria, she must remain civil with him for her friend's sake.

He closed the distance between them, until he occupied the step just below hers. "Are you ill, Isabel? Your cheeks are pale. You are shaking."

When he raised his hand to her face, she brushed his cool fingers aside. "Do not touch me. My health is not your concern."

"As usual, you find no pleasure in my company," he mused with a sardonic smile.

A knot formed in her stomach and grew with each steady intake of breath. "Did you hold the expectation? Why should you have believed I languished here awaiting your return? You mistake me for your betrothed. Have you given one thought to her in these long months?"

"She sent word to me of her departure to Kent. When the king comes again, she shall join me."

"Then by the Grace of God, I pray you may marry her and depart soon."

"Is it your heart's desire, to be so far from me?"

"You are betrothed!" She could have stomped her foot in frustration, if fear of the slick stairs had not impeded her. He remained as reckless with his declarations as he was with his betrothed's obvious feelings. If Amieria could not see his true nature, how little he cared for her, then she was a fool and deserved him. A deep, pained breath escaped her, filled with self-recrimination. She would not be the cause of Amieria's pain and should not disdain the girl for her lack of knowledge about William's inclinations.

He grasped her hand. "I have not forgotten. You must know my heart. I have never lied to you before and cannot do so now, even if it pains you. I do not love Amieria. I love you, Isabel."

Her heart pitched. Aghast, she would have struck him. His hold tightened.

"Let me go, milord."

"William. You never say my Christian name."

"It suggests familiarity between us when there is none." He could never know that she thought of him only in such terms now. "Release me, now."

"If only you might do the same for me." A wistful sigh escaped him. "You have claimed me."

Why must he say such dangerous words? "I do not want you! You forget yourself and who I am."

"I cannot forget you are the Comtesse de Meulan, wife to Robert. I bring word of your husband even now."

Despite the bruising pressure of his fingers, her struggles ceased. His mention of Robert sobered her frazzled state in an instant. "What news?" A harsh breath escaped her. "Speak! Has something happened to him?"

"Your cousin, King Louis of France, has pillaged Robert's border estates."

She covered her mouth before lowering her hand. "He has not dared! Why has Louis done this?"

"The French king has no claim against your husband. Rather, King Henry has drawn Louis' ire by refusal of the usual demands for homage and castles. The king of France strikes out at your husband because Robert is Henry's chief counselor and Robert's lands are within your royal cousin's domain."

"How have you received word of these attacks?"

"Before I crossed the Channel, I was with the king and your husband."

"What does my husband intend? Robert cannot mean to avenge himself against my royal cousin."

"Would you have the French king pillage and destroy your husband's demesne while he does nothing?"

She glared at him. "Robert is not the man he might have been in his youth. I would not see him injured or meet his death in a battle against France."

"He'll do as he must. If Henry would have returned the castles along the Epte and done homage, Louis would not have struck out at Robert."

"You blame our king for these troubles, yet you hold no sympathy for the danger my husband faces. Are you so oblivious?"

"I do not doubt the courage of a hero of Senlac. My father raised me on tales of the bravery of the Conqueror's companions. Your husband has no need for my pity. He shall avenge himself on your cousin, despite what you may believe of diminished capacity in his advanced years."

"You admire Robert," she whispered, almost in awe at the realization.

"How could I not?" His dark gaze melded with hers. "His fortunes have advanced. The wealth he owns rivals what I gained upon my father's death. I admire and hate him, for he possesses the only thing I now covet. Your loyal heart."

She broke their mutual stares, her hand pressing on the wall. He raised the other he held and pressed her fingers to his cheek. Rough stubble chafed at her palm.

"You are impetuous, milord."

"I did not want this." His voice did not rise above a murmur. "If you only knew how I have fought against such sinful thoughts of you. For years, I believed it only a lustful envy of Robert's delight, petty jealousy of his happiness. I deceived myself. I have had women as fair as you are. None has ever rivaled your hold upon me. In every instance of our encounters, my feelings grow."

"What of your betrothed and the regard you should have for her?"

"In time, I am certain she shall endear herself to me. I have admired her beauty and her sweetness of spirit, while desiring the match only because she is Henry's daughter. I have never loved her. I do not know if it is possible. All I know is you."

She glanced at him, wordless. He stepped closer until little space remained to draw breath between them.

"My dear, sweet Isabel, you are the only woman I have ever loved. I shall worship you until I draw my last breath."

She swayed and her knees wobbled. The steady knot in her belly tightened. "Amieria does not deserve your faithlessness." Her voice shook.

"None of us deserves this folly. Your friend is doomed to a mockery of a marriage, while I must forever mourn your absence from my arms. You hate me. My betrothed is your dearest companion. Would that God could look down and release us from this misery."

"There is no such hope. I cannot remain here, knowing you harbor such feelings for me."

He lifted her hand, fingers closing on hers again. "You believe me in my love?"

"You must see the impossibility of your wishes. My husband commands my fealty. I owe all to him. I cannot betray him, no more than I could forsake the bonds of friendship with Amieria."

"Then tell me the truth and it may ease my pains. Tell me you despise me above all others and there is nothing worse in the world you might imagine than being the object of my affections. Tell me you could never love me as you have loved your husband."

A teardrop spilled upon her cheek, followed by another. He released her, yet reached for her face. He stroked the tears away with his thumb. "Say it, Isabel."

"Why must you press me for the truth when you know it? Must I be cruel, so you could claim it as a kindness?"

A rueful laugh rumbled his chest. "I have despaired of your kindness. Shall I force my attentions upon you in the hope you may fully express your loathing?"

He joined her on the step suddenly and forced her against the stonework, his arms braced, palms flat on either side of her head.

She twisted and steadied herself against the wall, shaking her head. "Do not do this, William."

"You say my name at last. It fills me with the same hope I once carried, anticipation you would whisper it one day in a moment of passion."

"It is false hope! I do not desire you."

Perched precariously on the stairs, she could not dispel the shaking in her limbs, as he leaned closer and dipped his head. "Show me! Strike me or spit in my face if you must. I shall have the final proof of your hatred."

He cupped her neck and pressed his body against hers. Delicious warmth radiated from him and chased away the cold. "Tell me, Isabel. Tell me you feel nothing for me."

Her throat tightened as if robbed of speech. His fingers caressed her skin even as he pulled her closer. He would kiss her and she would let him. His lips hovered just beyond her reach. She only had to give in to the desire in his tremulous voice. It would be so easy, effortless.

"Isabel?" A final warning laced his guttural tone.

"I cannot!" Her scream echoed. She pressed a trembling hand to her mouth as if it would hold back the terrible truth. "God, forgive me, I cannot speak the lie."

She sagged as his lips pressed against her brow. His arms came about her, encasing her in his solid embrace. "Then we are both fools." She surrendered to him in full as he braced her with all his might when she would have fallen at his feet, weeping.

She sobbed against his neck, her heart hammering. He rubbed her back and murmured to her. If he meant to offer comfort, his gestures only pained her more. How had she allowed him past her heart's defenses? At last, she recognized that he had always been there, since their meeting at Vatteville, where he offered Lovvet. His obvious attraction for Isabel had long awakened and stirred something inside her that Robert had never touched. The desire to love and to share love with another beyond a sense of duty, or what was right or honorable. She could not deny William's feelings or her own any longer.

When she looked up, he cupped her wet face in his hands. "Come with me to Castle Acre, now. I shall claim you for my own. Not even your husband or King Henry's wrath would stop me."

His impetuous vow should have frightened her. It did not. Instead, a thrill raced through her. She could have laughed through her useless tears.

"You cannot mean it! Have you lost your senses and your heart before me? The scandal would destroy us both."

She slid her hand between their bodies, beneath his mantle and pressed the point where his heart pounded, strong and steady. "I cannot leave with you. Nor can I forsake my marital bonds and sin with my body as I would in my heart."

When he would have spoken, her forefinger against his lips stilled him. "I may have betrayed Robert and Amieria's friendship this day. I cannot commit adultery. Duty compels us. I remain bound to my husband and you to the king's wishes for his daughter. Whatever I may feel for you, I cannot injure Robert or Amieria. They must never know of this betrayal. It would destroy them, as it would doom us."

Voices and a feminine laugh drifted down the stairs. She cupped his cheek. "Release me if you love me, William. You must do it now or risk our ruin."

"One day, I shall have all I desire of you." He grasped her hand and placed a firm kiss against her palm before he hastened up the steps.

Isabel pressed her hand against the wall while continuing down the steps and through a doorway. Thick white vapor greeted her, enshrouding the bushes and trees. At her first step in the frost-covered garden, a heavy sob escaped her. Tears would not help her undo the day's madness. She stumbled on the protruding root of a withered tree and crumbled against it. After a short time, the rough bark bit into her back and the rime penetrated her cloak.

She felt more a fool than William. He had never hidden his attraction for her since he first came to Vatteville, while she strove in vain against him. She could not pretend now. She knew her own heart. It did not love him, yet he stirred deep feelings from its depths. He always had. Somehow, she must keep them at bay. They would bring about the ruination of those whom she loved. She had betrayed her husband and Amieria, in spoken word, if not in deed. Her traitorous sentiments were enough to damn her to hellfire forever. How could she remain Amieria's faithful friend when William would one day be her husband? How could Robert ever hold dominion over her heart again if William now claimed part of it?

A black shape parted the mist. She pressed against the tree in horror.

Brother Thorold bowed before her, his tonsured head appeared disembodied. "I find you all alone on the cold ground. Why are your attendants absent? I wish you would get up. It would pain the Comte de Meulan so much if you caught your death from cold and died."

With steady, even breaths she regained her composure and stood. She would not allow him to tower over her with his condescending tone. "Do not think me a fool, Thorold. You could care less for my health. You speak only for my husband's sake. Why are you here?"

"I sought you out."

"Why? When did my whereabouts suddenly become your concern, Thorold?"

"You were not at dinner. When I inquired, your attendants did not know where you had gone. They said you had dismissed them. I caution you against such an ill-advised move ever again."

"Do we have reason to fear in the king's court? Henry's laws protect us. Besides, why should it matter if I had dismissed my servants? They are mine to command." Before she finished, she knew the truth. "I am wrong. They are your minions, spies, aren't they?"

Cold malice shimmered in the monk's unapologetic gaze. "They are not mine."

Isabel took a step closer. "Robert's then? Are they his daughters?"

Thorold hid his fingers in the voluminous sleeves of his Benedictine robe before he answered, "You know enough of your husband's children. Robert's seed is strong and all of his offspring bear a resemblance to him."

"Did my husband ask you and those women to spy upon me in his absence?"

The monk's thin eyebrows arched. "Does he have a reason to spy upon his devoted wife?"

She knew she would get no answers from Robert's clerk. Only her husband could explain whether the monk lingered for his sake. Robert could also verify the identity and role of her new attendants. She already anticipated his response. He no longer trusted her. Given her perfidy with William a moment ago, she could not blame Robert for his suspicions.

With a swipe along her mantle, she removed ice granules and dried, deadened leaves and bypassed the monk.

"Are you aware of William de Warenne's return?"

She froze. "More impertinent questions. Why should I be aware of the comings and goings of the Earl of Surrey? Is he my husband? Should I take note of every action he undertakes? I do not like your suggestion."

Thorold halted at her side, a cold sneer twisting his lips. "I did not mean to imply anything untoward. The earl entered the hall just before I left it. I had thought you were aware of his return, because of your closeness to his betrothed, of course. She is a friend of yours."

A scant distance separated her from Brother Thorold. It would have been so easy to raise her hand and strike him for his insolence. All at once, she became intensely aware of how her abhorrence of him had burdened her long years. Why did Robert trust this man and keep him underfoot? She had long surrendered all hope of the monk's dismissal. Robert would never give him up.

She said, "I do not have to suffer your insinuations. We have made our disdain for each other apparent from our first meeting. I believe you disliked me even before we ever met."

"You injure me."

"Spare me your falsehoods, Thorold. Artifice does not suit you, not when your very mood is perceptible. You have never held a good opinion of me. I share the same lack of regard for you and while I have my reasons, I do not know what I have ever done to earn your disapproval. Your opinions have rarely concerned me. They trouble me even less now, since I have duly borne your insufferable presence for all the years of my wedded life with Robert. After you have collected my sons from their lessons with the abbot of Abingdon, return them and keep far from me during the duration of our time at court."

His jawline hardened. Then he bowed. "As you say."

Westminster, England: June 1109

Five months later, Isabel stood beneath an eastward facing window in the great hall of Westminster. She blinked hard against a beam of sunlight. Across the room, Amieria sobbed piteously.

The king held his natural daughter in his arms and whispered soothing words to her. "Do not weep, my girl. Anselm is not the final authority. I shall take this matter to Paschal if I must."

Isabel's husband leaned against a wall beside her. He pushed away from it now. "The pope is not inclined toward a dispensation as he was for your parents' marriage, Your Grace. Paschal has a long, bitter memory. Anselm might have persuaded him, if the archbishop had viewed the union differently, if it had concerned the princess. You have Anselm's last letter before his death in April. He believed an insurmountable impendent existed in the proposed union between William, Earl of Surrey and the Lady Amieria, in the sixth and fourth degrees of consanguinity. The blood relations date back to the time of Gunnora, Duchess of Normandy, who was grandmother to Your Grace's grandfather, Robert the Magnificent."

"Don't lecture me about the ducal dynasty, Robert!" Henry snapped. "I know who Gunnora was! We all do. I do not need you to recite my family's heritage."

The comte bowed with a flourish. "Forgive my attempt, Your Grace."

Amieria's bitter cries echoed to the rafters. The king's soothing murmurs followed. Then he asked, "Have Anselm's clerks thoroughly researched both lineages?"

"All those present here share a kinship with the Duchess Gunnora, no less removed than mine." William's voice echoed from the southern boundary of the hall. "I do not doubt the archbishop's clerks discovered what my father told me as a boy. Our bloodline derives from Duchess Gunnora's siblings. I cannot marry the Lady Amieria under such circumstances."

"Then she shall have another husband," the king

said.

Isabel clutched her chest, stunned at Henry's pragmatism. The king could barter away the bride he would have given William to another, without regard for his daughter's opinions. He had the right. It did not lessen his callousness.

"Please, Your Grace," Amieria sniffled and murmured. "Let me return to Kent."

The king said, "Your mother would pack you off to Montivilliers with the rest of her family. Consider it carefully—a cloistered life where you'll never know the joy of your own children."

"I can learn to accept such a life, Your Grace. My grandmother did after her husband died. My aunt Cecilia has only known the abbey's walls and grounds. I will not suffer alone or without comfort. I shall seek refuge in prayer. Please, if you have any affection for me, as a loyal subject of your realm, let me find my place in God's house."

"You are the natural daughter of the king of England! You shall not squander the possibilities for a marital alliance, not with royal blood in your veins!" Henry's answer spoke volumes of his role as sovereign, not as father. "Return to your mother in Kent if you must. Under my strict order as your king, you shall not retire to Montivilliers or any religious house within or outside my realm. Another suitable match shall arise. For now, I shall make provision for your escort home. Remain there, unencumbered and await my summons."

Isabel feared her shock matched the evident surprise in her husband's reddened face. She turned from Henry's visage filled with rage, fearsome in his determination.

Robert said, "Your Grace, our concern should be the envoys who are here to finalize the arrangements of your royal daughter's betrothal."

"Would a few knights ordered into Kent alter our plans for the Whitsun court? Arrange for Amieria's travel. Do not forget she is as much my daughter as Maud!"

A slow ache welled in the back of Isabel's throat. She would have to say goodbye to Amieria again, her only friend and sole comfort in Henry's miserable court. Robert glanced at her, yet he offered no consolation.

Was he so blind to her misery or simply uncaring? Robert was a cold-hearted wretch and he had made a mockery of her opinion of him throughout the years of their marriage. To think, she once believed him kind. In his view, Amieria's lowly birth merited less concern from the king than the marriage of Princess Maud, when both girls were Henry's children. Amieria would fade and lose her bloom awaiting a marriage, while the king's legitimate child married the ruler of an empire.

Then Henry said, "Out, all of you. This discussion has soured my mood and I am poor company. Get out!"

With an impatient wave, the king pointed to the door. When Robert offered Isabel his arm, she glared at him before drawing near to Amieria. She enfolded the younger woman in her arms before escorting her. They preceded the men. Heat swept up Isabel's spine. She never looked behind her, not knowing if she would meet her husband's baleful stare or William's tortured own.

Isabel helped Amieria as she packed her belongings, although the attendants the king had provided his child remained available. Later, Isabel and Amieria walked arm-in-arm, exiting Westminster in silence. Henry's knights awaited Amieria. A portion of William's household guards joined them, with the king's consent.

William stood at the base of the steps beside his constable. Isabel could not meet his stare, even when he spoke. "Rudolf shall ensure your safe return, Amieria."

Isabel released her friend and Amieria dipped into a low curtsy before William. "Thank you. Your kindness endures."

"Would that I could have shown you more." He raised Amieria and his hands settled on her shoulders. "I wish you well and pray you shall find the happiness you so richly deserve."

When he released her, she turned from him and

Isabel hugged her. Even when she would have extracted herself from the embrace, Isabel would not let her go. Their soft sobs vied with each other. Isabel wept for her friend's misery, as much as her own.

Amieria was as much a pawn in her father's hands as Isabel had been of Hugh de Vermandois. Was this the fate of all women, their wills, even their very lives, subservient to the dominion of fathers and husbands? Men could determine their own fates – was there no choice offered to women?

Amieria sniffled. "I am only sorry we must part and wonder if I shall ever see you again."

Isabel nodded. "If only we could exchange letters."

"Without the benefit of lessons in reading or writing, your letters would do me little good. You must know, no matter how far apart we are, I shall always think of you fondly."

"I wish your fate had been different, Amieria."

"Regardless of it, I shall always do the king's bidding. I am a loyal subject of His Grace."

Isabel framed Amieria's face between her hands. "Henry is cruel to consign you to another term of misery. He is your father."

"He is the king of England first. My will has been subject to his whims forever. Do you think I have no understanding of what it means to be a king's bastard? I have always known and accepted it. Do not grieve for me. Now, you must let me go. I would not delay the earl's constable or the king's knights."

Isabel kissed both her cheeks. "Before you depart, grant me one small kindness. Do not address your leave-taking to the Comtesse de Meulan. You must call me by my Christian name."

Amieria smiled despite her tears. "Then, I bid you farewell, Isabel, my friend."

Isabel grasped both of the woman's hands in her own and pressed her lips against them. Then Isabel released her.

Rudolf aided Amieria into the saddle before he

claimed his own mount. Henry's knights charged out of the bailey, the king's daughter in their midst, followed by William's men.

Isabel stood with William, her gaze straining for a final view. William's hand brushed against her arm and lingered. Where his fingers touched, her flesh burned.

Act IV: Consumed

(May 1113 – October 1129)

Chapter Eighteen – The Lovers
Leicester, England: May 1113

Isabel chewed a slice of roasted venison in silence, seated on a long bench with Robert in the hall at Leicester. Her husband had ignored her for most of the meal, engrossed in discussion with Brother Thorold, who occupied the space at his right. The entire household, excluding Isabel's eldest sons, dined at noon. Next to Isabel, her eldest daughter, Emma, sulked as she ignored the trencher she shared with her mother.

Still, Isabel asked, "Are you not hungry, child?"

Emma's wide, wet stare met hers. "I am not, milady."

Upon arriving at Leicester in the previous week, Robert had decreed Emma would not marry Amaury de Montfort, given the man's earlier intrigues with France and Flanders against King Henry. Although Henry had reconciled with Amaury in the spring, his chief counselor believed Amaury required only time and opportunity for his natural disposition toward strife to arise. Robert would not allow the marriage, despite any offense Queen Bertrade of France might take on her brother's behalf. Instead, Emma would become a bride of Christ at Saint Leger-de-Préaux, where Robert's sister Aubree had been the abbess until her death. The abbey offered one respite. It would spare Emma a regrettable association with the royal consort of France, a woman disliked by many, including Isabel.

Isabel said, "You should eat. Nothing can come of starving yourself, including altering your father's decision."

Emma sniffled and swallowed her tears before she picked at the cold pigeon pie.

Isabel watched her from beneath lowered eyelids, feeling her daughter's despair as keenly as she experienced her own melancholy. She hesitated to reach for the girl's hand beneath the white tablecloth. Would such a gesture console Emma or see her withdraw into further misery? The will of God and her parents had consigned Isabel to marriage with a man she no longer trusted or respected. Fate would be kinder to Emma behind abbey walls. Isabel also knew such a view would be cold comfort to the child, who clearly did not wish for a life devoted to Christ.

Having finished her food, Isabel left without a word to Robert, who remained intent on his conversation with Thorold. A swift glance told her Robert's bastards Beatrice and Mabel, more guardians than attendants, trailed her. Both women did their duty as required, but lacked Petronilla's warmth and attentiveness. More importantly, Isabel did not trust either of the women.

She paused in the doorway. Beatrice's mouth pursed, as if she realized Isabel had caught her unawares. Isabel ignored her and her strange sister, whose vacant stare alighted on the pillar closest to the door with feigned interest. Their clumsy attempts to remain unobtrusive aside, Isabel peered beyond the women. Robert and Brother Thorold stood near the dais, in the glare of noonday sunlight streaming through the hall's north-facing window. Side-by-side with the profiles of their wizened features illuminated, the similarities between them struck her. From their lines etched into their sloping brows, ice blue eyes and hooked noses, a stranger would have believed them part of the same family.

Isabel recalled a night many years past at Vatteville, where she and Robert had long been absent each other. She had sought a tincture from Brother Thorold for her dying nursemaid, Claremond. Thorold spoke of his descent from a line of healers. He never mentioned his father. The Benedictine also talked of her husband's childhood then, especially a former fondness for cats. It suggested an intimacy borne out of their youthful time at Beaumont. What had happened between a healer's son and the heir of a Norman magnate to engender such a lingering bond?

The hall had nearly emptied. Isabel left it. Nothing sensible would come of an attempt at understanding Robert's attachment to Thorold. It remained an enigma, as did the Benedictine who had brought word of her marriage to Crépy-en-Valois many years before.

Seated alone on a wooden bench beside a window, Isabel gazed out on what should have been an idyllic scene for any mother. Emma, all her solemnity and forlornness forgotten beneath a shimmering afternoon sky, played with her youngest sister, Isabel's namesake, beside a beech tree. Isabel had borne her last daughter a few months ago. Nearby, the children's nursemaid, Agatha, kept charge of Aubree, while Adelina and little Maud gathered wild flowers. The children had escaped the castle for the hillside just below Leicester's palisade. Even at such a distance, Aubree's pealing laughter rang through the countryside. Isabel's third son, Hugh, did not share their companionship. Perhaps he gazed with longing at her husband's men-at-arms at the quintain on the practice field, dreaming of the day when he might join them rather than wielding his wooden sword.

Three sons and five daughters should have granted Isabel the greatest joy. The children were hearty and robust, all in the image of their father, as Beaumont children tended to be. Isabel's husband adored them and remained as affectionate to his daughters as he was with the nine-year-old twins Robert and Waleran and their youngest son Hugh. Isabel missed her eldest boys dreadfully, each under the tutelage and care of Faritius at Abingdon Abbey. Four years had passed since the abbot had taken charge of her sons' education. She had last seen them at Christmas for a month. So much had happened since then. With a soft sob, she pressed her forehead against the cold masonry.

William! From the deepest recesses of her mind, his name resounded in a desperate plea. Where was he? She had not heard any word of him after her return to Leicester in the weeks following Amieria's departure. She could not have stayed in such close proximity to the man, certain of Robert's suspicions about William's interest. As long months stretched into years, Isabel wished she could have forgotten everything about him. Still, his fervent whispers of devoted love taunted her. How easy it would have been if she pretended he had never existed, not pledged his heart and never evoked unexpected feelings. Hope remained paramount among them. A fool's hope, for no circumstances could alter her life and see her to William's arms, as she often imagined whenever her husband came to their bed. Robert demanded her passionate responses. She feigned them all and found her sole joy in imagining William took her husband's place.

She brushed aside the tears on her cheeks and sniffled. Despite all his failings, Robert did not deserve her disloyalty. She had never lain with William, never even touched him except for their brief encounter on the stairs at Winchester. In her mind, she had done so and more a thousand times over. Robert would have cast her aside in his heart, if he had ever guessed how often she sinned with William in her thoughts. Vows compelled her, the bonds of matrimony and her duty as mother of Robert's children. Somehow, she had to forget William, as he seemed to have disremembered her.

She gasped at the hand suddenly pressed on her shoulder. She eyed Robert.

He looked at her askance. "You're crying. Did I frighten you so badly?"

"You know you did!"

"I never intended such." He glanced over his shoulder, a dark green mantle covering him. She followed his stare. Beatrice and Mabel lingered in the shadows of the corridor. "They told me where I might find you."

Isabel glared at the women. "I thought I had escaped them for one afternoon."

Robert beckoned the women. "Why would you wish to evade them, my dear?"

Beatrice's sallow-faced expression partly hidden beneath a low hood, she held out Isabel's mantle. Robert nodded and extended his hand. "Come, wife."

"Are we going somewhere?"

"I have sent Thorold, my clerks, the constable and the provost to record and oversee collection of this week's rents from the market stalls. Henry's charter permits the operation of the market this year and I anticipate an increase in the toll revenue. The time outdoors would do us both some good. Accompany me."

"If I must, at your command."

"It is a request. I return to court at the week's end and would like to discuss my plans for Emma with you."

"I am pleased you choose to share her future with me."

"You seem surprised. I fear you still do not know me as well as you should."

Sometimes, she wondered if she truly knew her husband at all. Isabel kept such concerns to herself as she stood. Beatrice arranged the dark blue mantle around her mistress' shoulders. Isabel waved the woman off and tied the golden cords herself. Robert claimed her hand.

At the entryway, the doorkeeper bowed before them, as did Sieur Josceline, the constable's young son. He followed with eight men at arms and Isabel's attendants. Grooms had saddled horses and awaited them in the castle's forecourt.

"You would not have the children accompany us?" Isabel asked. "I'm certain they would enjoy the fair."

"They might, but not today." Robert tucked her hand in the crook of his arm. Her fingers flexed and rested there. He covered them with his other hand. They walked down the sloping bank of the castle's mound.

Mud from the morning's rainfall squelched beneath Isabel's shoes, as they covered ground at a brisk pace. Robert's vigor in all things at his age still surprised her.

She began, "You recognize Emma's disappointment."

Robert nodded. "Our daughter cannot marry Amaury de Montfort. In these last three years, he has incited Queen Bertrade's son Fulk, Count of Anjou and Louis, King of France against Henry in Normandy. I would not give my daughter to such a man."

"You told me Henry has pardoned him."

"I care nothing for the king's amnesty, when Amaury has proven he is a dangerous fool, who needs no motive and scant opportunity to cause trouble. When I depart Leicester, Emma shall accompany me. By my leave, Thorold escorts her on to Saint Leger."

Isabel stopped and nearly wrenched her arm from the socket. "You're taking her away so soon?"

Robert chuckled. "Would you pretend a show of motherly devotion? You have never coddled our children, except Waleran and my namesake. Why should it matter when Emma leaves? We have other girls."

She turned aside, as pained by his casual brutality as the truth behind it. She had never been an affectionate mother and would never be. Robert had forbidden it at each opportunity and in truth, she never knew how. Tears pricked her eyes at the possibility of Emma's withdrawal into a nunnery. Isabel's sons gone to Abingdon, now a daughter would leave her and she might never see the girl again.

Robert cupped her chin. "We have no time for affectation. Emma's been promised. You understand my honor is at stake."

"Your honor? What of our daughter's feelings? Do you care nothing for them?"

He reached for her, gingerly at first. Then his arms came about her shoulders and he kissed the crown of her head. "Do not fear for Emma. She shall accept life behind the abbey walls. Now come for I would have an accounting from the market before day's end."

With Robert's aid, Isabel mounted her horse. The pair rode through the gatehouse with guardsmen protecting them on all sides outside the bailey of Leicester. Josceline's mount trotted at the forefront. At the tollgate, the riders headed northbound. Tracts of green meadows and forest bounded the dirt trail. Some villagers tended the thriving crops of Robert's demesne under the afternoon sun. Geese honked and sheep shorn of their wool mingled with a tide of merchants. At Josceline's stern command, carts traveling to and from the market on the road gave way to the riders from the castle.

When they entered the marketplace, stalls lined all sides of the square in a haphazardly fashion. While Robert maneuvered his big bay stallion, she trailed behind him. A minstrel wound his way through the growing crowd, who paid him scant attention except to shove past him. Traders and craftsmen hawked their wares—offerings of cloth, leather and salt. Sunlight glinted off metals. A woman selling a variety of breads screamed before a small child dashed across the square, a stolen loaf in hand. Two men on foot gave chase. Isabel lost sight of them and the errant boy in the bustling market. One stall owner displayed gauzy material Isabel had never seen before, fabric so thin, she could imagine a garment fashioned from it would only shame the wearer.

Josceline struck out at a man who strayed into Robert's path. "Would you have the horse trample you?"

Hemmed in on all sides, sudden terror almost took hold of Isabel. A wave of heat swept up her back, coupled with a distinct feeling of someone watching her. She spied Thorold adjacent a cloth weaver's stall at the eastern fringe of the square. The clerk could not have noticed her, or if he had, the weaver held his attention now. Tears streamed down the woman's cheeks as she gripped a wooden crossbar for support. The constable, Josceline's father, stood at Thorold's back.

"Wife?" Robert's voice beckoned. He approached her on horseback, his stare intent on the direction she had gazed. "Ah, you've found Thorold. Good."

Isabel followed her husband. She remained at some distance as Robert dismounted. She did not overhear the resultant exchange between her husband, his clerk and the weaver. Likely, it related to the rent for the stall. Isabel could not dispel the sensation of being watched, always arising from the direction of where Thorold stood. She did not recognize anyone else in the sea of faces. She dismissed the niggling doubt. No one had reason to scan the crowd for her, yet she remained grateful for the cadre of guards nearby.

Robert remained at the marketplace for several hours, even when the bells of Saint Mary de Castro pealed for Nones. The setting sun framed the sky in a garish gold, as Isabel left under Josceline's escort. With Beatrice and Mabel's unwelcome aid, Isabel changed her mud-stained garments for fresh clothing and went to the hall, where she would await Robert's arrival. He ate one meal per day and often enjoyed a late evening game of chess at a trestle table.

Torchlight beckoned from the doorway, slightly ajar. She peered inside. Robert and Thorold stood alone together. The clerk leaned against a column on the left, closest to the entryway. Thorold sighed, his expression downcast. Robert grasped his chin and lifted it, exposing the monk's haggard face. Isabel had never seen her adversary so careworn. He might be observing one of the ritual fasts again. Then she remembered he had dined with Robert earlier in the day.

Thorold sulked, his brow furrowed. "You send me from your side. Any of your chaplains or clerks could escort your daughter to Saint Leger."

"I trust few men as I trust you." Robert patted the man's cheek. "I'm not asking you to remain in Normandy for long. Return to me at court as soon as you have delivered Emma."

"The abbess shall be pleased to receive her as an oblate, even if your wife does not feel the same."

"You mistake Isabel's melancholy. My wife is

unsentimental where our children are concerned, just like her mother."

Isabel glanced both ways along the corridor before edging a little closer to the portal.

Did Robert truly think her unsentimental after he had taken every opportunity to correct her inclination toward their children? Even after so many years of marriage, he knew nothing of her heart and her true feelings.

"The comtesse shall remain here?"

"I would not have her at court to tempt William de Warenne. As I have told you, I do not like his covetous glances at my wife, especially when he thinks I do not notice him. It is more than lust. I have seen the look in his eyes. He wants more from her than a night's pleasure. He wants the heart that should be mine. It is mine."

Isabel pressed against the cool wall, her heart thudding. It was true. Robert knew of William's affection for her.

Thorold said, "I had thought the Earl of Surrey remained in Normandy, far from His Grace."

Robert chuckled. "After William gained the castellanship of Saint-Saens, he remained in Normandy. Henry has recalled him. William hastened his return."

"Hence your swift departure for court."

"I do not believe William seeks to supplant me, far from it. Still, after Henry sought to marry off one of his bastards to the man, His Grace has come to rely on William increasingly."

Isabel smothered a sigh, as a brief worry over Amieria's unknown fate plagued her, before Thorold spoke again.

"The king is not the only one who looks upon William with increasing favor. I have warned you. Your wife wants William as well. She would give him her body and her heart, if she could."

"I'll hear no more of your conjecture about my wife." Robert's smooth tone hardened like forged iron. "Isabel remains faithful to me in body, if not in her heart. For a long time, I have known she remains susceptible to the earl. Still, Beatrice and Mabel have assured me of her fidelity during my absences. She has had no reason to think of William for years. I would keep her here so as not to tempt the earl, or her inclination for him."

Guilt tormented Isabel. It was worse than she had feared. Robert suspected her divided loyalties and the change in her sentiments toward William. How could she have been so imprudent?

A brief wind stirred the door. She dashed around the adjacent corner, fearful the men in the room might have heard and looked outside. When no footfalls resounded, she peeked around the wall. Her chest heaving, she crept toward the hall again.

The pair remained inside, closer to each other than before. Robert nuzzled Thorold's forehead. "You have always been so jealous of Isabel."

"I have reason."

"You do not. My affection for you has remained unchanged since I married her."

"You love your wife."

"As much as I have loved you."

The monk sighed and rested his head on Robert's shoulder. They embraced in silence, no further words passing between them.

Betrayal knifed Isabel's heart. With a hand covering her lips, she stumbled backward, turned from the door and fled.

Later, in the darkness of the room she shared with Robert at the top of the tower, Isabel sat on the bed and braided her hair. She had dismissed Beatrice and Mabel for the night. Even when Agatha had brought the girls to bid her goodnight, she barely acknowledged them beyond a murmured blessing. She did not want anyone else around her. Her heart pounded, fear and revulsion taking hold of her.

Candlelight preceded Robert's entry. She did not look up when he came in. Her fingers shook. Still, she twined blue ribbons through her plaits.

"My dear, I thought you would be sleeping." Robert set the candle down near the shuttered window and removed his shoes. He had dismissed his squire.

Hose and mantle in hand, he sat beside her. She stared straight ahead.

"Dearest, you seem preoccupied. Is there something troubling you?" Robert asked.

Isabel's hands halted in midair before she settled them in her lap. Eyes watering, she bowed her head. "How long have you and Thorold been lovers, Robert? Did your liaison begin before or after we wed?"

The mutual sounds of their breathing filled the otherwise quiet chamber. With a loud swallow, she turned to her husband. He stared at the floor, stone-faced, his clothing held precariously between his fingers.

"Robert, please tell me the truth. You have always shielded me from matters you believed I could not understand or accept."

"I have protected you, Isabel, for your own good."

"You have kept me in ignorance, Robert. I am no fool. I have never supposed I might have been before, until tonight. After our long years of marriage and eight children, I deserve to know the full truth about you and your clerk. He is more than a boyhood friend. You feel for him what a man would feel for a woman. You have lain with him as you have with me. You cannot deny my words, for I feel the same certainty of them, as when I saw you with him in the hall earlier. I witnessed your proclamation of love for him. I did not intend to spy upon you. Now, I cannot forget all I have seen. So I ask again, when did your love affair with Thorold begin?"

As he shifted, the bed frame creaked beneath his weight. His shoulders hunched, he bowed his head. "It started long ago, before you and I were wed, when Thorold and I were young men at Beaumont."

Isabel looked away, a harsh sigh drawn from her depths. Robert threw his garments across the room before his hand covered hers. She did not flinch or withdraw.

"How did it begin, Robert?"

"You would have me lay bare my shame before you? Despite what you may think of me, I still care for your feelings, Isabel."

"Then tell me this, have you lain with him since we married?"

"I have been faithful throughout our union."

"In body, but not in your heart."

He nodded, although she had not asked a question. He cupped her chin between his thumb and forefinger. "Do you believe it so impossible to love more than one person with the fullness of your heart and find yourself undivided by equal passions?"

She would not, could not answer him. It would have been so easy to scorn him, bedevil him with her true feelings for William. Still, she could not hurt him. Instead, she said, "You were the first person I have ever loved, born of my duty to you, not attachment. You saved me from a miserable existence. I shall always be grateful. I do not know what it is to love with passion."

"You yearn for it with William de Warenne."

When she would have avoided his stark gape, Robert's fingers pressed into her flesh. The weight of the truth burdened her more than his painful touch.

"Have we both been faithless in our hearts, Isabel? Do you love him?"

She said nothing. The pressure of his hand increased in the lengthening silence. "Do not lie to me. You demanded the dreadful truth about Thorold. I want the same candor from you."

"I do not love him, Robert." The lie stabbed at her. She instinctively knew Robert would not have accepted any other answer.

He withdrew his touch. "I do not believe you." When she said nothing, he continued, "Tell me this truthfully, if you can. Have you lain with him? Thorold has accused you of adultery with William."

"Your clerk deceives you! His opinion is biased. The

monk is envious of me. He admitted it to you earlier this evening."

Robert rose from the bed. "Still, it would seem he is right to caution me." He clasped his hands together and looked down at her. "This night has brought both of us to an understanding. I give you my word. All I have said of my relations with Thorold is true. I require your pledge. Tell me you have not lied about William. You have not sullied your body by committing adultery with him."

She grasped his age-spotted hand and brought it to her lips. "I swear I have not lied." Tears stung her eyes. She held them back. "I promise I shall remain loyal to you. I would never abandon you for William's sake."

He smoothed his thumb across her trembling lips. "Good, for on the day you ever break your vow, I swear William shall die by my hands."

She stared up at him, horrified. "Do not make such a murderous vow, please. I have given you my assurances."

Robert chuckled. "Do you fear I would die in the attempt? You must think me an incapable old man. If I must, I can take William's head in a trial by combat. God would not deem it murder. I would have justice for how the Earl of Surrey has wronged me."

"You could be excommunicated!"

"Archbishop Anselm and the pope have threatened me with excommunication from holy mother Church before. I am unafraid. Besides, any of the clergy would grant me absolution if I defended my honor against William's attentions toward you."

She scrutinized him. Shivers tingled along her spine. When had he ever faced the denial of communion? Another long-held secret about the man she thought she knew.

In her mind's eye, she could almost see Robert and William hacking at each other, their swords clashing until one slaughtered the other. He had the right. The Church would think him justified. She feared her husband would not triumph. The admission would only earn his wrath.

"Robert, I do not doubt the sincerity of your vow or the strength of your cause. Is it not enough I have forsworn myself? I have borne your own regard for Thorold and still pledge myself to remain at your side!"

"It is your duty! You are mother to our children! Would you abandon them for your lover? Your lies unravel so easily, Isabel."

"My lies? What about you? You have hidden your relations with Thorold for years. I do not shrink from you. I would still embrace you as my husband. Must I also tolerate Thorold under the same roof, knowing how he is jealous of me and desires you still? Christ's blood, Robert, the man is enamored of you and reviles me! I have given all to you! You've demanded my apologies and vows, yet offer nothing of the same."

"I owe you nothing! You owe all to me. I will have proof of your penitence. Your words are not enough." He went from the chamber into the passage.

She rose from the bed, her fingers clasped together. She became vividly aware of much at once. The rise and fall of her chest with each breath and the shaking of her hands, robbed of all warmth.

Robert's sudden return startled her.

"You must seek forgiveness and endure penance, Isabel, the sins of your body driven out. Only then can you truly return to me as the woman you were before the Earl of Surrey tempted you from my side."

She bowed in resignation. "I shall make my confession to your chaplain before Matins."

"We do not wait until morning." He came around the bed and seized her arm.

She stilled the desire to pull away. "You would have me attend confession tonight? What can either of us gain before the morning?"

"A measure of peace. Now, come."

He tugged her with him down the dim passageway, lit only with torches in brackets along the wall. Two sentries eyed them in silence and remained stalwart.

Isabel stared at them in mute appeal. Neither man moved. Tears of shame streamed down her cheeks.

Robert's grip tightened. "Do not cry, my Isabel. I am cursed too, my sweet. Despite your failings, your perfidy, I still want you at my side. Do you understand? I shall never give you up. The earl has sown iniquity in your heart. Your atonement shall drive it out."

They went down the stairs to the hall. Faint light beckoned from the door of the small chapel at the opposite end of the corridor. Robert wrenched Isabel's arm. She gasped as he turned at the landing to another door, the scriptorium, where her husband's clerks often wrote his letters.

Oak wood creaked as the portal swung back on its iron hinges. Thorold bowed, the black cowl of his habit framing his rounded head. "I received your message, milord."

Isabel struggled against her husband. "You cannot mean to give me over to him! Robert, do not."

He propelled her before him into the room. "Thorold shall drive the wickedness from you."

She whimpered. "He'll enjoy it and you'll let him. How can you speak of loving me? I beg you, for your soul's sake, do not be so cruel. Do not let him ruin what remains of us. He shall destroy any feelings I have for you as he batters my body."

At Robert's curt nod, Thorold grabbed her. She struggled against him at each step. Shards of pain stabbed her arms in his viselike grip. Isabel screamed, though she knew no one else would seek the cause of her cries. Robert could do as he pleased.

Her unfinished braid loosened and streamed around her shoulders. She jerked against Thorold's rough hold. He held her tight against him.

"How can you do this? Robert, I am the mother of your children! Have pity."

Behind her, he said, "I do. I still love you, Isabel."

"You cannot love me if you would let him hurt me. Robert, if you have ever truly cared for me, you cannot let Thorold do this. He is evil. He still wants you for himself, has hated me from the start because of his unnatural desire for you."

"Be quiet, adulterous whore!" Thorold shook Isabel so hard, her teeth rattled. He bent her over the carrel and held her with one hand. The high, wooden desk pressed her chest inward and she gasped for air.

Robert appeared before her. She offered another plea in a soft whimper, as the enormity of what she now faced robbed her of speech. She could not speak, as her husband secured her hands to the wooden base of the carrel with a rope Thorold gave him.

Behind her, the Benedictine muttered in Latin about the virtues of confession. She could not understand his ravings, issued in a guttural, almost animalistic tone.

Robert framed her face in his hands. A smile that did not quite reach his watering eyes beamed down upon her. She barely recognized the man she had married. His relationship with Thorold and her betrayal had twisted his soul.

As he leaned forward and kissed her forehead, she turned her face from him. He grasped her chin. "Thorold loves me more than you ever could. You will never understand his feelings for me because you cannot understand the nature of our bond. He's more than my clerk or friend."

She gasped as her chest tightened, already having guessed at what Robert would now reveal. Still, she whispered, "You cannot mean—"

"Thorold is the bastard son of Roger de Beaumont and the village healer, though my father never acknowledged him. He is my brother. He loves me so. He shall never leave my side. He cannot, for the bond of blood binds us closer than anything else ever could."

As the truth tore through her heart, the first lash sliced across her back.

Chapter Nineteen – A Captive
Leicester, England: March 1116

Despite woolen gloves and a warm mantle, Isabel shivered and her teeth chattered as she walked the muddy path between Saint Mary de Castro and the castle's bailey. She had attended Mass at Sext, seeking a comfort prayer had never provided. While she stood in the church with the congregation and prayed for peace within her heart, it remained elusive.

She followed the knight, Josceline. He paused and looked over his shoulder at intervals. Concern furrowed his brow. Nearing the walls of the bailey, he halted again. "Are you well? Does the walk tire you?"

She could have laughed, not knowing whether his concern should amuse or insult her. A few years separated him from her age of thirty-one. "I promise you the walk does not tax my strength."

"You have been ill of late, milady."

In recent weeks, a fever had claimed the life of Beatrice. At first, it afflicted her sister, Mabel, before spreading through the household to infect Isabel and her youngest daughters. Isabel banished her attendants from the castle while ensuring a physician attended them. In time, all those who had been ill regained their strength although Mabel seemed too weak still. Isabel did not miss the company of her or her sister, though she knew such thoughts were uncharitable.

She said, "Josceline, your concern is unnecessary. You have known me since the first days in which I married. I have always borne travails with little complaint."

Including Thorold's chastisement, to which she had submitted each time Robert had demanded it. Resistance only worsened her punishments. No one showed an interest in her bent and bowed form in the days afterward or ever mentioned the horrific screams at night, which must have echoed beyond the scriptorium. Her husband's men never risked protecting her from the cruelty his minion meted out. As in her childhood, she lacked a protector.

Josceline resumed his pace. "As you say, milady, though I know your husband would never forgive me if —"

The ground rumbled beneath their feet.

"Milady! Come away from the footpath now!"

Josceline's sudden cry startled her, before she recognized the neigh of a horse. As the knight drew his sword, the sudden grip of a mailed arm came around her waist and lifted her bodily. She screeched in fury and fright. The iron hold of her abductor kept her restrained. Still, she struggled as he maneuvered her onto her stomach, across the back of an unsaddled horse.

"Josceline, help me!"

"Silence, woman!" Her captor's snarl sent a shiver along her spine. "We ride now!"

Isabel could hardly breathe. A cacophony of hooves sounded and warned her of aides in the man's mischief. Leicester's townspeople raised the alarm, but none was louder than Josceline.

"Milady! Comtesse Isabel! They are stealing the comte's wife! Bar the exits."

Hooves clattered across a wooden bridge. The riders fled as though the Devil chased them through the open city gateway. Tradesmen entering Leicester for its market day scattered.

Jarred from her shocking ordeal, Isabel screamed and bit the leg of the one who had dared abscond with her. His grunt preceded a stinging slap on her rump.

"My husband will destroy you for this! Do you understand me? He shall never give me up!"

"He's an old fool! Unless you want me to gag you, be quiet."

The men never slowed their mounts as they vanished into the thick woodlands. Isabel fought all the way, though fearful of sliding to her death from the horse's back, where the beast's hooves would certainly strike and kill her. Blood roared in her ears each time she raised her head. A well-aimed blow to the inner thigh of her abductor left him howling. His hand descended again with the fury of hellfire.

"Christ's blood, woman! Someone help me! Bind her before she kills us both!"

The riders slowed and before she might renew her efforts, coarse ropes entangled her hands and feet. She screeched anew, furious at how they had trussed her like a deer in the forest. Bound, a strip of cloth went over her eyes before someone else raked a dank, moldy strip between her lips. Blind and robbed of speech, fear took hold of her heart in a viselike clutch. She steeled herself against tears of frustration. Crying had never aided her before now.

An interminable time passed in which they stopped only once. Two pairs of strong hands hefted her down on the uneven ground. Pain shot through her cramped limbs. The men forced her against a tree trunk. Rough bark pressed into her back. The wailing wind stirred an earthy smell.

Leaves crackled underfoot and as the sound faded, replaced by quiet conversations and the occasional snort or labored huff from the horses, she wondered if the men had given her solitude. She guessed the riders remained secreted in some forestland. She could not run with her ankles and wrists tied.

Where could she run? The men could have taken her anywhere.

"Do you want to make your water now? My squire will give you a measure of privacy. He will also remain mindful of your actions and whereabouts. My men and I are tolerant, not foolish."

She jerked away from the voice on the left. Could they not have left her in solitude? The gag prevented her from uttering a furious reply. Then someone with wit at her right untied the cloth and she spat it out. She barely registered the presence of another person before her screams echoed. Frightened birds squawked and scattered, rustling leaves and branches in their wake.

A mailed hand grasped her chin. Iron links pressed

into her flesh. She bit back a wince until blood tainted her tongue.

"Scream again and you will be sorry."

"He said no harm must come to her." The words startled her less than the tone, youthful compared to the voice of her principal abductor, whom she now recognized. The other man who unknotted her gag must be his squire.

"He was always a fool for her sake. I spoke to her for kindness' sake. Now, she can piss herself for all I care!"

Then men hauled Isabel through the detritus of the forest floor. At a sudden halt, the rope around her feet loosened.

"You have your own mount now, milady. You ride with us. You must do as you are told."

Though robbed of her sight, Isabel turned in the direction of the firm voice at her ear. "If you think I will submit easily, you are as much a fool as the one whom you serve!"

Still, she mounted the horse with help. With a heavy-handed slap to the beast's rump, the riders sped off. At each jarring turn along the path they rode, she cursed her fate.

At some indeterminable moment, the men slowed. She recognized the winding of a winch and the presence of more men. Through the thin fibers of her blindfold, she became aware of torchlight. Night had likely fallen. The men must have reached their destination.

She ground her teeth together, fury boiling in her blood. She let the men aid her dismount. They untied her hands and removed the blindfold. Her first glimpse in hours fell on her abductor. He studied her with the familiar overconfidence she had grown accustomed to from his master, an arrogance that seemed a familial trait.

She looked toward the base of a motte, where blue flowers clustered. Her gaze rose to the summit, topped by a rectangular wood-framed building, with windows near the top. The banks of a steep ditch rose and encircled both the inner and outer bailey. More wildflowers clustered at the rounded corners of a wooden palisade.

One man emerged from the stone building, his blue mantle billowing on the evening wind. White hounds yipped and followed him. With a firm hand, he stayed them at the bottom of the steps. A strong gust swept dark hair threaded with stands of gray from his furrowed brow. A smile softened his craggy features. She did not return the gesture.

She passed through the gatehouse alone. He closed the distance between in great strides and tugged her into his arms.

"At last. My Isabel!"

"Do not call me that. Robert always did."

She shrugged from his hold and stared at his beloved visage, before she raised her hand and slapped him across the cheek.

"William, you selfish, ill-bred fool! Do you know what you have done? You have ruined both of our lives!"

Isabel stood with her arms folded beside the hearth in William's great hall. Despite the warmth in the chamber, she shivered. "Why did you risk this madness? What do you think my husband will do when he discovers you have abducted me? He is no simpleton. He will know. He has long suspected your regard for me."

"I do not doubt he will realize what I have done, with time." At her shoulder, William's low voice rose above the crackling fire. "We parted from each other a few days ago. At Passion Sunday, we swore the king's oath to uphold the claim of his heir. Then His Grace charged us to deliver his ultimatum to Archbishop Thurstan of York, requiring his submission to the primacy of Canterbury."

"You raced home afterward, intent on stealing Robert's wife."

"*Non.* I have labored over this plot for years, had Rudolf monitoring your every movement outside of the castle. I had to be certain he and my men could capture you when the time arrived."

She whirled toward him, would have struck him again if he had not caught her hand in his. He kissed the center of her palm.

"You knew there was no other course, Isabel. Despite my wishes to the contrary, Robert would not die at his great age and leave you a widow. Your royal cousin, Louis, could not kill him in the seemingly endless quarrels between England and France. I have waited far too long. I must have you for my own."

She wrenched her fingers from his grasp. "You have never accepted the simple truth. I cannot be yours! Robert is my husband. There is no other option for me."

He drew nearer. "Duty before desire? Surrender to the will of others, forever forsaking your own needs?"

"Always! It is all I've ever known." When tears threatened, she turned from him.

He came around her and tipped her chin up. "Let me show you another way."

"The way of sin! Would you make an adulteress of me in body and mind?"

"I would make you my beloved, my beating heart, my very soul, if you desired it. You married for duty's sake and bore your husband's children as he wished. I offer you a different choice, one where your happiness remains paramount."

She laughed in his face. "You have taken me from Robert and call it choice? People once thought my husband a monk. Now, he shall be a cuckold. Did you consider his feelings or my own? Did you think of how my children might suffer such a scandal? You are a prideful man, William, even more so than my husband."

His hand slid to her shoulder. "Forgive me. I have suffered too long without your love."

She pulled away. "You know nothing of suffering. Let me show you all I have endured, because my husband doubted whether my heart belonged only to him."

Although her fingers shook, she untied the cords of her dirtied mantle. The lacing at the back of her linen robe proved more difficult. She loosened the strings eventually and rolled the bodice down her torso to her hips. William's dark gaze dropped to the rounded circles poking through chainsil, the thin fabric of her chemise. She held him entranced, as she slid the white sleeves down her arms. When she revealed the tops of her breasts, William's throaty groan filled the room, until she turned her back on him. She gathered the crinkled chainsil at her waist.

His harsh intake of breath warned of his shock. Were the scars as bad as she had always imagined? She had never touched them herself, only remained quiet afterward while Constance tended to her. Constance, younger sister to Wulfwyn at Leicester, had often soothed her battered flesh with cool poultices and tended to the welts until they subsided. The evidence of Thorold and Robert's cruelty lingered in Isabel's mind. No amount of aid would ever banish the memories.

"I swear I will kill your husband for what he's done to you."

"You dare not harm him!" Only the crackling of the hearth fire vied with Isabel's heated command. "I have done this to myself. My selfishness mirrored your own. I could not accept the gifts God had given me. I forsook the comforts of home and the joy of children, yearning for more. For you. This is my punishment."

A long sigh escaped her. "Even as I desire you, long for you from the depths of my soul, I shall always be Robert's wife. Take what you will from me. Even your touch cannot erase the scars his minion has left upon me."

"You think your desire for me is a punishment for your failing as a wife and mother."

"What else could it be?"

"Your heart and love would be the greatest gifts I have ever received. I know you would not give your body alone."

"Do you? I speak of lust and you speak of hearts and love. Why do you love me, William?"

"You might ask me why I breathe or live instead. I have felt this way for too long to remember when it first started. In later years, I have recalled how we met when you first married Robert. Even as a child, you possessed more courage than any female of my acquaintance. Afterward, I pretended not to know you at Vatteville from the first, because I could not fathom how the child had grown into such a beguiling young woman. You upbraided and laughed at me for my arrogance. It produced the opposite effect than you might have intended. No woman ever showed such daring. I kept away from Normandy and never expected to see you again, until you came to England. Your affinity with Robert inspired my resentment. I despised him increasingly for siring children upon your body. He had the life I wanted with you. When Amieria chose you as her companion at court, I only wished to be near you again, even if for brief moments. Robert's jealousy and callous treatment would have broken any other woman, one who did not possess your courage. You ask why I love you and think it is only for your beauty. It is borne out of traits only those who come to understand you can see. I adore your strength and devotion, your patience and instinct to endure, no matter the trials you have faced. I admire your conviction, which will not let you surrender to me and betray your marital vows, although I want you at my side."

She sighed. "We cannot pretend this desire we feel for each other means more than the fulfillment of our carnal natures."

"If desire alone ruled me, you would have been stripped bare and your legs pried apart at Vatteville years ago. I would have taken your maidenhead upon the altar of your husband's chapel, without a care for your heart or Robert's wrath. I want more. So do you. You only have to ask, Isabel."

She turned and gaped at him, her vulnerable state long forgotten. William left her alone. The door swung violently on its hinges. She stared at the heavy thick wood in his wake before she pulled up her garments and wrapped herself in the warmth of the mantle again.

At length, a red-haired, pale woman appeared beside her and spread her skirts in a deep curtsy. She revealed her slightly rounded belly jutting beneath the robe. "Milady, I am Mildrith, wife of Sieur Rudolf. The earl has ordered me to attend you, if it would please you. He bid me escort you above stairs."

Isabel eyed her. "Have your husband or the Earl of Surrey told you I am a captive of this place?"

Mildrith's double chin dipped toward her chest before she nodded.

Isabel asked, "Will you tell me where I must suffer this imprisonment?"

"At Castle Acre, in Norfolk, milady."

"Is your husband still so wrathful with me? I bit his leg and would have done further harm to his manly parts, had he not restrained me."

Mildrith smiled. "I know how to soothe my Rudolf's parts well enough. He shall offer you naught but smiles tomorrow, milady. It would be my pleasure to ensure it."

Isabel followed Mildrith from the hall.

Castle Acre, England: April 1116

One month after Isabel's abduction, she sat alone on a wooden stool, in the chamber William had vacated on her behalf. Midmorning light revealed a thin layer of dust on the sparse furnishings and bedding. Despite the herbs and fresh wildflowers Mildrith brought up every day, the room still smelled of the earl, the odors of iron and horses comingled. William bedded down in the hall with his knights. When she dined with him, dark circles shadowed his eyes. He traded increasingly resentful glares between her and his constable, who often drew his breeding wife on to his lap for a quick kiss or fondle during the meal. William's chaplain always blushed and averted his eyes, while the knights and men-at-arms encouraged Rudolf's antics.

During her time at Castle Acre, Isabel learned more about William and Rudolf's relationship. They shared the same grandfather. Rudolf was a descendant of a younger, bastard son with no hope of inheritance. William's father had been generous to the family and Rudolf shared a bond of genuine friendship with his cousin ever after.

William's people were kind and solicitous, no more than required. She had shared her concerns for Robert's ruin to Mildrith and gained only sympathetic nods. The chaplain informed her he had previously counseled the earl against his rash actions. Even the cleric seemed too devoted and forgiving of William's faults. No one cared if she belonged to another man.

Yet, she did. The burden of her marital vows would not allow her to pretend otherwise, no matter William's desires or her own.

With a sigh, Isabel rested her hands in her lap and stared out of the only window in the chamber, which Mildrith had flung wide each morning after Isabel promised she would not tie the bed curtains together as a means of escape.

In the last several weeks, she had considered the women in her acquaintance, those who had influenced her views of life for better or worse. Her mother, a cruel tyrant like Isabel's father, who despised her husband in public, yet thrilled at his caresses during the night. Then there was Claremond, who had sullied herself by claiming the man her sister had wished to marry, suffering a lifetime of regrets in the aftermath. Petronilla had given herself to the bastard FitzRobert wholeheartedly, then killed herself rather than endure a life without him. If all these women remained with Isabel, what would each of them make of her current circumstances? How would they have judged her relations with Robert and William?

Movement on the horizon caught her attention through the window. Gold and red pennons upon lances fluttered in the spring breeze. A long train of riders approached the gatehouse of Castle Acre. Even at this distance, she spied the porter with ease. When her stare trained on the familiar features of the man whom he spoke with, her heart thrummed.

"Great God! It's the king."

Mildrith entered the chamber. "Milady."

Isabel whispered. "The king is here."

Mildrith advanced and peered through the window. "I know. My Rudolf's been snarling at the men in the bailey since the bells for Tierce rang. All this trouble for a king."

While Isabel glared at the woman as if she had grown another head, Mildrith tapped her fingers on her rounded belly. "A herald arrived after dawn. The earl and Rudolf spoke in a corner by the hearth, so even I could not overhear. The king's arrival is sudden, but also anticipated."

Dread filled Isabel's heart. "He is here because of me."

Mildrith asked, "Are you so certain?"

Isabel would have clouted her if she could have risked it. William had given her no leave to chastise his servants.

"Mildrith, I have only known you for a few weeks. You never seemed a foolish woman before. The king must be aware of what William has done with me."

"The earl loves you. Everyone here can see. He shall never let you return to your husband."

"If the king commands him, William must."

"Why are you so eager to return to your husband?"

Isabel blanched. "How dare you even ask?"

Mildrith snorted. "I would not care for any man who beat me, father or husband. I saw those silver stripes and faded bruises on your back when I attended at your Easter bath. Some of the whip marks had faded, crisscrossed by fresh ones."

"You should not speak when you know nothing of my past or circumstances!"

"Humph. As you say, milady."

"Christ's blood, you remind me of my Petronilla!"

"Who?"

"It is no concern of yours. Fetch my mantle. I shall greet the king and beg his mercy."

Mildrith's laughter pealed to the wooden rafters. "There are always guards outside your door for a reason. You will not see the king if the earl does not wish it. He does not."

"Please, you must help me!"

"You would escape from the arms of a man who loves and worships you, who gazes upon you as though you are an angel come down from heaven? The earl has been good to me and mine. He has never abused a woman here. I have heard whispers he has two bastards in Normandy. I do not believe he neglects their needs. His father treated my parents well, though they were English and his son has the same generous spirit. I would never betray him. He has not harmed or threatened you. He provides fine clothes, good wines and entertainment at dinner just for you. He has never forced his desires upon you, though obvious they may be. He sleeps in his hall at night, no woman to warm him.

"You should know better than to ask for aid, milady. Everyone would be happy if the earl finally bedded you. Lord knows how much more the man can bear, keeping himself like a monk for weeks, while you dine at his table in all your finery and beauty. It is unnatural to withhold your seed from a woman so long. I know you desire him. You think he does not notice the faint blush upon your cheek, the admiration in your gaze when he enters the hall. You love him, though you refuse to accept it. There is no shame in loving the earl, milady. The heart chooses."

Isabel blinked back tears, brought to the fore by the words of a woman who barely knew her. Mildrith's sentiments cut to the heart of her feelings, through a morass of guilt and uncertainty.

She sighed. "Love is impossible."

The pair lapsed into silence until Isabel rose from the

stool. She cleared her throat. "Bring my mantle."

"I will not."

"You must, because you must accompany me to the minstrels' gallery, where we shall await the king's arrival. He and William must have entered the hall by now. I wish to hear their exchange. I shall not reveal myself. Neither man will know I am there."

Mildrith scratched the rounded tip of her bulbous nose. "Swear upon something you value. You do not prattle on with pieties like the earl's mother did, so no swearing on a saint's bones either, as they likely mean nothing to you."

"I vow upon William's life, I shall not betray my presence in the gallery."

"Wait here for me." Mildrith's broad smile lent her features a glow of childlike happiness.

She left the room and returned with Isabel's mantle. "Say nothing when we leave this room."

When they stepped into the corridor, two guardsmen stood on either side of the door.

Mildrith mumbled, "The earl wants her."

One of the men raised an eyebrow. "Sieur Rudolf never told either of us."

"I'm his wife, oaf!" Mildrith rested her fingers on her ample hips. "Why send word to either of you when I can carry out milord's wishes?"

She grasped Isabel's arm. "This way, milady."

Near the landing, Isabel whispered, "I should not ask you to undertake such trouble for me. What if William discovers it?"

"Keep your vow and you will have no cause for worry."

They went down one flight of stairs and through a small door. Mildrith tugged Isabel into the shadow of the gallery, lined with columns and archways. Dank air permeated the space. The women stood beside a cool wall, as the hall door creaked below. Heavy footfalls stamped across the floor.

"Where is she?"

Isabel pressed against the cold masonry at her back, startled by Henry's brusque speech. Silence followed.

"Christ's bones, William, do you assume I'm an old fool too, as you've perceived Robert must be?"

"I would never judge you for a fool, Your Grace," William answered with a firm tone.

Isabel wondered at the strength of his composure when faced with the king's accusations.

"You will tell me the truth. Where is Isabel de Vermandois? Do you keep Robert's wife here or at Lewes?"

"Does Robert believe she is with me?"

"I thought you were more sensible than this. You never took to my Amieria, too busy sniffing at Isabel's skirts like one of your hounds. Well, my daughter is best left where she is."

Isabel waited and prayed Henry might reveal something of Amieria's fate. He did not speak further of her. Had she married according to his wishes or settled for a life at Montivilliers?

In either circumstance, she hoped Amieria would find the happiness she deserved. Isabel prayed the young woman would never discover the truth about William's abduction. Amieria would never forgive either of them—the man she had hoped to marry or the women she considered a dear friend.

"Shall I have your castle searched, William? Do I order your arrest? I do not need this trouble between my earls now, not when concerns in Normandy plague me. I grant you, Isabel is beyond fair. Even I looked at her with a foolish eye at times, but she is the wife of my greatest counselor. He would never have forgiven me. Do you understand what you and she have done? You have broken the man! The clerk who was with him when he received the news tried to calm him. Robert banished the man from his sight. I have never seen him as distraught as over his wife's betrayal."

"Her betrayal?"

Isabel would have edged closer to be within better

earshot. Her thoughts were a dizzying circle. Robert relied most upon Thorold as his clerk and had always kept the monk near. Had Robert now dismissed her tormentor?

When she moved, Mildrith clamped a hand on her arm.

Below, King Henry continued, "Robert told me everything, how he had seen your brazen interest in his wife grow over the years. Only when she came to court as companion to my Amieria did he believe she returned your sentiments. Tell me the truth now. Did Isabel come to you of her own free will? Did she run to you?"

"I can only say Robert's wife never sought me out. Have you never considered why a woman, if she is so beloved by her husband, would turn to another man?"

"I do not care why she has done it. Enough women with husbands have lifted their skirts for me to prove love or lack of it is no motivation. My only concern is for the turmoil you and Isabel have unleashed. Robert is no use to me. I have urged him home to Leicester, when he would have besieged you here instead."

"He would go to war with me on suspicion alone, Your Grace?"

"You have not denied stealing his wife. Do you think the man such a doddering simpleton in his old age? Give her up! Let Isabel return home. Let me have peace between my earls again."

William's long sigh echoed to the wooden beams in the rafters. "I cannot. It is beyond my power now."

"You cannot or will not? You dare defy your king. Christ, has she already bewitched you with the honey between her legs?"

"I have not touched the lady."

"You long for it! I saw the lust in your eyes for years, how you watched her, wanted her as I did. Now, I know your regard has progressed beyond base desire. You love the woman. If so, you are an addlepated fool. She is one, too, if she shares your hopes."

The hint of incredulity and envy in Henry's voice

stunned Isabel. However cynical the king must be regarding William's love for her, His Grace also begrudged them such happiness. Had Henry never known love in his endless affairs with women of the realm? How dare he judge William when his own sordid past outmatched some of the most lecherous men at court? Henry had no right to judge William or her.

Henry's demands and those of her soul be damned. She would never bend her will to suit another's own again. Her father. Her husband. The king. All of them had sought to control her fate. Even William had brought her here against her will. He would not keep her now by virtue of his power alone. This time, she would govern her fate. No one else would hold sway over it ever again.

The king continued, "Love is for those who have choices. You have none. Return Isabel to Robert and set this matter to right again. I will not have my earls at each other's throats like dogs fighting over a bitch in heat."

"Isabel is no bitch, Your Grace and I would not have her named so. Not even by you."

"You will do as I have ordered before my return from Normandy, or by all the power I possess, I shall seize everything you hold and raze your castles to their foundation stones! Do not gainsay me. Give her up! Isabel can never be yours."

Chapter Twenty – Choices
Castle Acre, England: April 1116

A burning candle scented the air in William's chamber with smoke and beeswax. In the hours after King Henry's furious leave-taking, Isabel sat on the bed with the curtains drawn, while Mildrith brushed her hair down her back. She wore her chemise and a blanket on her shoulders. Beyond the castle walls, the bells at the parish church and the priory of Castle Acre pealed the hour of Compline.

"Shall I braid milady's hair with ribbons?" Mildrith asked.

Isabel clenched her shaking fingers in the coverlet. "Not tonight. You may leave me."

"As you wish." Mildrith came around the bed and dipped into an awkward curtsy. Her rounded belly wobbled. "Is there nothing more you would have of me?"

Isabel knew her cheeks must appear flushed despite the lowlight. She gathered her courage. "If the earl is not asleep, I wish you to ask him to come here. I wish to speak with him."

Mildrith bobbed her head. "You want to speak with him only?"

At Isabel's exasperated sigh, the woman laughed and left her. Isabel stood. Her heart raced with pent-up emotions, anticipation chief among them. Fear remained absent. Up until today, before the king's arrival, guilt and fettered longing mired the path before her. Now, no such concern plagued her. Fear of the unknown would never govern her choices again. How had her feelings altered? Had William had bewitched her in the same manner the king had accused her of doing? She knew the thought could not be true. William was no more capable of sorcery than she might be.

When she had gone to the gallery earlier, she had still planned on some action or noise, which would reveal her presence to the king. Yet, his exchange with William had resulted in another inclination, toward the opposite effect of Henry's purpose and her own. In demanding William's submission and with it, hers, Henry had stoked bold fires in her heart. She would thwart the king and her husband and free herself from their commands forever.

All her life, she had lived by the dictates of her parents and her husband. Their choices directed her own. Even marriage to Robert had not gained her the independence she still desperately longed for, the power to govern her own fate. William had stolen her away from Robert, denied her the choice of remaining with her husband. Could she have borne a life without William, forever divided from him?

God would judge her for her sins. When He cast her into hellfire for all her misdeeds, it would be enough to know for a brief moment, she had made her life and destiny her own, subject to the commands of none other than her free will. Was it such a terrible wish to live as she chose?

A knock at the door startled her from reverie. She held her breath until the sound penetrated the wood again. William's voice followed.

"Isabel, are you unwell?"

"You may enter and see for yourself." She gripped the blanket and summoned all her courage.

The oak creaked before William stood framed in the doorway. His haggard countenance betrayed red-rimmed eyes, puffy cheeks and a rough pelt of hair on his face. Two dark stains splattered his green *cotte*. He had removed the belt and his shoes. He wore braies and green garters held his hose in place.

He remained just outside the chamber. "You summoned me."

She forced a smile. "I hope I have not troubled you at this hour."

"You could never trouble me. I was not abed. I was in the scriptorium, writing a letter to my sister, Edith, in France."

She gasped and turned away. "The scriptorium—"

Blood roared in her ears and queasiness gathered in her stomach. Just when she feared a faint might overcome her, William's hand caught her elbow. He bolstered her with his body, warmer than the blanket around her shoulders.

"Do not cry, my Isabel."

She leaned into him, foolish tears trickling across her cheeks. "Please, I have asked you never to call me so. Robert did, even when he set his creature Thorold to beating me for my sins."

"Who is this Thorold?" William murmured against her hair.

"One of Robert's clerks, a Benedictine monk. They have known each other since boyhood."

"Was he the sole person among the comte's retinue who ever hit you?" Fury laced his tone.

"Yes, always at Robert's command only."

"Why did Robert set him to your chastisement?"

Her throat tightened. Could she reveal all she had discovered in her last years as Robert's wife? What of his predilections, including decades-long incest with his own half-blood brother? How would a man like William act, if he held such information about the king's most loyal counselor? While she trusted William and knew instinctively he would never do anything to make her unhappy, he held no such regard for her husband. His jealousy and resentment of Robert would never permit it. Her years of loyalty and esteem for her husband could not countenance the stain upon his reputation throughout the realm.

Non, she could never humiliate him nor allow anyone else to do so, including William, no matter what Robert has forced upon her. He had not driven compassion from her. To the last, for his pride and the honor of their children, she would keep his secrets and never reveal Robert's shame.

"Isabel?" The concern in William's voice urged a response.

"The man displayed a keen interest in punishment

and in fulfilling Robert's wishes, nothing more." She sighed. "Thorold often conducted his whippings in the scriptorium at night, after all were abed. The sentries never helped me above stairs afterward nor inquired about the blood on my back, the torn cloth, or the screams at night. Only the healer at Leicester, a gentle woman named Constance, aided me. In her kindness, your Mildrith reminds me of her. Mildrith also has a sharp tongue like my former attendant, Petronilla."

He stroked her forearm. "I will never allow anyone to hurt you again as long as I am alive."

She inhaled the now familiar scent of him and leaned into his warm embrace. "I believe you."

"The king arrived today. He is on his way to Normandy. You must have seen his banners and those of his knights and clergymen from the window." When she nodded, he continued, "Henry demanded I give you up, or he would raze my castles. He said I had no choice. You must understand I love you too much to ever let you go."

"Then never let me go."

When his breathing stilled, she turned toward him and shrugged off the blanket. He looked down between their bodies. She experienced no embarrassment at the thinness of the fine chainsil of her chemise, which revealed as much as it covered. There could be no shame in standing before William as God had fashioned her, not when his eyes glittered with such pleasure and desire. She placed a hand on his chest, above his heart, which beat furiously. His fingers covered her own.

"Are you certain, Isabel?" His voice, deep and rough, washed over her and stirred embers of longing to life again.

"I am. God may damn me because of it."

"He shall condemn us both, for I shall be at your side in the pit of despair. I would join you gladly, having known your heart, your passion."

"I want a life with you, for as long as God shall permit it. I choose you." Her voice, thick with desire, startled her.

He bent his head slightly, his gaze wide and searching her features. His hesitation and uncertainty, even at the moment when the fulfillment of both of their wishes awaited them, delighted her. She laughed, a throaty sound she had never issued before, and framed his visage between her hands.

"Nothing and no one shall ever part us again, William."

His lips hovered just above hers. "You say I must not call you my Isabel, but you are mine! Now and forever, you are my life."

The first furtive touch of his mouth against hers set her blood boiling. Her stomach tightened. Desire made her bold. She tugged his face down to hers, arched against him and surrendered to the fervent feel of his lips on her. He lifted her as if she weighed nothing. His hands swept down to her hips and pressed himself against her. A low moan died inside her throat, swallowed up as she returned his feverish kisses. He broke their embrace, his ragged breath at her ear, before his mouth dipped to the hollow of her throat.

Her nails raked through his hair and across his scalp. "May I see your face when we are abed?"

His low chuckle warmed her neck, before he raised his head. "Isabel, what nonsense do you ask? Of course, you may. Why would you ever question it?"

"It is only because Robert would always take me from behind. At least, after he came to believe we would conceive sons in this way. He found proof for his superstition when our twins entered the world. My husband insisted upon the position ever afterward."

He cupped her cheek and kissed her there, lightly, before his lips trailed across her nose to the other cheek. Rough stubble grazed her tender skin. Then he sat on the bed and drew her onto his lap, astride him. His calloused hands pushed the chainsil garment up until he revealed her knees, which sunk into the bedding. The underside of her thighs throbbed.

She sputtered, "William! What are you doing?"

"You have never been atop before now."

Grateful for the fading light in the room to hide her blushes, she lowered her gaze. "Doesn't the Church forbid it?"

He touched her chin. "You have never seemed a pious woman who cares for the Church's dictates."

She slapped his hand away. "Now you would name me an adulteress and blasphemer."

"I would simply call you my own and watch you gain your pleasure in my arms. I would please you if you showed me how."

"You care for a woman's pleasure. My husband did when he thought it might avail him. Are you like him, William? Do you say and do what you must only for your gain?"

He kissed her throat and shoulders, nibbled her ear lobe and licked at the tender spot throbbing at the base of her throat. A jolt rippled from her breast through her belly. His fingers threaded through the hair cascading down her back.

"Do not doubt me now. I am a man in love. Such a man does not seek his fulfillment alone. Everything you want is permissible, my sweet Isabel. Let me show you."

He tugged the chemise down her arms and torso. He bared her to the waist. Then he withdrew his touch and braced himself on his elbows.

Cool air in the chamber danced across her florid skin, pimpled with gooseflesh. "Why did you stop?"

"I told you, I am not your husband, a man who would place his joy above your own. I do not seek to take what you would so willingly give. As you are mine, I am yours, to do with as you please."

She gazed at him, uncertain. "I do not think I should behave this way. Robert always cautioned me against wanton actions."

He reached for her. His thumb trailed across her lower lip. Despite the slow, deliberate path he traced, his hand shook before it fell away.

"He is not here. I am. You may do as you please with me."

She drew in a deep breath before she grabbed the hem of the chemise and pulled it up and over her head. He sucked in his breath as she revealed herself. His hands clenched and the knuckles whitened, while he admired her. She leaned forward and stroked a fingertip from his brow to the bridge of his nose and then across his rough cheek. He turned his head and his mouth caught her fingertip. She tugged her hand away and palmed his chest as it rose and fell, felt the rhythm of each harsh breath torn from him. Her fingers slipped beneath the *cotte* at the neckline. Even in the cold climate and drafts of Castle Acre, he wore no *sherte* beneath the tunic, which allowed her to feel the full strength of him.

She reveled in his nearness, guessing at the power his clothing covered. She had only ever seen Robert naked and then in brief interludes where he removed his clothes for a bath or to share the bed with her. He had always insisted on removing his garments. After years together, he stopped caring whether she did the same. Even at his great age, Robert's stomach and limbs had remained firm, without the paunch her father had developed. Still, Robert could not compare to William's strength and size, evidenced in her lover's broad shoulders, powerful arms and massive legs.

"Sit up and remove your *cotte*." She scooted back and rested her bottom on his legs.

He chuckled. "You are enjoying this."

At her soft giggle, he complied, almost ripping a seam of the cloth in his haste. She sighed at the mass of scars and cuts on his shoulders and arms. A jagged pink scab peeked between his black chest hairs. It snaked across his breastbone to the middle of his stomach.

"Am I too ugly for the likes of you, sweet lady?" he asked, naked uncertainty apparent in his stare. When she did not respond immediately, his heavy brow knitted and thick, black eyebrows flared. She wrapped her arms around his neck, her fingers stroking his nape. Her breasts felt fuller and heavier, than even when she had borne children for Robert. The tips of her nipples tightened almost painfully as they grazed him. He groaned. She could only guess at the internal struggle he endured as he refrained from touching her.

"You are beautiful in my eyes, William."

He chuckled. "Men are not beautiful, my Isabel."

"You are," she murmured, with a light kiss on a moon-shaped scar at the apex of his arm. His skin felt hotter than hers did. She trailed a line of kisses across his collarbone and reveled in his nearness.

Her hands slid from his neck, around his broad shoulders and pressed against his chest. "Lie down."

As she kissed the hairs down his belly, Isabel's hair blanketed them. Candlelight set the red-gold ends aglow.

"Christ's blood, you are beyond fair!" Despite his exclamation, he remained quiet beneath her.

She chuckled against his stomach and blew against the fine line of hairs at his waist. The muscles in his belly clenched beneath her fingers.

"Isabel."

The warning in his tone only emboldened her. She sat on his thighs again, her fingers on the bulge beneath his hose. "I would touch you here."

"I'll die if you do not." He ground the words out.

She rose and peeled back the garments from his legs, revealing thin wisps of hair. When they were both naked, she clambered atop him again. Her fingers curled around the hardness of him.

"Woman!" William's hips jerked against hers. "I beg you, end my torment."

"My own, as well?" With her free hand, she laced her fingers with his and dragged them to her breast. "Touch me as you would please. I give you all you would not take from me."

He brushed aside her hands and kneaded her flesh before his mouth closed on her other nipple. His teeth nipped before he sucked hard. His iron grip clamped on her waist again and pulled her close. She did not doubt the bruises of his lovemaking would mar her fair skin in the morning. His hardness surged between her legs.

Before the heat of their desires consumed her, Isabel sighed raggedly and murmured against his hair, "Never let me go."

"You said you were writing to your sister Edith earlier," she said later, while his fingers stroked the length of her arm. "Did you mention me to her?"

"I did, including my abduction of you. I have never hidden anything from my sister. It would have been useless, when she has always known of my heart's true desire. She never cautioned me against loving you, only counseled me to be careful and avoid rash action."

Isabel laughed. "It would seem you have ignored her warning. Men never listen to women."

He tickled her ribs while she squirmed.

"William, mercy, please!"

Laughter rumbled his chest. "Quiet! What would you have my men below stairs think I'm doing to you?"

"Pleasuring me beyond all dreams and desires. Loving me."

He caressed her back and kissed her hair with a sigh. "Edith shall be displeased. In time, she will forgive me. My sister desires my happiness in the same measure as I wish for hers."

William rolled on his side and took her with him. Her leg draped his massive thigh, their bodies still joined. Isabel gasped at the feel of him deep inside her. Languid, she contented herself with admiring the breadth of him. For now.

He propped himself up on one elbow, while her fingers roamed over his shoulder and upper back. He said, "I have admitted my feelings for you to one other person."

She giggled. "Rudolf was so determined to bring me here. I must apologize to your constable for my ferocity. I fought him at every step to Castle Acre."

"My cousin warned against your unladylike behavior. He said you were a little hellion who would scratch my eyes out before you let me bed you." When she laughed again, he added, "I did not mean him, though, you mistook my meaning."

She sobered and her hand stilled. Unease stirred in her belly. "Please do not say you told Amieria of your regard."

"She deserved the truth from me, even if it might have hurt her. A year after we parted from her at Westminster, she remained unmarried. I journeyed into Kent. She had won the king's concession and an endowment for a life at Montivilliers. She swore she would prefer it. I confessed my feelings for you and begged her forgiveness for the deception during our betrothal."

Isabel held her breath until he spoke again.

"She did not grant me her favor. She returned to her stepfather's manor house and never spoke with me again. Her gentle mother offered some consideration. The lady had no cause for anxiety, when I had wronged her daughter from the first. When Amieria entered the abbey, I bestowed gifts upon Montivilliers for her benefit, through the priory of Saint Pancras of Rome at Lewes. If the abbess has ever wondered at the generosity of Prior Hugh, I will never know. It is enough Amieria has accepted a new life."

"If she knows of the gifts, she will think it a credit to her father's wishes."

"Henry may claim the honor. His daughter's comfort is enough for me."

Isabel snuggled against him. "I regret the pain we have both caused. I shall never be sorry for choosing a life with you. I want to be at your side forever."

He kissed her brow. "I would marry you, Isabel, if I could."

Silence fell over them. She did not speak for fear the tears would ruin her joy.

Then she whispered, "I belong to you now, body and

soul. It must be enough, for both of us."

Lewes, England: February 1117

Isabel sat up in bed while the bells of the priory church at Lewes pealed a sonorous tone. She clutched the edge of a wooden cross William had presented to her, tied to a length of red twine. Through the sole window, she glimpsed snow atop the high flint walls of Saint Pancras, below the motte. In the fifth month of her new life with William, he had left Castle Acre for Lewes where they had resided for another five months. She had welcomed the change, concerned for the king's sudden reappearance. William had reason to fear for her safety and his own. He stood a greater chance against Henry here. Castle Acre's poor defenses could not compare to the fortress at Lewes, its walls and all the buildings in the bailey constructed of limestone.

At a knock on the chamber door, William entered. Mildrith trailed him. Both of them smiled at her.

Mildrith curtsied beside the bed. "How do you fare, milady?"

"Well, as before when you last inquired. You need not worry for me."

William sat down and the mattresses shifted beneath his weight. "You have birthed several babies before our child was born, which must help." He did not look up at Mildrith's frown, as he peeled back the swaddling around the squirming bundle in his arms.

Mildrith peered at the newborn. "None as large as Lady Gundred?"

Isabel also stared at the mottled face peering with wide eyes from the blanket. "None of my other children was this big at birth. She is strong and takes after you, William."

He said, "I pray she has your beauty, not my features, dearest. Are you certain you still do not wish to hold her?"

"William, it would not be appropriate for me."

"Why would it be inappropriate for the mother of my child to hold her?"

At his raised voice, Gundred let out a piercing screech, her face even more reddened than before. Mildrith held out her arms for the twitching child.

"Give her to me. This girl has a hearty appetite to match my new son's own. Thank God, I have ample milk for both of them. You should join your men on the practice field, milord." She took the baby from him and settled on a stool beside the window. Soon, Gundred made loud, smacking sounds.

William eyed the wet nurse, his lips tightly pressed together. The fine lines etched across his brow deepened. Then he rose from the bed and bowed to Isabel, before leaving the room. As he went, he murmured something she could not hear, except, "Damned women. I'm dismissed from my own chamber."

Isabel released a pent-up breath. The cross fell from between her fingers. She clasped her shaking hands beneath the wool blanket. She would never make him understand. He must have thought her the worst mother in the world.

Though she faced the window, Mildrith said, "The earl looked ready to hit something. Best if he expends such energy with his men. I doubt my Rudolf will agree. He will be sore tonight. I know just how to ease him."

Isabel murmured, "I do not doubt you do."

"There is no great art to keeping a man happy, milady. You must have learned by now."

"There are times I am uncertain where William is concerned." A little sob escaped Isabel. Tears trickled before she could think of stopping them.

Mildrith said nothing, only attended to the baby while Isabel cried silently. When Gundred had her fill and drifted asleep, her nurse placed the child in the cradle beside the bed.

"Milady, did your husband forbid you to hold your children?" she asked.

Isabel sniffled. "Robert did not encourage it. He

wanted me only for the sons I could bear. Motherhood has always been difficult. I am unsure it suits me. My mother was not an affectionate person, my father even less. They would both frown upon a parent coddling a child. In truth, I do not know what to do with a babe."

"They are easier to understand than men, milady. They only want you to hold, feed and love them. There is no mystery. Besides, your mother cannot dictate what you may do with any child of yours. Your husband is not here either. You may be as affectionate as you please."

"You mistake me. I do not know how."

Mildrith lifted Gundred from the cradle. "Then start now."

A tide of panic rose up from the pit of Isabel's stomach. "What are you doing? Leave her be." Her protest proved in vain, as the wet nurse deposited the baby on her lap.

"Look at your daughter, milady. She is fair like you, but a sizable babe. She has fine red hair, just like her grandmother Countess Gundred did. The earl's mother, God rest her soul, died at Castle Acre in the year of my birth. My mother told me she was a kind, pious woman. She never hid her opinions from her husband, even if they differed from his. I wish she had lived to know her granddaughter and the woman her son has grown to love."

Isabel stared at the child who dozed on, oblivious to the attention she had garnered. On impulse, she stroked her fingertip across a full, rosy cheek, which dimpled in response. The child's skin felt warm and soft at her touch.

"If she were here, my old nurse, Claremond, would say the child has the red hair of my grandmother, Anne of Kiev. She was a princess of Rus, a land of frozen rivers and snow. I never met her. She died before I was born. Claremond always spoke of her compassion and piety, much like your Countess Gundred." Isabel chuckled, as her musing sparked another memory. "Queen Anne often did as she pleased. She risked great shame. After the death of her husband, the king, she desired Comte Ralph de Valois and married him, although he already had a living wife."

"So, your love of milord would not be the first scandal among your family," Mildrith observed.

Isabel gawked at her in silence, before she chuckled. "My uncle, King Philip of France, was excommunicated for his second marriage."

"As I have said, the heart chooses, milady. I notice you do not deny your devotion to Earl William."

A warning blush heated Isabel's cheeks. "God love you, Mildrith. You are a bold one."

"I know only how to speak the truth, milady. If I wished, I could blame indulgent parents or a tolerant husband. As it is, Rudolf forgives much of my sharp tongue. When he first noticed me, I was a girl of sixteen and him, newly knighted. I wanted nothing to do with him. He won me over by his patience. When milord allowed us to wed, it was the second happiest day of my life. The first was when we pledged our hearts to each other. If you've not told the earl of your feelings, you should."

"Do I have to speak? I have cast off my husband and children and risked the ire of a king. I have given my body to William and shared his bed more often than I can recall. I have borne his child. Can he still be uncertain of my feelings for him?"

"Everyone wants to hear the words, milady. Word and deed are of equal importance."

Gundred squirmed and whimpered in her sleep.

"You had best take her, Mildrith," Isabel insisted.

The wet nurse lifted the babe, who barely stirred. Isabel contented herself with watching Gundred while she slept in her crib. With a protracted sigh, she considered the children she had left behind, those who no longer had a mother by their side.

The regrets she carried would burden her until death. She could not deserve the happiness this babe could bring, not when she had abandoned the children God has already given her.

In the late evening, when William had not returned to the chamber, Isabel threw off the bedclothes in exasperation. He was obviously still displeased with her reticence toward Gundred and punishing her with his absence. If he thought he could ignore her all day, he would soon learn differently!

As she shoved her feet into her shoes, she peeked at Gundred, again nestled snugly in her wet nurse's arms. Mildrith snored lightly, her mouth gaping. Isabel smiled at the pair before she pulled on the robe she had last worn. Her hair remained unbound, as when she had delivered the child. She did not care if the lack of a *couvrechef* would scandalize William. After all, he shared his bed with another man's wife. He would be a simpleton if concern for Isabel's loose hair troubled him.

She fled the chamber and barely acknowledged the nods of two sentries stationed in the corridor. She chafed at their nearness, a constant reminder of William's vigilance against her leave-taking. Even after ten months, he still doubted her.

Isabel paused at the top of the landing, her hand splayed across her breastbone. What if Mildrith was right? Isabel knew William loved her, but he did not trust whether she might remain with him even with the babe they shared. He still believed shame and fear would drive her back to Robert's arms. Would he believe in her devotion, if she told him of her devotion? She doubted it would be so easy to convince him. Deep in her heart, she loved him. She did not know when her feelings had burgeoned. Their intensity often overwhelmed her. The long years apart after William's first declaration had not dulled her yearning for him. She had dreamt of him at night as Robert used her body. She often pretended William's arms held her instead. Her affection for him swelled deep within her heart, unfathomable and stronger than she had ever deemed possible.

"He must know of my feelings now."

With a sigh, she crept down the stairs. Servants on their way to the hall with tablecloths, cups and spoons bowed or curtsied. She nodded to each of them whom she bypassed. Only the Lord knew how the scullery maids and pageboys must gossip of her affair with William in private. Still, they showed her the deference of a woman of her station and treated her with the appropriate courtesy. What must they be thinking now, since she had borne their lord a bastard?

She gripped the hall door, a pained wheeze escaping her at the thought.

"Milady, should you be out of bed?"

Rudolf approached, rubbing his shoulder. A thin cut blemished his chin. William had pushed his men too hard.

Isabel had soothed the constable's ill will toward her in previous months. Still, she often felt he watched her with a wary gaze. He also needed convincing of her love for his cousin.

"I delivered a babe two weeks ago. I am well, Rudolf. Thank you."

"Why isn't my Mildrith with you?"

"I need no escort to find William. Your wife takes a much-needed rest. It is a wonder she can bear the hungry demands of Gundred and your babe. She is a good and patient woman."

A smile relaxed the constable's brow. "She is a blessing, far better than I deserve." He sighed. "If you're seeking milord, he's within."

At his gesture, Isabel thanked Rudolf and entered the hall. William stood by the hearth dressed all in gray, his face in profile. He did not offer her the usual, warm smile. Instead, worry lines marred his expression. He gripped a roll of parchment in his hand tightly. The young men setting up the tables and benches stopped their work at her sudden, unkempt appearance. She ignored them and raced toward him.

"What news do you have, milord? Is it the king? Does he move against you?"

When she touched his shoulder, William sighed and covered her fingers with his own. "Do not fear. It is a family matter, naught more."

"Will you speak to me of it?"

"I would not burden you."

Her hand fell away. "When will you realize your burdens are mine? You share a bed with me, yet you think less to tell me of your family's concerns. What am I to you, William? Your *leman?* The mother of your bastard only? Will you treat me with the disdain my husband offered? Will you never see me as a kindred spirit, someone in whom you might confide and trust?"

The activity in the hall ceased. He scowled at her, red-faced. His fist closed on the parchment.

His anger roused, she feared the results. She should not have spoken so! If he was angry before over her attitude toward Gundred, she had made him furious now.

Her heart raced as she turned to the servants. "Leave us. Now!"

Some measure of satisfaction filled her as the hall's occupants scurried.

She stood alone with William. "My greatest faults are lack of forethought and pride. Forgive me. I should not have spoken so carelessly before your household, or ordered them out as if they are mine."

"You should not have done so."

He hauled her into his arms, his lips seeking hers. He tasted of wine and the smoke from the hearth. If he had sought to punish her in his possessive hold, his embrace had the opposite effect on both of them. Her fingers delved in his dark hair, nails raking his scalp. He backed her against a trestle table. When he deepened their kiss, cupped her breast through the robe and nearly crushed her against him, she broke the kiss.

"Stop it! Do not try to silence or dominate me with your will. Do not treat me the way Robert did. I love you, William. If we are to share a life together, you must trust me in all things. No more guards. No secrets between us.

I will stay with you, always. I will learn to be a proper mother to our child. Others will shun her for her birth. We shall shield our daughter from their slights. You do not understand my reserve toward her. If only you had known what I endured as a child, you would find no fault with me. There is time for me to learn to love our daughter, for you to understand the woman you have chosen. You must give me time.

"For now, I want your pledge, a solemn promise from you. Never let your love make you conceal the past or present truths from me, even if they would hurt. I have lived ignorant of the confidences and concerns of others who thought they were protecting me. I will not suffer more. Do you understand? I ask for your confidence, your respect and love of me wholly. As I love you."

He kissed her brow, a grin on his lips. "Say it again."

"You cannot expect me to repeat everything."

"Only the part about loving me."

"Oh. Of course, I love you."

"You have never said so before. I would hear it again."

"I love you."

"Once more?"

"William, for the love of all that is good in this world, I love you!" When he laughed, picked her up and swung her around, she groaned. "Heavens! I will say it as often as you wish. Only please put me down before I'm overcome with faint!"

His warm, wide lips covered hers. She laughed and clung to him. "I still require your pledge."

He raised his head and nodded. "I give it freely. I shall never conceal the truth from you in any matter, even if it would cause you great pain."

When he set her on her feet again, Isabel touched the parchment in his hand. "Who sent you this?"

His frown returned. "Edith writes from France. Her son with Gerard de Gournay is a young man, easily influenced by the whim of others. Hugh is my eldest nephew and I love him for my sister's sake. After

Gerard's death, Hugh served as a page and squire at Henry's court. Edith did not agree with his placement. Henry insisted upon it as one condition of my restoration to Surrey."

"You are being overly kind. You mean to say the king took your nephew as a hostage, ensuring your loyalty, before the battle at Tinchebrai against his brother Robert Curthose."

"It seems my assurances were in vain. When my nephew gained his inheritance and a knighthood from the king himself, Hugh crossed over to France. His mother and I expected he would sojourn at the castle La Ferté-en-Bray. Instead, after a month, he went to the court of Count Baldwin of Flanders for a year. Baldwin is Henry's rival. The Flemish count has corrupted my nephew. The king took Hugh prisoner at Rouen. Edith writes in the hopes I might intercede and persuade you to join me."

"I would do whatever I could, but I do not understand how I might assist you with Hugh de Gournay."

William shook his head. "Perhaps you are right. Truly, your estrangement from your family at Crépy-en-Valois is one I can hardly fathom. If some attachment remained between you and your younger sisters, you would know Beatrice de Vermandois is the wife of Hugh de Gournay. You would call my sister's son a brother by marriage, Isabel, if you knew him."

Isabel stared at him, open-mouthed, as she recalled mention of her sister's marriage in one of Comtesse Adelaide's letters. The name of the bridegroom had remained a mystery until now.

William smiled. "It would seem there was always meant to be some bond between us, Isabel, whether in the union of your younger sister and my nephew or the love we share."

She nodded. "My mother did not encourage affection between her children. Beatrice, all my sisters and brothers, would be as strangers to me if I saw them now.

I am truly sorry, William. I cannot influence Beatrice to counsel her husband Hugh against his folly."

"I understand. The task remains before me to influence my nephew and persuade the king against killing him. I fear—"

"Henry is unlikely to favor your plea, because of your conduct with me," Isabel finished for him. She turned to the hearth and stared into the crackling flames.

William loved her so. He would have kept even this trifle of Henry's displeasure with them from her, to spare her regrets. What did she care for the will of kings now? She served her own desires. She had made her choice to live at William's side forever. She must show him her worth and allow him to know she could be his helpmate in every way. If she could not help him through her relations with Beatrice, another means might exist.

She said, "If your pledge would not satisfy the king, then Hugh must guarantee his own conduct. Your sister Edith had two children with Gerard de Gournay?"

"There is my niece also, a child who shares our daughter's name. She is young, unwed."

Isabel perceived how she might help William resolve his family's crisis. "Henry is always looking for young heiresses to forestall his rebellious nobles. If this Gundred were to wed a nobleman of the king's choosing, their union might seal the breach between Henry and your nephew. Suggest it. Henry might be amenable."

"When I was last at court, the king sought a bride for Nigel d'Aubigny."

"We may have found her."

William grasped her shoulders and tugged her against him. "With your wisdom to guide me, with you at my side, all things may be possible."

Chapter Twenty-One – The Blood Debt
Lewes, England: July to October 1118

Isabel hastened to the hall, Mildrith breathing raggedly at her back, as she carried Gundred. The women nearly collided with the herald from Normandy, who begged their pardon with a bow. William awaited them. Isabel approached him, her hand on her stomach where their second child nestled. The midwife had confirmed her suspicions earlier, after weeks of retching in her chamber pot each morning. William knew, had suspected it even before Isabel did. His frigid gaze made her wonder whether the news would please him.

Each day at William's side filled Isabel with more trepidation that at any moment, Henry would end her idyllic happiness. His siege engines would batter Lewes Castle, while his men dragged wooden belfries up to the walls, raining arrows on the defenders until they forced the surrender of William and his men. Had the dreaded day come at last?

"You summoned me," she whispered.

He nodded. "First, tell me what the village midwife said."

"It is true. You are to be a father again."

William crossed the room and kissed Gundred's plump hands as she reached for him. "Return with her above stairs, Mildrith."

The wet nurse curtsied. "As you wish, milord."

Gundred wailed for her father as Mildrith took her away. Isabel wondered whether her daughter would ever feel such attachment to her. Though she had grown more comfortable with the child, the wet nurse still knew best how to interpret Gundred's needs. Even William was more at ease with their child than she had ever been.

When they were alone, William took Isabel in his arms. She heard the rapid beating of his heart. She pushed aside her concerns about Gundred.

"What is it, my love? You're frightening me."

"I do not mean to. The herald brought word of

Robert. Your husband is dead."

Isabel drew back in the circle of his arms. She stared up at him, wordless.

"Late last year, he retired to Saint Pierre-de-Préaux and took up the habit of the Benedictines. His last will and testament stipulated the care of his children would reside with King Henry. Robert died at the beginning of last month. At Saint Pierre-de-Préaux, Abbot Richard de Forneaux prayed with him often in his last hours. The archbishops of Rouen and Canterbury also arrived at the abbey. They came from Rouen expressly to intercede for Robert's soul. Archbishop Ralph d'Escures of Canterbury sent his herald to us, after Robert's death.

"The archbishop of Rouen asked Robert, on pain of denying him the Extreme Unction, if he would not renounce the lands he had stolen at Leicester from Ivo de Grentmesnil and his two sons. Robert refused, though he did repent of his sins against the abbey of La Croix Saint-Leuffroy, from which he had also taken lands inappropriately. He said his honors belonged to his heirs, the twins Robert, Earl of Leicester and Waleran, Comte de Meulan. They would act accordingly for his soul. Robert's body lies buried at Saint Pierre-de-Préaux. The abbot ordered his heart carried to his monastic foundation at Brackley."

Isabel pulled away and walked toward the hearth, her footsteps heavy. She sank down on a nearby stool. William hovered. "Though you may not believe it, I grieve for your pain, my love. I would never wish to see you hurt by such news, though I know you must be."

She reached for his hand. "I believe you. You would never lie to me."

A deep sigh rattled her chest. She had been unable to imagine a future without Robert for so long, first as his wife and afterward, when she had turned from him for a life with William. More than any other man, including her father, Robert had dominated her existence for so long. After twenty years, she was free of him forever.

She flinched as a phantom ache crisscrossed her back.

William soothed her with his gentle touch. She grasped his hand again and kissed it. When he stood with her, she found courage to banish the nightmares of the past.

Where were the tears of grief and sadness? Should she not have shed some for her children bereft of a mother and father by now? Her twin son in Henry's clutches. Could she entrust their lives and wellbeing to the king without the kindly influence of Faritius of Abingdon? The abbot had died in the same year of Gundred's birth. Was there any other choice when Robert's will and testament specified his precise direction?

Though Isabel longed for news of her sons, she knew better than to expect it. She assumed they had gone with Henry to Normandy and prayed each day for their safety. More so, she prayed one day all of her children might forgive her.

"There is more," William said.

"Tell me everything."

"The king's decree accompanies the archbishop's words from Rouen. Henry demands we end this illicit liaison and marry. Upon our wedding, a council of four men shall administer the honors Robert's heirs have attained."

Although Isabel had guessed at what William would say, she asked, "Who are these men?"

"First, Morin du Pin, the steward of your husband's Norman and French castles."

Isabel nodded, remembering the chestnut-haired young man at Vatteville. "He is loyal and will take good care of Waleran's interests."

"Ralph the comte's butler shall serve your second son. The other guardians of their welfare shall be Nigel d'Aubigny, Henry's friend and the betrothed of my niece Gundred de Gournay, and me, if I am stepfather to your children."

"Henry moves you and my sons, even me, as if we were all naught more than pieces on a chess board. His Grace has acknowledged more than a dozen bastards and brought them and their mothers to court. He was always shameless before his queen. Now she has gone to her grave before her lecherous husband's time. To think, we have Gundred alone and Henry judges our love an illicit liaison! The king of England is a hypocrite, if you will forgive me."

"It is Henry's privilege to call our love what he will. We know the truth." William knelt beside her, his fingers still intertwined with hers. "I shall be here for you always, even at this loss."

"It is no true loss. I lost Robert years before his death. He never gave his whole heart to me." She guessed at the question in William's eyes and rushed on before he could ask it. "I did not do the same for him. Until you, I never recognized true love and knew I wished to give and receive it. I am free to love, but more importantly, to choose."

"When the requisite mourning period ends, I would claim you for my wife and the Countess of Surrey, if you will have me."

She reached for his cheek and rested her hand there. He turned slightly and kissed her palm. For more than two years, she had been by his side, loving him as a wife might. He could not have doubts regarding her commitment. If he did, she would reassure him now.

"My heart has already chosen you, William. I will be your wife and countess."

Five months later, Isabel sat near the hearth after dinner. The thin cloak on her shoulders offered no respite from the chill in William's great hall. Beneath the wool, she rested a hand on her swollen belly. The coming of a new year would also signal the arrival of the babe growing within her. After the meal, when William had left her for a meeting with Prior Hugh at Saint Pancras and Mildrith withdrew with Gundred, Isabel sat alone thinking of her other children. The sons and daughters she had left behind at Leicester after William's abduction.

Her eldest ones would not have been in the castle to

know firsthand of her disappearance. The world outside Saint Leger would have been a mystery for Emma, now in her fourth year at the abbey. Since Emma's departure, Robert had inquired annually after the health of their daughter. Isabel knew nothing now. The fate of her sons also remained a partial mystery. Whatever troubles Henry faced in Normandy, she prayed Waleran and Robert remained safe.

She pondered the fates of the others, her son Hugh and her daughters Aubree, Adelina, Maud and young Isabel. Bereft of the mother who had abandoned them, their father's death had left the younger children orphaned. Robert's will and testament designated his first two sons as his heirs, his namesake to succeed him to the earldom in England, while Waleran became the Comte de Meulan in his father's stead. The boys were only fourteen and no one could expect them to make provision for their younger siblings. Isabel did not doubt the members of Robert's household under nominal charge from Ralph the butler would provide for her children's needs, better than she ever could have as Robert's widow. What had they told her son and daughters at Leicester of her disappearance?

After so many children, God's purpose for her in their lives remained uncertain. She had not been cruel to her own as her mother had been. Still, willful neglect had to be as harmful to the soul as a whip plied upon a child's back daily. What must her children think of her? Would they believe that she had feared for their wellbeing? How had Robert explained her absence? Did their children think she was dead? Did they fear she had abandoned them forever?

She cupped the mound of her stomach as a heavy weight settled like a stone inside her. Even Gundred preferred her father to her mother. Truly, Isabel had done nothing to deserve the love of her children with Robert.

She blinked back tears when the door creaked.

"Isabel, why are you here alone?"

She stared into the fire. Several dogs barked outside the hall.

William's hands settled on her back. "Still so cold, my love?"

"Not when you are near. Your visit with Prior Hugh went well?"

"As always, the prior is a blessing, a courteous and generous man much like his predecessor, Lanzo. With the death of my clerk, Prior Hugh has granted me another to take his place, who returned with me to the castle. He attends to his duties in the scriptorium."

"Who is he?"

"Peter of Heacham, from one of the priory's daughter houses. When my mother died, my father granted Heacham manor, north of Castle Acre, to monks from Saint Pancras. Prior Lanzo had sent them into Norfolk to found another dependency. The monks still offer daily prayers for my mother's soul."

He knelt beside her and the dogs crowded around him. Try as she might, Isabel could not allow herself to grow attached to the hounds again. Whenever they followed him around the castle, she remembered the alaunt, Lovvet, William's first gift to her. Since then, he had given her so much more.

He said, "Five months have passed since Robert's death."

"I know. Each day, I have prayed for his soul."

"Why have you sent no letters to your children of your good health or our impending nuptials?"

"Would they be pleased to hear from me? What words of comfort could I offer in the aftermath of their father's death? Even if they ever forgave my absence from Leicester and gave their blessing to our union, it would not change how I have failed them in the past. I have been inattentive to their needs throughout my life. I still struggle so much for an understanding of Gundred. When I reach for her, she recoils from me and whimpers if she thinks Mildrith will give her over. She does not act in such ways with you. This child shall be no different.

My children are born with a keen understanding that I do not know how to love them."

"You have told me much of what your childhood was like and how you left your children with Robert to the care of their nurse. Do you remember what you said on the day the midwife confirmed your pregnancy with Gundred?"

She recalled the softening of William's craggy features when she had confessed her secret, of a child conceived in love at Castle Acre.

"You were worried for how I feel about bearing your child, one whom the Church would deem a bastard upon her birth. I told you the past would never govern me again." She touched his shoulder. "Oh, my William, I held only a fool's hope."

He cupped her chin. "It was not. You know how to love, Isabel. You show me the proof each day. Our children shall know your feelings."

A woman's scream echoed from beneath the rafters. William stood and looked up.

"That's Mildrith's voice, I would know it anywhere."

Isabel pushed herself up from the low stool. "Gundred is with her."

He raced ahead of her and encountered Rudolf already on the steps.

The constable looked over his shoulder. "My wife, where is she?"

"She must be in the chamber with Gundred." Isabel dashed up the stairs, despite the cumbersome bulk of her belly and almost tripped on the hem of her robe. William turned swiftly and clutched at her arm. He tugged her behind him. They reached the entrance to William's chamber a moment after Rudolf did.

"Come closer and the child dies as the woman did."

A familiar voice out of Isabel's dreaded nightmares echoed from the room. She peered over William and Rudolf's shoulders, knowing what she would see.

The monk, Thorold de Saint Pierre-de-Préaux, stood near the opened window, towering over Mildrith. She stretched out prone on the floor. Blood trickled from her forehead and saturated a tear across her stomach. Rudolf's anguished cry stirred Gundred, held against the monk's chest.

"Whoever you are, you will die as my wife has," the constable swore.

"Do you think earthly concerns touch me? I am already dead to all who knew me," Thorold whispered.

Isabel said, "Not to me. You have haunted my most horrible dreams at night."

William glanced at her for the briefest moment before his gaze returned to Gundred, who had started wailing. Her cries brought the guardsmen up, along with William's hounds, their teeth bared and low growls in their throats.

When one of the beasts would have lunged at Thorold, Isabel grabbed its collar and pleaded, "*Non*, get the dogs back. Please, everyone stay away from this man!"

William gestured for one of his men, who subdued the snarling mastiff. William asked, "Isabel, how do you know him? This is Peter of Heacham, who came with me from the priory this afternoon."

"He is not from Heacham. His monastic order is that of Saint Pierre or Peter. He gave a false name, a clever disguise. He is my husband's clerk, Thorold, the one who Robert set to beating me," she answered.

The clerk railed at her, "As you deserved! After Robert dismissed me, the brothers of Heacham took me in. I knew you would have run to your lover. I knew I would have seen you again. I told Robert he should have locked you away. You lived only to shame him. I hold the proof of your lust in my hand."

Gundred screeched in Thorold's grasp. William dived for her. The monk's hand lashed and William clutched his forearm. Blood seeped between his fingers and coated the thin edge of Thorold's knife.

"I have no wish to bleed you, milord, but I'll stab you and kill this bastard babe of yours before you can reach her. You cannot help how this woman has bedeviled you. She did it to Robert. Hers is the blood I seek, for the pains she has caused him."

Isabel sidestepped William, who blocked her with his injured arm. "Get back! I won't risk losing you and our daughter."

She glanced at him. "You must see I am not afraid of him. I will never fear him again."

"Are you afraid for your child, whore?" Thorold taunted her, the blade against Gundred's tender cheek. The child wriggled and screamed anew as the blade cut her.

Isabel said, "You gain nothing by this perfidy, Thorold. Robert is dead. He will never come back to you. You have your liberty, as I do."

Thorold eyes were reddened and wild like an animal cornered before the hounds. "I never wanted to be free of him! He cast me far from his sight because of you. You destroyed him and his feelings for me. He said God had judged us for his cruelty to you by taking you from him. He could not see the blessing. I did."

"Isabel, what is this man talking about?" William asked.

"William, for the love of Gundred, be silent! Let me talk to him."

She held up her hands, a plea on her trembling lips. Thorold pressed the blade into Gundred's wound. The agony of her child propelled Isabel. In Gundred's desperate need, Isabel had found the courage to reach for the babe at last.

"One more step and I toss her from the window," Thorold warned. He stretched out his arm and dangled the child by her tunic.

Cries of dismay echoed behind Isabel. She hovered beside Mildrith, whose fingers brushed against her ankle. Isabel dared not look down before Thorold realized life remained in the woman he thought he had killed. He had not murdered Mildrith and he would not kill Gundred. Isabel would not let him.

She willed courage to imbue her speech. "Even if you should take this child from its father, what will you have, Thorold? The blood of an innocent babe on your hands before William murders you."

"You will know pain, bitch, as you never have before when I have killed your child."

"What is one child's life to me? Children die each day." The icy reserve in her tone startled even her. She hoped it would also lull Thorold.

"Isabel! Have you lost your mind? Think of our daughter." William's fury struck her deeper than any powerful lash of Thorold's whip, but she ignored the man she loved.

Please, let William forgive her later. He had to see she had to do this for Gundred's sake. She could not show Thorold how much the babe meant to her or the monk would kill her child! She would not lose another child, not her Gundred.

Her focus remained on the monk. "Have you ever known me to think of a babe as mine, to show such attachment to it as a mother might feel? I abandoned my children for my lover. What makes you think I could ever love William de Warenne's bastard, when I could not care for the children I bore Robert? The girl is nothing to me. She is William's own, not mine."

For the first time, lines crisscrossed his brow. "You lie! You love this babe as you adore the Earl of Surrey."

Isabel lifted her chin and eyed him. "I am incapable of such affection. You once told me, attachment is useless. Everyone and everything we love leaves us."

Tears seeped from beneath Thorold's lowered lids. "As Robert left me. He loved me and then he left me."

In the moment of his distraction, Isabel lunged for Gundred. She caught Thorold by surprise as she snatched her screaming daughter and held her tight, turning away from the monk. He lunged for her back, the knife clenched in his fist.

Mildrith grabbed Thorold's ankle. Startled, he fell backward against the window and bashed his head against the casement. A crimson stain marred the lime wash.

Rudolf knelt beside his wife, who moaned in her torpor. William held Isabel against his body, his chest rising and falling rapidly. His murderous glare fell on the monk, who rose and cupped the back of his head. Isabel soothed Gundred, though she never took her gaze off Thorold. She could not believe she still lived and she had saved her daughter from the man who intended to kill them both. He stepped back a pace and clambered up on the windowsill.

"Let me kill him, milord," Rudolf demanded.

"You will not need to, constable," Isabel whispered. She did not even blink as Thorold slipped backward and out through the window.

William gathered Isabel and their child in his arms. He kissed both of their heads.

Rudolf hefted his wife, her limbs lank around his neck. She groaned and whimpered his name.

William nodded to him. "Attend to Mildrith's care quickly. The wound in her stomach looks very bad. I will send others below to remove the monk's body."

As Rudolf took Mildrith away, William ordered the remainder of his men out into the bailey. Alone with Isabel, he kissed her brow again and held out his hands for the baby. "Let me take Gundred. We must ensure her wound is not too deep. She may bear the scar for the rest of her life."

Isabel clutched her child. "I will take her down the stairs."

"Dearest, this has been a shock for you. Would you endanger yourself and our second child?"

She shied away. When Gundred whimpered, Isabel cradled her against her chest. "I will never let anyone take a child of mine from my arms again. Not even you, her father."

"Then let us see to her care, together."

In the evening, William left Isabel and Gundred with

several guards stationed outside the hall. Though certain the Benedictine acted alone, he would not allow any strangers into Lewes or see his beloved or their child left alone. With Isabel's assurances, he sought his chaplain for a quiet hour of prayer and thanksgiving.

She held Gundred, her cut washed and bandaged with a poultice of herbs to ward off infection. Although Isabel waved him away, William lingered in the doorway, a slight smile on his lips. Isabel kissed the golden red fuzz upon her daughter's head and crooned softly in the ear of the child, who clung to her mother at last.

Chapter Twenty-Two – The Countess
Lewes, England: October 1129

A cool autumnal breeze rustled Isabel's cloak and nearly ripped her veil from her head. She clutched the folds of cambric before the veil could whip across Gundred's face. At twelve years old, her daughter had surpassed Isabel's height and did not seem as though she would ever stop growing. In all things except her beauty and hair color, she was the image of her father. She had inherited his stocky build, a love of horses and an unabashed manner. When Isabel looked in her daughter's large eyes, she saw William's fire and passion burned within her child. Gundred possessed her mother's features along with the red-gold hair of her paternal grandmother and maternal great-grandmother—a distraction for many. Each time Gundred drew near or entered a room, the squires in her father's household ceased their conversation and activities. Admiring glances followed the girl everywhere she went. Time had faded the scar on her cheek where Thorold's dagger had cut her to a thin streak.

Gundred said, "The rains may have delayed them and made the roads impassable, *Maman*."

Isabel smiled. "Do you fear Roger of Warwick will disappoint you, my dear?"

A flush crept up Gundred's face. She stared hard at the ground. Then she met Isabel's gaze. "He would not dare upset his betrothed."

Beside Isabel, William chuckled. "Or her father."

Isabel chuckled at his protectiveness. Although William would never admit it, she knew the eldest child among their five remained her father's favorite.

Nine-year-old Adeline stood before her mother. She looked up at Isabel. "I still do not understand how Gundred can marry Roger of Warwick, if he's our cousin! You told me close families aren't allowed to wed, *Maman*."

Her eldest brother, William's heir and namesake,

buried his face behind his hands with a smothered sigh of exasperation. Then he lowered his small fists. "Ada, how many times must Father and *Maman* or I explain this to you? Roger is not our cousin!"

"He is cousin to our brothers, the Earl of Leicester and the Comte de Meulan!" Ada insisted.

Isabel laid her fingers on the shoulders of her argumentative young daughter. "Ada, dearest, you are right. Roger is the cousin of my sons Robert and Waleran, because their fathers were brothers. Roger is no relation to Gundred, so it is permissible for them to marry."

Ada asked, "Must Gundred live at Warwick Castle? Why can't she stay here with us?"

Her brother groaned. "After a girl marries, she always lives with her husband's family, Why are you so ignorant, Ada?"

"Will." His father's tone, laced with impatience, carried a heavy warning.

"Father, she's always asking questions even an addlepated fool would know!"

William laid a firm hand on his heir's shoulder. "Ada is young and you must learn to have more patience for her. When I was your age, your aunt Edith was the most vexing creature God ever placed on this earth to torment a young boy. You never knew your uncle or my fondness for him. We fought on opposing sides at Tinchebrai. I miss our closeness. Edith and Reginald are not with me to my sole regret. After the bond of husband and wife, there is no closer tie than the love of brothers and sisters. When your mother and I are gone, Will, look to your siblings for comfort and courage."

"As you say, Father."

Ada ruined her father's attempt to placate young William by sticking out her tongue.

Then she called out, "They're here! Look, *Maman*, Father."

Isabel awaited the arrival of her children with Robert who still resided in England. Her gaze encompassed in the mud-slick slope of the motte and the gatehouse of the outer bailey. A large party of riders awaited the porter. Even at a distance, she glimpsed a flag tied to a lance, embroidered with the image of a bear.

A heavy weight settled in the empty pit of her stomach. The dinner hour would arrive soon. She wondered whether she could keep anything down today with her nerves so frayed. She stood with most of her and William's family within the inner bailey. Mildrith kept her two youngest sons, both sick with colds, above stairs in the castle. Isabel had left them earlier with kisses on their warm brows and a brew of dried heartsease.

Gundred must have seen the riders. A wide toothy grin made her impossibly beautiful. "At last."

Isabel wondered at the rapid passing of time. Gone were the days in which her eldest daughter with William led her younger siblings in a merry chase around the castle, or tweaked Ada's plaits and teased her little brothers, Reginald and Ralph. Soon, Gundred would marry and be the chatelaine of Warwick Castle, aged only two years older than Isabel was at her first marriage.

When she sniffled, Gundred's hand alighted on her arm. "Roger isn't taking me away today, *Maman*. Besides, you promised not to cry until after the wedding. It is still several months away."

Isabel covered her daughter's fingers with her own. Gundred knew her mother's moods, joys and heartbreak, almost as well as William did.

"You do well to remind me, daughter. I shall keep my pledge."

Gundred kissed her cheek. "Even after I marry, you and my father shall never be far from my thoughts or my heart. I could never love anyone as much as my parents, not even Roger."

William chuckled. "We will not hold you to such a promise, my girl. The man comes now."

Isabel had known Roger, named for his famed grandfather, since his birth. William was right. A man of more than ten years Gundred's senior seated his mount, instead of the sullen, reserved boy at Warwick Castle. The wind rustled the hay-colored hair shading his blue eyes.

Isabel looked to the others, who accompanied Gundred's betrothed. Several years had passed in which she had first reunited with her twin sons, Waleran and Robert. After William carried her off, she did not see her eldest sons again until a year after their father's death. William went to court as part of Henry's war band in Normandy. Isabel had accompanied him, although her meeting with her sons meant leaving Gundred and young Will in Mildrith's keeping. While William fought off French invaders at the battle of Brémule, Isabel had seen her twins at Rouen. As she had expected, their reticence and her uncertainty strained the meeting. Years of terse exchanges in letters followed. Their forgiveness of her betrayal might never come.

God alone knew what Henry and his courtiers had filled their heads with about her love for William. Isabel would have to live with the regret at causing her children pain. She would never be sorry for her choices in life, especially her devotion to William.

She raised her chin a little, as the frigid stares of her sons met hers, before she turned her attention to the women in the party. Robert's countess was Amice, heiress of the honor of Breteuil. King Henry had arranged the marriage eight years ago. Amice's soft, doe-eyed gaze hinted at a quiet temperament, which probably suited Robert's contemplative, pragmatic nature. The couple had made Isabel the grandmother of children she had never met, a boy, another Robert like his father and grandfather and a girl, Margaret. Robert's pale hand rested on the rounded belly jutting beneath his wife's mantle.

Isabel's namesake stood beside her sister in-law. Eyebrows the same auburn color as Isabel's own arched slightly at the sight of her mother, though Isabel did not know the reason. A servant girl clambered down from a horse litter, a squirming bundle in her arms.

William's herald, who had stood with them, stepped forward. William waved him off and greeted their guests. The men bowed and the women curtsied.

William said, "Welcome to Lewes. I present my family. My heir William. My eldest daughter, Gundred and her sister, Adeline."

His youngest daughter interjected, "Ada, Father! No one calls me Adeline, except when I've been wicked."

She rushed past her father and stared up her half-sister. "Your face looks like mine. We both have *Maman's* eyes, nose and lips. Is your hair red?"

Young Isabel chuckled, a deep rich sound. "I am older than you, so I believe it is more appropriate to say you look like me."

"Ada, please come back here," her mother said with an irritated sigh.

When the girl complied, William sighed and glanced from his youngest daughter to Isabel, who struggled against a smile. He continued, "As I was saying, my youngest daughter, Ada. You already know my wife, the countess of Surrey."

Isabel and her children with William exchanged murmured greetings with Roger of Warwick and his companions. Roger and Gundred only had eyes for each other. When he bowed before her, she blushed furiously. William frowned at his daughter's open affection. Isabel caught his hard gaze and shook her head. She prayed Gundred would be happy in the choice her parents had made for her.

Ada tugged at the sleeve of her father's *cotte* and drew his unrepentant stare from Gundred and her betrothed. "Father, I'm hungry."

William nodded to their guests. "Let us enjoy a fine feast and entertainment before my youngest daughter expires from starvation."

"My men have brought casks of wine from Meulan," Waleran said.

"You are generous with your stores, milord. I thank you for the addition to our meal," William said as he offered Isabel his arm.

She shied away. "Please, lead them on. I would speak with my Isabel before we dine."

Robert and Waleran colored hotly, each sharing a glance with their full-blood sister. She waved them ahead. Though puzzled, William escorted his children and Isabel's relations into the castle.

Robert's marshal, the knight Josceline, bowed. "Milady."

"I am pleased to see you again, marshal. You prosper in my son's household?"

"Earl Robert is a worthy and just lord." Josceline paused and studied her. "If you'll forgive my observation, you seem more content here than ever at Leicester. I am grateful for it."

"Thank you, as always, for your kindness."

Josceline bowed again before he started barking orders to the rest of her son's men. Isabel directed their guests' retainers to the kitchen with the wine and the stables for the horses. At last, she stood with her namesake and the servant girl, who carried a red-faced babe.

Isabel held out her hands. "May I hold my grandchild?"

Her daughter nodded to her attendant, who placed the child in her grandmother's arms. Isabel kissed the babe's dark, curly hair.

"She looks like you, my daughter, but this black hair is her father's own."

"King Henry has less of it now than you might remember, milady."

"His Grace is kind to you and the child?"

"We want for nothing. The king is a generous father, a temperate man. He considers a match for me with the Clare family. Waleran insists upon my marriage."

"Your brother concerns himself with dishonor now? He rebelled against Henry. He lost his estates, saw his castle at Vatteville razed to the ground and found himself Henry's prisoner for five years. He let the king bed his own young sister in exchange for his release."

"Do not be angry with Waleran. He did not put me into Henry's bed. I sought the king's attentions and gained my brother's release. Two years ago at Leicester, I witnessed the sorrow in Robert's eyes as he contemplated another season without Waleran. You must remember their closeness. When the king condemned our brother, it was as if Robert had lost an arm or foot. He was bereft, not even his gentle Amice could comfort him. Once, when he and Waleran were deep in their cups at a happier time, I remembered them talking of how the king had drunkenly confessed his lust for you. Henry had said he regretted not having had the audacity of William de Warenne. From my girlhood, everyone told me I favored you. Today, the proof of our resemblance to each other startled me."

Isabel stared at the mirror image of her younger self in wonderment. There was more of her own passion and willfulness in her children than she realized. Her youngest was a mother at sixteen, a year younger than she had been at the birth of Emma. Robert had entrusted their children to Henry's care. His affections for the king had blinded him to Henry's base nature. What would Robert say of His Grace now, if he knew how Henry had abused his trust and sired another one of his bastards upon their young girl's innocent body?

"I do not judge you, my child. I have no right. I brought shame upon your father's head and abandoned our children to Henry's lustful whims. My regrets have not faded."

"Father rests in peace and you are happy here. Your children have gained. Even my brother Hugh enjoys a friendship with Henry's nephew, Stephen de Blois. My sisters Aubree, Adelina and Maud have their own families. We are not at the mercy of fate, or a lecherous old king. Our parents bequeathed their ambition and pride to us. We will choose our own fates."

Isabel nodded and led her daughter up the stairs and into Lewes Castle. "You have a wisdom I did not own at your age. His Grace has always been kind to the mothers of his children. The Clare family has also thrived under Henry's reign. Earl Gilbert has five sons. Whom does the king consider among them as a suitable husband for you?"

"The youngest, Earl Gilbert's namesake."

Glorious orange burnished the sky as Isabel rode with her twins, beside the River Ouse at the outskirts of Lewes Castle. They had lingered for hours at dinner. Now, the evening's light shimmered with a brilliant sheen upon the water. Waleran's mount snorted as he slowed the horse to a walk.

Isabel mirrored his action with her own mare and continued the discussion she had started when they left the castle precincts. "William knows all of my wishes, should I depart from life before he does. My marriage portion at Elbeuf shall come to you, Waleran."

When her eldest son made no reply, his twin asked, "Why speak of death now? Are you ill?"

Isabel said, "I am in good health. Each day a new ache affirms my mortality. I have two families. It is only right to consider the disposition of all I own, even if I trust my husband would not deny your father's offspring their due."

"You have two families. You just love the rest more than you love the former!" Waleran kicked his horse into a canter and left Isabel and his brother in shock.

Robert called out, "Waleran! Brother, come back!"

Isabel's hand pressed against her breastbone. A ragged sigh escaped her lips. Waleran would never forgive her. She had lost him forever.

Robert turned to her. "I will go after him and make him see reason, *Maman*."

Her heart pitched at his lapse. He had not referred to her as his mother in years. "Do not go. Waleran's anger is justified. I left him, both of you, to Henry's care and sought my own happiness with William."

"You made provision for Waleran at Elbeuf to assuage

your guilt over loving the Earl of Surrey?"

In his blatant stare and bland tone, she recognized the traits of his father. When she looked at her sons, her first husband's features and personality were evident. She had given them little of herself, except a remarkable heritage and her pride.

"I have bequeathed Elbeuf to your brother because it came to me out of marriage to your father. The honor is dear to me, as Waleran is. You are both my sons, but he is the eldest. I trust him to provide for his younger brothers and sisters. There are times I have wondered whether my faith was misplaced."

Robert's cheeks reddened. "You blame us for Henry's liaison with our sister."

Isabel touched his arm. When he flinched, she still kept her hand steady.

"I blame no one, my son. Each of us must bear the responsibility for our choices in life. I have done so. Your sister, you and your brother must do the same. If you wish me to say I am sorry for abandoning you, I am sorry. If you have thought my betrayal of Robert caused me grief, then know his aches are still mine. Yet, if you want me to deny my love for William or our children, I must disappoint you."

"Your regrets are not half enough," Robert muttered. "You do not understand how much we endured at the king's court. You cannot know the debauched life Henry and his courtiers enjoyed. The things Waleran and I have seen changed us forever. We ceased to be children far too soon."

"I remember the court well, Robert. You should not have seen such things."

"I witnessed worse at Leicester. You remember good Abbot Faritius permitted us to return home each Yuletide?" When she nodded, he continued, "A full year before you left us, I was at home one night and could not sleep. I heard a woman weeping—screaming, I should say."

Tears flooded Isabel's gaze. Her fingers touched her

mouth. "Oh, Robert, please do not say you saw me."

"I crept down the stairs. The door of the scriptorium was slightly ajar. Piteous noises came from the room. For many years afterward when I closed my eyes at night, I could still recall the sounds and sights. You bent over the carrel, Father standing over you, while his clerk Thorold flayed the flesh from your back."

Isabel turned away. Shame overwhelmed her.

Robert clutched her hand and drew it to his lips. He kissed her fingertips. "I watched the Benedictine beat you several times afterward during that stay, as my father exhorted him to ply his whip. When I told Waleran about the beatings, he said our father could not have committed such cruelty."

"You must not blame your father entirely. Thorold led him astray. The monk met his end here, at Lewes. He tried to kill Gundred. He fell from the window."

Robert released his hold on her. "A deserved end for a monstrous man. Your pity surprises me. You still have compassion for Father's soul after all you have endured."

"When I am in William's arms, the past does not touch me."

"Then, you are happy with him? I could not bear it if you were ever ill-treated again, *Maman*."

His declaration emboldened her. "I am loved. The prosperity of both my families completes my happiness." When her mount shifted, the breath hitched in her chest. She continued, "You must grant me another visitation. When you return, bring your children."

"I shall come again. We will make the journey after Amice has delivered our child. My countess hopes for a girl with her mother's quiet beauty. We plan to name such a babe Isabel."

Afterward, they rode side-by-side and returned to the castle just before dusk. At the stables, Isabel noted the return of the horse Waleran had ridden. She did not see her eldest son. As she and Robert mounted the stairs, he offered his arm. At the entry to the hall, she gestured for him to enter. She remained just outside the doorway.

Torches set in wall brackets illuminated an idyllic scene. Young Isabel and Gundred sat close together. Gundred held her black-haired niece on her lap, while the baby cooed and played with her aunt's fingers. Roger of Warwick hovered beside them, his meaty hand on his betrothed's shoulder. Waleran displayed his fine sword to an over-awed Will. Amice and Ada sat near the hearth, some of the castle's hounds curled at their feet with full bellies. Robert's countess rose from the bench, welcomed him with a generous smile and offered a cup of wine.

William's hand alighted on Isabel's arm. "I wondered when you and the earl might return. Waleran came back alone."

She turned to her husband. The rest of his dogs loped behind him. Her forefinger smoothed his frown of concern.

"Impulsiveness rules my eldest son. He does not bear slights easily. He lacks his twin brother's temperament."

When William tugged her hand, she held back. "*Non,* we should not intrude. I have no wish to ruin their happiness."

"It is ours to share, Isabel. Neither of us could have expected such a day, where our children and yours by Robert would sit in my hall, sharing a cask of wine from Meulan's vineyards."

"I have no wish to irritate Waleran. He is still having a hard time accepting our life here."

"Remember what you once said. Fear will never rule you again. Waleran is a young man, unwed. Let him look to his own future. I have mine with my countess."

He kissed her fingers, dark hair threaded with gray falling over his eyes. "My love for you will always burn bright, Isabel."

When William straightened, she clasped hands with him and let him lead her into the hall.

THE END

Characters
(In order of appearance)

*Based on historical figures

In the Kingdom of France

<u>At Crépy-en-Valois</u>

*__Isabel de Vermandois__ - daughter of Hugh, Comte de Vermandois and Adelaide, Comtesse de Vermandois, born circa 1085

Claremond – Isabel's nurse

*__Hugh, Comte de Vermandois__ – Isabel's father, third son of Henry I, King of France and Anne of Kiev, Queen Consort of France, born 1057, died October 1101

*__Adelaide, Comtesse de Vermandois__ – Isabel's mother

Thorold de Saint Pierre-de-Préaux - a Benedictine monk, clerk to Robert de Beaumont, Comte de Meulan

Petronilla – Isabel's attendant and Claremond's niece

<u>At Paris</u>

*__Bertrade de Montfort, Queen Consort of France__ – second wife of Philip, King of France, died February 1117

*__Philip, King of France__ – Isabel's uncle, eldest son of Henry I, King of France and Anne of Kiev, Queen Consort of France, born 1052, died July 1108

*__Robert de Beaumont, Comte de Meulan__ – eldest son of Roger de Beaumont and Adeline de Meulan, born 1046, died June 5 1118

***William de Warenne, second Earl of Surrey** – eldest son of William de Warenne, Earl of Surrey and Gundred, Countess of Surrey, died May 11 1138

FitzRobert – a squire in the service of Robert de Beaumont, Comte de Meulan

***William de Montfort, Bishop of Paris** – brother to Bertrade de Montfort, Queen Consort of France

***Gerard de Gournay** – brother by marriage of William de Warenne, Earl of Surrey, died 1098

Rudolf – constable of Castle Acre in service of William de Warenne, Earl of Surrey

In the Duchy of Normandy

<u>At Vatteville</u>

***William** – constable in the service of Robert de Beaumont, Comte de Meulan

***Josceline** – son of William the constable

Sieur Miles de Brotonne – a knight in the service of Robert de Beaumont, Comte de Meulan

***William de Fortmoville** – steward in the service of Robert de Beaumont, Comte de Meulan

***Anschetil** – butler in the service of Robert de Beaumont, Comte de Meulan

***Morin du Pin** – another steward in the service of Robert de Beaumont, Comte de Meulan

Lovvet – Isabel's dog, an alaunt

<u>At Elbeuf</u>

***Edith de Warenne** – sister of William de Warenne, Earl of Surrey, wife of Gerard de Gournay (until 1098)

Judith – an attendant to Edith de Warenne

In the Kingdom of England

<u>At Warwick</u>

***Henri de Beaumont, Earl of Warwick** – second son of Roger de Beaumont and Adeline de Meulan, born 1048

***Margaret de Perche, Countess of Warwick** – wife of Henri de Beaumont, Earl of Warwick

<u>At the English court</u>

***Henry I, King of England** – fourth son of William, King of England and Duke of Normandy and Matilda of Flanders, Queen of England and Duchess of Normandy, born circa 1068

***Anselm of Bec, Archbishop of Canterbury** – son of Gundulf of Aosta and Ermenberga, born circa 1033

***Matilda, Queen of England** – daughter of Malcolm Canmore, King of Scotland and Queen Margaret. Wife of Henry I, King of England, born circa 1080, died May 1 1118

***Robert Curthose, Duke of Normandy** - eldest son of William, King of England and Duke of Normandy and Matilda of Flanders, Queen of England and Duchess of Normandy

***Amieria** – natural daughter of Henry I, King of England

***Sybilla Corbet of Alcester** – daughter of Robert Corbet, Earl of Cornwall. Mistress of Henry King of England

***Faritius, Abbot of Abingdon** – royal physician until 1117

<u>At Leicester</u>

Hild – an English midwife

Wulfwyn – Hild's eldest daughter, also a midwife

Agatha – Hild's second daughter, nursemaid to Isabel's children

Constance – Hild's third daughter, a healer and assistant to Wulfwyn

***Emma de Beaumont** – Isabel's first daughter with Robert de Beaumont, Comte de Meulan, born 1102

***Waleran de Beaumont, Comte de Meulan** – Isabel's first son with Robert de Beaumont, Comte de Meulan, born 1104

***Robert de Beaumont, second Earl of Leicester** – Isabel's second son with Robert de Beaumont, Comte de Meulan and Waleran's twin, born 1104

***Hugh de Beaumont** – Isabel's third son with Robert de Beaumont, Comte de Meulan, born circa 1106

***Aubree de Beaumont** - Isabel's second daughter with Robert de Beaumont, Comte de Meulan, born circa 1108

***Adelina de Beaumont** – Isabel's third daughter with Robert de Beaumont, Comte de Meulan, born circa 1110

***Maud de Beaumont** – Isabel's fourth daughter with Robert de Beaumont, Comte de Meulan, born circa 1112

***Isabel de Beaumont** – Isabel's fifth daughter with Robert de Beaumont, Comte de Meulan, born circa 1113

-**Beatrice and Mabel** – Isabel's other attendants

<u>At Castle Acre & Lewes</u>

-**Mildrith** – wife of Rudolf

***Gundred de Warenne** - Isabel's first daughter with William de Warenne, Earl of Surrey, born circa 1117

***William (Will) de Warenne** – Isabel's first son with William de Warenne, Earl of Surrey, born 1119

***Adeline (Ada) de Warenne** - Isabel's second daughter with William de Warenne, Earl of Surrey, born circa 1120

***Reginald de Warenne** – Isabel's second son with William de Warenne, Earl of Surrey

***Ralph de Warenne** – Isabel's third son with William de Warenne, Earl of Surrey

***Roger de Beaumont, Earl of Warwick** – eldest son of Henri de Beaumont, Earl of Warwick and Margaret de Perche, Countess of Warwick

***Amice de Gael** – Countess of Leicester, wife of Robert de Beaumont, second Earl of Leicester

Author's Note

Born in medieval France, Isabel de Vermandois lived the majority of her years in England. Isabel's paternal grandparents were the Capetian King Henry I and his wife, Anne of Kiev, a daughter of Grand Prince Yaroslav the Wise of Russia. In 1096, Isabel became the wife of a hero of Hastings, Robert de Beaumont, Comte de Meulan. She gave birth to eight of his children, five daughters and three sons.

Within two decades of her marriage to Robert, William de Warenne, the second Earl of Surrey abducted her. They enjoyed a love affair, which likely resulted in the birth of William's daughter, Gundred during Isabel's separation from Robert. After he died on June 5, 1118, William and Isabel married and had four more children. William died in May 1138. Isabel survived by a few years, but her date of death remains unclear.

Earlier sources list her death incorrectly as February 1131. Her eldest son, Waleran, did not inherit her dower estate at Elbeuf until 1141. Since several personal details of her life remain unknown, I speculated about certain aspects, keeping to the mantra "all within the realm of possibility." During most of her years in England, both of Isabel's husbands served King Henry I.

King Henry I

King Henry I was born circa May 1068 or 1069, near Selby, Yorkshire. His father was King William I of England, the duke of Normandy, also known as the Conqueror. Henry's mother was Matilda of Flanders. Henry had three elder brothers. Robert Curthose succeeded to the duchy, Richard died in a hunting accident and William Rufus became the king of England. Henry's sisters included his favorite, Countess Adela of Blois, Abbess Cecilia of Holy Trinity at Caen, Matilda,

Constance, Adeliza / Adelaide and possibly Agatha. Henry became a count of the Contentin (1088 - 1091) and later the king of England, after he seized the crown upon the death of his brother King William Rufus II in August 1101.

Around the time of Henry's birth, his parents were in the north for the dedication of a new Norman abbey. A turbulent world awaited the young prince. His father had defeated Harold Godwinson at Hastings only three years ago and resistance to the Norman conquest of England would rage during Henry's formative years. As the youngest among his brothers, Henry must not have expected to gain much at their father's death. His eldest brother, Robert, coveted his inheritance at Normandy and revolted against King William to gain it prematurely. The king had designated William Rufus his heir in England. At their father's eventual passing, Henry received money only. There must have been a bit of a rivalry between Henry and his elder brothers while growing up. Their mother had left Henry English lands, which William Rufus denied him. Robert and William Rufus also swore an agreement that if either man died, Henry could not claim the succession to Normandy or England. Due to Robert's mismanagement of his finances, Henry gave him money and bought the title of the comte of the Contentin, a peninsula encompassing Cherbourg, Valonges and Bayeux.

Then in August 1100, King William Rufus died by a stray arrow, while hunting with Henry, his companion Robert de Beaumont, Comte de Meulan and others. Some historians have suggested Henry might have arranged the assassination during the hunt. The man who allegedly shot the arrow was Walter Tirel, who had married into the Clare family. The Clares, another Norman baronial house, benefitted greatly during Henry's rule. Henry was in another part of the forest when he heard of his brother's death. He and many others in the king's retinue immediately scattered. Henry and Robert de Beaumont rode for the capital and treasury at Winchester. Within days, Henry claimed the crown. His brother Duke Robert had gone on Crusade, but he soon returned.

Henry settled down to the business of the kingdom and chose a bride, Eadgyth (who later took the Anglo-Norman name of her husband's mother, Queen Matilda). Eadgyth was the daughter of Malcolm III of Scotland and Queen Margaret. Her birth fused the blood of Scottish kings and the old Anglo-Saxon royal line. Her mother Margaret's grandfather was King Edmund II of England, called Ironside and Margaret's brother was Edgar the Aetheling, the last legitimate Anglo-Saxon claimant of the crown after the Norman invasion. Henry married in November 1100 and became the father of Matilda, also called Maud. He named his son, William.

Henry is notorious for having publicly acknowledged at least 21 illegitimate children as his, more than any other English monarch has done. In fact, he did more than acknowledge them. His children became bishops and abbesses, earls and countesses, as well as the consorts of other powerful monarchs. The children were born from 1090 to as late as 1126. In *The Burning Candle*, an unnamed daughter of the king, whom he intended to wed with William de Warenne, is a strong secondary character. I called her Amieria. Her true name and final fate is lost to history. It is possible there are other illegitimate children belonging to Henry whom we will never know. The *Royal Bastards of Medieval England*, my primary source for knowledge of Henry's children, cites 21 bastards. Hollister's Henry I, mentions another daughter named Emma who is absent from other sources.

Henry enjoyed long-standing relationships with the mothers of his children. His mistress, Lady Sybilla Corbet of Alcester, bore him at least five children and might have been the mother of Robert Earl of Gloucester. Robert became a staunch supporter of his half-sister, Princess Matilda / Maud, in later years. Another daughter of Sybilla's, her mother's namesake, became wife of Alexander I of Scotland. Nest, the daughter of the Welsh monarch Rhys ap Tewdwr, also bore Henry a son. Yet another mistress in Henry's later years was Isabel, the young daughter of Robert de Beaumont. Henry did not always have the best relations with his illegitimate children. One of his daughters, Juliane, married the nobleman Eustace de Pacy. In later years, Eustace and Ralph Harnec, constable of the castle of Ivry exchanged their children as hostages. Eustace blinded Harnec's son for some unknown reason. As revenge, Harnec blinded Eustace and Juliane's two daughters. When Henry did not punish Harnec, Juliane and her husband rebelled. She shot a bolt from a crossbow and almost assassinated her father.

Henry's father raised him with the idea of the divine right of kings. From the beginning of Henry's reign, he clashed with Anselm, the archbishop of Canterbury and Pope Paschal II over the entitlement of kings to demand homage from clerics and invest laymen as clergy. Anselm accepted exile rather than tangle with Henry. Pope Paschal seemed to have been more belligerent of the three. Henry warred with his brother Robert over the latter's claim to England. In 1101, the brothers averted a crisis by agreeing to similar terms as Robert had with their brother William Rufus regarding the succession. Peace did not prevail. Five years later, Henry and Robert met at the battle of Tinchebrai. The king emerged victorious and kept his brother in custody for the rest of his life. As ruler of Normandy and England with an heir groomed for the succession, Henry seemed destined only for greatness.

Henry suffered several setbacks. After the tenth year of his reign, the counts of Flanders and their counterparts in France under King Louis VI attacked the borders of Normandy. Henry spent much of the latter part of his kingship fighting battles in Normandy. In 1118, he suffered two tragedies, when Queen Matilda died on May 1 and the life of his chief counselor, Robert de Beaumont, ended on June 5. Greater pain awaited the monarch. Two years later, Henry's heir, William, died on November 25, 1120. The White Ship, which brought the prince and his bride to Barfleur, France, struck submerged rocks. Henry made his nobles swear allegiance to his daughter Matilda / Maud, his only remaining legitimate child. Some in the kingdom considered her half-brother, Robert Earl of Gloucester, a candidate for the throne. Henry died in Normandy on December 1, 1135. William de Warenne, the second Earl of Surrey and his stepsons Robert de Beaumont, second Earl of Leicester and Waleran, Comte de Meulan, stood with others at the king's deathbed. Stephen, Henry's nephew by his favorite sister Adela and Henry's daughter Matilda / Maud, both claimed the crown. The period historians call the Anarchy followed and would last for 18 years.

Robert de Beaumont

Robert de Beaumont was born in 1046, the son of Roger de Beaumont and Adeline de Meulan, sister to Comte Hugh II. Robert was the eldest of the siblings Aubree, Abbess of St. Leger de Préaux and Henri, the Earl of Warwick. During his lifetime, Robert held the title of the Comte de Meulan, which he succeeded to upon the death of his maternal uncle Hugh in 1081. Robert also became Earl of Leicester under King Henry I of England in 1107.

To understand Robert's heritage, consider the Viking Age and the invasions of the Danes and Norwegians who carved out the Norman duchy in northern France after 911. Robert, like many of the magnates who would gain power in Normandy and later England, came from a baronial family. His great-grandfather Thorold held the lordship of Pont Audemer near the Risle River. Some historians believe Thorold was the maternal nephew of the Duchess Gunnora, wife to Robert I of Normandy (942-966). In the generation of Robert's grandfather, Humphrey, the family holdings increased. Vielles, Beaumont and Beaumontel came under their control. Humphrey married the heiress of the forest of Brotonne, Aubree de la Haie. Of their daughter, Dunelme and sons, William, Robert and Roger, the latter became a parent to Robert de Beaumont in 1046.

Medieval naming conventions have always interested me, especially among the nobility. Most took the names of their birthplaces or territories they seized or inherited. It would be a fair assumption Robert came into the world at Beaumont, where Roger had built a castle on the hill above Vielles. Roger had married Robert's mother Adeline a year before their eldest son's birth. Adeline's brother Hugh held rich territory to the east in the French Vexin. Roger and Adeline also became parents to Aubree and Henri. The sons of Roger would grow to have a special closeness with each other. From an early age, Roger ensured his sons were literate and taught them about administrative functions. Robert witnessed his first recorded charter, a gift to the abbey of Marmoutier, when he was only nine years old. He also became acquainted with the ducal court from an early age.

When William the Conqueror invaded England in September 1066, Robert represented his father's interests, while Roger aided Duchess Matilda at the ducal court. Robert would have been twenty years old, newly knighted by William, when he led a devastating cavalry charge and feint at the battle of Hastings. After the defeat of the English, Robert's brother Henri arrived from Normandy a year later. By 1068, he held the newly constructed Warwick Castle. Robert gained honors as well, including the worth of some eighty English manors. Above all, he prized the title 'Comte de Meulan' and often styled himself as such "by the grace of God."

When the Normans claimed the duchy, technically they owed fealty to the kings of France, which brought personal consequences to Robert later in life. With the accession to Meulan, Robert moved into the sphere of the French court and owed the king of France homage for the county of Meulan. He also owed loyalty to the dukes of Normandy. Despite his riches, Robert wanted more. In 1088, he appeared outside the abbey of Bec and demanded of Abbot Anselm a pledge of fealty. It would be the first of many troublesome encounters between Robert and Anselm. The new duke of Normandy arrested Robert for threatening the abbey. Failing his father's intervention, Robert would have remained imprisoned. After Roger's death in the 1090's, Robert became lord of the most important castles in his family's holdings at Beaumont, Pont Audemer, Vatteville and Brionne. Robert also served the successive Norman kings of England, William Rufus and Henry I, as chief counselor. Only one thing remained glaringly absent—a wife. Robert had opportunity and heiresses he or his father could have considered. Robert's younger brother had also married Margaret de Perche several decades earlier. It is unclear why there is no record of a marriage for Robert before he reached his fiftieth year.

He first proposed to marry Godehilde de Toeni, in an age where a betrothal could be tantamount to a full marriage with all the benefits. For unknown reasons, she later married Baldwin, the son of Comte Eustace de Boulogne. Godehilde died while accompanying her husband's crusading venture in the Holy Land. Robert chose another bride, Isabel, daughter of Comte Hugh de Vermandois. On her father's side, Isabel was a granddaughter of King Henry I of France. With the births of their children, Emma (1102), the twins Waleran and Robert (1104), Hugh (around 1106), Isabel (circa 1107 or 1113), Aubree (circa 1108-1109), Adelina and Maud, plus the newly created earldom of Leicester, Robert's future seemed bright.

Robert claimed Leicester by underhanded means, as described in the narrative. Ivo de Grentmesnil, the sheriff of Leicester, numbered among the rebels who had supported Duke Robert of Normandy against King Henry of England in 1101. Robert pleaded Ivo's case before the king and received a grant of Ivo's lands in exchange for money Robert offered Ivo to complete the Crusade. Ivo returned to England in later years, but he never retrieved his holdings from Robert. Ivo's sons never gained their rightful inheritance. Robert's mercurial personality allowed him to play various roles in medieval history. He could be a mediator and conciliator at court and an unrepentant opportunist concerning his personal interests and the wealth of his heirs.

After two decades of marriage, Robert lost Isabel to William de Warenne. Chroniclers of the period note he died a shamed and broken man, embittered by Isabel's betrayal. He withdrew to his family's monastic foundation at Saint Pierre-de-Préaux. In June 1118, his death neared. He took up the habit of the Benedictines. His last will and testament commended the care of his heirs, Robert and Waleran, to his master Henry. The archbishop of Rouen insisted the dying man renounce claim to the lands he had stolen in England and France, including Leicester and honors belonging to the abbey of La Croix Saint-Leuffroy. Robert refused most of the demands and stipulated his heirs would act on behalf of his soul. The twins did so, with later grants to Bec and Saint Pierre-de-Préaux. Robert died on June 5 and lay buried at the abbey. His heart went to another of his monastic foundations at Brackley. Within months, his widow remarried. In a few years, his heirs succeeded him as Robert, second Earl of Leicester and Waleran, Comte de Meulan.

William de Warenne

William de Warenne's birth date is unknown. His parents were William de Warenne, first Earl of Surrey and Gundred, sister of Gerbod the Fleming. William was the eldest child. His sister Edith became the wife of Gerard de Gournay (until 1098) and of Dreux de Monchy. William fought his brother Reynald / Reginald, at the battle of Tinchebrai. William succeeded to his father's title in 1088.

The surname ascribed to William by medieval convention suggests he was born in Varenne, Normandy. His Christian name came from his father, who served as a loyal companion of Duke William of Normandy, later the king of England. In 1088, the duke's successor King William Rufus II made his father's loyal companion, the first Earl of Surrey. The title soon fell to the younger William. His father died on June 24, 1088 of an arrow wound sustained during a siege of Pevensey Castle, when the leg turned gangrenous. William did not require a guardian. I assume he was born by at least 1070-1072, sixteen being around the age of majority.

The history of William's mother, Gundred, is slightly convoluted. For centuries, genealogists referred to her as a daughter of Matilda of Flanders, wife of Duke William of Normandy. Gundred was most likely the sister of Gerbod the Fleming, the Earl of Chester in 1070, of no relation to Matilda of Flanders. Gundred might have married William's father in the same year as her brother gained an earldom. Before Gundred's death in 1085, she and William's father founded the Clunaic monastic house at Lewes Priory.

As the eldest son, William inherited great wealth

from his father, including lands in over thirteen English counties and his father's seat at Castle Acre in Norfolk. In Normandy, the family holdings of Mortemer and Bellencombre would have been his also. Within a few years, William had settled on a prospective bride. She was Eadgyth, the daughter of Malcolm III of Scotland and his sainted queen, Margaret. Eadgyth had spent most of her life from the time she was six in 1086 at Romsey Abbey, near Southampton, but apparently never took the veil. She rejected William's proposal, whether of her own initiative or on the advice of others. In November 1100, she married King Henry I, who had just seized the throne of England.

At the death of King William Rufus while hunting in the New Forest in August 1100, England devolved into chaos. Henry along with several nobles, including Robert de Beaumont, raced to Winchester and claimed the treasury and crown. Henry and William Rufus' brother, Duke Robert Curthose held every expectation that he would have succeeded to the throne of England. The situation left Earl William of Surrey in a quagmire. He owed fealty to the king of England for his lands there. He could not risk losing his Norman estates. William chose to support Duke Robert. In July 1101, a Norman invasion force of 200 ships and 260 knights landed at Portsmouth, with William as part of the retinue. King Henry raced from Pevensey and met his brother the duke. The two sides came to an agreement, after which the duke returned to Normandy with William, who cannot have been a happy man at his departure. His men had supposedly raided some of his neighbors in Norfolk. For his failure to control them, William lost the earldom of Surrey, which he later regained in 1103. Afterward, William became a loyal supporter of King Henry and served as one of his commanders in 1106 at the battle of Tinchebrai, where Henry defeated his brother Robert and claimed Normandy.

As early as 1101-1103, King Henry might have been giving thought on how to placate William, bitter about the loss of his earldom and his prospective bride to the monarch. The king proposed a match between one of his unnamed bastard daughters to William. Anselm, the archbishop of Canterbury, rejected the union for concerns about blood ties between William and Henry. Anselm's letter to Henry regarding consanguinity strengthens the theory that William's mother cannot have descended from Henry's mother. The date of the letter has not been determined. Anselm could have written it as early as 1100 or before his death in April 1109. The letter states William and the unnamed daughter of the king could not marry because they were cousins in the fourth generation on the one part and in the sixth on the other. If William's mother Gundred had truly been a daughter of Matilda of Flanders, Gundred would have been a half-blood sister to King Henry. His illegitimate daughter and William de Warenne would have been first cousins. If the archbishop knew of such close kinship, he would not have mentioned lesser-prohibited degrees as a reason for banning the marriage.

William must have scandalized England when he seized Isabel de Vermandois. There is no record of when they first met. As part of the nobility with close ties to the king, William and Isabel would have encountered each other at court. Some chroniclers of the period suggested the abduction concealed a long-standing affair between the two, while others believe Isabel did not willingly abandon her first husband. The event likely dates to a period after February 1116. In the same month, King Henry had sent Robert de Beaumont, Isabel's husband and William to York. He tasked the men with bringing Archbishop Thurstan of York to heel. The archbishop refused to accept the supremacy of the archbishopric of Canterbury over his office. It is unlikely William and Robert would have cooperated in the venture if the former had stolen the latter's wife at any point before their journey to York. It is possible, though uncertain, Isabel conceived their daughter Gundred during the first year of the affair. Various dates exist for Isabel and William's children. After Robert de Beaumont's death on June 5, 1118, Isabel and William married. Their son, also William, was born likely in 1119, followed by another daughter, Adeline / Ada and their sons, Ralph and Reginald. Isabel's second husband died on May 11, 1138, according to the death registry at the Priory of Saint Pancras at Lewes. She survived him. Their eldest son, William, became the third Earl of Surrey.

Isabel de Vermandois

Isabel de Vermandois was born circa 1081 or 1085. Her parents were Hugh Magnus, Comte de Vermandois, younger son of the Capetian King Henry I and his wife Anne of Kiev and Adelaide / Adele Comtesse de Vermandois. Isabel's siblings included Ralph (who succeeded their father as Comte de Vermandois), Henry, Simon, William and her sisters, Matilda, Beatrice, Constance and Agnes. In her lifetime, Isabel was Comtesse de Meulan, wife to Robert de Beaumont from 1096 to 1118 and Countess of Surrey, wife to William de Warenne from 1118 to 1138.

Isabel's ancestry linked her with the most prestigious bloodlines throughout Europe. Her father Hugh was a younger son of King Henry I of France and Queen Anne of Kiev. Hugh married Adelaide / Adele, daughter of Herbert IV, Comte de Vermandois and Adele, Countess of Valois. Isabel's heritage included the Capetian dynasty (from Hugh Capet, first King of the Frankish domain), Carolingian dynasty (from Charles Martel, royal grandfather of Charlemagne) and Russian royalty (through Anne of Kiev, daughter of Yaroslav the Wise, Grand Prince of Russia). Isabel was the second or third daughter of her parents. Some historians refer to her as

Isabel de Crépy. She would have been born at Crépy-en-Valois, founded in the tenth century by the counts of Valois, just northeast of Paris. Her marriage to Robert de Beaumont occurred between the ages of 11 and 15 in 1096. As early as 1094, Isabel's mother had visited the Norman abbey of Bec, perhaps as an emissary for the negotiation of her daughter's union. Robert was several decades older than his prospective bride.

The marriage of Isabel and Robert faced an impediment before the union could take place. Bishop Ivo of Chartres raised an objection. The couple shared kinship within prohibited degrees. The exact connection is uncertain though it might pertain to a common ancestor among the counts of Valois. As a condition for the papal dispensation regarding Isabel's marriage, her father Hugh participated in the first Crusade. He reached the Holy Land, aided in the capture of Antioch and should have gone to Constantinople with a request for reinforcements. Instead, he returned to France. Facing Pope Paschal II's threat of excommunication, Hugh joined another crusade against the Turks in September 1101 and died of his wounds a month later at Tarsus.

Hugh's pledge to go on Crusade for the sake of his daughter's marriage became unnecessary because Robert and Isabel wed in 1096 without awaiting the papal dispensation. Their first child, a daughter, Emma, arrived in 1102, making Isabel either as young as 17 or as old as 22 when she first became a mother. Subsequent children included the twins Waleran and Robert, Hugh, Aubree, Adelina, Maud and Isabel.

After twenty years of marriage, Isabel surrendered to the temptation posed by William de Warenne, the second Earl of Surrey. Whether he seized her or they arranged the event beforehand, she never returned to Robert. Eventually, she and William would have five children together. The lives of Isabel's descendants by both her husbands are equally fascinating and complex. The children of both marriages founded an unexpected companionship. In December 1138, Isabel's eldest son Waleran and his younger half-brother William journeyed together to Rouen.

Of Isabel de Vermandois' children with Robert de Beaumont, Emma likely went to a convent. Despite her betrothal at the age of one to Amaury de Montfort, brother of Queen Bertrade of France, Emma never married Amaury. I have no further information on her life.

Waleran de Beaumont became the Comte de Meulan after his father's death and remained at the court of King Henry I with his twin Robert until he came into his patrimony. In 1122, he joined a rebellion against the king and gave three of his sisters, Aubree, Adelina and Maud in marriage to his confederates. Two years later, Henry seized him and demolished his castle at Vatteville. Waleran remained imprisoned at Wallingford Castle until 1129, when he regained his freedom. He was at Henry's deathbed on December 1, 1135. In the Anarchy, he supported King Stephen and accepted the offer of Stephen's two-year-old daughter as his future bride. In 1141, Henry's daughter Matilda / Maud, who continued warring with Stephen for the crown claimed Waleran's lands in Normandy. Waleran switched sides and allied himself with Geoffrey Plantagenet of Anjou and Matilda / Maud.

Waleran married Agnes d'Evreux in 1141 and she soon gave him a son, Robert, followed by seven other children. Waleran again looked to advance by other means and came into the sphere of French influence. Having completed one pilgrimage to Spain around 1143, he joined the second Crusade (1145-1149) and survived a shipwreck. The threat of war loomed between Duke

Henry of Normandy, son of Matilda / Maud, and the French court. Waleran found himself on the wrong side. His sister Adelina's son, Robert de Montfort, captured and imprisoned him in 1153. Duke Henry became Henry II of England in 1154. Whereas Waleran's father rose to preeminence under successive Norman kings, Waleran could not gain the same advantage. He founded several Cistercian abbeys before retiring to Saint Pierre-de-Préaux in March 1166. Waleran died there twenty days later on April 9, having taken the habit of the Benedictines. Waleran's granddaughter Clemence married Roger de Sable, a Grand Master of the Knights Templar.

Robert de Beaumont became the second Earl of Leicester. In 1121, he married Amice, the heiress of the honor of Breteuil. She gave him at least four children. Robert remained loyal to King Henry I until his death and thereafter, supported King Stephen and Henry II. He lost most of his estates in Normandy to those who supported the claim of Henry's daughter, Matilda / Maud. In 1155, King Henry II named Robert as his justiciar, responsible for the administration of England during the king's absences. Around this time, Robert married his eldest son and namesake to Petronilla de Grentmesnil, the great-niece of Ivo, who had lost Leicester to Robert's father. In his role as justiciar, Robert also became embroiled in the controversy between Archbishop Thomas Becket of Canterbury and the king. Becket threatened Robert with excommunication, but the earl died on April 5, 1168. His heart, like his father's own, went to Brackley. Countess Amice took the veil. Through Robert's granddaughter, Amicia, Isabel de Vermandois became the great-great-grandmother of Simon de Montfort, who rebelled against King Henry III.

Hugh de Beaumont became a great landowner of Bedfordshire in 1138. He may have gained the earldom of Bedford from King Stephen.

Aubree de Beaumont married Hugh fitz Gervase, one of her brother Waleran's co-conspirators against King Henry I. Hugh held lands in the county of Chartres. When the rebellion failed, Henry consigned Hugh to prison.

Adelina de Beaumont married Hugh de Montfort-sur-Risle before October 1123. Hugh, a grandson of one of the companions of William the Conqueror, had a few children with Adelina including Robert de Montfort. After the failed rebellion against King Henry I, Hugh, as one of Waleran's co-collaborators, endured imprisonment at Gloucester Castle. It is likely Hugh never left prison alive. Afterward, his son Robert de Montfort became the temporary ward of his uncle Waleran. Adelina may have remarried later. Isabel de Vermandois' descendants through Adelina's children were living up through 1667 in Staffordshire.

Maud de Beaumont married another rebel, William Louvel. He escaped into France after Waleran's capture and later became lord of Ivry and Bréval.

Isabel de Beaumont is the most controversial of the children. Her date of birth is uncertain. She may have been the youngest mistress of King Henry I. Before Waleran's release from Wallingford in 1129, Isabel had given the king a daughter, likely named Maud, who would later become abbess of Montivilliers. There are references to a second daughter, Isabel or Beatrice. After Waleran gained his freedom, Isabel de Beaumont married Gilbert de Clare, first Earl of Pembroke. Through this union, Isabel de Vermandois became the grandmother of Richard de Clare, also known as Strongbow, the Lord of Leinster and justiciar of Ireland. Richard's daughter and eventual heir, Isobel de Clare, married William Marshal. He served the English rulers

Henry II, Richard the Lionhearted, John and Henry III and became "the greatest knight that ever lived" according to Archbishop Stephen Langton of Canterbury. Through this union, Isabel de Vermandois became great-great-grandmother of William Marshal's ten children and ancestress of the dukes of Norfolk until 1307.

Of Isabel de Vermandois' five children with William de Warenne, Gundred de Warenne, married Roger de Beaumont, second Earl of Warwick. Roger was the heir of Isabel's brother in-law, Henri. In 1153 upon her husband's death, Gundred expelled King Stephen's garrison from Warwick and surrendered the castle to the future King Henry II. Gundred may have remarried after Roger's death. Through Gundred and Roger's union, Isabel de Vermandois became the ancestress of the Beauchamp earls of Warwick up through the 15th century. Her descendant, Edward Plantagenet, became the 17th earl of Warwick. King Henry VII kept him a prisoner of the Tower of London until 1499, when the king executed him for treason.

Young William de Warenne became the third earl of Surrey, loyal to King Stephen at the beginning of the Anarchy. He married Adela, a granddaughter of the infamous Robert de Belleme and had one child, Isabel de Warenne. Like his half-brother Waleran, he switched sides to Matilda / Maud briefly, but soon returned to Stephen. Later, William joined his maternal second cousin, Louis VII of France, on Crusade. William died fighting the Turks in 1148. His daughter first married William de Blois, King Stephen's second son. After her first husband died, Isabel wed Hamelin, an illegitimate son of Geoffrey de Anjou. Through Hamelin and Isabel de Warenne's marriage, Isabel de Vermandois is the ancestress of the Warenne earls of Surrey until 1347 and the FitzAlan earls of Arundel and Surrey until 1415.

Ada / Adeline de Warenne married Prince Henry of Scotland, son of King David and the maternal grandson of Earl Waltheof, the last Anglo-Saxon earl of preeminence under the Norman regime. Henry and Ada had seven children, including two future Scottish monarchs, Malcolm IV and William I, called the Lion. Through Ada, Isabel de Vermandois is the ancestress of Scottish rulers until Margaret, Maid of Norway, in 1290. Ada was also mother to David of Scotland, the Earl of Huntingdon. His daughter Isobel married Robert de Brus, fourth Lord of Annandale. By this union, the great Scotsman King Robert the Bruce descends from Isabel de Vermandois.

Ralph de Warenne is a mystery. His brother Reginald de Warenne, while he inherited some of his father's lands in Normandy and married Adeline de Wormegay, also left scant details of his life. Reginald's son, William, founded the priory of Wormegay during the reign of Richard the Lionhearted.

Thank you for purchasing and reading *The Burning Candle*. I hope you enjoyed its heroine, Isabel de Vermandois and the period in which she lived. Please consider leaving feedback where you purchased this book. Your opinion is helpful, both to me and to other potential readers.

To learn more about the Norman period in England, visit my website for a link to the Saxon and Norman periods. I love to hear from readers. You may also email me at lyarde1175@gmail.com.

Glossary

Braies: a medieval undergarment cinched with a drawstring at the waist or belted.

Candlemas: traditional observation of the presentation of Jesus at the temple, also known as the Feast of the Purification of the Virgin, observed in February.
Chainsil: fine linen for veils or screens hung around beds in Norman households to offer a modicum of privacy.
Churching: the ritual purification required of medieval women after childbirth.
Compline: the canonical hour observed at 9 PM.
Consanguinity: shared heritage within prohibited degrees of kinship that invalidated a marriage.
Cotte: a tunic.
Courses: menstruation.
Couvrechef: the headdress of a Norman woman, typically fashioned in cambric or fine linen.

Denier: the French equivalent of the medieval English penny.
Dovecote: housing for tamed doves.

Frumenty: a popular medieval dish primarily of boiled wheat, mixed with eggs, milk and various sweet fruits.

Godsibs: godparents of a child, typically neighbors or men and women of suitable rank. Medieval boys had two male godfathers and one female, with the reverse for medieval girls.
Gloria Patri: the doxology also known as Glory be to the Father.

Justiciar: a trusted official responsible for the administration of England in the king's absence.

Kyrie Eléison: the litany "Lord, have mercy."

Lauds: the canonical hour observed at 3 AM.
Leman: lover.

Maman: Norman French for mother.
Matins: the canonical hour observed at midnight.
Michaelmas: The Feast of Saint Michael the Archangel, observed September 29.
Motte and bailey castle: a wooden or stone structure built on a mound, with an enclosed courtyard.

Nones: the canonical hour observed at 3 PM.

Paternoster: the Lord's Prayer
Prime: the canonical hour observed at 6 AM.

Senlac: the Norman term for the area where the battle of Hastings occurred in 1066.
Sewer: the medieval officer who supervised hand washing before meals commenced.
Sext: the canonical hour observed at midday.
Sherte: undershirt.
Slavering cloth: a baby's bib.

Tierce: the canonical hour observed at 9 AM.

Vespers: the canonical hour observed at 6 PM.

Wattle and daub: a composite of natural materials for building the walls of medieval structures.

About the Author

Lisa J. Yarde writes fiction inspired by the Middle Ages in Europe. She is the author of two historical novels set in medieval England and Normandy, *The Burning Candle*, based on the life of Isabel de Vermandois, and *On Falcon's Wings*, chronicling the star-crossed romance between Norman and Saxon lovers. Lisa has also written three novels in a six-part series set in Moorish Spain, *Sultana, Sultana's Legacy*, and *Sultana: Two Sisters*, where rivalries and ambitions threaten the fragile bonds between members of a powerful family. Her short story, *The Legend Rises*, which chronicles Gwenllian of Gwynedd's valiant fight against English invaders, is included in Pagan Writers Press' 2013 HerStory anthology.

Born in Barbados, Lisa currently lives in New York City. She is also an avid blogger and moderates at Unusual Historicals. She is also a contributor at Historical Novel Reviews and History and Women. Her personal blog is The Brooklyn Scribbler.

Learn more about Lisa and her writing at the website www.lisajyarde.com. Follow her on Twitter (@lisajyarde) or become a Facebook fan (**Lisa J. Yarde**). For information on upcoming releases and freebies from Lisa, join her mailing list at http://eepurl.com/un8on.

www.ingramcontent.com/pod-product-compliance
Lightning Source LLC
Chambersburg PA
CBHW051001180726
48291CB00006B/1923